Ai Mi is a pseudonym. She lives in the United States, after having grown up in China.

'The period is drawn with convincing detail, evoked to illuminate how political repression and strict social mores affect two characters engaged in one of China's favourite literary themes – the melodramatically doomed love story' Isabel Hilton, *Guardian*

'An example of old-fashioned storytelling, written in the style of "scar literature" . . . this type of fiction became unfashionable . . . but, who knows, perhaps this book will kick-start a revival' John Sunyer, *Financial Times*

'The novel's depiction of life under communism is its strength, peopled by fascinating characters and conflicting attitudes, not unlike a Jane Austen tale' Natalie Bowen, *Irish Examiner*

'A tragic love story . . . This is the stuff of *Romeo and Juliet*: romance and tragedy. The ending is heartbreaking . . . This is a simple book about tragic love. But set in this time period, in this culture, the novel takes on a very complex topic: romantic versus political belief . . . This book should be read'
Michelle Berry, *Globe and Mail*

Under the Hawthorn Tree

Ai Mi

Translated from the Chinese by

Anna Holmwood

virago

VIRAGO

First published in Great Britain in 2011 by Virago Press
Published by arrangement with the
People's Literature Publishing House, China
This paperback edition published in 2012 by Virago Press

A CIP catalogue record for this book
is available from the British Library.

ISBN 978-1-84408-703-7

Typeset in Sabon by M Rules
Printed and bound in Great Britain by
Clays Ltd, St Ives plc

Papers used by Virago are from well-managed forests
and other responsible sources.

MIX
Paper from
responsible sources
FSC® C104740

Virago Press
An imprint of
Little, Brown Book Group
100 Victoria Embankment
London EC4Y 0DY

An Hachette UK Company
www.hachette.co.uk

www.virago.co.uk

The translator would like to thank the British Centre for Literary Translation and the Translators Association for their support throughout the translation mentoring programme, and she would also like to give particular thanks to her mentor, Nicky Harman, for her professional attention and kind friendship.

Translator's Introduction

Ai Mi's *Under the Hawthorn Tree* has been a publishing sensation in China since it first appeared on her website in 2007. The media attention intensified with the release of the film version by China's premier director Zhang Yimou (of *Raise the Red Lantern* fame) in 2010, and it continues to be the subject of impassioned debates on the internet. Somewhat unusually for a story set during the Cultural Revolution it has had real cross-generational success. It has sold millions of copies, which is particularly remarkable considering that Ai Mi (a pseudonym) makes it available for free on her blog so we can reasonably assume that the number of people who have read the story is even larger than the staggering sales figures suggest.

The Cultural Revolution (1966–76) looms large in the Chinese books that have been translated in recent years, and yet even now this period of political turmoil remains alien to Western readers. It was a world dominated by sloganeering and awkward political labels and at the height of Chinese Communist zeal every citizen was encouraged to make revolution. Chairman Mao's Red Guards were called on to challenge their parents and elders, and while some young people experienced it as a time of unbridled freedom, for many more it was filled with violence, political persecution and distress. While political sensitivities have continued to limit full historical and political analysis, novels were for a while – and perhaps even still are – the most fruitful way of coming to terms with this period. They became known as 'scar literature' or 'literature of the wounded' – a term coined after the publication of Lu Xinhua's novel *The Scar*. But for younger Chinese people born during the 1980s and afterwards, who have enjoyed greater personal freedoms, a nascent sexual revolution, and the lure of global consumerism, there has been a marked shift away from stories about the Cultural Revolution. That *Under the Hawthorn Tree* has proved so popular with them demonstrates how this story of thwarted love has transcended the political and historical, becoming a national story that touches the heart.

Some of this passionate response from readers in China is because Ai Mi tells her readers that it was inspired by a true story and that she was given Jingqiu's memoir. Many of the place names in the book were disguised in the original Chinese novel, resulting in an industry of speculation on the Chinese blogosphere as to the 'real' locations. In consultation with the author, I have chosen to follow the consensus that has formed on the web, one that bears scrutiny, and have used real city and village names in this translation.

Under the Hawthorn Tree has taken its place as part of China's collective project of remembering and yet this is not the story of national political struggles but an intensely personal story of the way those struggles affected human relations. Jingqiu's sexual naivety may strike the Western reader as rather incredible, yet it shows the startlingly intimate reach of politics in that period. Often referred to as the 'purest and cleanest of love stories' by Chinese critics, what is at stake in *Under the Hawthorn Tree* is innocence, both of the individual and of society at large, in the face of the corrupting influence of extreme politics.

The story starts as Jingqiu travels to the countryside to help her Educational Reform Association write a new history textbook based on the stories told by the local lower and middling peasants. This is where her education in love begins . . .

Anna Holmwood

Under the Hawthorn Tree

Chapter One

During the first weeks of spring 1974, when Jingqiu was still at senior high school, she and three other students were selected to take part in a project to compile a new school textbook. They were to travel to the homes of poor and lower peasants in West Village and interview them, turning their stories into a history book for use at No. 8 Middle School. Before the Cultural Revolution, textbooks were full of feudalism, capitalism and revisionism and, as Chairman Mao gloriously proclaimed, marked 'the rule by gifted scholars and fair ladies, emperors, generals and ministers, through the ages'. Now education 'needed reforming'.

The chosen few were students whose grades in essay writing were above average. They were collectively named the 'No. 8 Middle School Educational Reform Association'.

The four students struggled up the path across the mountain after Mr Zhang, the head of the village which would be their new home for the next few months, and their three teachers. It was not a large mountain, but with their packs tied to their backs and string bags in their hands they began to sweat heavily and it wasn't long before Mr Zhang became steadily weighed down with their luggage. Two of the three girls, even though now rid of their backpacks, still panted and puffed up the mountain.

Jingqiu was strong, and although she too was exhausted by the weight, she insisted upon carrying her own rucksack. The ability to endure hard work was the standard by which she measured other people, and she redeemed any political shortcomings by her reliably good performance, by not fearing hardship and by making sure that she never lagged behind.

Observing that each breath sounded like their last, Mr Zhang was endlessly encouraging. 'Not far now, just a bit further, once we get to the hawthorn tree we can take a rest.'

The fabled hawthorn tree reminded Jingqiu of the plum tree in the ancient story in which General Cao Cao made empty promises of refreshing fruit juice in order to spur his soldiers on. She also thought of a Soviet song she had learnt some years previously thanks to a trainee Russian teacher, Anli, who arrived at No. 8 Middle School from the provincial teacher training college. The twenty-six-year-old Anli was assigned to Jingqiu's class. She was tall and trim, with pearly white skin, pleasant features, and a straight, prominent nose. But her eyes were the best. They were large and crowned by remarkable eyelids. They weren't just double, but had two or maybe three creases. In fact, had her eyes been more deeply set, she would have been taken for a foreigner. The students, with their single eyelids, were so jealous.

Anli's father was some kind of chief in the second division artillery but, following the disgrace of Mao's second-in-command, Lin Biao, he was targeted and demoted, and Anli had suffered. Afterwards, her father came into favour again, and so he was able to recall Anli from the countryside and squeeze her into the provincial teacher training college. It was a mystery as to why she had decided to study Russian as by that time it was a subject that had long since ceased to be popular. Just after the Liberation, in the early 1950s, there had apparently been a craze for it, but then Sino-Russian relations soured, and the Soviet Union was branded revisionist because of its attempts to 'reform' Marxist Leninist theory. So then those same teachers changed back again to teaching English.

Anli took a liking to Jingqiu, and when she had time, she would teach her Russian songs such as 'The Hawthorn Tree'. Of course, this had to be done in secret. Not only had everything associated with the Soviet Union become dangerous but, just as importantly, anything contaminated by the idea of 'love' was considered the bad influence and the putrid remains of the capitalist class. 'The Hawthorn Tree' was deemed 'obscene', 'rotten and decayed', and of 'improper style' because the lyrics spoke of two young men who were both in love with the same young maiden. She liked them both and could not decide who she should choose. In order to make her decision she asked advice from the hawthorn tree. In the last lines she sang:

Oh! Sweet hawthorn tree, white buds on your branches,
Ah! Dear hawthorn tree, why so troubled?
Which is the bravest? Which is lovelier?
Oh, I beg you, hawthorn tree, tell me which one.

Anli had a lovely voice trained in what she called the 'beautiful Italian style' and it suited this song very well. At weekends she would come to Jingqiu's house and have Jingqiu accompany her on the accordion while she sang.

When Mr Zhang mentioned the hawthorn tree Jingqiu was surprised, but then she quickly realised that he was referring to a real tree, not the song, and that he had designated this tree the goal for the seven of them struggling up the hill.

Now Jingqiu's rucksack pressed hot and heavy on her sweaty back and the straps of her string bag dug hard into her palms. In order to relieve the pressure she passed it back and forth left to right, right to left. Just as she began to feel she could go no further Mr Zhang announced, 'We've arrived, let's rest our feet for a while.'

There was a collective sigh from the group – like the sound of men who have just been read their amnesty order – and they collapsed to the ground.

After they'd regained their strength one of them asked, 'Where is this hawthorn tree?'

'Over there,' Mr Zhang said, pointing to a tree not far away.

Jingqiu saw a rather unremarkable tree, six or seven metres tall. The air was still cold, and so not only were the white flowers yet to bloom, it was even bare of green leaves. Jingqiu was disappointed; the image the song had given her was far more poetic and charming. When she'd listened to 'The Hawthorn Tree' she imagined a scene of two handsome young men standing beneath the tree waiting for their dearest maiden. A young girl, wearing one of those dresses favoured by Russian women, walked towards them in rainbow-infused twilight. Which one should she choose?

Jingqiu asked Mr Zhang, 'Does this tree have white flowers?'

This question seemed to arouse something within old Zhang. 'Ah, this tree! Originally the flowers were white, but during the war against Japan countless brave men were executed beneath it, their blood watering the soil at its roots. From that time on the flowers on this tree started changing until all the flowers were red.'

The group sat silently, until Mr Lee – one of their teachers from the city – said to the students, 'Still not writing this down?'

Realising with a start that their work had begun, the four rushed to find their notebooks. Four or five scratching pens seemed to be an everyday occurrence for Mr Zhang, so he continued talking. Once he had told the story of the tree which had borne witness to the glorious deeds of the people of West Village, it was time to set out again.

After a while Jingqiu looked back to the hawthorn tree, now faint, and thought she could see a person standing beneath it. It wasn't a soldier from Mr Zhang's story, tied up tightly by those Japanese devils, but a handsome young man ... She scolded herself for her petty capitalist thoughts. She must focus on learning from the poor peasants, and work hard on writing this textbook. The hawthorn tree story would definitely be included in the textbook, but under what title? What about, 'The Blood-stained Hawthorn Tree'? Perhaps that was too gory. 'The Red-blossoming Hawthorn Tree' might be better. Or, simply, 'The Red Hawthorn Tree'.

Jingqiu's backpack and string bag felt heavier after the rest, not lighter. She thought, perhaps it's like clashing flavours: a little bit of sweetness before a mouthful of bitterness makes the bitter taste much more bitter. But not one of them dared to complain. To be afraid of struggle and exhaustion was for capitalists and to be labelled a capitalist was the one thing that scared Jingqiu. Her class background was bad, so she mustn't go around exploiting the peasants, making them carry her bags – that would mean elevating herself above the masses even more. The Party had a policy, 'You can't choose your class background, but you can choose your own path.' She knew that people like her had to be more careful than those with good class backgrounds.

But struggle and exhaustion didn't go away just because you didn't talk about them. Jingqiu wished that every aching nerve would wither and die. That way she wouldn't feel the weight on her back or the pain in her hands. She tried doing what she always did to help dismiss pain: she let her thoughts run wild. After a while she would almost feel that her body was elsewhere, as if her soul had flown away and was living a completely different life.

She didn't know why she kept thinking of the hawthorn tree. Images from Mr Zhang's story of the soldiers tied up alternated with the handsome young white-shirted Russian men from the song. In her imagination she became an anti-Japanese hero, punished by her enemies, and then she was the young Russian girl, wracked by indecision. Jingqiu couldn't honestly say if she were more of a Communist or more of a revisionist.

Eventually they reached the end of the mountain road and Mr Zhang, halting, pointed down the mountainside. 'That's West Village.'

The students rushed to the edge of the cliff to admire West Village spread out before them. They could see a small jade-green river that snaked down from the foot of the mountain and circled the village. Bathed in early spring sunlight and surrounded by bright mountains and crystal water, West Village was beautiful, prettier than the other villages Jingqiu had previously worked in. The panoramic view showed fields spread like a quilt across the mountainside in patches of green and brown scattered with small houses. A few buildings were concentrated in the middle, alongside a dam, which Mr Zhang said was the army base. According to the system in Yichang county each village had a large army detachment, and the head of the village was actually the army unit's Party secretary, so the villagers called him 'Village Head Zhang'.

The group walked down the mountain, arriving first at Mr Zhang's home which was located at the river's edge. His wife was at home and welcomed them, asking them to call her

Auntie. She said that the rest of the family was either in the fields or at school.

Once they were all rested, Mr Zhang began to arrange where they would stay. Two teachers, Mr Lee and Mr Chen, and the student Good Health Lee, were to live together with one family. The other, Mr Luo, would only be here for a short while, providing guidance on the writing – within a day or two he would need to return home to get back to school – so he would just squeeze in somewhere. One family had agreed to give one of their rooms to girls, but they only had space for two.

'Whoever is left over can live with me,' Mr Zhang said, deciding to set an example. 'I don't have any spare rooms, I'm afraid, so that girl will have to share a bed with my youngest daughter.'

The three girls looked at each other, dismayed. Jingqiu took a deep breath and volunteered. 'Why don't you two live together? I'll stay at Mr Zhang's.'

There were no activities planned for the rest of the day so they had time to settle in and have a rest. Work would start officially the next day. As well as interviewing the villagers and compiling the text, they knew that they would be working in the fields with the poorest farmers, experiencing peasant life.

Mr Zhang led the others to their new homes, leaving Jingqiu with Auntie Zhang. Auntie took Jingqiu to her daughter's room so that she could unpack. The room was like the other rural bedrooms she had been in, dark with a small window on one wall. It had no glass, just cellophane pasted to the frame.

Auntie switched on the light, dimly illuminating the room which was about fifteen square metres, tidy and clean. The bed was bigger than a single bed but smaller than a double. With two it would be tight, but adequate. Newly washed and starched, the sheets, more like cardboard than cloth, were spread tightly across the bed, on top of which lay a quilt folded into a triangle, the white lining turned out at two corners. Jingqiu pondered how it was folded and couldn't for the life of her work it out. Feeling a little flustered, she thought she would use her own blanket so that she wouldn't have to struggle to refold the quilt the next morning. Students who were sent to the countryside to live with lower and middle-ranking peasants knew they were to take their cue from the protocol used by the 8th Route Army during the civil war: use only that which the peasants use and return everything intact.

On the table by the window was a large square of glass used to display photographs, which Jingqiu knew was considered decadent. The photos lay on a dark green cloth. Curious, Jingqiu walked across the room to take a look. Auntie pointed to each photo in turn, explaining who everyone was. Sen, the eldest son, was a towering young man who looked completely unlike his parents. Maybe he's the odd one out, she thought. He worked at Yanjia River post office, and only came home once a week. His wife was called Yumin, and she taught at the village primary school. She had delicate, refined features and was tall and thin – a good match for Sen.

Fen was the eldest daughter. She was pretty, and Auntie told Jingqiu that after graduating from middle school Fen went to work in the village. The second daughter was called Fang. She looked very different from her sister, her mouth protruding, and her eyes smaller. Fang was still studying at Yanjia River Middle School, and only came home once or twice a week.

While they were talking Mr Zhang's second son, Lin, came home. He was there to fetch some water and to start preparing the food for the city guests. Jingqiu saw that he didn't resemble Sen, his older brother, but looked more like Mr Zhang. She was surprised. How could two brothers and two sisters look so different? It was as if when making the first son and daughter, the parents used up all the best possible ingredients so that by the time they came round to the next two, they'd just put them together any old how.

Jingqiu, feeling awkward, said, 'I'll help you collect water.'

'Can you manage?' Lin said quietly.

'Of course I can. I often come to the countryside to work on the land.'

Auntie Zhang said, 'You want to help him? I'll just cut some greens, and you can wash them in the river.' She picked up a bamboo basket and left the room.

Lin, left alone with Jingqiu, turned and scuttled off to the back of the house to get the water buckets. Auntie returned with two bundles of vegetables and gave them to Jingqiu.

Back with the buckets, eyes cast down to avoid her gaze, Lin said, 'Let's go.' Jingqiu picked up the basket and followed him, tracing the small road towards the river. Halfway, they bumped into a few young boys from the village who teased Lin. 'Your dad's got you a little bride, has he?' 'Oooh, she's from the city.' 'Things are looking up!'

Lin dropped the buckets and chased after the boys. Jingqiu called, 'Don't listen to them!' Lin returned, picked up the buckets, and flew off down the road. Jingqiu was confused, what did the boys mean? Why did they make a joke like that?

At the river Lin decided the water was too cold for Jingqiu, it would freeze her hands solid, he said. Jingqiu couldn't convince him otherwise, and so stood waiting and watching from the riverbank. Once he had finished washing the greens, he filled up the two buckets.

Jingqiu insisted that she should carry them. 'You didn't let me wash the vegetables, at least let me carry the water.' But Lin wouldn't let her, he picked up the buckets himself, and darted off towards home. And not long after they got back to the house, Lin quickly left.

Jingqiu tried to help Auntie cook but, again, wasn't given the opportunity. By now Lin's little nephew, Huan Huan, who had been sleeping next door, had woken up, and Auntie instructed him, 'Take your Aunt Jingqiu to fetch Uncle Old Third for dinner.'

Jingqiu didn't know that there was yet another son in the family. She asked Huan Huan, 'Do you know where Uncle Old Third is?'

'Yes, he's at the geobology camp.'

'The geobology camp?'

'He means the geological unit's camp,' Auntie explained smiling. The boy doesn't speak very clearly.'

Huan Huan pulled at Jingqiu's hand. 'Let's go, let's go, Old Third has sweets . . . '

Jingqiu followed Huan Huan only to find that after a very short while Huan Huan refused to walk. Opening his arms he said, 'Feet hurt. Can't move.'

Jingqiu started laughing and lifted him up. He might have looked small, but he was heavy. She'd already spent the best part of a day walking and carrying her bags, but if Huan Huan would not walk, she had no choice but to carry him a little way, put him down to rest, then lift him up and carry on, asking constantly, 'Are we nearly there yet? Have you forgotten the way?'

They had walked a long stretch of road and Jingqiu was just about to take another rest when she heard from far off the sounds of an accordion. Her instrument! She stopped and listened.

It was indeed an accordion, playing 'The Song of the Cavalryman', a tune that Jingqiu had played before, though she could really only play the right-hand part. This musician, however, played both parts very well. When they got to the rousing sections it sounded just like ten thousand horses galloping, winds howling, and clouds swirling. The music was coming from a building that looked like a worker's shed. Unlike the rest of the houses in the village, which were all detached, this building consisted of a long strip of huts joined together. It had to be the camp.

Huan Huan now found new, heroic, strength. His legs no longer hurt, and he wanted to throw off Jingqiu and run on ahead.

Keeping a firm hold of his hand, Jingqiu was dragged to where she could hear the music clearly. And now there was a new song. 'The Hawthorn Tree', this time joined by a chorus of male voices. She hadn't expected people in this little corner of the world to know 'The Hawthorn Tree'! She wondered if the villagers didn't know that it was a Soviet song, so freely were the men singing ... They sang along in Chinese, and she could hear that they were slightly distracted, as if also busy with their hands. But it was this distracted quality, the starting and stopping, the low humming, that made the song particularly beautiful.

Jingqiu was mesmerised; she felt that she had been transported into a fairy tale. Dusk enveloped them, kitchen smoke curled up to the sky, and village smells drifted through the air. Her ears were filled with the sounds of the accordion and the low rumbles of the men's voices. This strange mountain village was at once familiar; its flavour had to be savoured, she thought, as she struggled to express it in words. Her senses were steeped in what she could only think to describe as a petty capitalist atmosphere.

Huan Huan escaped Jingqiu's grip, and ran into the building. Jingqiu guessed that the accordion player must be Huan Huan's uncle Old Third, Mr Zhang's third son. She was curious. Would this third son look more like the eldest, Sen, or the second son, Lin? She secretly hoped that he would look more like Sen. Such lovely music couldn't possibly come from the hands of a man like Lin. She knew that she was being unfair to Lin, but still . . .

Chapter Two

A young man appeared carrying Huan Huan. He was wearing a dark blue, knee-length cotton coat, which must have been the geological unit's uniform. Huan Huan's little body obscured most of his face and it was not until he was almost in front of her and had put the little boy down that she saw his face properly.

Her rational eye told her, he's not the picture of a typical worker. His face isn't blackish-red, it's white; his figure is not robust 'like an iron tower', but is slender. And his eyebrows are bushy but not like those on the propaganda posters which slant upwards like two drawn daggers.

He made Jingqiu think of a film, made on the eve of the Cultural Revolution, called *The Young Generation*. In it, there was a character who had what was called at the time a 'backwards way of thinking'. Old Third didn't look a bit like a revolutionary or a brave soldier – he looked much more like a petty capitalist – and Jingqiu found herself admiring the non-revolutionary things about him.

She could feel her heart racing and she grew flustered, suddenly becoming aware of her appearance and clothes. She was wearing an old padded cotton outfit her brother used to wear, which looked a bit like a Mao suit except that the jacket only had one pocket. The standing collars on these suits were short, and Jingqiu's neck was particularly long. She was convinced she must look like a giraffe. Because her father had been sent to a labour reform camp in the countryside when she was young, the family had had to survive on their mother's salary. They were always short of money, so Jingqiu wore her brother's old clothes.

She couldn't remember ever before being so aware of what she was wearing; it was a first for her to worry about making a bad impression in this regard. She hadn't felt so self-conscious for a long time. When she was at primary and secondary school the other students bullied her, but once she got to senior high school none of them dared look her straight in the eye. The boys in her class seemed scared of her and turned red when she spoke to them so she had never given any thought as to whether they liked the way she looked or dressed. They were silly, just a bunch of little monsters.

But the well-dressed man before her made her so nervous her heart hurt. His brilliant white shirt sleeves peeped from under his unbuttoned blue overcoat. His shirt, so white, so neat and smooth, must have been made from polyester, which Jingqiu definitely couldn't afford. His rice-grey top looked homemade, and Jingqiu, who was good at knitting, could see that the pattern was difficult. On his feet he wore a pair of leather shoes. She looked down at her own faded 'Liberation shoes' and thought, he's rich, I'm poor, it's like we're from different worlds.

He also wore a slight smile, asking Huan Huan, 'Is this Auntie Jingqiu?' Addressing her, he said, 'Did you arrive today?'

He spoke Mandarin Chinese, not the local county dialect, nor her city dialect. Jingqiu wondered who he would speak Mandarin to around here. Her own Mandarin was excellent, and as a result she did the broadcasts at her school and was often picked to read out loud at gatherings and sports events.

But she felt embarrassed to speak it as, apart from when speaking with people from outside the county, it wasn't used in everyday life. Jingqiu didn't understand why he was speaking Mandarin with her. She gave a short 'mmm' in reply.

He asked, 'Did my writer comrade come via Yiling or Yanjia River?' His Mandarin was melodic.

'I'm not a writer,' Jingqiu replied, embarrassed. 'Don't call me that. I came via Yiling.'

'Then you must be exhausted, as from the town you have to walk, you can't even push a manual tractor up there.' As he spoke he held his hand towards her. 'Have a sweet.'

Jingqiu saw that he had two sweets wrapped in paper in his hand. They didn't look like the ones you could buy in the market at home. Shyly, she shook her head. 'I won't, thanks. Give them to the little one.'

'And you're too old for them?' He was certainly looking at her as if she were a child.

'Me? Didn't you hear Huan Huan call me Auntie?'

He started laughing. Jingqiu liked this laugh a lot. Some people only move their facial muscles when they laugh, their mouths appear happy while their eyes are not, the expression in them cold and detached. But as he laughed small lines appeared at either side of his nose and his eyes squinted faintly. It was a laugh from deep within him, not at all mocking. It was heartfelt.

'You don't have to be a child to eat sweets,' he said, holding his hand out again. 'Take one, no need to be embarrassed.'

Jingqiu had no choice but to take a sweet, but she said, 'I'll take it for Huan Huan.' Huan Huan rushed over to her, begging to be carried. Jingqiu didn't know what she had done to secure his affection so easily and was a bit surprised. She lifted him up and said to Old Third, 'Auntie Zhang wants you to come home and eat dinner, we'd better go.'

'Let Uncle take you,' Old Third said. 'Your auntie has had a long day of walking, she must be very tired.' He scooped Huan Huan out of Jingqiu's arms, signalling to Jingqiu to start walking ahead. Jingqiu refused, for fear that he would watch her from behind and think her gait unattractive, or see that her clothes didn't fit. She said, 'You walk first. I . . . don't know the way.'

He didn't press her, and carrying Huan Huan went in front allowing Jingqiu to follow him. She watched, thinking that he walked like a well-trained soldier, marching with long rod-straight legs. He didn't look like either of his brothers, but as if he was from a different family altogether.

She asked, 'Just now, was that you playing the accordion?'

'Mmm-hmm, did you hear me? You must've heard all my mistakes.'

Jingqiu couldn't see his face, but she could sense that he was smiling. She stuttered, 'I . . . No, what mistakes? I don't really play, anyway.'

'Such modesty can only mean one thing: you must be an expert despite your young age.' He stopped and turned back. 'But lying is not good behaviour in children . . . So you can play. Did you bring one with you?' When Jingqiu shook her head he said, 'Then let's get mine, you can play a couple of tunes for me.'

Startled, Jingqiu waved her hands violently. 'No, no, I'm not good at it, you play . . . really well. I don't want to play.'

'Okay, another day then,' he said, and started walking again.

Jingqiu asked, 'How come people from around here know "The Hawthorn Tree"?'

'It's a famous song. It was popular around five or ten years ago, lots of people know it. Do you know the words?'

Her thoughts had jumped from the song to the hawthorn

tree up on the mountain. 'In the song, it says that hawthorn trees have white flowers, but today Mr Zhang said that the hawthorn tree up on the mountain has red flowers.'

'Yeah, some hawthorn trees have red flowers.'

'But with that tree, isn't it because the blood of those brave soldiers watered the tree's roots, turning the flowers red?' She felt a bit stupid. She thought he was laughing, so she asked, 'You think that question was stupid, don't you? I just wanted to be clear, you know, because I'm writing this textbook and I don't want to include any lies.'

'You don't need to lie. Whatever people tell you, you should write. Whether or not it's true, well, that's not your problem.'

'Do you believe that the flowers were coloured by the blood of those soldiers?'

'I don't believe so, no. From a scientific point of view it'd be impossible, they must've always been red. But it's what the people around here say, and of course it makes a nice story.'

'So you think everyone around here is telling lies?'

He laughed. 'Not telling lies exactly, they're just being poetic. The world exists objectively, but every person's experience of the world is different, and if you use a poet's eyes to look at the world, you see a different world.'

Jingqiu thought he could be quite 'literary', or as the king of spelling mistakes in her class would have said, 'aerodite'. 'Have you ever seen this hawthorn tree in bloom?'

'Uh-huh, it flowers every May.'

'Oh, I'm leaving at the end of April so I won't get to see it.'

'You can always come back to visit. This year, when it flowers, I'll let you know and you can come and see.'

'How will you let me know?'

He laughed again. 'There's always a way.' He was just making empty promises. Telephones were rare. No. 8 Middle School only had one, and if you wanted to make a long-distance call you had to trudge all the way to the telecommunications bureau on the other side of the city. A place like West Village probably didn't even have a phone.

He seemed to be thinking over the same problem. 'There's no phone in this village, but of course I could write you a letter.'

If he wrote a letter to her her mother would definitely get it first, and it'd no doubt scare her to death. Ever since she was small her mother had told her, one slip leads down a road of hardship. Even though her mother had never actually explained what 'one slip' meant, Jingqiu guessed that just having contact with a boy was probably enough. 'Don't write a letter, don't write,' she said. 'If my mother sees, what would she think?'

He turned round. 'Don't worry, if you don't want me to write, I won't write. Hawthorn trees don't just flower for one night and then die. The tree will be in bloom for a while. Just pick a Sunday in May, come back and take a look.'

Once they got to Mr Zhang's house he put Huan Huan down and went in with Jingqiu. Everyone in the family was back. Fen first introduced herself, and then introduced everyone else, this is my youngest brother, this is my sister-in-law. Jingqiu echoed, brother, sister-in-law, and everyone smiled, happy to have her with them.

Fen pointed to Old Third last and said, 'This is my third brother, say hello.'

Jingqiu was obedient, and greeted him, 'third brother', at which everyone laughed.

Jingqiu didn't understand what was so funny and blushed.

Old Third explained, 'I'm not really one of the family, I

stayed here before like you are now, but they like to call me that. You don't need to. My name is Sun Jianxin, you can call me by my real name, or what everyone else calls me, Old Third.'

Chapter Three

The next day, Yichang No. 8 Middle School Educational Reform Association got to work. In the following days and weeks they interviewed villagers, listening to their stories from the war against the Japanese, stories of being a 'village for the study of agriculture', stories of how they had struggled against such and such a capitalist in power. Sometimes they went to visit local sites of historical importance.

After the day's interviews were finished, the association's members would discuss together what they were going to write, and who was going to write what. They'd split up and write their sections, before coming together again to read out what they had written and noting down suggestions for revisions. In addition to working on the textbook, they spent one day a week in the fields with the farmers from the commune. The commune didn't rest on Sundays, so neither did Jingqiu. The Educational Reform Association members would take turns to return to their homes in Yichang city in order to report on their progress, and once home they were allowed to rest for two days.

Every Wednesday and Sunday the Zhang family's second daughter Fang returned from school in Yanjia River. She was of a similar age to Jingqiu, and as they slept in the same bed, they quickly became close friends. Fang taught Jingqiu how to fold the quilt into the special triangle shape, and Jingqiu helped Fang with her essays. In the evenings, they would stay awake late, talking, mostly about Fang's second brother, Lin, whom they called 'Old Second', and her sort-of-brother, 'Old Third'.

The custom of the village was that the sons in every family were nicknamed according to their age, so the oldest would be called Old First, the second son, Old Second, and the third, Old Third. This was not the custom for the daughters; for them, the family would just add the affectionate term yatou, or 'little girl', to their names, so Fang was called Fang yatou, and Fen, Fen yatou. This, of course, was only so long as they were still 'part of the family', as once married they would leave to join their husband's family; a married daughter was said to be like spilt water.

Fang said to Jingqiu, 'Mum says that since you've been here Old Second has become really hard-working. He's back a few times a day, bringing water because he's worried you city girls like to wash more than us country girls. And he thinks you're not used to the water being cold, so every day he boils lots of bottles so that you have water to drink and to wash in. Mum's really happy – she thinks he's trying to make you his wife.'

Jingqiu felt uneasy. She knew she couldn't repay Lin's kindness in a way that he might want.

Fang said, 'Old Third is also good to you. Mother said that he's been here replacing your light bulb, saying that the one we had here was too dark and it would be bad for your eyes. He also gave Mum some money and told her it's for the electricity bill.'

Jingqiu was overjoyed, but merely replied, 'That's only because he's worried about your eyes, it's your room after all.'

'This has been my room for a long time, but has he ever come to change my light bulb before?'

When Jingqiu next bumped into Old Third she tried to give

him some money but he wouldn't accept it. They argued until Jingqiu gave up. As she was preparing to leave, however, she put a bit of money on the table and left a note, just like the 8th Route Army used to do. No one had ever been so openly attentive to her since she had been burdened by her 'bad class background'. She felt that she had stolen a new life as Auntie and the rest of the family didn't know about her background. Just wait until they find out, she thought, they won't look at me in the same way.

One morning, Jingqiu got up and went to fold the quilt, only to discover an egg-sized blood-stain on the sheet. Her 'old friend' was back. It always made an appearance just before something important was about to happen, and now it was conducting its usual pre-emptive attack. Whenever her class had to go learn industrial production, study agriculture or do their military exercises, her 'old friend' would arrive unannounced. Jingqiu rushed to remove the sheet. She wanted to scrub the stain discreetly, but felt embarrassed about washing the sheet in the house. That day it happened to be raining so she had to wait until midday when it finally stopped, in order to go clean the sheet in the river.

She knew she shouldn't get into the cold water during a visit from her 'old friend' – her mother was always reminding her about this, explaining over and over the dangers. You mustn't drink cold water, you mustn't eat cold food, and you mustn't wash in cold water, otherwise you'll get toothache, headaches, and muscle aches. But that day she didn't have a choice. Standing on two large stones in the river she lowered the sheet into the water but it was shallow and as soon as she did so it got muddied by the riverbed. The more she washed the dirtier it became. Just do it, take off your shoes and get into deeper water, she thought.

As she was taking off her shoes she heard a voice say,

'You're here? Lucky I saw you, I was about to go upstream to wash my rubber boots. The mud would have made your sheets dirty.'

It was Old Third. Ever since she had called him 'brother' and been laughed at she didn't know what to call him, and even had she known what to say it wouldn't have mattered as she wouldn't have been able to get the words out anyway. Everything connected to him had become a taboo, and her mouth declined to offend. But to her eyes and ears and heart everything about him was as dear as Mao's Little Red Book; she wanted to read, and listen, and think about him all day.

He was still wearing the half-length cotton coat, but on his feet he wore a pair of long rubber boots, slathered in mud. She was diffident; it's raining so hard today, and here I am washing my sheets, he must be able to guess what's happened. She feared he might ask, so she turned the thoughts over madly in her head, desperately drafting a lie.

But he didn't ask her anything, just said, 'Let me, I'm wearing rubber boots, I can wade into deeper water.'

Jingqiu refused, but he had already removed his cotton coat, put it into her hands and grabbed the sheet. She cuddled his jacket close and stood by the bank, watching him push his sleeves up and stride into the deep water. First he used one hand to clean the mud off his boots, then started to pound the sheets.

After a while he took the sheet into his hands and, as if casting a net, spread it out on the water. The red stain bobbed on the surface. He let go and waited until the sheet was nearly swept away by the current, and Jingqiu became frightened, and called out. He reached into the water and pulled up the sheet. He played with the sheet like this a few times until Jingqiu was no longer disturbed by the prospect of the sheet floating away, and instead looked on in silence.

This time he didn't grab the sheet, and it was snatched by

the current. She watched it float further and further away until finally, as Old Third still hadn't reached out to grab it, she couldn't hold back any longer. She bellowed, making him laugh, and he ran through the choppy water to fetch it back.

Standing in the water, he turned back to look at her and said, 'Are you cold? If you are, wear my coat.'

'I'm not cold.'

He jumped up on to the bank and draped his coat over her shoulders, looked her up and down, and then shook with laughter.

'What? What is it?' she asked. 'Does it look that bad?'

'No, it's just too big, that's all. With it draped across you like that, you look like a mushroom.'

Seeing his hands were red with cold she asked, 'Aren't you cold?'

'I'd be lying if I said I wasn't,' he laughed, 'but I'll be all right in a minute.'

He went back into the water to continue washing the sheet, then after wringing it out, climbed back on to the bank. She passed him his coat and he picked up the wash basin with the sheet in it.

Jingqiu tried to wrestle the basin from him saying, 'You get to work, I'll take this back, thank you, very much.'

He wouldn't give it to her. 'It's lunchtime. I'm working near here now, so I'm off to take my break at Auntie's.'

Back at home, he showed her the bamboo pole used for drying clothes that was situated under the eaves at the back of the house, found a cloth to wipe the pole clean, and then helped her hang and peg the sheet to let it dry in the sun.

It all came so naturally to him. 'How come you're so good at housework?'

'I've lived away from home for a long time, I do everything myself.'

Auntie heard this and teased him. 'What a boaster! My Fen washes your quilt and your sheets.'

Fen must like him, Jingqiu thought, otherwise why would she wash his sheets?

During those weeks, Old Third came to Auntie's house almost every day at lunchtime. Sometimes he'd take a nap, sometimes he'd stop to say a few words to Jingqiu, and sometimes he would bring some eggs and meat so that Auntie could cook them for everyone. No one knew where he got them from as these things were rationed. On occasion he would even bring fruit, which was a rare treat indeed, so his visits made everyone happy.

Once he asked Jingqiu to let him see what she had written, saying, 'Comrade, I know a good craftsman doesn't show his uncut jade, but your writing is not rough, it's the history of the village, won't you let me see what you've written?'

Jingqiu was unable to dissuade him, so she let him read her work. He read it carefully, and then returned it to her. 'You've certainly got talent, but making you write this stuff, well, it's a waste.'

'Why?'

'These are all incidental essays, each one unconnected. They're not very interesting.'

His words shocked Jingqiu, he sounded so reactionary. Deep down she didn't like writing these essays either, but she didn't have any choice.

He could see that she put a lot of effort into her writing, so comforted her, 'Just write whatever, it'll be fine. Don't put so much energy into writing this stuff.'

She checked there was no one else around, and asked him, 'You say "don't put so much energy into writing this stuff". Well, what should I spend my energy on?'

'What you want to write. Have you ever written any stories, or poems?'

'No. How could someone like me write a story?'

He was amused. 'What kind of person do you think writes stories? I think you have the makings of a writer, you have a good style, and more importantly, you have a pair of poetic eyes, you can see the poetry in life.'

Jingqiu thought he was being 'aerodite' again, so said, 'You're always talking about being "poetic", everything's "poetic". What exactly do you mean by "poetic"?'

'In the past, I would have meant just that, "poetic". Nowadays, of course, I'm referring to "revolutionary romanticism".'

'You seem to know what you're talking about, why don't you write a story?'

'I want to write, but they're the kinds of things that no one would dare publish. The kinds of things that can be published, I don't want to write,' he laughed. 'The Cultural Revolution must have started just as you started school, but I was at senior high school at the time, I've been more deeply influenced by the capitalist period than you. I always wanted to go to university, Beijing University or Qinghua, but I was born too late.'

'Workers, farmers, and soldiers can study, why don't you do that?'

'What's the point? You don't learn anything at university now,' he said, shaking his head. 'What are you going to do once you finish school?'

'Work in the fields.'

'And after that?'

Jingqiu was upset – she didn't see that she had an 'after that'. Like all the other youths from the city, her brother had been sent down to the countryside a few years ago and had no way of returning. He was very good at the violin, and both the county performance troupe and the Army and Navy Political Song and Dance Ensemble had invited him to join them, but each time he came up for political review, the invitation was withdrawn. Hurt, she said, 'There is no "and after that". After I get sent to the countryside there's no way I'll get to come back, because my family's class status is bad.'

He reassured her. 'That's not true, of course you'll be able to come back, it'll only be a matter of when. Don't think too much about it or that far into the future. The world is changing every day. Who knows, by the time you finish school the policy might have been revoked, and you might not get sent at all.'

Jingqiu felt she had nothing else to say to him – he was the son of an official, and despite having suffered a little as well, everything was fine for him now. He'd never been sent down to learn from the peasants, but had been assigned to the geological unit straight away. People like him can't understand people like me, she thought, can't understand why I worry.

'I want to get back to writing,' she said, picking up her pen and pretending to start. He didn't say anything else, but left to take a nap and play with Huan Huan until he had to go back to work.

One day, he gave her a thick book, *Jean-Christophe* by Romain Rolland. 'Have you read it?'

'No, how did you get it?' Jingqiu asked him.

'My mum bought it. My dad is an official, but my mum isn't. You probably already know this, but just after Liberation, in the early 1950s, a new marriage law was passed. Lots of cadres abandoned their wives in the countryside and took new, pretty, educated city girls as wives. My mum was one of those young girls, the daughter of a capitalist family. Maybe she married my dad in order to change her class status, who knows? But she thought my dad didn't understand her so she was bitter and depressed, and lived most of her life through books. She loved reading and had lots of books, but when the Cultural Revolution started she was a coward and burnt most of them. My younger brother and I saved a few. Are you interested?'

Jingqiu said, 'It's capitalist, but I suppose we could absorb it critically?'

Again, he looked at her as if she were a child. 'They're all world-famous books. It's just that . . . right now in China, well, it's an unfortunate time. But famous works are famous for a reason, and don't become rubbish just because of some temporary changes. I have more if you're interested, but you can't read too many, otherwise it'll show in your writing. Or I could help you with your writing.'

There and then he sat down to help her with some paragraphs. 'I know a lot about the history of West Village. I'll write a bit and you can take it to your teachers and friends and see if they notice. If they don't, I'll carry on helping you.'

When she took her work to the group it seemed that no one could tell she had not written it herself. So, he became her 'hired hand'. He came every day at lunchtime to help her write her textbook, and she spent the time reading novels.

Chapter Four

One day the Educational Reform Association went to the eastern end of the village to visit a mountain cave, Heiwu Cliff, which was said to have been a hiding place during the war against Japan. A traitor had revealed its location to the Japanese who then surrounded the cave, trapping twenty or so villagers sheltering inside, and set it alight; those who ran out were shot, those who didn't were burned alive. You could still see the scorch marks on its dank walls.

This was the grisliest page in the history of West Village, and as the group listened their eyes filled with tears. After their visit they were supposed to have some food, but no one felt like eating, agreeing we're only alive today because these revolutionary martyrs spilt their blood and sacrificed their lives; surely we can eat a bit later? They started to discuss how to write up the events as a chapter of the textbook, talking without a break until two in the afternoon.

Jingqiu returned to Auntie's house but couldn't see Old Third. He must have come round, and then gone back to work. She wolfed down some leftovers, and hurried to her room to write up all she had heard that morning. The next day Old Third didn't come, leaving Jingqiu apprehensive. Did he come yesterday and get angry because I wasn't here? Won't he come back? This was impossible; since when was I so important as to arouse such feelings in Old Third?

For days Old Third didn't come. Jingqiu felt dispirited and tried to work out what she had done wrong. She couldn't write, couldn't eat, but could only think over and over, why isn't Old Third coming? She thought of asking Auntie and the family if they knew where he had gone, but she didn't dare in case people thought there was something between them.

In the evening, using Huan Huan as a cover, she took him to the geological unit's camp to find Old Third. When they drew close Jingqiu couldn't hear his accordion. She lingered a long time, but she didn't have the courage to enter the long building to ask after him, so they hurried back. Eventually she could bear it no longer and, attempting to be subtle, asked Auntie, 'Huan Huan was just asking, why hasn't Old Third come round for the last few days?'

'I was also wondering why. Maybe he's home visiting his family.'

Jingqiu went cold. Home visiting his family? Is he already married? She'd never asked him if he was married, and he had never mentioned it. Neither had Fang, but then, she had never said that he wasn't married either. Old Third said he was a senior high school student when the Cultural Revolution started, so that means he must be seven or eight years older than me, she thought, as I was in primary two at the time. If he hadn't followed the Party's appeal for later marriages, he could well be married. The thought of it pained her, made her feel cheated. But she thought through every moment they'd spent together and realised he hadn't cheated her, not really. They'd talked, he'd helped her with her writing, nothing else, he'd neither said nor done anything improper.

There was a picture of him under the glass plate in her room, a very small one, about one inch across, which must have been taken for some kind of official document. Often, when no one was around, Jingqiu lost herself looking at this photograph. Since meeting him she no longer took pleasure in the proletarian aesthetic, she only liked looking at his kind of face, his kind of outline, listening to his words, thinking about his sort of smile. Blackish-red faces, iron-like bodies, they could all go to hell. But he doesn't come here any more, maybe he can sense how I feel and is hiding from me? She'd be leaving West Village soon, and might never see him again. If she was this upset by not seeing him for a few days, how would she cope with never seeing him again?

It often happens that a person doesn't realise they are in love until they are suddenly separated from the object of their affection. Only then do they realise how deep their feelings run. Jingqiu had never before experienced this kind of longing. She felt that she had unconsciously given him her heart to take away, and now he had it with him, wherever he was. If he wanted to hurt her, all he had to do was give it a pinch; if he wanted to make her happy, all he had to do was smile upon it. She didn't know how she could have been so careless. They were from two different worlds, how could she have let herself fall in love with him?

There was nothing about her worthy of Old Third's affection, and he only came to Auntie's house because he had nothing else to do and wanted to rest. Maybe he was one of those flirts you read about in books who has his tricks for making girls fall into his arms. Old Third must have tricked her because now she couldn't give him up, and he knew that. This must be what her mother meant by 'one slip'. She recalled a scene from *Jane Eyre* in which, in order to let go of her love for Rochester, Jane looks in the mirror and says something like, You're a plain girl, you're not worthy of his love, never forget that.

In the last page of her notebook she wrote an oath: 'I promise to draw a line between myself and any capitalist thoughts, and put all my efforts into studying, working, writing this textbook, and taking concrete actions to thank the leaders of my school for the trust they have put in me.' She had to be discreet but she knew what she meant by 'capitalist thoughts'. A few days later, however, her 'capitalist thoughts' resurfaced. It was afternoon, nearly five o'clock, and Jingqiu was writing in her room when she heard Auntie say, 'You're back? Did you visit your family?'

A voice that made her tremble replied, 'No, I went to work over at the second division.'

'Huan Huan has been asking after you. We missed you.'

Jingqiu started and then reflected, well, at least she didn't say I was asking, Huan Huan can get the blame. She heard the scapegoat scampering about in the living room, before he came in to give her some sweets, from Old Third apparently. She accepted them, and then changing her mind, gave them back to Huan Huan, and smiled as he ripped open two at once and stuffed them into his mouth, swelling both cheeks.

She was resolute; she would sit still in her room, she would not go out to see Old Third. She listened to him chatting to Auntie. She let out a long breath, and within those moments forgot her oath. She desperately wanted to see him and exchange a few words with him, but then told herself, Jingqiu, this is the moment of truth, you've got to stand by your words. So she sat stone-still, refusing to go out and meet him.

After a while she couldn't hear his voice any more and, realising that he'd left, was full of regret. I've wasted a rare opportunity to see him, haven't I? She rose to her feet, flustered, wanting to see where he had gone. A glimpse would be enough to settle her. She stood up and turned, only to see him leaning against the door frame, looking at her.

'Where are you off to?' he asked.

'I'm . . . going round the back.'

There was a crude outhouse in the yard, and 'going round the back' was short for making a visit to this toilet. He smiled, and said, 'Off you go, I won't get in the way, I'll wait for you here.'

Dumbly, she looked at him, noticing that he'd got thinner; his cheeks were sunken and bristles were appearing on his chin. She'd never seen him like this, his chin was normally smooth-shaven. She asked, 'It must've been tiring work . . . over there?'

'Not really, technical stuff isn't too physically demanding.' He stroked his face, and asked, 'Thinner, aren't I? I haven't been sleeping.'

He stared at her and she grew more nervous. Maybe my cheeks have hollowed too. She said quietly, 'How come you went without saying anything to Auntie? Huan Huan was asking after you.'

He was still staring at her but, matching her soft tone, he replied, 'I had to leave in a hurry. I planned to come over and tell you . . . all, but I did go to the post office while I was waiting for the bus at Yanjia River and told Sen. Maybe he forgot. In the future I won't rely on someone else to give you the message, I'll come and tell you myself.'

Jingqiu froze, what did he mean? Can he read my mind? Does he know how much I've been missing him? 'Why tell me? What do I care . . . where you go?'

'You don't care where I go, but I want to tell you, is that okay?' He tilted his head, and spoke with an edge in his voice.

Embarrassed, she didn't know what to say and rushed off to the back of the house. When she went back to her room she found Old Third sitting at her desk leafing through her notebook. She charged at him, slammed shut the book, and said, 'How can you go looking through people's stuff without asking?'

He smiled, and mimicked her. 'How can you go writing about people without asking?'

'Where have I written anything about you? Have I written your name anywhere? It was a . . . resolution, that's all.'

'I didn't say you wrote about me, I meant you didn't ask permission from those anti-Japanese soldiers. Have you written about me? Where? Isn't this the village history?'

She was mortified that she'd mentioned the resolution; he'd obviously just been looking through the stories in the opening pages. Thankfully he didn't keep asking and instead brought out a brand new fountain pen. 'Use this pen from now on. I've been wanting to give you one for a while, I just didn't have the chance. Yours leaks, your middle finger is always covered in ink.'

He always had lots of pens lined up in his top coat pocket, and once she had laughed at him. 'You're such an intellectual, with so many pens.'

He'd answered then, 'Haven't you heard? One pen means you're a student, two pens means you're a professor, and three pens . . . ' He had paused.

'What? Who has three pens? A writer?'

'Three pens and you're a pen repairman.'

'So you're a pen repairman?' she had laughed.

'Uh-huh, I like to tinker with things, repair fountain pens, watches, clocks, I've even taken apart an accordion just to have a look inside. But I had a look at your old pen, and it can't be fixed, it needs to be replaced. When I get the chance, I'll buy you a new one. Aren't you afraid of getting ink on your face when you use this old pen? You girls find that particularly embarrassing.'

She hadn't replied. Her family was poor so she couldn't afford a new pen. This old pen, in its day, had also been a present.

Now he passed her the new pen. 'Do you like it?'

Jingqiu took it. It was a handsome Gold Star brand fountain pen, so lovely. She couldn't bear the thought of putting ink into it. She thought she could maybe take it and pay him back later, but then she remembered, even the money her mother had had to pay in advance to cover her food on this expedition was borrowed. Reminded of this, and feeling ashamed, she returned the pen to Old Third. 'I don't want it, my pen works fine.'

'Why don't you want it? Don't you like it? When I was buying it I thought, you probably don't like black, but this type doesn't come in any other colours. I think it's a good pen, the nib is fine, perfect for your delicate characters.' He paused. 'Use this pen for now, next time I'll buy you a better one.'

'No, don't. It's not that I don't like this one, it's nice, too nice ... and expensive.'

He relaxed. 'It wasn't expensive. As long as you like it. Why don't you put some ink in it and give it a try?' As he spoke he took her ink bottle and filled the pen himself. Before writing he swayed the pen from side to side, as if mulling over a tricky problem. After performing this ritual, he wrote quickly in her notebook.

Over his shoulder, she could see that he'd written a poem.

If life is lived in single file, please walk in front so I can
watch you all the time;
if life's road is walked in two lanes, side by side,
let me take you by the hand, so when we walk through
life's sea of people,
forever you will be mine.

She really liked it. 'Who wrote it?'

'I just wrote whatever came into my head. It's not a poem,

really.' He insisted she take the pen, saying that if she didn't take it he would go to her association and tell them that the pen was a donation given especially to Jingqiu to allow her to write the distinguished history of West Village. Jingqiu wasn't sure if he was teasing and worried that he really might do this, and then everyone would know, she decided to take it. But she promised to pay him back once she had earned some money.

'Fine,' he said, 'I'll wait.'

Chapter Five

The following Wednesday and Thursday it was Jingqiu's turn to return home to Yichang. She had given her first two allocated holidays to a fellow student, Good Health Lee, because in fact he wasn't in good health at all. His face was constantly covered in blotches which required regular hospital check-ups. But another reason Jingqiu let him go in her place was that she didn't actually have the money to get home. Her mother's salary was just over forty yuan a month and that had to pay for her mother and sister's living costs, pocket money for her brother, and some had to go to help her father in the labour camp. Each month their expenditure exceeded their income. But her form teacher had sent a letter back with a member of Jingqiu's association. The school was going to put on a show, and the class needed Jingqiu to choreograph the steps for their performance. They'd already collected the money she would need for the bus so she had no choice.

Jingqiu's mother taught at No. 8 Middle School's adjoining primary school, and was a colleague of Jingqiu's form teacher. The form teacher knew that Jingqiu's family was poor, and at registration each term she arranged to let Jingqiu suspend payment of her fees. The family couldn't afford even these three or four yuan. Jingqiu's teacher would also try to get her to claim a bursary of fifteen yuan a term from the school, but

Jingqiu refused; the application required the approval of her class, and she didn't want them to know her situation.

Instead, every year during the summer holidays she would look for temporary work, mostly doing odd jobs on construction sites: moving bricks, mixing mortar and shovelling it into wooden buckets for the bricklayer. It meant she had to stand high up on ladders to catch bricks hurled from below, and sometimes she'd have to help carry heavy cement panels. It was arduous and dangerous work, but she could earn one or two yuan per day so she went back every year.

The thought of returning home now made her both happy and anxious. She was happy that she would get to see her mother and sister. Her mother wasn't very strong and her sister was still young, so Jingqiu worried about them. She knew she could help them buy coal and rice and do some of the heavier work around the house. But the truth was she didn't want to leave Old Third. Two days at home would mean two days of not seeing him, and she knew she didn't have much time left in West Village before she had to return to Yichang for good.

When Auntie heard that Jingqiu was going home for two days she tried to insist that Lin should accompany her over the mountain to the bus. Jingqiu refused saying she didn't want to get in the way of his work, but really it was because she knew she would never be able to repay his kindness in the way he wanted. She knew from Fang that a few years earlier Lin had fallen for a young city girl who had been sent down to learn from the peasants in West Village. It was likely that she had only returned Lin's affections once conscious of Mr Zhang's influential position in the village. She later made Lin a solemn promise that if he were to arrange for her return to the city she would marry him. Lin did so, asking his father to organise the transfer. She left without ever returning, saying to people that it was Lin's fault for being so stupid, that he hadn't cooked his rice in time. Had he proposed to her she couldn't have left him in the lurch like that. The episode had made Lin a laughing stock of the whole village, and even the young children taunted him, 'Stupid Lin, Stupid Lin, the chicken's flown off, and the egg is bust; she's gone to the city, can't see her for dust.'

For a long time Lin's face had been lined with sorrow. He was listless, refusing all offers of matchmaking from friends and family. But ever since Jingqiu arrived, his spirits had been revived and seeing this Auntie encouraged Fang to propose the match to Jingqiu. Jingqiu thought that a graceful way to avoid it all was to ask Fang to tell Auntie that because her class background was bad, she wouldn't be a good match for Lin. On hearing this Auntie rushed over herself to speak to Jingqiu. 'What does it matter if your class status is bad? If you marry Lin it will improve, as will your children's.'

Jingqiu blushed crimson, and silently begged for a hole to appear and swallow her up. She said, 'I'm young, I'm young. I'm not planning to find a partner so soon, I'm still at school, and they're encouraging later marriages. I can't think about this until after I turn twenty-five.'

'Marry at twenty-five? You'll be so old your bones will slap together like a wooden clapper. The girls in our village marry early. The production unit can get you a licence anytime so you can marry whenever you like.' Auntie Zhang reassured Jingqiu, 'I don't want you to marry this instant, I just wanted to say that as long as our Lin is in your heart, that's all that matters.'

Jingqiu didn't know what to say to Auntie and so pleaded with Fang to explain. 'Old Second and me, well it's not possible. I ... don't know what else to say, just that it's not possible.'

Fang was highly amused by it all. 'I know it's not possible, but I'm not going to be the bearer of bad news, you'll have to say it yourself.'

The day before Jingqiu was to leave for Yichang Lin came to find her, his face flushed. 'Mother has told me to accompany you tomorrow. The mountain road is empty and not safe, and it's far ... and the water levels could rise.'

Jingqiu desperately tried to make excuses, repeating, 'There's no need, I can go myself.' Then a thought occurred to her. 'Are there tigers on the mountain?'

Lin was honest in his reply. 'No, this mountain's not big, I've never heard of any wild animals. My mother just said she's afraid there might be ... villains.'

Actually, the truth was that Jingqiu really did want someone to accompany her over the mountain as she didn't feel brave enough to walk it alone, but she preferred to risk the dangers of the road alone rather than finding herself in Lin's debt.

That evening Old Third came round. Jingqiu wanted to tell him that she was leaving the next day and would be in Yichang for two days, but somehow couldn't find the right moment. She hoped that someone else would mention it but no one did. Maybe there's no need to tell him, she thought, he probably won't even come over, and if he does, he probably won't be upset at not seeing me. She got up from the living room and returned to her bedroom pretending that she needed to write a few reports. She kept her ears pricked for activity in the living room. I'll just wait until he says goodbye and then sneak out to tell him, she promised herself.

She waited in her room without writing a single word. When it was nearly ten she heard him saying goodbye and while she was panicking, thinking of a way to slip out and tell him, he suddenly entered her room, removed the pen from her hand and scrawled a few words on a piece of paper. Tomorrow go to the mountain road, I'll be waiting for you. Eight o'clock.

She raised her head to look at him, and watched as a smile inched across his face. He was waiting for her reply, but before she had a chance to answer him Auntie walked in.

Old Third spoke loudly. 'Thank you, I'll be off,' and left.

'What was he thanking you for?' Auntie was suspicious.

'Oh, he asked me to buy some things for him in Yichang.'

'I also wanted to ask you to get me something.' Auntie took out some money and said, 'Could you buy some wool for Lin and knit him a new jumper? You can decide the colour and pattern. Yumin told me that you're very good at it.'

Jingqiu felt she couldn't say no to this request, so she took the money. She consoled herself, I can't be Auntie's daughter-in-law, but knitting him a jumper can be my repayment.

That evening, she couldn't sleep. She kept taking out the piece of paper with his handwriting on it. How did he know she was leaving tomorrow? Doesn't he have work? What will he say, what will he do? She was delighted that he was going to escort her, but then she became worried. Girls were supposed to be on their guard with men, and wasn't he a man? Us two, alone on that road. If he wants to do something to me, can I defend myself? Isn't a man a threat? She really had little idea, didn't know what exactly that threat was. You'd often see posters plastered around with men's names on them, crossed out in red. Some had committed crimes for which they had been executed, and of course she'd heard the word 'rape' before. There had been a few 'rapists' on those posters, and sometimes there would even be a description of the crime, but only in the vaguest terms so you couldn't tell exactly what had happened.

Jingqiu remembered once seeing one of these posters. It had said the man had been 'exceedingly cruel, and had forced a screwdriver into the woman's lower regions'. She had discussed it with some female friends. Where are a woman's 'lower regions'? They agreed it must be below the waist, but where exactly had this rapist put the screwdriver? She had never managed to work it out. All of Jingqiu's friends were students at No. 8 Middle School, or else daughters of teachers at the adjoining primary school. Some of them were a bit older, and seemed to know more about life, but they enjoyed revealing only half-truths and fragments of their knowledge. To Jingqiu, puzzling it all out was like wandering around in a fog.

She had heard people saying that so-and-so had been 'knocked up', had had their 'belly made big' by so-and-so. She had tried to figure it out herself. She gathered it involved 'sleeping' with a man, valuable information gleaned from her mother's colleague whose son had been dumped by his girlfriend. Angered, the mother had gone around saying to people, 'That girl slept with my son, got knocked up, and now she doesn't want him. We'll see if anyone wants her.'

Mulling over all these stories and gossip, Jingqiu came up with a plan: tomorrow she would walk over the mountain with Old Third, but she would be vigilant. Since she wouldn't be sleeping on the mountain there shouldn't be any risk of getting 'knocked up', but it would be better to let him walk in front, that way he wouldn't be able to surprise her, or press her to the ground. The only worry left was if anyone saw them and told her association. That would be a disaster.

At seven o'clock the next morning Jingqiu got up, combed her hair, said goodbye to Auntie, and left the house on her own. She first walked to the upper reaches of the river, crossed on the small boat, and started to climb the mountain. She didn't have much with her, so the walk took less effort than last time. She had just reached the top when she saw Old Third. He wasn't wearing his blue uniform, but rather a short jacket she had never seen before which revealed the entire length of his long legs. She suddenly found she liked men with long legs. As soon as she saw him she forgot the previous night's pledge.

Smiling, he watched her as she approached. 'I saw you leave. When I started out I thought you might not come.'

'Aren't you working today?'

'I took the day off.' He reached into his backpack, took out an apple and gave it to her. 'Have you eaten yet?'

'No. Have you?'

'I haven't either. We can get something in town.' He took her bag from her. 'You're very brave. Were you prepared to cross the mountain on your own? Aren't you afraid of jackals, tigers, or panthers?'

'Lin told me there aren't any wild animals up here. He said I should only be careful of villains.'

Old Third laughed. 'And am I one of these villains?'

'I don't know.'

'I'm not a villain. You'll come to realise that.'

'You were brave yesterday, Auntie nearly saw that note.' Saying this made her feel like they were up to no good, and as the feeling of complicity came over her, her face reddened.

But he didn't notice. 'It wouldn't have mattered if she'd seen, she can't read. And anyway, my handwriting's messy. I was only worried you wouldn't be able to understand my characters.'

The mountain road was too narrow for them to walk side by side, so he walked ahead and had to turn around to talk. 'What did Auntie say?'

'She wanted me to buy some wool for Lin and knit him a jumper.'

'Auntie wants you for her daughter-in-law, that's what she wants. Did you know that?'

'She said.'

'Did you ... say yes?'

Jingqiu nearly fell over with shock. 'What are you talking about? I'm still at school.'

'Does that mean if you weren't at school you would say yes?' Old Third teased. 'Did you agree to make him a jumper?'

'Yes.'

'Well, if you agreed to knit him a jumper then you can make me one too!'

'You sound like a child! Someone gets a jumper, so you have to have one too?' She gained courage. 'Are you sure you want me to knit you one? What would your wife say?'

He was startled. 'What wife? Who told you I have a wife?'

So he isn't married. She was rapturous, but continued to push him. 'Auntie said you had a wife, that last time you left you went home to visit your family.'

'I'm not married yet, so what wife is that? She must have been trying to get you and Lin together, otherwise why would she say that? You ask the men at my unit, they'll tell you if I'm married or not. If you don't believe me, you'll believe my unit, yes?'

'Why would I ask your unit? What's it got to do with me whether you're married or not?'

'I was just worried you'd got the wrong idea,' Old Third replied.

He must like me, otherwise why would he worry that I'd got the wrong idea, Jingqiu thought. But something stopped her from persisting. She'd approached an exciting but dangerous point and she could see that he didn't seem to want to continue either, instead changing the topic of conversation to her family. She decided to be candid, that she would tell him the truth to test him. She spoke of her father's denunciation, how he had been driven out to the countryside, how both he and her brother had no chance of returning, she told him all of it. He listened, never interrupting and asking questions only when she faltered.

Jingqiu said, 'I remember at the beginning of the Cultural Revolution and my mother still hadn't been hunted down. One evening, when I was with my friends, we ran to the meeting hall at my mother's school as we heard noise and we wanted to see what it was all about. We knew they often held struggle meetings there. We thought struggle sessions were fun, watching people being criticised as traitors to the revolution. That day a teacher called Zhu Jiajing was confessing to being a traitor, but only in order to save her skin. She said she had never defected, and had never betrayed a comrade. She was often pulled out for struggle sessions but was always perfectly calm, would raise her head, and say coldly, "You're not talking sense. This is not true, and I can't be bothered to respond." One day, I went with my friends to the meeting hall as usual to see what was going on, and this time I saw my mother in the middle of the crowd being criticised, her head lowered. My friends started laughing at me and copying my mother. I was so scared I ran home, hid and cried. When my mother returned she didn't say anything, because she thought I hadn't seen.

'When the day came for her to be publicly criticised, she knew she couldn't hide it from us any more, so at lunchtime she gave my sister and me some money and told us to go to the market across the river, and not to come back before dinner. We stayed away until five o'clock. As soon as we entered the school gate we saw a poster so big it could have covered the sky, and on it was my mother's name, written upside down with a red cross over it, calling her a historical counter-revolutionary.

'Back at home I saw that mother had cried till her eyes were red-raw, her face was swollen on one side, as were her lips, and her head was shaved. She sat in front of the mirror, trying to neaten the tufts of her hair with some scissors. She's a proud person, with a strong sense of self-worth. She couldn't bear being criticised in public like that. She held us as we cried, and told us if it weren't for us three children she wouldn't be able to go on.'

Old Third said softly, 'You have a wonderfully strong mother who can bear such pain and humiliation for her children. Don't be too upset, lots of people have had similar experiences; you just need to get through it. Be like that Zhu woman, raise your head, be proud, and don't let it get to you.'

Jingqiu thought his class alignment was confused; how can he compare my mother's actions with that traitor Zhu? She was upset. 'My mother isn't an historical counter-revolutionary, she was liberated. She's allowed to teach. Those people made a mistake. My mother's father joined the Communist Party but when he moved he couldn't find his new local branch. People claimed that he'd left voluntarily. Around the time of the Liberation he was arrested, and before they bothered to get the whole story clear he got sick and died in custody. But that's not my mother's fault.'

Old Third tried to comfort her. 'The most important thing is that you believe in her, because even if she were a historical counter-revolutionary, she is still a wonderful mother. Politics . . . who knows? Don't use political labels to judge your loved ones.'

Jingqiu was exasperated. 'You sound exactly like that traitor Zhu. Her daughter asked her why she had turned herself in, saying if she hadn't, by now she'd have become a revolutionary martyr. Her mother replied, "I'm not afraid of being beaten, nor of death, but your father is in prison and if I don't confess you'll all starve to death."'

Old Third let out a breath. 'On the one hand she has to

think of her children, and on the other, the cause. I suppose it was hard for her to choose. But if she hadn't betrayed anyone there was no need to punish her like that. At that time the Party had a policy – to help them stay in power – that after being imprisoned you were allowed to leave the Party if you made an announcement in the newspaper. As long as you hadn't betrayed anyone, it was fine. Some people who had been in leadership positions, but were later imprisoned, did this.'

He rattled off a few names as examples. Jingqiu listened, stunned. 'You're such a reactionary!'

He laughed. 'What, are you going to expose me? These things are all open secrets in the Party's upper circles, even people lower down the hierarchy know about some of it,' he teased. 'You're just too innocent. If you want to expose me, I'll confess and die in your arms, perfectly contented. All I ask is that after I'm dead and buried, you come put some hawthorn flowers on my grave, and erect a stone with the words, here lies the person I loved.'

She raised her arm and pretended to hit him, threatening, 'Don't talk rubbish, or I won't listen.'

He bent his head towards her and waited for her to hit him, but seeing that she would not come closer he leaned back. 'My mother's story might be even more tragic than your mother's. When she was young she was progressive, very revolutionary; she personally led the factory's guards to look for her capitalist father's hidden property. She watched with her own eyes, unaffected, as people interrogated and tortured him. She thought it was all for the revolution. After she married, however she kept a low profile, working as a cadre in the city community arts centre. She was married to my father for many years, and during that time was estranged from her own father, but in her bones she was still a capitalist intellectual. She liked literature, romance, and beautiful things. She read lots of books, and loved poetry – she even wrote some herself – but she didn't show it to anyone because she knew that it would be considered bourgeois.

'During the Cultural Revolution my father was condemned as a "capitalist roader", was criticised and ostracised, and we were forced out of our army residence. My mother too was called a capitalist, and a corrupt cadre. They used cruel methods to lure my father into dangerous waters. At that time the community arts centre was covered in vulgar posters that described my mother as a filthy, shameless woman.

'Like your mother, she was proud. She'd never suffered a smear campaign like that before so she had no way of coping. She argued with them, speaking in her own defence, but the more she did so the worse it got. They used different ways to humiliate her, forced her to pass on details that would trap my father. Every day, when she got home, she would spend a long time washing, trying to scrub away the dirt of their insults. They hit her until she couldn't get up, and only then would they let her go home to dress her wounds.

'During this time my father was being criticised in the provincial and metropolitan newspapers. The pages and pages of articles got steadily more offensive, saying his lifestyle was seedy, that he had seduced and raped nurses, secretaries and office workers. My mother struggled on, but she was defeated finally by what she believed was my father's betrayal. She took a white scarf, and with it, ended her life. She left us a note: "Though pure in essence, when of impure destiny, and when born at the wrong time, regret can come only after death."'

Jingqiu asked quietly, 'Did your father really do those things?'

'I don't know. I think my father loved my mother, although

he didn't know how to love her in the right way, in a way that satisfied her. But still, he loved her. It's been years since my mother died, and my father was reinstated at an early stage. Lots of people tried to set him up with other women but he has never remarried. My father is always saying that Chairman Mao understood life when he said, "Victory comes only after further struggle." Sometimes when you feel you have reached an impasse, when you think there is no hope left, if you struggle on a bit more, and a bit more, you'll see the glimmer of success.'

Jingqiu was shocked that he'd experienced such sorrow. She wanted to comfort him, but didn't know what to say. They walked on in silence until he surprised her with a question: 'Can I come with you to Yichang?'

'Why do you want to come with me to Yichang? If my mother sees, or my teacher or classmates, they'll think ...' She broke off.

'What will they think?'

'They'll think, they'll think ... well it would create a bad impression.'

He laughed. 'I've scared you so much you can't speak. Calm down. If you say I can't come with you I won't. Your words are my command.' He continued carefully, 'Then can I wait for you in town when you come back? You'll be using this road on the way back, won't you? How can I relax knowing you're walking back this way alone?'

She was grateful to him for obliging her. She said he couldn't come with her to Yichang so he wasn't coming. 'I'll be on the four o'clock bus tomorrow, so I'll arrive at five.'

'I'll wait for you at the station.'

They carried on, happy in their silence, until Jingqiu said, 'Tell me a story. You've read so many books, you've probably got lots of stories stored up. Tell me one.'

He told her a few stories, and after each one came to an end Jingqiu prompted, 'Another one?' They continued in this way until finally he told her a story about a young man who, in order to further his father's career, had agreed to marry the daughter of his father's boss. But because the young man was not in love he was forever postponing the wedding. Then, one day, he met a girl that he really did fall for and wanted to marry. The only problem was that when the girl found out that he was engaged she told him she could not trust him.

At this point, he stopped.

'And then what? Finish the story.'

'I don't know the end of the story. If you were that girl – I mean, if you were the girl that the young man fell in love with – what would you do?'

Jingqiu pondered his question. 'I think, if that young man could go back on a promise to another girl, then . . . if I were that second girl I wouldn't trust him either.' She had a moment of suspicion. 'Is this your story? Are you talking about yourself?'

He shook his head. 'No, I took it from books I've read. All love stories are much the same. Have you read *Romeo and Juliet*? Romeo really loves Juliet, right? But you mustn't forget, before meeting Juliet he liked another girl.'

'Really?'

'Have you forgotten? Romeo first meets Juliet at a party where he's gone to find another girl, but when he sees Juliet he falls in love. So, can you say that just because he let the first girl down, he was definitely going to do the same to Juliet?'

Jingqiu thought about it, then said, 'But he didn't have time to let Juliet down because he died so soon after meeting her.'

'I've just thought of the ending to my story: the young man goes crazy and tries looking for the girl everywhere but can't find her, and unable to live without her, he kills himself.'

'You've definitely made that up.'

CHAPTER SIX

On Thursday afternoon Jingqiu ran to the long-distance bus station and crammed herself into the last bus headed for Yiling. But the plans she'd made with Old Third hadn't allowed for the possibility of the bus breaking down on an empty stretch of road far from any village, or for it being stuck there for over an hour before the bus rattled into action again. Jingqiu was extremely anxious, for it would be past seven before they got to the town, the station would be closed, and who knew if Old Third would still be waiting. If he's gone, I've got no way of getting back to West Village, she thought. I'll have to find somewhere to stay in town. But she had very little money. If absolutely necessary, I'll have to use the change left from what Auntie gave me for Lin's wool.

As the bus approached the station she was relieved to see Old Third standing in the yellow light of dusk, underneath a street lamp, waiting for her. As soon as the bus stopped he bounded up and eagerly squeezed along the middle of the bus towards her.

'I thought you weren't coming or that the bus had crashed. Hungry? Let's find somewhere to eat.' He took her bags, smiling. 'So much stuff? Are you carrying things for other people?' Without waiting for an explanation, he grabbed her hand and led her off the bus to find a restaurant. She tried to tug back her hand but he was holding it tight, and as it was evening, she figured no one could see anyway, so she let herself be led.

The town was small and most of the restaurants had closed for the evening. 'If you've eaten, we don't need to find somewhere,' Jingqiu said. 'I can eat back at West Village.'

Old Third pulled her by the hand. 'Come with me, I've got an idea.' He took her to an area of farmland on the outskirts of town. As long as you had money there was always food to be found. After walking a while he saw a house. 'This one. The house is big, and so is the pigsty, so they'll have some left-over pork. Let's eat here.'

They knocked on the door and a middle-aged woman opened it. On hearing that they were looking for food, and seeing coins gleaming in Old Third's hand, she led them into the house. Old Third gave her some money, and the woman started to prepare the meal. Old Third went to help to light the fire, first sitting on a pile of hay in front of the stove. Like a seasoned expert, he stacked the firewood and lit it, and then pulled Jingqiu to sit beside him. The heap of hay was small so they had to squeeze together to fit, but despite having to almost lean against him, she wasn't scared or nervous. After all, the people in this house didn't know them.

The light of the flames from the stove flickered on Old Third's face and he looked particularly handsome. Jingqiu kept stealing glances at him, as did he at her. When their eyes met he asked, 'Are you having fun?'

'Yes.'

Jingqiu had rarely had such a sumptuous meal. The rice was fresh, simply boiled and delicious, and the dishes were flavourful and fragrant: one bowl of pan-fried tofu, one of bottle-green oily spinach, some pickles, and two handmade sausages. Old Third gave them both to her. 'I know how much you like sausages, so I asked especially, saying if she didn't have any we'd go elsewhere.'

'How do you know I like sausages?' She couldn't eat both, he had to have one.

'I don't like them that much, honestly. I like pickled vegetables, we don't get them at the camp.'

She knew he was just saying that so she would take them both. Who doesn't love sausages? She insisted that he eat one, and that if he didn't she wouldn't eat any either. They squabbled until the woman, looking on, laughed. 'You two are so funny. Do you want me to cook another two?'

Old Third quickly pulled out some more money. 'Cook two more, yes, we can eat them on the road.'

After they had finished he asked Jingqiu, 'Do you still want to go back today?'

'Of course, where else would we go?' she said, startled.

'We could find somewhere to stay.' He smiled, then said, 'Let's go back, otherwise you'll worry yourself sick about what people will say.'

When they got outside he took her hand saying it was dark and that he didn't want her to fall. 'You're not scared of me holding your hand like this, are you?'

'Uh-uh.'

'Has anyone ever held your hand before?'

'No. Have you ever held someone else's hand?'

It took some time for him to reply. Eventually he said, 'If I had, would you think me a villain?'

'Then you definitely have.'

'Holding hands and *holding hands* are two different things. Sometimes you do it because of responsibility, because you don't have a choice, and sometimes you do it . . . out of love.'

People usually used other words, not love. Something

caught in her throat as he said this. She fell silent, unsure of what he would say next.

'There's the hawthorn tree. Do you want to go over and sit for a while?'

'No. Lots of soldiers were killed there, and in the dark, it'd be scary.'

'You believe in Communism and ghosts?' he joked.

Jingqiu was embarrassed. 'I don't believe in ghosts, I just don't like the darkness of the forest, that's all.' Suddenly she remembered the first time she'd seen the hawthorn tree and asked him, 'The day I came to West Village, I thought I saw someone standing underneath the tree, wearing a white shirt. Did you stop at this tree that day?'

'Someone in a shirt on such a cold day?' Old Third said. 'They'd have frozen to death. Maybe one of the Japanese soldiers' wronged spirit looks like me. Maybe that day he appeared, and you just happened to see him, so you thought it was me. Look! He's appeared again.'

Jingqiu didn't dare look around. Frightened, she started to run, but Old Third pulled her back into his arms, and holding her tight, he whispered, 'I was joking, there's no such thing as wronged spirits. I only said it to scare you.' He held her for a while, and then joked again, 'I wanted to scare you into my arms. I had no idea you would start running in the opposite direction. Obviously, you don't trust me.'

Jingqiu buried her head in his chest. She couldn't pull herself away – she really was scared – and so dug herself deeper into this body. He pulled tighter, until her cheek found itself up against his heart. She had no idea men's bodies smelt like this, so indescribably wonderful that it made her giddy. She thought, if I had someone to depend on and trust, I wouldn't be afraid of the dark, nor of ghosts. Only of other people seeing us.

'But you're scared too.' She raised her head to look up at him. 'Your heart is beating very fast.'

'I'm really scared,' he said. 'Listen to my heart beating, beating so hard it's going to jump out of my mouth.'

'Can your heart jump out of your mouth?' Jingqiu laughed.

'Why not? Haven't you ever read that in books?'

'It says that in books?'

'Of course. His heart was beating so fast it was almost in his mouth.'

Jingqiu felt her heart, and with a hint of suspicion asked, 'It's not fast, certainly not as fast as yours, so how could it nearly be in my mouth?'

'You can't feel it yourself? If you don't believe me, open your mouth and I'll see if it's in there.'

Before she had time to react he had already leant down to kiss her. Jingqiu tried to force him off. But he didn't pay any attention and continued kissing her, stretching his tongue so far into her mouth that she almost gagged. It's obscene, how can he do this? No one had ever said that kissing was like this. He can't be doing this for any honourable reason, she thought, so I'll have to try to stop him. She bit together so he could only slide his tongue between her lips and her teeth but his assault continued, and she continued to lock her jaw shut.

'Don't . . . you like it?' he asked.

'No.' That actually wasn't the truth. It wasn't that she didn't like it, it was just that the way it made her feel, the way she wanted to respond startled her. It made her feel wanton and depraved. She liked having his face close to hers, she liked discovering that a boy's face could be warm and soft; she had always thought them cold and hard like stone.

He laughed, and relaxed his hold a little. 'You're certainly making me work hard.' He put her backpack back on. 'Let's go.' For the rest of the way he didn't hold her hand, just walked beside her.

Jingqiu asked cautiously, 'Are you angry?'

'I'm not angry, I'm just concerned that you don't like holding my hand.'

'I didn't say I didn't like it.'

He grabbed hold of it. 'So you do like it?'

'You know so why ask?'

'I don't know, and you're teasing me. I want to hear you say it.'

Still she didn't answer and he persisted in squeezing her hand as they walked down the mountain.

The man who operated the small ferry had shut down for the day. 'Let's not shout for the boat,' Old Third said. 'There's a saying around here to describe unresponsive people, it goes, speaking to them is like calling for the ferry after hours. I'll carry you on my back instead.'

As he spoke he took off his shoes and socks, and after stuffing his socks into his shoes he tied them together with his laces and hung them around his neck. Next he fastened his bags around his neck in a similar fashion. He knelt down in front of her so she could climb on, but she refused. 'I'll go myself.'

'Don't be embarrassed. Come on, it's not good for girls to walk in cold water. It's dark, no one can see. Jump up.'

She climbed on to his back reluctantly, and clasped his shoulders, trying hard to make sure her breasts didn't touch his back. 'Lean over, and put your arms around my neck otherwise it won't be my fault if you fall in the water.' At that moment he seemed to slip, tilting sharply to one side, so she threw herself forward and flung her arms around his neck, her breasts pressing against his back. It was strangely comfortable. He, however, was shivering all over.

'Am I too heavy?'

He didn't reply, trembled for a while, and then settled. Carrying her, he slowly waded across the river. Midway, he said, 'We have a saying where I'm from, "an old man needs to be married, an old woman needs to be carried". I'll carry you whether you're old or not. How does that sound?'

She blushed, and blurted out, 'How can you say something like that? Say it again and I'll jump into the water.'

Old Third didn't respond to this but nodded downstream. 'Your brother Lin's standing over there.'

Jingqiu saw Lin sitting by the river with a water bucket to either side of him. Old Third climbed on to the bank, released Jingqiu, and while putting on his shoes and socks said, 'You wait here, and I'll go talk to him.' In a low voice he spoke a few words to Lin and then returned to Jingqiu. 'You go home with him, I'll go back to camp from here.' With that, he slipped out into the night.

Lin collected water in the two buckets, swung them on to his shoulders, and walked back to the house without uttering a word. Jingqiu followed behind, terror-stricken. Is he going to tell everyone about this, tell my association? I'm finished. She wanted to use the time before they got home to speak with Lin: 'Lin, don't be mistaken, he only accompanied me. We . . .'

'He said.'

'Don't tell anyone else, people won't understand.'

'He said.'

Everyone was surprised that she had arrived so late. Auntie asked repeatedly, 'Did you come back on your own? Over the mountain? Oh, you're so brave; I don't even dare walk that way on my own during the day.'

Chapter Seven

Jingqiu was so apprehensive that Lin would tell other people what he had seen at the river that she took a long time to get to sleep. He hadn't told anyone yet, but wasn't that because she was there? Once my back is turned, he's going to tell Auntie, isn't he? If he really was waiting by the river for her return then he'd be sure to blab, because she knew he couldn't stand seeing her with Old Third. The worst scenario would be for Lin to tell people about her and Old Third, and for this information to find its way to the ears of her association, and through it to her school. What would happen if the school found out?

Her bad class status worried her for although her mother had been 'liberated' and was now serving as a teacher to the masses, her father was still a landowner. Of the five bad elements – landowner, rich peasant, counter-revolutionary, corrupt cadre, rightist – landowner was the stinkiest enemy to the working class of all of them. Her school would certainly seize upon any 'bad behaviour' and use it as a stick to beat a landowner's daughter like her. And they'd be sure to pull in the rest of her family too.

Her father's class label was extremely unfair. Not only had he left home at an early age to study, but his family had not taken rent from the tenants on their land, so he was doubly wronged and should never have been classed as a landowner.

He should have been seen as a progressive youth. He'd fled enemy territory for the liberated areas at least a couple of years before 1949, using his musical talents to serve the people by organising a choir for propagating Communism and Mao Zedong, teaching the masses 'A liberated sky is a brilliant sky'. No one knew why, but once the Cultural Revolution started he was singled out and accused of being an undercover agent in the service of the Nationalists. Eventually he was branded a landowner, and sent to labour camp. The truth of the matter was that they couldn't give him more than one label, and so only the one capable of causing the most harm would do; 'secret agent to Chiang Kai-shek', 'active counter-revolutionary' and heaven knows what else simply weren't injurious enough.

Even the smallest error on her part, therefore, would bring about even greater misfortune. These thoughts filled her with remorse for her actions. She couldn't work out what had come over her, it was as if she had taken some kind of bewitching drug. Old Third told her to take the mountain road, so she took the mountain road. Old Third said he wanted to wait for her in town, so she let him wait in town. Afterwards, she let him take her by the hand, let him hold her, let him kiss her. And the worst of it all was that Lin had seen him carrying her across the river. What now? The worry consumed her. How can I stop Lin from saying something, and if he does, what do I do then? She didn't have the energy to even think about what she felt about Old Third.

The following few days Jingqiu was on edge, conscious of every word she said to Auntie and Lin, and scrutinising Auntie for evidence of his betrayal. She realised that Lin did not have a loose tongue; he was like a sealed calabash. It was Auntie she was worried about. If she were to hear about it, then it would definitely get out. Jingqiu felt trapped by the threads of the thoughts as they wound themselves around her. Sometimes Auntie displayed an all-knowing look, but other times she was quiet, as if unruffled by suggestions or wafts of gossip.

Old Third still came to Auntie's house, but his place of work had moved to another part of the village so he couldn't come at lunchtimes. He often came in the evenings, however, and each time he would bring food. Twice he brought sausages that he had bought from a local farmer. Auntie cooked them, cut them into pieces, and prepared vegetables as accompaniments. One such evening, Jingqiu discovered a chunk of sausage hidden beneath the rice in her bowl. She knew Old Third must have put it there. Knowing as he did that she liked sausage, he was making sure she received more than the others.

She didn't know what to do with the extra piece of meat. It disarmed her. Her mother had narrated stories from the old days in which loving husbands from the countryside would hide meat in their wives' rice bowls. Young wives had no status in the family, and had to yield constantly to everyone else. If there was ever something nice to eat she would have to wait for her husband's parents to eat first, then her husband, then any uncles and aunts, and finally her own children. By the time it came to her turn, only vegetables would remain.

Husbands didn't dare display love in front of their parents, so if they wanted to give their beloved wives a piece of meat they'd have to resort to tricks. Her mother told Jingqiu the way such a favoured young wife would eat the hidden meat: first, furtively, she would mash it up, then, lifting the bowl to her mouth, she would dig the meat out from the bottom of the bowl as if excavating a tunnel, pretending only to be shovelling rice. Quietly, she would chew, while ploughing the remaining meat back 'underground'. She had to be careful not to eat up all the rice before taking a second helping, thereby uncovering the buried treasure. But you couldn't go for another helping of rice without having finished the first because if her parents-in-law saw she would get a terrible telling-off.

Her mother told her about a young girl who, because of her husband's love, choked to death. He hid a boiled egg in her bowl, the family's only egg, and scared that she would be discovered she stuffed it into her mouth in one go. Just as she was about to chew her mother-in-law asked her a question, and so in order to answer, she swallowed it whole. The egg got stuck in her throat and she died.

Jingqiu looked down into her bowl, her heart thumping in her chest. If Auntie sees, won't it be used as evidence against me? If a young wife was caught, she was decried as a temptress who had seduced her husband. If Jingqiu let anyone find out now, she'd be in an even worse position than those wives, and the news would definitely reach her colleagues in the Educational Reform Association.

Jingqiu glanced over at Old Third and saw him looking back at her, his expression seemingly asking, 'Delicious?' He was artful, and she longed to strike him with her chopsticks. This piece of hidden sausage was a minefield. She was too scared to dig it out from her rice, but if she didn't eat it her rice would soon be gone and the offending sausage would be revealed. Half a bowl in, she rushed into the kitchen and flicked the piece of meat into the bucket for the pig.

After returning to the table she didn't look at him again, but lowered her head over her bowl. Whether she reached for more food she did not know, nor was she aware of what she was putting in her mouth; she was conscious only of the need to empty her bowl. But he was in total ignorance of her turmoil, and picking up another piece of sausage with his chopsticks, gracefully plopped it into her bowl. Enraged, she struck her chopsticks against his. 'What are you doing? I have my own hands.'

He looked back at her in surprise.

Ever since the day he had walked her back over the mountain she had been snapping at him, and especially when they had an audience she exhibited a particular ferociousness, as if to advertise that there could be nothing between them. He, on the other hand, behaved in the opposite manner. Before, he had spoken to her as an adult does to a child, teasing her, admonishing her. But now he had become cowardly, always trying to guess her thoughts and make himself agreeable to her. She reproved him, and he gazed back at her, pitiable rather than angry, lacking the courage to pick playful fights. The more wretched he looked, the angrier she got: he was giving away their secret.

The first days after she got back Old Third was still trying to carry on as before; coming in to help her whenever he saw her in her room writing. She hissed, 'What are you doing coming in here? Go, quickly, before anyone sees.' And he was brazen no longer. When she told him to leave he stood in the doorway, mute, before leaving obediently. She could hear him talking with others in the family, and sometimes she would have to pass through the living room in order to go round the back. He would break off mid-sentence and watch her pass through without saying anything to her, forgetting to reply to whoever else was there.

She heard Auntie's daughter-in-law, Yumin, say, 'Isn't that so, Old Third?'

He grunted an 'Mmm' in reply, and then, confused, asked, 'Isn't what so?'

Yumin laughed at him. 'How come you're so distracted lately? I have to repeat myself several times, and you still don't understand. You're just like my naughtiest students, never listening in class.'

Jingqiu discovered sausage, and even egg, buried in her

bowl a few more times, and each time she was wild with anger. She decided to tell Old Third that if he ever did that again someone would find out. He obviously wasn't scared; he was a working man, it was natural for him to have a girlfriend, but she was still at school. His behaviour was putting her in danger.

One day the oldest brother, Sen, arrived home from Yanjia River, bringing with him a friend called Qian, a driver, who, the previous evening, had run down a wild deer. He and some other drivers had slaughtered it and divided up the meat. Sen had received some and had taken it home so everyone could have a taste. Sen sent Jingqiu to fetch Old Third; Qian's watch was broken and he'd come to ask if Old Third could fix it.

Some distance before the geological unit's camp, she heard the sounds of Old Third's accordion. He was playing the polka – a tune she knew well. She came to a stop and thought of her first day in West Village, and the first time she heard Old Third's accordion playing. It was right at this very spot. That day her thoughts extended only as far as meeting him and exchanging a few words by way of a greeting. Afterwards she had started longing for him, becoming distracted if she went a few days without seeing him. But from the day she had walked with him back over the mountain her feelings had changed. Now she was tormented by the thought of being caught. My capitalist thoughts are deep-seated, and I'm such a hypocrite, I only worry about someone finding out about them. If Lin hadn't seen us that day I'd probably still be longing to be with him. Lin has saved me from sliding deeper into this abyss.

Her thoughts were swirling. Eventually, she mustered the courage to collect Old Third. He opened the door and said, 'How come you're here?'

'Sen asked me to come and get you for dinner.'

He found her a chair and poured her a glass of water. 'I've already eaten, but tell me what good things Sen has brought to eat and perhaps you can persuade me.'

Jingqiu continued to stand, and said, 'Big brother wants you to come now. Someone's come with a broken watch and he wants you to fix it. He also brought some venison and he wants you to have some.'

Overhearing this, one of Old Third's middle-aged room-mates teased, 'Little Sun, venison's no joking matter. Don't you know it stokes the fires, and you've got no means of putting a fire like that out. Wouldn't that be terrible? Take my advice, don't go.'

Jingqiu was afraid that Old Third would not come on account of this advice. 'Don't worry, venison is indeed a warming food, but we can ask Auntie to cook some mung bean soup. That's supposed to be good for cooling you down.'

The other men guffawed, and one said, 'Okay, okay, so that's how you reduce heat, eh? Eat mung bean soup.'

Old Third was visibly uncomfortable and once outside, apologised to her. 'Those men have been away from their families for a long time so they're a bit careless with their words. They're always making jokes like that. Don't take any notice.'

Jingqiu didn't understand. Surely someone saying venison was a warming food wasn't something that needed an apology? Whenever she ate warming foods, like chilli for example, her mouth would blister and sometimes her teeth would hurt, so she had to be careful not to eat too much. And what do liking jokes and not being around your family have to do with each other? Their meaning may have remained a mystery to her, and seemed rather incoherent, but she didn't give it too much thought – she was otherwise occupied with finding a way of telling him not to hide any more food under her rice.

They walked back on the same small road they had walked

along before, balanced between the fields. After a while Old Third asked, 'Are you angry with me?'

'Why would I be angry?'

'Maybe I'm too sensitive. I thought you might have been angry because of that day up on the mountain.' He turned to look at her and slowly retraced his steps towards her. 'That day, I was a bit too forceful. But don't think ill of me.'

'I don't intend to talk about what happened that day,' she said quickly. 'You forget it too, and as long as we don't make the same mistake, it'll be fine. I'm just worried Lin has misunderstood, and if it gets out . . . '

'He won't tell anyone, don't worry, I've spoken with him.'

'What? And just because you've spoken with him, he won't say? He listens to you?'

He hesitated before replying. 'Men often carry women across the water like that around here. Before, they didn't have a ferry, men carried people across – young girls, old people, children. If it had been Lin accompanying you, he would have done the same. Really, it's nothing. Don't worry so much.'

'But Lin must have guessed that we came together from the town. It couldn't have been a coincidence, you happening to run into me on the mountain.'

'Even if he does guess he won't say anything. He is very honest and keeps his promises. I know you've been worrying about this, and I wanted to talk to you about it, but you're always avoiding me. Don't worry. Even if Lin does say something, as long as we both deny it no one will believe him.'

'You want us to lie?'

'That kind of lie wouldn't hurt anyone, it's not a major crime. Even if people believe Lin, I'll say it has nothing to do with you, that I'm chasing you.'

This word, 'chasing', sent shocks through Jingqiu's body. She'd never heard anyone say this word straight out. At most people said 'so-and-so has developed deep proletarian feelings for so-and-so'.

'Don't worry so much.' He was begging now. 'Look at you. In these last few days you've got so thin and your eyes are all sunken.'

She looked back at him in the twilight. He too looked thinner. She concentrated on him, and preoccupied in this manner, nearly tumbled off the ridge and into the field.

'There's no one here, let me hold your hand.'

She twisted and turned, looking all around, and indeed, there wasn't a soul. But still, she couldn't be sure that someone wouldn't suddenly appear, or that there wasn't someone watching them from a hiding place somewhere. Keeping her hands glued to her side she said, 'Forget it, let's not make more trouble. Also, from now on don't hide things in my rice bowl. If Auntie sees she'll use it as proof.'

'Hide things in your rice bowl? I haven't,' he said, confused.

'Admit it, because if it wasn't you, who was it? I'm always finding sausage, or egg, or whatever, when you come round. I have to act like those wives in imperial times, scared out of their wits. I throw it all into the pig's bucket.'

He stopped and looked at her. 'It really isn't me. Maybe it's Lin. You say it's every time I come, but maybe that's because that's when you're having something for dinner worth hiding. But I haven't put anything in your bowl, I know you'd go crazy.'

'It's not you? Then who is it? It must be Lin.' She thought for a moment, and said, 'In that case, I'm not worried.'

His face twisted with displeasure. 'Why aren't you worried that people will think something's going on between the two of you?'

Chapter Eight

A few days passed without the merest ripple of gossip, and Jingqiu began to believe that perhaps there was nothing to worry about after all. Lin seemed a trustworthy person, and having agreed to Old Third's request not to say anything, appeared to be sticking to his promise. So, Jingqiu managed to relax a little. Reassured, she started knitting the jumper for Lin. She had made a guess at his height and chest size, and had picked out a straightforward pattern. Every evening she sat knitting late into the night in order to get it finished before she left for good.

Seeing her working so hard, Auntie Zhang said, 'No need to rush, if you don't finish you can always take it home with you. Once it's done Lin can go and fetch it, or you can bring it when you come to visit.'

As soon as Jingqiu heard this she began to work even harder to finish it; she didn't want to leave any loose ends that meant she would have to meet Lin again. The strange thing was, she didn't worry that people would mistake her efforts for affection, only that Lin might do so. When the time came for her to refuse him it would hurt him even more.

One day, as Auntie Zhang and Jingqiu were chatting, Jingqiu mentioned her mother's ongoing health problems. She often had blood in her urine, but the doctor couldn't find the cause. He had begun to write out prescriptions so that her mother could buy walnuts and rock sugar, which were said to be able to cure it, and so far they had helped. But walnuts and rock sugar were scarce, and even with a prescription they were hard to come by.

'Yumin says they have walnut trees at her old family home,' Auntie Zhang said. 'I'll ask her to bring some when she next goes there and you can take them back for your mother.'

Jingqiu was ecstatic. Her mother had been ill for a long time, and they had tried everything to cure her; chicken blood injections, hand-waving therapy, anything, as long as it didn't cost too much, but all to no avail. At her worst, her mother's samples were the colour of blood. She ran over immediately to ask Yumin, who replied, 'We do indeed have walnuts where I grew up, but it's very far away, and I don't know when I'll be going next. But I will write a letter home and ask them to save some for you, and when I next go I'll bring them back.'

'Um ... how much do you sell a pound of walnuts for?'

'They're all our own trees, we don't want money! It's remote, and besides, we can't come down from the mountain to sell them, we're supposed to be "cutting the tail of capitalism". They collect the things we grow on these hilly scraps of land, which are supposed to be for our own use. When do they let us sell any of it? Besides, we all consider you a part of the family. As long as we can help your mother get better you can have a whole tree's worth, it's no bother.'

Jingqiu was moved. 'Thank you so much, whenever you have the time to write the letter would be fine ... I'll find the time to go myself, just as long as my mother gets better. I'm so afraid that one day she'll bleed herself dry.'

A few days later, Lin came to Jingqiu's room carrying a bamboo basket. 'Check to see if you think that's enough.' With that, he turned and left. Jingqiu peered into the basket and found it full of walnuts. She was stunned. Yumin must have told him to go all the way to get them. She was furious, and spent most of the day holding back her tears. A long time ago she had made herself a promise, no more tears. Her father and brother were in the countryside, her mother was ill, and her sister was five years younger than her, so she had to be the rock of the family. She had her own slogan: bleed, sweat, but don't cry.

She hurried to find Lin. He was sitting by the gable wall of the house, eating. She walked across to him, then stood watching him eat mouthful after mouthful. He looked ravenous.

'Did you go to our sister-in-law's family home?' she asked.

'Mmm.'

'Was it far?'

'No.'

Jingqiu looked down at his feet. His shoes were worn through from walking and the sole of his foot was poking through. She couldn't summon any words, but just looked at his shoes, mute. He followed her gaze, and quickly removed the shoes, covering them with his feet. Ashamed, he said, 'I walk with heavy steps, so I wear shoes out quickly. I was going to go barefoot, but it's cold on the mountain.'

She choked, forcing back her tears. 'Did she send you?'

'No. I just thought your mother could use them as soon as possible.' He finished scraping the last grains of rice from the bowl and said, 'I'm off to work. I can still fit in a half-day.' He walked off, only to hurry back a short while later with a hoe balanced on his shoulder. 'Find a piece of paper to cover the basket, otherwise Huan Huan will eat them all. Don't think just because he's small he doesn't have his ways.'

Jingqiu watched him stuff his worn shoes into the pile of firewood outside the door. He turned around and told her, 'Don't tell my mother, she'll only tell me off and call me spoiled.'

Lin left. Jingqiu picked the shoes out from amongst the firewood and examined them. She wanted to repair them but as the sole of one of them was already worn right through they'd be impossible to fix. She forced them back into the pile.

She was overcome. She stood, thinking, if she accepted Lin's help, how was she supposed to repay him? She decided to take the walnuts, but only because they would help her mother get better. She was wearing herself out, and had too many worries. Whenever she was less anxious her symptoms eased. When there were things to worry about, however, or whenever work was too exhausting, she would bleed again. The walnuts and rock sugar made it stop.

Jingqiu returned to her room and crouched down before the basket of walnuts. She touched each one in turn. There must have been more than twenty pounds of walnuts. Were she to ask the doctor for a prescription, she'd probably need over ten in order to buy that many, not to mention the money. She was desperate to deliver the basket of walnuts to her mother right away, but without the sugar they'd be of no use, and without a doctor's note she wouldn't be able to get hold of any. The doctor only wrote a prescription once her mother's illness had flared up.

Nevertheless, there were enough walnuts to last her mother a long time. Her sister would also be delighted, as she loved nothing more than cracking walnuts. Indeed, she was an expert. She'd hold the walnut upright, and using a small claw hammer would lightly tap the top until the shell split in four directions. There, in the middle, would stand the perfectly formed nut. Sometimes, of course, it would break. Then her sister would use a needle to fish out the pieces. She'd mix these pieces with the rock sugar and give them to their mother to eat. Her mother, however, would refuse, telling the two daughters to eat the mixture. Mother's health is not so bad, there's nothing wrong, you two are both still growing, eat some. The two girls would respond that the walnuts were too bitter, and that they didn't like them.

Jingqiu knelt, thinking, Lin was really too good to her. She had heard stories from before the revolution about 'filial daughters' who used to sell their bodies to support their mothers. She thought she could understand them. What else could a young girl do to support her mother in those days? Even now in this new society, apart from her own body, what else did a girl like Jingqiu have to support her mother? Now, with this basket of walnuts before her, she was afraid; if this basket of walnuts cures my mother, shouldn't I agree to marry Lin? Now they were part of the new society where you couldn't buy and sell people, she couldn't 'sell' herself to him. Only marry him instead.

As she contemplated how to repay Lin's kindness, she began thinking of Old Third. In her heart she wished it had been Old Third who had brought the walnuts as this problem would then easily be resolved; she would happily 'sell' herself to him. She reproached herself. In what ways, exactly, was Lin inferior to Old Third? Was it that he was a bit shorter, did not have the same 'petty capitalist' look as Old Third? But shouldn't we look at what's on a person's inside, not just the outside?

Instantly, she chastised herself again; how can you say that Old Third does not have Lin's kind nature? Doesn't he take care of you? Also, he's always helping others, repairing their pens, clocks, watches, spending money to buy the spares and never collecting a penny from anyone. Isn't that proof of his good nature? People said that he was named the model solider of their geological unit.

Having been tangled up in these thoughts for some time, she roused herself and laughed wryly. Neither of these two have actually said they're interested, why are you getting yourself so worked up? She decided to make some new shoes for Lin so that his mother wouldn't scold him, and so that he wouldn't have to go barefoot on cold days. She knew that Auntie Zhang's sewing basket was full of padded soles which had yet to be stitched up, and uppers which had been glued but not yet welded. It would only take a couple of evenings to turn these half-finished bits into a pair of shoes.

She ran off to find Auntie, and told her she wished to make a pair of shoes for Lin. Auntie's eyes flashed with pleasure, and she instantly hurried off to find the ready prepared uppers and soles, along with thread, needles, and heels to give to Jingqiu. She stood to one side, watching tenderly as Jingqiu sewed together the soles.

'I'd never have guessed, you city girls know how to sew!' Auntie exclaimed, after a while. 'You've put together that sole faster than I could, and with tighter stitches. Your mother really is a good teacher; she's raised a very capable daughter.'

Jingqiu was embarrassed and told Auntie Zhang that the only reason she could make shoes was because her family was poor. They couldn't afford to buy shoes, so her mother made them herself. With a foot of black cotton she could make the front parts for two pairs of shoes. With some more old bits of cloth she could stick together the lining and make the uppers. As for the soles, she had to make them herself. The hardest part was stitching together the sole with the upper, but Jingqiu had learnt each step. Most of the time she wore shoes she had sewn herself, and only when it rained, or when she was to travel far away, or when they had military training at school did she wear her army-green canvas 'Liberation shoes'. Her feet were understanding; once they reached size 35 they had stopped growing, as if scared that they would outgrow her Liberation shoes.

'Neither your cousin Fen nor Fang can make shoes. Who knows what they'll do once they are married off.'

Jingqiu comforted her. 'These days, lots of people don't wear homemade shoes. They'll buy shoes once they're married.'

'But bought shoes are not nearly as comfortable as homemade ones. I can't get used to those gym shoes. They are so sweaty, and when you take them off they're hot and stinky.' Auntie looked down at Jingqiu's feet and gasped, 'Oh! Your feet are so small, just like those girls from rich families before the revolution. No girl who works out on the fields can have feet that pretty.'

Jingqiu reddened. These feet must have come from her landowning father. Her father's feet were considered small, whereas her mother's were not, proof that her mother's family were of good working stock, whereas her father's relied on exploiting the masses for a living.

'They're probably from my father,' she said frankly. 'My father ... his family were landowners. When it comes to my thinking, I've drawn a clear line between my father and I, but when it comes to my feet ...'

'What's the big deal with being a landowner? You need both good luck and skill in household management to amass land. Those of us without fields, who rent land and pay rent to others, we also have our place. I don't like those people who are jealous of landowners and their money, they're just finding any excuse to denounce people.'

Jingqiu thought she was having hearing problems. Auntie's ancestors were all poor peasants, how could she say such reactionary things? She was sure that Auntie Zhang was testing her, and it was vital that she pass. She didn't dare to take the bait, choosing instead to bury her head in her sewing.

Two nights of toil and Jingqiu finished Lin's shoes. She asked him to try them on. He brought in a basin of water and carefully washed his feet, slipping them humbly into his new shoes. He called to Huan Huan to bring him a piece of paper which he laid out on the floor before taking a few measured steps.

'Too tight? Too small? Do they pinch?' Jingqiu asked anxiously.

Lin smiled. 'They're more comfortable than my mother's.'

Auntie Zhang laughed, and chided him playfully, 'People do say "Find a wife, forget your mother". But now, you—'

Interrupting, Jingqiu hurried to explain, 'I made these shoes to thank Lin for getting the walnuts for my mother, there's nothing more to it than that.'

Two days later Old Third arrived with a big bag of rock sugar and gave it to Jingqiu to give to her mother. Jingqiu started with surprise. 'You . . . how did you know my mother needs this sugar?'

'You didn't tell me, but did you stop others from telling me?' He looked irked. 'How come you can tell them, but you can't tell me?'

'Tell who?'

'What do you mean, who? Lin told me, that's who, said he could only get hold of the walnuts but not the sugar, and without the sugar the walnuts would be of no use.'

'Such a big bag of sugar . . . how . . . how much was it?'

'Such a big basket of walnuts, how much were they?'

'The walnuts were picked from a tree . . . '

'Sugar also grows on trees.'

So, he was bantering with her again. She giggled. 'You're talking rubbish, sugar doesn't grow on trees . . . does it?'

He brightened on seeing her smile. 'Wait till you earn some money and you can pay me back, fair and square. I'll make a note of it. How does that sound?'

Great, she thought, now I'm in trouble. If Lin and Old

Third were working together to help her mother, did that mean she had to marry them both? She could only respond by laughing at herself again: Have either of them asked you to marry them? With a background like yours, it'd be a miracle if anyone ever wanted that from you.

Chapter Nine

People say 'once the scar's healed you forget the pain', and of course they're completely right. As the days passed Jingqiu's anxiety abated until she grew bold enough to talk to Old Third again. Auntie and Mr Zhang had left for Auntie's home town and Yumin had taken Huan Huan to Yanjia River to visit her husband, so Jingqiu, Lin and Fen were alone in the house.

After finishing work Old Third would rush over to help make food, preferring to eat with Jingqiu rather than at the camp. One tended the fire while the other fried the vegetables, making an excellent team. Old Third had perfected the art of making crispy rice. First he boiled the rice, and once it was cooked he scooped it out of the pan and put it into a cast iron bowl, sprinkled it with salt and drizzled it with oil, and then tossed the rice over a low heat until it was fragrant and crisp. Jingqiu adored it. She could eat just this for dinner and be satisfied. Indeed her fondness for this dish amazed people – give her the option of fresh white rice or Old Third's crispy rice and she would, without fail, choose the latter. City people were odd.

Fen took the opportunity to bring her boyfriend back for dinner. Jingqiu had heard Auntie say of this young man that he was 'all face', untrustworthy and a fly-by-night. He didn't do his farming work in the village but was always running around making small business deals. Auntie and Mr Zhang didn't like him and forbade Fen from bringing him to the house. Fen would sneak off to see him, but now her parents weren't at home she made a show of bringing 'the face' back with her.

Jingqiu thought that 'the face' was all right. He was tall, knowledgeable, and good to Fen. He also brought Jingqiu some hair bands with flowers on them, which he normally went from house to house selling, so she could put her hair in plaits. Fen held out her arm to show Jingqiu her new watch. 'Nice, isn't it? He bought it for me. It cost one hundred and twenty yuan.'

One hundred and twenty yuan! That was the equivalent of nearly three months of her mother's wages. Fen refused to wash any vegetables or dishes while wearing it in case it got splashed with water.

As they ate, Old Third used his chopsticks to place food into Jingqiu's bowl, and 'the face' did the same for Fen. Lin, partnerless, was left to scoop up a bowl of rice, take some vegetables, and disappear off on his own. Once he'd finished he would come back to leave his bowl and then slink off somewhere – no one knew where – returning only to go to bed.

In the evenings Fen and 'the face' would shut themselves up in the room next door to do goodness knows what. Fen and Fang's rooms were only divided by a wall of about their own height, leaving an opening up to the roof. Needless to say, it was not soundproof. When Jingqiu was in her room, writing, she could hear Fen giggling as if she were being tickled.

Old Third sat in Jingqiu's bedroom helping her with the textbook. Occasionally she would knit while he sat opposite, feeding her the yarn. But sometimes she could see his mind wandering, his eyes still and fixed on her, and in this state he would forget to unravel the wool until she tugged at the other end of it. Pulled awake, his focus would return and he would apologise before letting out a long length of wool.

Jingqiu asked in a low voice, 'That day, you weren't just being contrary when you said you wanted me to knit you a jumper, were you? How come you haven't bought any wool?'

'I bought some. I just didn't know if I should bring it over.'

He must have seen how busy I've been these last days, and didn't want to trouble me, she realised. His kindness touched her, but this was a problem; whenever she was affected by someone's kindness she would make promises she shouldn't. 'Bring the wool over, and once I finish this one I'll start yours.'

The next day Old Third brought the wool in a big bag – there was a lot of it. It was red; not vermilion but more of a rose-red, almost pink, and the same colour as azaleas. This was her favourite kind of red, but very few men wore this colour.

'It's the same colour as the flowers of the hawthorn tree. Didn't you say you wanted to see them?'

'Are you going to show me those flowers by wearing this jumper?' she laughed.

He didn't reply, but rather looked down at the collar of her jumper poking up over her cotton padded jacket. He must have bought the wool for me.

'Promise you won't get angry?' he said. 'I bought it for you.'

But she was angry. He must have taken a close look at her on that walk over the mountain and noticed how worn out her jumper was; otherwise why would he buy her wool? Her jumper was tight and short, and clung to her body. Her breasts were a bit big, and although she used a vest-like bra to rein them in they still protruded from under her jumper. Neither did her jumper cover her bottom. She had a bump at the front and a bump at the back, and knew herself to be a repulsive shape. Girls at school had a test for determining whether a girl had a good figure. If, while standing up against a wall, she could press her body flat against it, then she had a straight, and so attractive, body shape. Jingqiu had never passed this test. At the front her breasts stuck out too much, and with her back against the wall there were also gaps. Her friends laughed at her, calling her 'three mile bend'.

Her mother had bought the wool for this jumper when Jingqiu was three or four years old. She didn't know how to knit, so had paid someone else to do it for her, but despite the large quantities of yarn – and due to this person knowingly wasting wool – she had got only two jumpers out of it, one for Jingqiu and one for Jingqiu's brother.

Subsequently, Jingqiu had learned to knit, and unravelled the two jumpers to knit the wool into one. After a few years she unravelled it again, added some cotton and knitted it into another jumper. Another two years passed and it was time to unravel the jumper again and add more wool. It had evolved into an explosion of colours, but as she was such a skilled knitter people thought the patchwork was of her design. However, it was an old jumper, and the wool had already become brittle, snapping easily into lengths. At first she tried twisting the ends together so you couldn't see the breaks, but there were too many to fix – each one was met by another – so she had to knot them together and forget about it. So, from the outside, her jumper was a seamless hotchpotch of abstract colours, the joins unfathomable. The reverse side, however, held a secret; it was covered in blisters and pimples, just like the sheepskin jacket Chairman Mao wore on Jinggang Mountain, its strands of wool curled back to their natural state.

Old Third must have seen these blemishes at some point and pitied me. He wants me to knit myself a new jumper. She was furious. 'What's wrong with you? What business did you have . . . looking inside my jumper?'

'The inside of your jumper? What's wrong with the inside of your jumper?'

He looked so innocent that she thought she had mistreated him. Maybe he hadn't seen it after all. They had walked together the whole way and he hadn't had any opportunity to look at the inside of her jumper. Maybe he thought the wool was a nice colour, reminding him of the flowers of the hawthorn tree, and simply bought it for her.

'Nothing, I was joking.'

He looked relieved. 'Oh, you're joking. I thought you were angry with me.'

Is he scared of me being angry? This thought puffed her up. I have the power to affect his emotions. He is the son of a cadre, is clever and capable, and looks like a capitalist, but in front of me he is earnest, as fearful as a mouse, and scared of making me angry. She felt like she was floating. She was playing with him, she was both conscious and unconscious of that; his alarm was confirmation of her influence over him. She knew she was being vain, and she did try not to be lured into this bad behaviour.

She wrapped up the wool and gave it back to him. 'I can't take your wool, how would I explain it to my mother? She'd say I'd stolen it.'

He took it and replied quietly, 'I hadn't thought about that. Can't you say you bought it yourself?'

'I don't have one penny to my name, how could I afford that much wool?' She was squaring up to him now, using her economic situation as a weapon, as if to say, my family is so poor, what do you say to that? Do you look down on us? If so, then you'd better forget about it now.

He stood still, his face pained. 'I hadn't realised. I hadn't realised.'

'You hadn't noticed? There are lots of things you haven't noticed, your eyesight can't be up to much. But don't worry, I'm telling the truth when I say I'll pay you back the money for the sugar, and the pen. I take temporary work during the summer holidays, and as long as I don't take any breaks I can earn thirty-six yuan a month – it'll only take me that to pay you back.'

'What kind of temporary work?'

'You don't even know about that? I work on building sites, or shovelling coal on the docks, or painting in factories. Sometimes I make cardboard boxes – whatever. Why? What else would you call temporary work?' She was boasting now. 'Not everyone can find temporary work. The reason I can is that the mother of a classmate is the head of a neighbourhood committee. She's in charge of that sort of stuff.'

She continued with a few amusing anecdotes but after a while noticed that Old Third wasn't laughing along with her stories, but instead was staring back at her, upset.

'Gluing boxes sounds okay,' he said, 'but don't work on a building site, and especially don't work at the docks, it's dangerous.' His voice was raspy. 'A young girl like you doesn't have the strength for such work. You could be crushed to death or knocked down by a vehicle, and then what?'

She comforted him, 'You've never done temporary work, so you think it sounds terrible, but in reality—'

'I haven't done temporary work, no, but I have seen how the men on the docks shovel coal into steep piles. They don't hold the steering wheel and nearly drive the vehicles into the river. I've also seen how the men at building sites repair walls and tile roofs, with things dropping from ladders. They're all heavy, dangerous, jobs, otherwise they wouldn't give them to temps, the regular workers would do them. How come you don't worry about doing such dangerous work? Your mother must do.'

Her mother did worry, indeed, she was constantly fretting while Jingqiu was out working, worried that she would get hurt. Were that to happen, when she didn't have any worker's insurance, that would be the end of it. 'A few pence here or there' are inconsequential, your life is not.' But she knew that 'a few pence here or there' were not inconsequential; without money you were without rice. You were hungry. Her family wasn't just short of 'a few pence'; they were short of a lot of pence. Her mother frequently borrowed money from other teachers, and as soon as she got her wages it would all go to paying back debts, only for the borrowing to start again the next day. The family would often give away their meat and egg rations as they didn't have the money to buy them anyway. Furthermore, her brother's earnings were never enough. All sent down youths had to ask for money, their status being so low that their work points weren't even enough to cover their rice ration.

These last few years Jingqiu had been lucky enough to work every summer to help her family. She would comfort her mother, 'I've been doing this for so long, it'll all be fine. Lots of people do it. Have you ever heard of anyone getting injured? Accidents can happen at home too.' As Old Third had adopted such a motherly tone, she repeated this line of argument to him.

He wouldn't let her finish, interrupting her. 'You shouldn't do that kind of work, truly. It's dangerous. If you get injured, or exhausted, it'll affect you for the rest of your life. If you need money I've got some, we work outdoors, so our pay is pretty good, and we get subsidies. I've got savings, so you can borrow that first, and then I can give you thirty to fifty yuan a month. That should be enough, right?'

She didn't like him like this, all high and mighty with his high wages. He was looking down on her, treating her like a charity case. She replied proudly, 'Your money is your business, I don't want it.'

'You can borrow it, if that's what you'd prefer. You can pay me back once you start working.'

'Who says I'll be able to get a job.' She adopted an ironic tone; 'Your father's not that powerful a cadre, I doubt he'd be able to fix me up with an outdoor job. I'm prepared. Once I get sent down I won't be coming back, and my mother won't need to borrow for my rice ration. But when that time comes what money will I have to repay you?'

'If you don't have it, you don't need to repay. I'm not using it. Don't be so stubborn, you're wearing yourself out over a few pence. You could end up bedridden for the rest of your life the way you're going, and wouldn't that be worse?'

'A few pence'? He does look down on me, making me sound like someone who loves money as much as life itself. 'That's right, I'm a slave to money,' she retorted. 'But I'd rather get injured or exhaust myself doing temporary work than take yours.'

Old Third looked like he had been stabbed in the chest. 'You – I—' he mumbled, unable to formulate a response, looking at her with pitiable eyes. He reminded her of a dog she used to look after that had been taken away by the dog catchers, his mouth tied, his eyes staring up at her, knowing that this was the end, begging for his life.

Chapter Ten

Yumin returned after a couple of days and the house settled again. Fen's boyfriend 'the face' didn't come round any more and that evening Old Third's unit was having a meeting so he didn't have time to visit. Instead, Yumin brought a colleague, Mrs Ye, who wanted to ask Jingqiu how to knit the front of a pair of men's woollen longjohns.

Jingqiu was able to help, but Mrs Ye was not only asking how to knit the opening, but also about its appropriate size so as to be comfortable for her husband when he relieved himself. Jingqiu had learnt the pattern from someone else, but had never stopped to think about what it was for. When Mrs Ye said 'relieve himself' Jingqiu blushed. 'Just let me knit it,' she said, sweeping up the needles and starting to knit.

Mrs Ye chatted to Yumin while she waited for Jingqiu to finish. 'Qiu yatou is very capable, and pretty. No wonder your mother-in-law is so keen to have her for Old Second. Qiu yatou, why don't you marry him? That way we can come over whenever we have problems with our knitting, and we'll all learn properly.'

'Don't say that, Jingqiu's very shy,' Yumin replied, but then continued, 'Jingqiu is from the city, she eats government supplied grain, how could she possibly think of us from out here in the sticks. Someone like Qiu yatou wants to marry another city person, isn't that right, Jingqiu?'

Jingqiu turned even redder. 'I'm still young, I haven't given it any thought.'

'You want to marry a city boy?' Mrs Ye asked her. 'Better find one from the geological unit. That way she gets to marry a city boy and we still get help with our knitting, win-win.' Mrs Ye thought this over a bit more and said to Yumin, 'That Sun boy's not too bad, he can play the accordion, he'd suit Qiu well. He's often coming round here, he must have her in his sights.'

Yumin chuckled. 'You're sharp. He was avoiding us because I mentioned our Fen to him, but now he can't stay away. He's here nearly every day.'

Jingqiu listened, tense and silent.

'Isn't your mother nervous as hell? Here she's found such a good girl, and she's being poached by an outsider.'

'No, Jingqiu is without a doubt part of our family. Anyway, that Sun boy has a fiancée waiting at home.'

Jingqiu heard a buzzing sound and felt that she was about to topple over. But rather than faint, she began to imagine herself flying up over her body, and as if watching herself teeter on the edge of a stage and yet somehow delighted by her own misfortune, she thought, Jingqiu, you're always saying one should be optimistic in all situations. Well, now's the time to test your resolution.

Yumin and Mrs Ye continued chattering and laughing, but Jingqiu's mind was fixed on one sentence: 'That Sun boy has a fiancée waiting at home.' She was unconscious of the movements of her hands, oblivious to every word of the conversation, and when Mrs Ye came over to look at Jingqiu's work, she discovered that the girl had made the flap for the front opening nearly a foot long.

Mrs Ye burst into laughter. 'This will certainly do for my husband. They're like a pair of toddler's open-crotch trousers!'

Jingqiu wanted to unravel it at once.

'It doesn't need to be unravelled, just use a needle and thread to sew up the surplus,' Yumin said.

'You're right, it would be a shame to unravel such a lot of knitting,' Mrs Ye conceded.

Once Mrs Ye left, Jingqiu rushed to her room. She climbed into bed, dragged the quilt over her head, and pretended to sleep. She shivered under the thick quilt, from fear, from cold, or from some other feeling she didn't know, and cursed Old Third furiously. 'Cheating liar! If you've got a fiancée, why did you act like this? Is that how someone with a fiancée behaves?'

Pained, she realised cursing him was of no use. There were liars and cheats everywhere in this world, and cursing them didn't kill them off, or even hurt them. You could only blame yourself, blame your own bad eyesight for not spotting one when he was in front of you.

The scenes from their walk on the mountain road flashed through her mind, one by one, like a film. She couldn't make them stop. A whole string of them flashed by, her head was spinning, she didn't know what to think, say, or do. The memories went round and round like a stack of photos, each one capturing its own moment. The image that appeared and reappeared was when Old Third had startled her, telling her there was a ghost that looked like him under the tree, and before she had known what was happening he had grabbed her, kissed her, and tried to press his tongue in her mouth.

Knowing now that he was engaged, it was as if the photos had aged, their clarity faded. Whenever she was with Old Third she felt lighter, as though her proud judgement, her restraint, were falling away. He was a strong wind that blew her feet from the ground when they walked together.

She thought of the day she had left West Village, when they walked together over the mountain and he had told her stories.

He had used the story of Romeo and Juliet as an example to defend a man who had dumped his fiancée, but now she knew he had been talking about himself. The next evening he also admitted, inadvertently, to having held someone else's hand. She was eaten up with regret. Why didn't I understand? Had she understood, she would have lost her temper with him when he came to hug her, she would have stood her ground and shown him how much she hated him doing that. The worst of it was, not only had she not lost her temper, she had admitted to liking holding his hand. She couldn't understand why she had done such a stupid thing.

So she let him hold her, kiss her, and all along he had a fiancée. Hadn't she been cheated? Jingqiu's mother had always said one slip leads to a road of hardship, but at first she had misunderstood even this simple sentence, thinking her mother had said 'one's lip leads down a road of hardship', and even after the real meaning became clear to her, that one small error could lead to untold misfortune, she still hadn't really understood the meaning of this word, 'slip'. In her opinion, letting a boy know you loved him was a 'slip', because he could boast about it to his friends and destroy your reputation. Jingqiu knew of many such stories, and not just stories, but real girls who had been treated this way. She was always careful not to make that kind of mistake, and the best method, she thought, was to not fall in love – that way you couldn't possibly lose your footing.

She was no longer trembling so forcefully. She decided not to bother with him any more. She should act as if none of it had ever happened. He had a fiancée, so probably he wouldn't tell anyone about it, and she could erase the episode entirely from her life. She thought of a phrase that went: 'If no one knows it's not a scandal.' She hoped that this at least was true.

The only problem that remained was what to do with the

bag of sugar. Her mother really did need it, and she would have no opportunity to buy it once back in Yichang, so she would keep it. But she would pay him back, and quickly. She could first borrow money from her association and pay them back once they were home. She climbed out of bed, determined to go immediately to borrow money from one of the teachers, Mr Lee, but at that moment Yumin came in and began at once to talk.

'My mother-in-law has wanted me to speak to you about Lin for a while now, but I haven't mentioned it to you because I didn't think it possible. You're from the city, and a senior high school student. Lin is a country boy, who hasn't even graduated from junior middle school, he couldn't hope for a match like you.'

'It's not that I look down on him, it's just—'

'Later, I heard about your family's situation, and I thought maybe I should have a talk with you, speak to you about your experiences. It might be of use.' Yumin let out a long breath, and continued. 'When I look at you it's like seeing myself at that age. I was also a city girl, but my parents were labelled rightists and lost their government positions. Unemployed, they survived on odd jobs. Later, the city was cleaned up and people like my parents were driven out to the countryside. My whole family came to this poor mountain area.'

'You've also had a rough ride,' Jingqiu sympathised. 'I always thought you seemed different from the people around here.'

'I've become one of them, haven't I?' Yumin said. 'You'll also be sent down to the countryside, you just don't know where. But here we're close to the town, and not too far from Yichang. Actually this area is considered prosperous. You've lived here a few months, and as I'm sure you can see for yourself, Auntie's family is a good one. If you were to marry Lin the whole family would treat you like a goddess.'

'You must have felt frustrated since coming to the countryside,' Jingqiu said, trying to change the direction of the conversation.

'It's fate, no matter how hard you try you can't overcome it.' Yumin sighed. 'But I still consider myself lucky, I married Sen. His father is a lower-level official, and he got Sen a state-allocated job and me a teaching position. Although I don't get state rations, teaching is much better than labouring. When you come back to West Village, as long as Lin's father still has his post, he'll definitely get you a job as a teacher.'

Jingqiu had never before thought of marriage as a way of altering her future; she was going to be sent down and she would never come back, and that was that. Her family was poor, and she did want to change that, but she refused to rely on marriage as a means of improving her situation. She'd rather rob a bank. For her, everything – school, finding work, joining the Youth League and so on – was out of her control. Only her private feelings were her domain, the only area of her life she could govern through her own free will. It was a question of motivation; she could marry out of gratitude, to repay their kindness, and she could save someone out of sympathy, but she couldn't override her emotions in exchange for money or position.

'I know you won't take Lin because you like Old Third.'

'Who says I like Old Third?' Jingqiu said, 'You said you "mentioned" Fen to him. What exactly did you mean?'

'Oh, before, when Old Third and the unit first arrived here, the unit's buildings weren't finished, so they had to stay with families in the village. Old Third lived with us. Fen loves singing and Old Third plays the accordion, so she let him accompany her, and after spending time with him she started to like him. She was too embarrassed to say anything herself so she asked me to talk to him. He responded that he had a fiancée back at home.'

'Maybe he was just saying that as an excuse?'

'No, he showed me a photo of them together. She's beautiful, and the daughter of a cadre. They're a very good match.' As she spoke she walked across to the table. 'The photo is tucked under the windowsill, I'll show you.' Yumin searched the windowsill for a while. 'Huh? I can't find it. Where's it gone?' Jingqiu thought that Old Third had probably taken it so that she wouldn't see it. Further proof of his treachery. Sly, furtive, shameful! 'After that, he didn't come back. Auntie is still very good to him, and despite her failure, she still likes him, and invites him over if there's anything nice to eat. Fen eventually found someone else, and it was all forgotten.'

'Have you met his fiancée?'

'No, she's from Wuhan, and her father has a powerful post. There's no way she'd come all the way out here. Take my advice, don't set your heart on Old Third. Forget him. In my experience the sons and daughters of officials are not available to people like us. Before my family was driven to the countryside I had a boyfriend whose father was a cadre – albeit not as important as Old Third's father, apparently he's military commander of a whole region. My boyfriend's father was just an officer in a regiment. But all official families are the same; they're educated, experienced, and well-connected. They needn't worry about finding good partners for their children. At first, my boyfriend's family didn't allow us to be together. Those families pay a lot of attention to background. My boyfriend insisted that I was a nice girl, but he hadn't the courage to make me one of his family. When he heard that my family were to be sent down, he panicked. But he wasn't very good at all that, and he broke up with me in the end. Thankfully I had kept control of myself and didn't allow him to come too close so I was able to marry someone else. Had I given everything to him, done things with him, the day he dumped me would have been my last.'

Jingqiu shook as she listened. 'Why would it have been ... your last?'

'If a girl lets a boy get close and is then dumped, who's going to have her after that? Or if he discovers on your wedding night that you're not a maiden, he'll have his way but he won't respect you. Qiu yatou, you're much more attractive to the opposite sex than I was at that age; you're destined to have men pester you your whole life. If you don't hold steady, you'll be in trouble.'

Jingqiu was flustered. She knew that 'sharing a room', and 'sleeping together' were dangerous, but now she had to add 'getting close' to the list of forbidden activities. When Old Third embraced her, did he 'get close'? She decided to risk the question. 'When you say let him ... get close, what exactly do you mean?' She regretted asking as soon as she said it.

'You are innocent, aren't you? It means sharing a bedroom, sleeping together, doing the things husbands and wives do.'

Jingqiu was two-thirds relieved. She hadn't shared a room with Old Third, and they hadn't slept together. The only thing she couldn't be sure of was whether they'd done the things husbands and wives do. But she couldn't continue asking for fear of arousing Yumin's suspicions. Why did a young girl like her want to know about this sort of stuff?

The next day she steeled herself to borrow money from her friends in the Educational Reform Association, explaining that she needed it to buy sugar for her mother, and Mr Lee and Mr Chen between them scraped together eighteen yuan to lend to her.

The evening that Auntie and the rest of the family returned home Jingqiu spied Old Third in the main room. She fetched her newly borrowed money and marched in, to find him sitting on a low bench with Huan Huan on his shoulders, playing affectionately. Old Third raised his head to say hello but she had no greeting for him, and instead dropped the money on his lap in an angry fashion, saying, 'Thank you for buying the sugar for me. Check to see if this is enough.'

As the money fell into his lap, his face looked as if it had been branded with an iron. He didn't reach out to touch it. Feebly, he raised his head begging for an explanation.

Somehow, it seemed, she had the right to be angry with him. 'Is it enough? If not, tell me, I'll get some more.'

'How come suddenly you have enough to pay me back?'

'I borrowed it from my association.'

'If you have to borrow the money anyway, why ask them?' he said, injured.

'I'll borrow from whoever I please. Thank you, on behalf of my mother.' She turned and went back to her room. She was trembling.

He followed her in and stood behind her. 'What's happened? Tell me. Don't be like this, something must have happened. The day before yesterday everything was fine, and now you're like this? What's changed?'

'What do you mean the day before yesterday? I've always said I don't want your money.'

'Is it because I said I'd give you money, is that why you're so angry now? You said you didn't want it, and I didn't insist. I know you're proud, and don't want to accept other people's help, but you .... you shouldn't think of me as ... just anyone.'

She said nothing, but her mind churned: You're a con artist, the words flow like honey from your mouth. If I hadn't found out the truth, you would have fooled me again. You tricked me, and you'll trick others. Someone as upright as Lin wouldn't trick people.

Without turning around she said, 'Don't stand there. Go. I want to write.'

She could feel he was still standing behind her but still she didn't turn to look at him, and trembling, picked up her pen to write. After some time she sensed that he had gone, turned, and indeed found the room empty. She felt deflated. She had been convinced that he would stand a little longer, or perhaps keep standing there, forever. No, what was wrong with her? She'd forget him, yes, forget him, think of him no more. It would be easy. She already found it easy to speak to him in brutal tones. Whenever he looked back at her with those wretched eyes she was resolute and unmoved. But she was resentful. How could he do this? I only said those few words, and he's run off?

Then she thought her behaviour disgraceful. She told herself off now. He's good to you, afraid of making you angry, and you purposefully hurt him in such a cavalier manner, and worse of all, you only regret it now he's run off? She scolded herself and pretended to go round the back to see if he really had left. She passed through the main room and kitchen on her way; he wasn't in either. She listened carefully, but she couldn't hear his voice. He really had gone. Dejected, she continued searching, desperate now to find him.

He was in the mill, turning it as Auntie fed it. As soon as she saw him, knew that he hadn't left, the confusion fell away and distrust engulfed her again. Under her breath she cursed him as 'a cheat', turned, and went back to her room.

For the next few days she ignored him. He tried to find chances to speak to her and ask her what was going on, but she wouldn't reply, until eventually she snapped, 'Deep down you know your own actions, good or otherwise.'

'I don't understand,' he pleaded. 'Tell me, what exactly have I done?'

She ignored him, and went to her room to pretend to write. She knew he wouldn't leave in anger, so she became impudent and was even colder with him, giving him no explanations.

She let him sweat. For some reason this was her right, to torment him. Was it because she could? Or was it because he had taken advantage of her, that day on the mountain? Was she punishing him?

Chapter Eleven

By the time the Educational Reform Association was ready to return to Yichang, Jingqiu realised she still had the problem of how to get the walnuts home. She knew she didn't want Lin to take them, still less Old Third. She couldn't look to her group to help her as they were all carrying luggage – it was bad enough with your own stuff. Who would have the strength to help her carry a basket of walnuts?

'Let Lin take them,' Yumin suggested. 'He rarely gets to go to Yichang, it'd be fun for him. If you want, we can ask my father-in-law to send Lin on a work trip. He can be sending off your group, and could even get work points from the brigade for it.'

Jingqiu thought this suggestion sounded even worse. Dragging Mr Zhang into it would make her into even more of the daughter-in-law.

It was only on the day before she was due to leave and Fang had returned from Yanjia River that Jingqiu was saved from her predicament. Fang would send the group off, but as she couldn't carry the basket herself, Lin would come too to help in that capacity. Their primary task was to accompany the group to the city, and it just so happened they could also help with Jingqiu's walnuts. Fang said she had long been wanting to go to Yichang, but she hadn't had anyone to go with before. Now was her chance. Auntie and Yumin also had a few things they wanted Fang to buy in the city. Jingqiu couldn't think of a better solution, and realising that this arrangement would be a good way of punishing Old Third, she agreed.

Lin was extremely excited, as was Auntie. She gathered together his best clothes and taught him all the appropriate etiquette she could think of for his trip away from home. She instructed him to call Jingqiu's mother 'teacher', and not to stand around like a lump of wood. When eating he should chew carefully and swallow slowly, and not eat as if he'd just been let out of the workhouse. His walk should be light and his arms should swing gently by his side, and he shouldn't ram into things. Each possible situation and potential event – no matter how big or small – was explained and re-clarified. It was as if she was dying to go in his place herself.

In the evening Old Third came to visit. The whole family was animated and nervous, adding the finishing touches to their preparations for Lin's trip. Auntie and Yumin tipped the walnuts into a bag, and added some dried string beans, dried cabbage and dried salt vegetables as presents for Jingqiu's family.

Jingqiu became more anxious as the preparations became more complex, far exceeding her expectations. She tried to explain that it was just brother and sister coming to visit Yichang, and to help bring the walnuts, but the others were acting as if Lin was preparing to leave home for the first time to meet his new parents-in-law. She wanted to stop the whole trip but she couldn't get the words out; it was too difficult to turn down an offer made with such warmth, it would be like punching a smiling face, and how could she do that? Auntie hadn't told Lin to call her mother 'mother-in-law', after all, but just 'teacher'. And after living for so long with Auntie's family, how could she refuse to let her son and daughter visit?

Old Third was lost and unsure as everyone busied themselves, his expression changing only when he heard that Lin was to go with Jingqiu to Yichang. He froze to the spot, still in the midst of the whirl of activity.

Jingqiu looked at him, and a certain sense of satisfaction at his distress came over her. If you're allowed a fiancée, am I not allowed someone to lend me a hand? She had been regretting allowing Lin to bring the walnuts, afraid of the extra trouble it would cause, but now she could see the decision was an excellent one. It was the perfect form of retaliation.

'Do you have an extra travelling bag?' Yumin asked Old Third. 'One that he can carry in his hand is fine. He won't look presentable in the city without a bag.'

He hesitated, then said, 'I have one I use when going away. I'll bring it over.' It was a long time before he returned with a couple of bags, and giving one to Lin said, 'Can you carry it all on your own? If not, I can come tomorrow and help. I've got the day off.'

'I can carry them, didn't I bring that basket of walnuts back from my aunt's house, after all? Not only can I carry the walnuts, I can also help them with their bags. You don't need to come.'

Old Third glanced over towards Jingqiu, as if asking for an invitation. She dodged his gaze and returned to her room to collect her things. Old Third followed her in, asking: 'Is there anything I can do to help?'

'No.'

'Why did you ask Lin? If he goes, he'll miss work. I've got the day off tomorrow – why don't . . . '

'Forget it, it's too much bother.'

He stood to the side, mute, responding only after watching her trying to stuff her things into an army shoulder bag. 'I brought a few bags with me, do you need one?'

'No. I'll go back with the same bag I arrived with.'

He continued to watch as she crossly squashed her things

into the bag. 'When you get back please tell your mother from me that I hope she gets better soon.' After some moments of silence he added, 'Tell me as soon as she's finished the sugar and I'll get some more.'

'Thank you, but there's no need.'

'But your mother must get better as soon as possible!'

'I know.'

After another period of silence he said, 'Come back when you get the chance. Come see the hawthorn flowers in May or June.'

That first day, when we met, he invited me to come see the flowers then too. She had been certain she would return to see them, but now she didn't know how to answer. Somehow, the hawthorn flowers had lost their meaning. She was downcast at the thought of leaving this place, she didn't want to go, even with this cheat standing before her. She looked at him, and saw the same sadness in his face, the face that once she said goodbye to she would never see again.

The two of them stood in silence, until she said, 'If you stay here Fang won't dare come in to go to bed. Go back.'

'OK, I'm going.' But he didn't move. 'You're about to leave, and you still won't tell me why you're angry with me.'

She didn't answer, her throat choked with rising sobs.

'Have you ... said yes?' he asked.

'Said yes to what?'

'The thing with Lin.'

'None of your business.'

Old Third paused to regain his composure. 'When I went to get my bags just now I wrote you a letter, to make my feelings clear.' He dropped the letter on her table, his eyes lingered on her, and then he left.

Jingqiu looked at the letter, which was folded into the shape of a dove. This must be a break-up letter because he wrote it when he knew Lin was coming with me. What else would he be saying? She didn't have the courage to open it, but stared at it instead, hating him.

She also wanted to write him a letter, to have a go at him. She grabbed the letter, wanting to see what he had to say for himself. It was short:

> Tomorrow you're going and Lin is going to accompany you, so I won't. You've made your decision, and I respect that, but I only hope it came from your heart. You've got real artistic talent, but you were born at the wrong time, and so cannot let it run free. Don't underestimate yourself. You must believe, 'If heaven made me I must be of use.' One day, your talents will be recognised.
>
> Your parents are the victims of injustice, which wasn't their fault. You mustn't think that you are inferior because of your background, they have never done anything that is worthy of condemnation. For thirty years the river flows east, for forty years the river flows west; those on the bottom rung today might well be on top tomorrow, so don't denigrate yourself.
>
> I know you don't like me asking about your temporary work, but I still want to say that those tasks are too dangerous, so don't do them. If something were to happen your mother would be even more upset. Physical strength is not there to be flaunted, and if you can't lift something you shouldn't force yourself to lift it; if you can't pull a vehicle you shouldn't pull it. Your body is capital for the revolution, if you wear it out, you won't be able to achieve anything.
>
> You ignore me, and I don't blame you. You are intelligent and wise, and you must have your reasons, even if you won't tell me what they are. I won't force you, but if ever you want to tell me, then please do.

Getting to know you these past months has made me happy and fulfilled. You have helped me experience a kind of happiness I have never known before, and I treasure it. During this time, if I have done anything wrong, or anything to upset you, then I hope you will forgive me.

Chapter Twelve

Jingqiu and the Educational Reform Association left on Sunday at eight in the morning. At first Jingqiu was worried that the group would criticise her for bringing Fang and Lin with her, but in fact her teachers praised her for having integrated so well with the poor and lower peasants, citing it as evidence of the formation of deep proletarian feelings.

Lin was carrying the big bag of walnuts as well as Jingqiu's personal effects, and Fang helped the other two girls carry their luggage. The atmosphere was boisterous as everyone chatted and laughed. Strangely, it did not seem the same endless mountain road of their initial journey to the village but perhaps having got to know the way and with their attention turned towards home, it felt like only a matter of moments before they arrived at the hawthorn tree. It was the end of April and it was yet to blossom.

Jingqiu was hot, and while everyone was taking a rest under the tree, she darted to one side to take off her jumper. As she was pulling it off she thought of the day she had walked here with Old Third. She looked over to the spot where he had stood that day. She gazed at it for a while, uncertain of the feeling that had swept over her.

Jingqiu returned home to discover her mother very unwell and lying, pale-faced, in bed. Her sister was balancing a curved length of wood on a large piece of stone outside the school canteen, attempting to chop it into kindling. The scene made Jingqiu's heart hurt, and she rushed over to her, grabbed the axe from her sister's hands and started to chop herself, instructing her sister to start cracking walnuts for their mother.

'Brother, why don't you help with the wood?' Fang said to Lin. As if woken from a dream, Lin stepped forward, wrestled the axe from Jingqiu, and started chopping.

At that time everyone used coal to make their fires. Kindling was part of the planned economy, so each family only received a fifteen pound supply of wood every month which once used up was impossible to replenish. In order to cope, lots of families never put their fires out. At night, using thin shavings of coal, they banked up the fire, before stoking it with fresh piles of coal the next morning. Maybe they hadn't looked after the fire properly yesterday and it went out. Last time Jingqiu had cut kindling she had made a large pile, but this was all gone now. Thankfully Jingqiu had now returned, otherwise they wouldn't have been able to cook any food that evening.

Lin cut the family's remaining firewood into kindling, and stacked it for later use. Fang laughed at the small pieces of wood Jingqiu's family used to light their fire, each piece being around three inches long. At her house they stuffed whole branches into the stove. Lin heard Jingqiu say that her family only had three to five branches to use for the whole month, and so he promised to bring firewood from home next time.

They lit the fire, but for a long time it wouldn't take, so using a fan Jingqiu flapped furiously at the flames. She hurried to get the food finished quickly so that Lin and Fang would have time for a walk around the city after the meal before taking the bus home. Fang wanted to help, but despite searching high and low she couldn't find the kitchen cupboard, nor their chopping board. 'Where's the kitchenware?'

'We don't have any.'

They really didn't have anything – they were destitute. Their table was an old school desk, students had sat on their stools, and their beds were made from school benches with planks of wood fixed across them. The sheets were clean, but patched. Bowls were stored in an old wash basin, and the chopping board was made from the top of a desk.

Lin huffed and puffed with shock. 'How can you be poorer than us country people?' Fang looked sharply at her brother in order to shut him up.

With great effort they had managed to cook a meal, and together they sat down to eat. The house was composed of an old school room divided in two, fourteen square metres in total. Her brother used to live in the outer room, while Jingqiu, her mother and sister had slept in the inner room. Ever since her brother had been sent to the countryside Jingqiu had slept in the outer room, where they also ate, and her mother and sister in the inner room.

As they were eating a gust of wind blew in, bringing with it flakes of what looked like black snow. 'Damn it,' Jingqiu exclaimed. She leapt up to fetch some newspaper to cover the food on the table and called to everyone to cover their bowls, but they had already received a sprinkling of the mysterious dust. Fang asked what it was, and Jingqiu replied that it was dust from roasting rice husks that had blown across from the canteen opposite. The chimney of No. 8 Middle School's canteen was always spewing out these burnt husks, and as Jingqiu's home didn't have a ceiling, as soon as the wind picked up the husks would blow through the cracks between the roof tiles. Two families used to live next door, but finding the black snow unbearable, they had asked the school for new accommodation and had moved away. The school treated her mother differently, however, so they hadn't been assigned a new place to live, and had to make do.

Jingqiu was distressed. She hadn't planned to reveal all these details of her family's poverty to Fang and Lin. But she was grateful for one thing: that Old Third hadn't come instead. Were Old Third, who grew up in a cadre household, to see this he'd turn and run, wouldn't he? That would be worse than just telling her to go to hell.

After they finished eating Jingqiu took her two guests into the city, but as it was nearly four o'clock they didn't have time to go shopping. Instead they ran to the long-distance bus station and bought tickets for the last bus back to the county town. Jingqiu felt ashamed; they had wasted money on bus tickets only to help her deliver some walnuts to her mother.

Once back home, as Jingqiu put away her things, she made a surprise discovery: someone had put the money she had borrowed and given to Old Third into her army bag. In her mind, she sifted through everything that had happened after she gave him the money, but there had been no opportunity for him to put it there. Had he followed her today? If so, how could he possibly have put the money into her bag? She decided to pay the money she owed Mr Lee and Mr Chen tomorrow, while looking for a way to pay back Old Third. Finding a way of returning the money, of seeing Old Third again, was like covering live cinders in order to remake a fire, and that thought made her happy.

Again, her mind turned to Old Third's letter and the poem he wrote in her notebook. She had to take care to hide them, for it would be bad enough for her mother to see them, and worry, let alone for anyone else to find them. She read over his letter a few more times, still unable to determine what type of letter it was. It wasn't quite a summation, rather a sort of 'looking back while looking forward', saying that in the future they must 'make persistent efforts', that was to say, their 'friendship will last for years', or something like that. Like he's putting a full stop on these last months, and deep down he's saying 'Those months were glorious, but they are now in the past.'

Jingqiu was known for her ability to interpret texts; she was the writer of her class. Her teachers always picked her to join the propaganda team, to be responsible for their magazine. At that time, every class had to take turns painting big character posters with brush and ink. These would criticise some or other person or idea, or otherwise report on the progress the class was making in their industrial, agricultural and military education. Jingqiu was good at writing and painting, both with a single brush or with a row of brushes tied together, big characters or small characters. She was good at everything like that. She could do a whole wall of posters all by herself.

Her Chinese teachers always praised her essays in highest terms, especially Mr Luo, who deemed them 'full of wit and talent'. He read her essays out in front of the class and commended them to the city-level ministry of education, and always included them in his booklet, 'Best of Yichang No. 8 Middle School Student Writing'. The school had organised two essay writing competitions in the past, and Jingqiu had won both times, gaining her fame among all the students. Jingqiu's classmates, including the boys, would bring things to Jingqiu that they didn't understand, such as love letters and break-up notes, in part because they knew she would keep her mouth shut, and also because the teacher kept extolling her 'superior powers of understanding'. She could grab the core of an idea quickly, even those written in the windiest, most circular prose.

But even with her 'superior powers of understanding', she couldn't make out exactly what it was Old Third was trying to say in his 'essay'. Was it a love letter, or a break-up note? The break-up letters she'd read before all started with things like 'the wind and rain send spring away, the flying snow welcomes spring back'. She didn't know who came up with it, but it seemed that break-up letters were always full of the changing seasons symbolising a changing heart.

Jingqiu had read quite a few love letters. Crass, mischievous boys would usually ask directly, 'Do you want to go out with me?' or 'D'you want to be my bird?' Once, her class was preparing to denounce a classmate and they asked Jingqiu to look over the materials. The obscene love letter contained the sentence 'garlic nuts smell good'. She knew it was a hidden code and that she was supposed to rearrange the letters of 'garlic nuts', but despite trying for hours, she couldn't work it out.

The relatively cultured love letters that Jingqiu had read mostly used maxims from Mao's Little Red Book or lines from his poetry. At that time the most popular one, a particular favourite of the boys, was, 'Wait until the mountain flowers bloom, and out from the thicket she will smile'. She remembered once one boy had misunderstood this line, and wrote 'and out from the crickets she will smile', but luckily he had given this love letter to Jingqiu to give the once over. Jingqiu laughed until her belly ached, and helped him rewrite it, sentence by sentence, explaining each mistake carefully. He gasped in realisation, 'I was also wondering why he was talking about crickets.'

Old Third's letter definitely couldn't be called a love letter because nowhere did he use the phrase 'and out from the thicket she will smile', nor did he ask 'will you go out with me?', not to mention the absence of 'could our relationship take the next step beyond being just comrades?'. He had referred to her as simply Jingqiu, he hadn't added 'my dear'. In signing off he had dropped his last name, Sun, and had just written Jianxin, which sounded a bit creepy, but not too creepy, because it was normal to miss out a character in a three-letter name. Most people would call him that.

So, Jingqiu decided, this letter was primarily a summation, a bit like the song they always sang at the end of meetings, 'Sailing the Ocean Needs a Helmsman'; as soon as you heard the opening chords you knew things were drawing to a close. She remembered how when she was small she used to go with her father to a teahouse to listen to readings. When reciting his favourite line the story-teller used a judge's gavel, striking the beat, 'Two flowers bloom, each on its own stem'. Perhaps Old Third was also using this narrative technique? Their time together had been a branch in bloom, and now the display of flowers was over, he was gathering everything up and going home to his other branch.

Jingqiu decided not to reply. Were anyone else to see Old Third's letter they probably wouldn't investigate it as a love letter, but it would be viewed as a reactionary piece of writing. 'For thirty years the river flows east, for forty years the river flows west' had the tone of a class enemy's wishful thinking. Furthermore, phrases such as 'you were born at the wrong time', 'your parents are the victims of injustice' et cetera, all displayed a certain resentment against society, and were exceedingly reactionary. If found, this letter would finish Old Third off, and as his protector and accomplice in propagating these reactionary views, that'd be it for her too.

In the past few years active counter-revolutionaries had been treated harshly, and reactionary views that showed dissatisfaction with prevailing social realities were resolutely attacked. Every now and again reactionary posters would surface in No. 8 Middle School, and as soon as they did the school would be cloaked in terror, making everyone feel insecure. Jingqiu remembered once playing out on the sports field when the loudspeaker suddenly screeched into action announcing the appearance of a reactionary poster.

Jingqiu was terrified of these investigations. She had held her brush and stared dumbly at the white piece of paper placed in front of her, unable to make a mark. What would she do if her handwriting just happened to be the same as that of the big character poster? With her class background, did she stand a chance? How could you guarantee that your handwriting wasn't the same as in the poster?

Jingqiu hated the people who wrote these reactionary posters – what was the use? Sure, you could write away merrily, but it was other people who suffered from your actions. Jingqiu was sure that a considerable number of her brain cells popped of fright every time they conducted one of these investigations. Once, one of the offending posters appeared in her classroom. That day she happened to have been writing the bulletin for her year group on the blackboard outside her classroom. She hadn't finished when she heard a voice from the school's loudspeaker calling everyone to the sports ground, the announcement containing the dreaded words 'reactionary poster', and its location: the blackboard of year one, class one.

Jingqiu had nearly fainted. Did I make a mistake while writing on the blackboard? Her class was ushered into a different classroom and asked to write the stipulated sentences on a sheet of white paper. That time they were quick to find the culprit, a foolish classmate of hers called Tu Jianshe. After school, bored and with nothing to do, he had taken a piece of chalk and started scribbling and drawing, absent-mindedly writing some words from Mao's Little Red Book: 'never forget class struggle'. But he had been careless, and forgot 'forget', so that instead he had written 'never class struggle'. The worst of it was that he came from a bad class family. He was taken away on the spot, and Jingqiu had no idea what happened to him after that.

Jingqiu agonised, but couldn't bring herself to rip up Old Third's letter. Instead she tore off the geological unit's printed header, her name and Old Third's name, and dropped the pieces in the toilet. Then, she found a piece of cloth and sewed a small pocket into her padded jacket, slipped his letter and poem into this hiding place, and sewed it shut. Her needlework was exceptionally fine, and as she used hidden stitches it was impossible to see that there was any patch at all without peering at it closely.

Chapter Thirteen

Jingqiu started back at school the day after her return but the students weren't spending much time in the classroom. They studied industrial production, agriculture, military training, medicine – lots of things really, as long as they weren't from books. Jingqiu's class were to start their studies in medicine not long after her return from West Village. Most of the students went to a town called Guanlin, where they were to stay with local peasants and take classes at the local military hospital. As Jingqiu could afford neither the bus ticket nor the mess fee she stayed in Yichang along with the other poor children, to be sent to hospitals around the city. Since these students were not going to experience the destitution of rural life, a deprivation that was deemed detrimental to their development, the school decided to send the headteacher of No. 8 Middle School's adjoining primary school, Mr Zheng, to lead them in the study of traditional Chinese medicine.

They were kept busy. Weekends consisted only of Sundays, and while from Monday to Saturday Jingqiu had to go to the hospital to study medicine, clocking on and off with the nurses, Sundays were spent with Mr Zheng. Occasional trips to the outskirts of the city to pick herbs to make into medicine for the poor and lower peasants only added to their hectic schedule.

On their herb-picking expeditions they walked along small country roads, and as dusk spread across the sky, and smoke from nearby kitchens curled up into the twilight, Jingqiu would think of her time in West Village, and the first time she had laid eyes on Old Third. A bewildering sort of grief surged in her chest, and she felt like crying. On these evenings, once home, she would bury herself under her quilt, open the secret pocket in her padded jacket, remove Old Third's sewn-in letter, and pore over it. Mostly she just wanted to see his writing; the content she had long since memorised. She had always liked his handwriting, it was special, most notably when he wrote his name. He wrote the 'xin' of Sun Jianxin – which meant new – in two sweeping strokes. She surreptitiously traced along the lines, copying sections of the village history he had helped her to write, until she succeeded in mastering its exact likeness.

There was a popular song at the time called 'I Read Chairman Mao's Books', that went:

Chairman Mao's books, my most beloved books,
a thousand times, oh! ten thousand times, I'll read them through;
his deep reasoning, my careful reading, it fires me up!

Hey! Just like dry land drinks timely showers,
young sprouts draped in strung pearls of rain.
Mao's thinking arms me hey-ho,
with strength to make revolution.

There was supposed to be a musical interlude between the verses, but as people usually sang unaccompanied, they would have to croon the part, 'la-do-la-do-lai-lai', instead.

Previously, when Jingqiu had sung along, she had been like a young monk reciting the scriptures, all words but no heart, but now, reading Old Third's letter, she finally understood the feeling this song described. Of course, she knew that was like comparing Old Third to their great leader, and that was naturally an extremely reactionary thing to do, but the more she read his letter the more she loved reading it. Gradually, she came to realise that he too had deep reasoning, and it inspired her.

When he said that she should believe that 'if heaven made me, I must be of use', he was saying she had talent, and that having talent was a good thing. Whenever anyone said she was talented she got very nervous, 'you're talented' could well mean 'you're concentrating on apolitical, technical matters', and being 'technical' was the opposite of being 'red'. According to the wisdom of the time, when satellites ascend to the sky the red flag will fall to the earth, so 'technical' people and their knowledge had to be overthrown.

Old Third's letter comforted her. Her favourite sentence was 'if ever you want to tell me, then please do'. She hadn't given it much thought the first time she had read it, but now she saw that it meant he wanted her to tell him, he was waiting for her to tell him.

She really wanted to go to West Village to see the hawthorn tree again. Maybe then she would bump into him at Auntie's house. Maybe he'll come with me, and I'll tell him the reason why I'm angry, and he'll explain, and tell me he doesn't have a fiancée, that Yumin was wrong. But to spend five or six yuan on a bus fare to see a hawthorn tree was simply out of the question. What's more, she didn't have time. Also his story indicated that he had agreed to marry the daughter of his dad's boss. And that he held that girl's hand.

One Sunday at the end of May, when the weather was fine, Jingqiu got up earlier than usual to wash the family's sheets before the afternoon's acupuncture lesson with Mr Zheng. Just as she opened the door she saw some young boys hurtling away from her house. She didn't bother to chase after them as there was nothing worth stealing or breaking. She glanced over to an old desk they kept outside and was surprised to see a glass bottle with a bunch of bright red flowers and green leaves sticking out of it. The bottle had toppled over and water was running out over the table. One flower had been pulled out of the bottle and flung on the ground. It must have been one of those little kids. They had probably made a grab for the flower as she opened the door.

Were these hawthorn flowers? She had seen peach blossoms, plum blossoms, azaleas, but these were unlike any of those flowers. They were very similar in colour to the wool Old Third had bought, so they must be hawthorn flowers. That meant Old Third came by with them that day. Maybe he had been waiting for her to come back to West Village to see the hawthorn flowers, and as she hadn't made an appearance, he had picked some and delivered them to her house? But how did he know where she lived? There's always a way, he had said, the first day they had met. He must have served in reconnaissance missions before, she thought.

Her heart was thumping. She took the bottle and filled it with water, rearranged the flowers and put them on the small table by her bed. She stared at them, transfixed: he remembers me, he remembered how much I wanted to see the hawthorn flowers. He's come all this way just for me. Then, she thought, did he leave me a note beside the flowers? He wouldn't put these flowers here, and then leave without a word, surely? If he left a letter, where has it gone?

The area outside her door was like a bustling high street, it was the busiest area on the campus. The school only had two places to draw water and both were located by Jingqiu's house. Furthermore, the back door to the school's canteen was directly opposite. Everyone who came to wash or get food in the canteen came past this spot, and everyone who wanted to use the taps to wash clothes and vegetables or fill bottles would see the table outside her door as they did so.

Growing fearful, she recalled something that had happened a few years before. At primary school she had a classmate called Zhang Keshu. His skin was dark and his figure spindly, and he was a clever student. Zhang Keshu's parents worked in the Yichang ship building factory, and his mother was also a low-level cadre. Later, the factory set up its own school for the children of its workers, and from then on, Zhang Keshu and Jingqiu were no longer in the same class. She couldn't remember when exactly it had all begun, but Keshu had started writing her love letters. He wrote well – the letters were clear and succinct – but for some reason Jingqiu couldn't stand him. She warned him several times but he wouldn't listen, and continued writing to her.

One day Keshu put a letter in an old shoe outside Jingqiu's door. He must have come round very early in the morning before school when no one in Jingqiu's house was up. The next-door neighbour, Yan Chang, got up before them and saw the letter, and unconcerned by whether or not he had the right to do so, took it upon himself to open it and read it. The letter started with a discussion of the excellent international and domestic circumstances in which China currently found herself, before moving on to the fortunate conditions of their very province and city and those of his school and class. These thoughts took a good two or three pages, but that was how people wrote in those days, no one was in a position to ignore such formalities. It was only at the end of the letter that Keshu wrote how much he admired and respected Jingqiu's talents, as one intelligent person to another, just as a hero recognises heroism in his companion. And of course, he didn't forget to ask if Jingqiu would like to be his girlfriend.

Even a character like this Mr Yan could see that Jingqiu was in no way responsible for the affair, so he passed the letter on to Jingqiu's mother, instructing her to have a good talk with her daughter about the importance of studying and not being negligent in her thinking. Mr Yan also trumpeted his success in public, saying that it was lucky he had seen the letter first as if someone else had, who knows what gossip might have spread about.

The whole affair scared Jingqiu's mother half to death, and inevitably she went back to repeating her mantra, one slip leads down a road of hardship. Jingqiu hated Keshu for his actions, but she wasn't particularly worried, because they couldn't accuse her of anything. She had a clear conscience. She had never spoken to him, let alone actually done anything with him.

But when it came to Old Third, Jingqiu couldn't take the same comfort. The more she thought about it, the more anxious she became; Old Third must have written a letter. He's so 'aerodite', and took the trouble to write me a letter when he was only popping home for a bag, would he really not write a letter now? Maybe he put the letter on the table along with the flowers, and some shifty passer-by took the letter, leaving the flowers behind. Her heart burning with anxiety, she ran to find the small children, but they claimed not to have seen any letter, they had only wanted a flower to play with, they didn't know anything else about it. When she asked them if they had seen who put the flowers there, again they claimed ignorance.

Jingqiu's feeling of delight had by now dissipated and, almost mad with worry, she thought the matter through: if Old Third wrote a letter, what would he have written? If he only suggested that it was he who was chasing after her, she wouldn't be too worried, it couldn't be a crime to be chased. But she could almost guarantee that Old Third wouldn't write that, he would definitely have written about what had happened between them, something like: 'Do you still remember the day when we walked over the mountain, and you let me take you by the hand and hold you tight in my arms?' If anyone were to get their hands on a letter like that she'd be done for. They'd criticise her for her indecent behaviour, which would not only ruin her life, but would also implicate her mother and sister. And it would only be worse if Old Third had repeated any of his reactionary ideas.

With these thoughts in mind, she decided it would be better not to keep the flowers; they could provide the vital clue in someone's investigations. She cut the flowers into pieces and threw them down the toilet, before depositing the glass bottle into a rubbish dump far away.

That evening she was so nervous she couldn't sleep, and for the next few nights she was plagued by nightmares. In one nightmare, a teacher was forcing her away, while in his hand he waved a letter, telling her to confess her sins, and confirm that it was indeed when writing a textbook in West Village that she had committed her crime. She explained and defended herself, but no one believed her. In the end they called Old Third to the stand and he confessed, passing the responsibility to her. She hadn't imagined that he would do this, and wanted to curse him but couldn't get the words out. She was paraded down the street with a string of worn-out shoes tied around her neck, a gong in her left hand and a hammer in her right. She walked while banging the gong, calling to the crowd, 'I'm a loose woman, loose like a worn-out shoe! Everyone come denounce me!' and 'I am a disgraced stinky hag! I've committed adultery!'

She woke, her body covered in sweat. It took her a long time to believe that it had all been a dream. But these scenes were not entirely creations of her imagination; there had been a similar public denunciation when she was still at primary school. It was said that the woman had been a prostitute before Liberation, but had since reformed and had even got married and raised a son, who was in Jingqiu's class. Only a few days after being paraded through the streets she drowned herself in a nearby reservoir. Her belly was swollen with water, and the body floated in the water for days as everyone refused to dirty their hands by removing it. Jingqiu had no idea why loose women were called 'worn-out shoes', nor why they called it committing 'illicit relations', but ever since that day, she had refused to wear worn-out shoes – she would rather go barefoot – and she felt sick at the mere mention of the word 'relations', let alone 'illicit'.

She was on tenterhooks, convinced that Old Third's letter had been distributed to her school teachers, reading into their glances signs of her disgrace. After a week of this her nerves were ready to collapse. She decided to write a letter to Old Third to warn him that he was driving perilously close to the edge. She wrote and rewrote it, and fearing that the school was already investigating her dealings with him, decided not to sign her name so that it could not be used as evidence against her. She begged him to forget her and not to send her any more flowers or letters. He held both of their futures in his hands.

But this draft wouldn't do. What if someone sees it? They will know at once that something has happened between us, otherwise why would I ask him to forget me, and why would our futures be ruined?

She rewrote it, in a fiercer tone: 'I don't know you, I don't know why you are pestering me, please behave in a more dignified manner.'

But this didn't seem right either. Such a frosty and ferocious tone might shame Old Third and make him resentful. It could prompt him to write a confession, even to make his own embellishments, and give it to her school. Wouldn't that be even worse? He was the son of a military commanding officer, she the daughter of a landowner. It was obvious who the school was going to believe.

She wrote, scribbled out, wrote, and scribbled out again like this for a whole day until she finally produced a letter that satisfied her. She tried to be detached, but polite, so as to deter him without blaming him. She decided on the following: 'A sea of suffering has no horizon, repent and make your way back to the shore. Let's put it behind us, and not have it repeated.'

Jingqiu didn't know Old Third's exact mailing address, so she merely wrote 'geological unit camp, West Village' on the envelope. She assumed he must have received her letter, as she received no more gifts.

Chapter Fourteen

The really exciting thing was that summer was soon upon them, and Jingqiu could go out to work. She was preparing to work every day, without rest, the whole summer. Optimistically, she calculated that she could make up to eighty or ninety yuan. Even before it reached her pocket, she was deciding how to spend her earnings. First she would pay back the money she owed Old Third, and then she would buy her mother a hot-water bottle. Her mother often suffered back aches that required the warming effects of just such a piece of equipment. Currently, she used a glass bottle filled with hot water, but sometimes it leaked and its surface area was limited.

She was also going to buy half a pig's head – a half-kilo meat ticket bought you one kilo's worth of pig's head. Pig's ear and tongue could be stewed in soy sauce, the cheeks could be used to make twice-cooked pork, and the scraps left over could be used for soup. Just the thought of twice-cooked pork, fried with garlic sprouts, was enough to make her mouth water, and she longed to buy some right away. Her family often went months without tasting meat, and she had felt pangs of guilt when eating the meat brought by Old Third back in West Village that she couldn't take any home for her mother and sister.

Her wages would also stretch to material to make her sister a spring outfit. She had long since decided that her sister was not going to experience the same kind of humiliation she'd endured. She wanted to buy her sister a pair of medium-high rubber boots. It was a bit extravagant, but her sister had wanted them for such a long time. Jingqiu detected a look of envy in her sister's eyes every time she saw someone else wearing a pair.

Her brother still owed money for his rice rations, so she hoped she could use some of the money to pay back at least part of his debt. Students sent to the countryside often went hungry, so sometimes they would steal vegetables and chickens from the lower and middling peasants. In many places the students had made enemies of the local peasants, and they often came to blows. Sometimes peasants from several villages would band together to beat up the city kids, and groups of the sent-down students would join together in response. Recently her brother had been wounded by a group of peasants. He said he had been very lucky as the other students had sustained serious injuries. Some couldn't walk and had to be carried back. Only his little group had been able to run away fast enough, suffering only surface wounds as a result.

Following this incident the beaten-up students and their parents met up in Yichang to discuss their options. The students maintained that the peasants had made a mistake, that they hadn't stolen anything. The city people reported the incident to the brigade and the commune, then to the prefectural Party committee, and eventually the Party committee agreed to send someone to meet them and listen to their grievances.

That evening Jingqiu had gone to the meeting with her mother and brother. They waited for hours. No one knew the source of the rumour, but word spread that the secretary had been wining and dining a guest, and being a bit tipsy, wasn't sure he could receive them that day. Some of the students were laid out in the hall, unable to move after the beatings, some sat, their faces swollen and limbs broken from the blows, and around them their parents' chests burned with anger. And this secretary still dares to go off boozing?

A feeling of hatred gripped Jingqiu. She knew that Yichang constituted a separate military area, and that Old Third's father was a military commander of a rank most definitely above the regional level. She imagined that Old Third must have grown up in a compound with armed guards, along with his fiancée. She thought of what Yumin had said to her: We're not made to be friends with high officials. She had understood the words, but only by seeing the Party committee's compound with her own eyes could she really absorb their meaning. She and Old Third were from two different worlds. Waiting for the Party secretary, she imagined she was waiting for Old Third's father and she was overflowing with resentment.

After waiting some time a few of the parents became fearful; could it be a trap? They'll round us all up, and all they need do is accuse us of 'attacking a government organisation' and we'll be tossed into jail. Everyone grew steadily more nervous, and Jingqiu's mother said, 'Let's go. Maybe the others can make this sort of stand, but people like us can't. A beating's a beating. I mean, sure, we can feel sorry for ourselves, but can we really expect a Party secretary to catch those peasants?'

Jingqiu hated her mother's cowardice, and she insisted they wait a little longer, saying, 'If you're scared, then I'll wait by myself.' Jingqiu's mother had no choice but to wait with her. When at last a cadre arrived it wasn't the secretary, no one knew what his rank was, but he told them he was representing the secretary and scribbled down their statements before sending them back home.

They never heard anything more on the matter. Jingqiu's

mother comforted herself: 'Never mind, that's how it goes.' Swallowing her tears, she sent her son, who had yet to recover from his injuries, back to the countryside. Fortunately he was put in charge of drying the crops, considerably easier work than going out on the fields but it only earned him half as many work points, so by the end of the year he would need even more money for his rice ration.

Filled with thoughts of these necessary expenditures, on the first day of the summer holidays Jingqiu asked her mother to take her to see the head of the neighbourhood committee, Director Li, so that she could find a job. Early that morning mother and daughter went to Director Li's house and waited. Jingqiu's mother had taught Director Li's son, Kunming, so Director Li was very polite to her. She asked Jingqiu's mother to return home while she sorted out a job for her daughter. Every year Jingqiu would allow her mother to present her to Director Li before she too would insist that her mother go home. Jingqiu was a bit ashamed because at school Kunming and she didn't have much to say to each other, but now, here she was, waiting in his home and asking for his mother's help.

At that time, enterprises in need of temporary workers would send a manager to Director Li's house who would lodge his request before nine in the morning. If the jobseeker hadn't found employment by nine o'clock, there would be no chance of work that day. Most of the time, if you found a job it would last a good few days until the task in hand was completed, and then the temporary workers would head back to Director Li's house to wait for a new job.

That day there was an old, toothless granny of indeterminate age waiting with Jingqiu. Jingqiu recognised her; they had worked together before. People called her Granny Copper. Her real name was Tong, which meant 'child', but also sounded just like the character for 'copper'. Jingqiu thought this nickname suited her perfectly, considering the fact that she was still working at her advanced age. Apparently her son had been beaten to death during a struggle session and his wife had run away, leaving a boy of school age for Granny Copper to look after. Jingqiu couldn't bear to think about what would happen to the grandson were she to die.

They sat waiting for a while until they saw a manager arriving in search of workers. He needed muscle to unload sand from a ship that had docked on the river. Jingqiu boldly volunteered but the man was dissatisfied with the young girl standing before him; he didn't want a woman, women couldn't lift sand. Director Li told Jingqiu not to get flustered. 'I'll only let you take lighter work.'

She waited until another manager arrived looking for workers to tamp earth, but despite her valiant efforts he didn't want her either. She was too young and definitely not tough enough. Anyway, tampers needed to have big voices for singing. 'I'm not scared, I'll sing,' Jingqiu had replied.

'All right, sing me a song.'

'I'll sing, I can sing,' interjected Granny Copper. Shrivelling her nose she started singing, 'Nuns and monks have seen the light, hey-ho. They think of their lovers day and night, hey-ho ... '

What's all this nonsense about? Jingqiu wondered. I get that it's about boys and girls and all that ... Maybe she wasn't suitable for this job after all. She watched as Granny Copper left with the manager, the old woman as delighted as if her name had appeared on the list of successful candidates in the imperial examinations.

Jingqiu waited until ten o'clock but there were no jobs, so she gave up and went home. A whole day at home without work was like sitting on a carpet of nails, or worse, like someone reaching into your pocket and fishing out one yuan in cash. She longed for the following morning, when she could return to Director Li's house to wait for work.

But by the third day she still hadn't found a job; the only one available was shovelling sand. The manager told her that out of those he had hired just a few days before most hadn't been able to hack it and had run away. He had no choice but to return to look for more workers. Jingqiu begged for hours before he finally agreed to give her a try. 'But if you run off before the day's through I won't even pay half a day's wages.' Jingqiu agreed without hesitation.

She was ecstatic to have found a temporary job. She was one step closer to being a proper part of China's Communist revolution. She followed the manager to the dock, arriving just as the temporary workers were taking a rest. There was not a woman among them, and the men stared at her, bemused. In unfriendly tones, one said, 'If you've come to work we've had it, we'll have to waste our time helping you. Go and do piece-meal work, why don't you? That way you don't get paid for other people's hard work.'

'We work in teams of two,' another added. 'One lifts the sand off the boat, the other piles it up. But who's going to draw the short straw and work with you? They'll exhaust themselves bringing it down off the boat for you and then carrying it up to the pile, they'll have to walk miles extra.'

'Don't worry, I'll work by myself,' Jingqiu replied softly. 'I won't move less than you lot.'

The manager said, 'Just try it out first, if it's too much don't be pig-headed, you've got no work insurance here if you do yourself any damage.'

Someone who recognised her replied, 'Your mum's a teacher. What a greedy guts, why do you need this extra money?'

After the manager left another man leered, 'It's hot today,

having a girl around's a real hassle. Once we get sweaty we'll be taking our tops off, so don't go getting all shy, okay?'

Jingqiu paid no attention. If you're not too shy to take them off, then why should I be shy? She lowered her head and readied her bamboo basket and shoulder pole. It was time to start work so she followed the men to the riverbank. The ship was joined to the bank by a long thin plank only a foot wide that swayed underfoot. Beneath it the river water gushed and surged. Summer was the season for rising waters, and with it the river swept along mud and sand, painting red streaks in the yellow water. It was scary; cowards wouldn't walk along it empty handed, let alone while shouldering heavy baskets of sand.

It had been a long time since Jingqiu had carried anything on a shoulder pole, and her shoulders began to ache at once. Luckily her pole was a very good one; not too long and with some flex in it. As anyone who has ever used a shoulder pole will tell you, if your pole is too stiff and doesn't sway as you walk, it's exhausting to use, but just a bit of flexibility goes a long way to making your load feel lighter.

Each load weighed nearly fifty kilograms, and each time Jingqiu filled up her baskets and stepped on to the narrow plank she felt it rock alarmingly below her. She was scared that she would step out into mid-air and just plop into the river. She could swim, but the water was full of stones; she wouldn't drown, but most likely she would be killed by a rock. With her gaze fixed ahead, and holding her breath, she stepped on to the plank.

Once off the boat she had to pile up the sand. The bank was fairly level at first but then it rose up steeply. You would struggle empty handed, so you can imagine what it was like scrambling up there carting two heavy baskets of sand. She now understood why the men had divided themselves into teams of two; after the hair-raising experience on the plank her legs were like mush. If someone else took the sand up the bank she could have gone back to the boat and had a moment's rest, but as one person doing both jobs she had no option but to do it all in one go.

After two rounds her body was already drenched in sweat. In the sun it was blisteringly hot and, with no water to drink, she felt that she would faint from heatstroke. But then she remembered that she would receive one yuan and twenty cents for this day's work, and the fear of not finding a job for two days was fresh in her mind, so she gritted her teeth and carried on.

She didn't know how she managed to struggle through the day. Once at home she had to pretend to be fine so as not to worry her mother. That day she was so tired that after eating and a wash she collapsed into bed.

The following day she got up early. The previous day's pain was a trifle in comparison to what she felt now. Now she knew what it meant to ache in your whole body. The skin on both shoulders was red-raw, to the point where she couldn't put her clothes on. The skin on the back of her neck had also been rubbed away from constantly shifting the weight on her shoulders. Her legs were incomparably heavy and her face and arms were severely sunburnt. Just splashing water on them was painful.

Jingqiu's mother saw her daughter get up and rushed over to her. 'You're too tired, you groaned all night in your sleep. Don't go today.'

'I always groan in my sleep.'

Her mother grabbed Jingqiu's shoulder pole from her hands and begged, 'Jingqiu, don't go, my girl, it's heavy work and you could do so much damage. You say you're used to it and you don't get ill, but you don't normally groan in your sleep. You must have been very tired yesterday.'

'Don't worry, I know how things stand, I won't do anything too heavy,' she comforted her mother.

After two days of shovelling sand the attitude of her fellow workers started to improve. She may have been a girl, but they saw that she carried exactly as many loads as they did. One man called Wang volunteered to form a team with Jingqiu. 'Piling the sand is tiring, I'll do that, you lift it off the boat.' Wang struggled to unload his sand in time to take the load from her as soon as possible, that way each time Jingqiu would have to walk fewer steps. Once or twice Jingqiu had just come down from the boat when Wang met her for the pole, causing the others to laugh and embarrassing Jingqiu.

She worked for a few more days before the pain started to ease and she wasn't panting and puffing quite as much. Now all she worried about was that they might run out of work and she'd have to return to Director Li's house to wait goodness knows how long for another job. For her, piles of sand left to shift was the very definition of happiness, that is, endless work and an endless summer in which to do it.

Chapter Fifteen

The day before their work finished Jingqiu had just carried a load down from the boat when Wang came up to her and said, 'Let me, someone's come for you. They're waiting by the bank. Go.'

Who would come down here to find her? 'Do you know who it is?' she asked Wang.

'She looks like she could be your sister. No one I know.'

Her knees went weak at the word 'sister'. Something must have happened to her mother, as her sister would never run down here in the hot midday sun without a good reason. She had intended to take a load down off the boat with her but she couldn't lift anything after hearing the word 'sister'. She let Wang take over. 'I'm sorry to bother you,' she apologised, 'I'll go see what the matter is and come straight back.'

She scrambled up the bank and saw her sister standing in the shade of a tree, and beside her was another girl. She squinted. It was Fang. She let out a sigh of relief. 'Fang, what are you doing here? I thought . . . '

Fang was fanning herself with a handkerchief. 'Phew, it's hot. How come you're working here on such a hot day?'

Jingqiu walked over to the shade. 'Did you come today? Are you going back tonight?' Fang nodded. 'Then I'll ask for the rest of the day off.' She felt a bit awkward about asking for time off because she'd have to leave Wang to work on his own, and she thought that unfair. She saw Wang climbing up the slope with a load of sand so she ran over to him to discuss it.

'Take the day off, I can do it myself, no problem.'

Jingqiu asked the boss and then took Fang and her sister back to the house. Fang hadn't eaten yet so Jingqiu busied herself in preparing a meal to welcome Fang. They didn't have any fresh vegetables, so she used the salted beans and cabbage that Fang had brought with her on her last trip. She soaked them in hot water, fried up two bowls and added some pickles, and served them with mung bean congee. It was surprisingly tasty.

By the time Fang finished her bowl it was getting late and she wanted to go back to the city to catch her bus. Jingqiu invited her to stay for a few days but Fang declined. Time was getting on so she said she'd go with Fang to the bus station. They went to the jetty to cross the river in front of Jingqiu's house. 'Every time you come it's such a rush. You never get to enjoy yourself,' Jingqiu apologised.

'Today was my fault. I came on the eight o'clock bus and arrived here at nine, but I forgot the way to your house. I asked here, I asked there, until someone pointed me in the wrong direction. I walked a very long detour. I'm useless with directions.'

When the boat had rowed halfway, Fang pulled out an envelope from her pocket and gave it to Jingqiu. 'You're like a sister to me, and if you feel the same way too, then you'll take this. If you don't I'll be upset.'

Jingqiu opened it and found one hundred yuan tucked inside. She was flabbergasted. 'You ... you came to give me money?'

'So that you don't have to work.'

'Where did you get so much money?'

'It's my sister's. She sold the watch Zhao Jinhai gave her.'

Jinhai was Fen's 'face', that much Jingqiu knew. But why would Fen sell her watch to lend me money? She loved that watch, how could she just sell it like that? She pushed the money into Fang's hands. 'Thank your sister from me, but I can't take it. I can work and earn money, I don't like owing anyone anything.'

Fang resolutely refused to take the money. 'Didn't I just say you're my sister, how come you treat me like we're not family?'

The two of them pushed the envelope back and forth until the boatman called, 'D'you want to sink the boat?' scaring the two girls so they didn't dare move. Jingqiu was squeezing the money tight, racking her brains as to how she was going to slip it into Fang's bag once they got on shore.

'Look, it's such a hot day, and you're working outside loading sand,' Fang started earnestly. 'I couldn't do it, how can you? Not to mention towing trailers, working on building sites – they're not jobs for us girls.'

Jingqiu thought it strange as she'd never mentioned her work to Fang before. How does she know details like 'towing trailers' or 'working on building sites'? 'Is this really your sister's? If you don't tell me the truth I definitely won't take it.'

'If I tell you the truth, will you take it?'

'You tell me where the money's from, and I'll take your money.'

Fang hesitated. 'You better stick to your word. Don't go asking me for the truth and then not agree to take it.'

Jingqiu was now all the more certain that the money wasn't Fen's. She thought for a moment, and then said, 'Tell me whose money it is. You call me a sister, but you don't trust me?'

Fang said finally, 'Old Third asked me to give it to you, but he told me not to say. He said he didn't know how he'd offended you, but if you knew it was his, you wouldn't take it.'

Fang looked at Jingqiu holding the money and thought she was taking it. Smiling, she boasted, 'I said I could sort it out. Old Third didn't believe me, he thought I wouldn't be able to persuade you.' Fang took some coins out from her pocket, and rubbing them said proudly, 'Old Third also gave me money to take the bus once I got here to the city. He told me to take the bus to the last stop, then take the boat, and I'd be able to see your house. But I didn't take the bus as I was worried that I'd take the wrong one. So I got lost instead, but I did save the bus money.'

Jingqiu thought, perhaps he never got my letter. She thought it best not to mention the letter to Fang, so just asked, 'Old Third? Is he all right?'

'Why wouldn't he be? But he did say he's been anxious since the holidays started. He reckoned you'd gone out to work and he's worried you'll fall from a ladder or into the river or something. He's always talking about you to me. He was pressing me to deliver the money to you, saying that if I didn't go soon it might be too late and something might have already happened. It wasn't that I didn't want to come as soon as possible, it's just that our holidays start later than yours. In fact, I came as soon as I could. If I hadn't, he would have talked 'til my ears bled.'

Jingqiu fell silent. Then, pretending nothing had happened, she said, 'How could he tempt fate by saying things like that? Lots of people do extra work and how many of them have been killed or drowned?'

The boat reached the bank and the two girls stepped down. 'I'll take you on the bus,' Jingqiu said. 'That way, you'll get to know the route and next time you won't get lost.'

This was the first time Fang had ridden a city bus, and it was an exciting experience for her; she was too consumed with the view out of the window to chat to Jingqiu.

At their stop Fang followed Jingqiu, as they shoved their way off the bus. 'Such a short ride? We can't have gone far enough. It was really far when I walked, how can it be so quick on the bus?'

At the long distance bus station Fang bought one ticket for the three o'clock bus. 'Aren't you scared about walking on the mountain road alone?' Jingqiu asked.

'I won't walk that way, I'll go on the lower road where there're always lots of people.'

Jingqiu realised there would be no more opportunities to sneak the money into Fang's bag, so she'd just have to get tough. She grabbed Fang's hand, stuffed the money into it and then closed it. 'Thank Old Third for me, but I can't take his money. And tell him not to do this again.'

Fang's hand was clamped shut in Jingqiu's, and so she had no choice but to wait for another opportunity to give it back again. 'Why won't you take it? He's trying to help you, so let him. Are you only happy when he's worrying?'

'I don't want him to worry, and he needn't.' Jingqiu paused in thought, and continued, 'He has . . . a fiancée, he should be worrying about her.'

Jingqiu was longing to hear Fang say, What fiancée? He doesn't have a fiancée, but instead she asked, 'What has this got to do with his fiancée?'

'So he's really got . . . a fiancée?'

'Apparently their parents organised it, many years ago.'

Jingqiu was distressed, as subconsciously she had been hoping that it wasn't true. Dumbly, she asked, 'How do you know he has a fiancée?'

'He said so himself, and he gave my sister-in-law a picture of them together.'

'Yumin said that she put the photo under the windowsill in your room. How come I haven't seen it? He must have taken it and hidden it.'

'Don't go making false accusations, I was the one who took it. Someone told me that if you cut a photo of two people in half – without cutting into either person, mind – then you can split them up in real life. So, I cut them apart.'

Jingqiu thought this sounded very childish, not to mention superstitious, but also quite fascinating, if it really worked, that is. 'Did you manage to cut them apart perfectly?'

'Ah, more or less. But their shoulders were a bit close together. Old Third's shoulder was tucked behind her shoulder, so when I cut the photo Old Third lost a chunk of it. Don't tell him about this, it's bad luck.' Fang didn't look like she believed in all that, and started laughing. 'If Old Third had a sore shoulder that day, it's all my fault.'

'It'd serve him right. How can he do this? He's got a fiancée, and yet he's giving other people money?'

'Just because someone's got a fiancée, doesn't mean that they're not allowed to give other people money,' Fang said, surprised. 'He's got a good heart, he doesn't mean anything by it. Don't misunderstand him, and think he's got his eye on you. He's not that kind of person. He's got a soft heart and can't bear to see other people suffering. Didn't he help Cao Daxiu from the village, remember?'

'Who's Cao Daxiu?'

'You know, that girl whose father is an alcoholic – people call him "Three-slugs-a-day Cao". Have you forgotten? He once came round when Old Third was having dinner at ours and asked him for money.'

Jingqiu remembered, oh him. 'Old Third helped his daughter? How?'

'Daxiu's father loves drinking and brawling. Her mother died young – it's possible he beat her to death. He was always hitting her mother, no matter how much he had had to drink, and even when completely sober. Three times at the drink, and three times at it with his fists, why else would he be called "Three-slugs-a-day Cao"?

'Daxiu's mother died a few years ago, and as her father didn't do his work in the fields the production team put him in charge of the cows. But he still got drunk regularly and he let the cows out to eat the crops, so the production team deducted his work points. The worst of it was that as soon as he had a few pence in his pocket he would spend it on drink. When Daxiu reached fourteen or fifteen her father tried to marry her off so he could spend the money on booze.

'Daxiu didn't have a dowry, and with a father like that, no one in the village would have her. Her father promised her to Lao Meng's second son who has epilepsy. His fits frighten you half to death, his mouth froths, and he loses consciousness and falls to the ground wherever he happens to be. Everyone thought he was sure to die young. Daxiu refused to marry him and her father almost beat her to death, saying he'd raised her all these years for nothing. "Daughters are supposed to be wine jugs for their fathers, how did I produce a shit-and-piss pot like you?"'

'So Old Third agreed to marry her,' Jingqiu guessed, 'to save her life.'

'It wasn't like that. Old Third gave her father money for alcohol, and told him not to force his daughter into prostitution. Daxiu's father was only interested in booze, he didn't care who his daughter married, but in the end he didn't make her marry the boy with epilepsy. But Old Third couldn't escape some measure of responsibility now, so whenever Daxiu's father ran out of booze he would go find Old Third saying, "It's all your fault, if you hadn't got in the way my daughter would be married to a good person who would bring me money for my drink." Old Third was afraid he'd hit Daxiu, so he handed over the cash. Daxiu's father tried to force Old

Third to marry his daughter, that way he wouldn't have to worry about getting money for booze any more.

'In fact, Daxiu was hoping for the same outcome. Who wouldn't want to marry someone with state rations and an official for a father? Not to mention Old Third's good looks and good temper. Daxiu often went to find Old Third at his camp, offering to wash his quilt and help him with things, but Old Third wouldn't let her, nor would he let my sister. My sister had to steal his bedding to take it home to wash.

'She asked Yumin to talk to him about it, but Old Third said no because he already had a fiancée. My sister cried a few times, and made a promise never to marry. But then she got together with Zhao Jinhai, and obviously didn't stick to her vow – she spends her days all in a fluster about getting married to him now.'

'So when you cut up that photo you were helping out your sister?'

Fang looked embarrassed and laughed. 'How long ago was it that my sister liked him? Let's just say I cut up the picture quite a while afterwards.'

Jingqiu's heart started hammering; maybe Fang read my mind, and did it for me. 'So who did you do it for?'

'There's no point doing it for anyone else, it had to be for myself,' Fang said frankly. 'But it didn't do me much good, I could only cut them apart, not glue us together. Apparently Old Third has known his fiancée since they were young and their fathers are both officials, what are we in comparison? So, if you ask me, him lending you money is just to help you, it doesn't mean anything else. Take my advice, take the money because if you don't someone else will, and why should someone like "Three-slugs-a-day Cao" get it just to spend on alcohol?'

Jingqiu was forlorn, and the more Fang pleaded Old Third's

innocence the worse she felt. She believed Old Third had helped her because he liked her, and although her pride had made her refuse him, she had been genuinely touched. But Daxiu's story had turned her insides cold.

Old Third must have hugged Daxiu. He had no qualms about hugging me after such a short time, and he's known Daxiu much longer, so he must have hugged her, surely? She had been sullied by Old Third. When they hugged there had been a layer of clothing between them, and she had washed them and herself since, so it must be washed off by now? But his tongue had reached in between her lips and teeth. Just thinking of it made her feel nauseous, and she wanted to hawk and spit it out, but instead sat there, ashen-faced, without saying a word.

Fang tried to squeeze the money back into Jingqiu's hand. 'Take it, you said you would, you must stick to your word.'

Jingqiu jumped up as if she had been scalded, and the money dropped on to the floor. She refused to pick it up, and still standing, replied in a distant voice, 'I agreed to take your money, not his filthy cash. Take it back with you. Don't make me go to West Village tomorrow specially and risk losing my job.'

The tone of her voice and colour of her cheeks must have been terrible, as Fang returned her gaze, terror-stricken. 'What do you mean, filthy cash?'

Jingqiu couldn't bear to tell Fang about how Old Third had embraced her, so instead she replied, 'If you can't work it out, don't ask.'

Fang knelt down to pick up the money and faltered. 'Now what? I've used up the money he gave me for the bus and I've failed. What will I say to him? Take the money, for my sake.'

Jingqiu didn't want to get Fang in trouble. 'Don't worry, go back and tell him that I'm working at the cardboard factory gluing boxes. The money's good and the work's not hard, so

I don't need his money, nor his concern. If you say that, he won't blame you.'

Fang mulled over the excuse and agreed. 'I'll say it, but you have to help me with the details, otherwise I won't do it. I'm not good at lying, my heart pounds and it only takes a few questions before I'm found out. See? Old Third told me over and over not to say whose money it was, and yet it didn't take much for you to get it out of me.'

Jingqiu helped Fang to flesh out the details of the lie, including the address of the cardboard factory, the direction in which the main gate faced, that they had met at the factory and that Jingqiu would be working there all holiday.

'So don't do any dangerous work in real life, because if something happens Old Third will know I lied,' Fang pleaded.

After having sent Fang off Jingqiu decided not to spend even more money on another bus ticket so walked back, her head filled with images of Cao Daxiu. She had never seen her, but a clear picture floated in front of her eyes; despite her worn clothes she was an attractive young woman. Then came an image of Old Third hugging Daxiu on a mountain top. Old Third was kind to her, so whatever he wanted she must have given him; Old Third had reached his tongue into her mouth and Daxiu had done nothing to stop him.

She returned home with a headache, and without eating went to lie down. Her mother was alarmed, thinking the day had been too hot for work. She asked Jingqiu a few questions, but after receiving Jingqiu's clipped replies she decided not to persist.

Jingqiu slept for a while until Wang arrived to say that the boss wanted everyone to work overtime that evening. 'If the boat stays an extra day tomorrow the factory will have to pay an extra day's wages. If we work from six until nine tonight we'll get paid half a day's wages, for only three hours' work.'

As soon as Jingqiu heard this her head was too excited to hurt and she forgot to be angry any more. If she applied the Marxist theory she had learned at school to the situation, you could say it would be better to concentrate on her economic base first. She thanked Wang, gulped down two bowls of rice, grabbed her bamboo basket and shoulder pole, and rushed off to work. All the temporary workers were gathered at the river, and some had even brought family members. Who wouldn't do three hours' work for half a day's wages?

That evening they worked more than three hours, however, heaving the sand down from the boat, and so the boss offered to pay a full day's wages for their trouble. But now the work was finished, they weren't required the next day. If any more work came up he would call on them.

The thrill of hitting it big time was diluted in an instant by the news of their impending unemployment, and Jingqiu felt dejected. Tomorrow I have to go back to Director Li and who knows if there'll be a job. She had started to trudge with heavy steps back towards home when the boss came running up to her, offering her a few painting jobs if she was interested. She could start tomorrow at the factory repairs unit.

Jingqiu couldn't believe her ears.

'Will you do it? You're hard-working, and I trust you. Also, painting requires attention to detail, it's better for a woman to do it.'

Jingqiu was wild with joy. So this is what they mean by 'luck the doors can't keep out'! The next day she would go to the repair unit to paint. People said that the paint was poisonous, but the work was easy, and you got ten cents more per day. Who cared if it was poisonous or not?

That whole summer luck was on her side. To her surprise her lie to Old Third came true and she really did work at the cardboard factory for two weeks, gluing boxes. You were supposed to be struck by lightning for lying, and yet she had come out not only unscathed, but with an actual job at the factory'.

This time she would work at the machines with the regular workers. They gave her a white hat, and told her to tie her hair back with a leather belt from the workshop, in case her long hair caught in the machine. The regular workers were given white aprons which made them look like they worked in a textile factory, but the casual workers worked without, so it was obvious who had a permanent job and who was only temporary.

Jingqiu really wanted to sneak herself an apron and try it on: it felt truly wonderful to be employed. The work was simple, all she had to do was put two flat pieces of cardboard and one corrugated piece into a machine, and then it would swipe glue on them and press the three pieces together into one sheet. These could then be used to make boxes. The only technique she had to learn was to line up the corners when she put the cardboard into the machine, otherwise it would come out crooked and would have to be thrown away.

Jingqiu was a meticulous person, always striving to do her best, as well as a fast learner. The other workers on her machine liked her because she was quick and reliable, and never slacked off. A few of them let Jingqiu take care of everything while they slipped out the back door to browse in the nearby shop. Every day they finished their quota early and once the inspector had checked their work they were free go to the common room to rest until they were allowed to go home.

Once, the factory distributed pears, one and a half kilos to the regular workers and just one kilo to the temporary workers. At the end of the day, she carried the pears back home and presented them to her family as if she were a magician that had conjured them into existence. She told her sister to eat. Her sister was overjoyed; grabbing three pears she went to wash them so they could have one each. Jingqiu declined, saying she had already eaten some at the factory. 'That's the thing about pears, if you eat too many you get sick of them.'

Jingqiu watched her sister read while nibbling at a pear. After half an hour she still hadn't finished. Jingqiu's heart ached, and quietly she made a promise to herself: when I earn some money I will buy a big basket of pears so my sister can eat as many as she pleases, so many that she will never want to eat another pear again.

Unfortunately her job at the cardboard factory lasted barely two weeks. It was only when someone told her that she needn't come the next day that she really understood that she was just a temporary worker. She was reminded of a sentence in one of the classical poetry books Old Third had lent her: 'In dreams I know not that I am a guest, / a moment of stolen happiness.'

So she returned to Director Li's house to wait for a job, and the fear that went along with waiting. She was back to the exhaustion of it all. Old Third was but a remote concern compared to her nervousness and exhaustion.

Chapter Sixteen

In the days after starting back at school in the autumn Jingqiu was very busy, not with studying but with a confusion of other things. That term, apart from continuing on the girls' volleyball team, she was also training with the ping-pong team for a forthcoming competition. Normally the sports teams had an agreement that each student could only play for one team so that they could concentrate properly on one sport. But Jingqiu's circumstances were special; the two coaches, Mr Wang for ping-pong and Mr Quan for volleyball, had negotiated to let her play both.

Mr Wang thought Jingqiu a vital part of his team, not only because she was the best girl in the whole of No. 8 Middle School, but for another important, what you might call historical, reason.

Jingqiu had started on the ping-pong team at junior high. One year, there had been a city-wide competition in which Jingqiu had come in the top four. In the semi-finals she had met another student from her team, Liu Shiqiao, with whom she was often paired during practice. Jingqiu held her bat upright, in an attacking grip, whereas Shiqiao held hers in a horizontal, defensive grip. The coach knew that Shiqiao met the ball securely, but lacked ferociousness in her attacks, the killer instinct you might say, unlike Jingqiu who lashed and served the ball as if killing was in her blood. So the coach had taught Shiqiao to wear her opponent down through a process of attrition, slowly weakening her adversary rather than looking for the fatal shot. Then, when her opponent finally lost patience, it would be her own mistakes that finished her off. As they were both on the same team Jingqiu naturally knew Shiqiao's strengths and weaknesses, not to mention the coach's tactics, so she had perfected her own way of dealing with her. Usually during practice it was Jingqiu who came out on top.

They were playing instant knock-out. In the second round Jingqiu had been drawn against a player from the city sports academy. It was like a small theatrical troupe up against an operatic company, so Mr Wang told her he had no great hopes but that she should just 'Go for it, and try not to get skinned alive'. Her opponent must not take the glory in all three games. Mr Wang didn't even stay to watch the match on the grounds that it would be pointless to waste his energy over it. Even the umpire was not bothered to watch properly.

But who was to know that, perhaps because of a nearly absolute lack of expectation on the part of those around her, Jingqiu really did go for it. She thwacked from left and from right. Perhaps her fearless way of attacking had shocked her opponent. Or perhaps because her methods weren't particularly 'operatic' the girl hadn't known how to respond. Smashing this way, crashing that way, Jingqiu eventually knocked out the girl from the sports academy.

Mr Wang was jubilant but the rest of the competitors panicked. The girls who competed against her in the following rounds were beaten calmly and Jingqiu progressed through the competition. Shiqiao happened to have a lucky competition too, and so, in the semifinals, the two girls met.

After they had tossed for who was to play on what side and who was to start, Mr Wang walked over to Jingqiu and rasped under his breath, 'Let her win, d'you hear me?'

Jingqiu was given no explanation as to why she was supposed to let Shiqiao win, but she thought that maybe it was the coach's special tactic, that he was thinking of the glory of the whole school. Every ping-pong player at the time knew that the Chinese national team had the tradition that for the country to come on top individuals had to let their team members win sometimes. So, with a heavy heart, Jingqiu let Shiqiao win a game, only to have the same instructions repeated. Jingqiu put her doubts out of her mind and returned the ball sloppily, letting Shiqiao win the match.

Only afterwards did Jingqiu ask the coach, 'Why did I have to let her win? What tactic was that?'

'The people who get into the finals are invited to train with the provincial sports academy,' Mr Wang replied, 'but your class background is bad, they'd reject you as soon as you got there. You'd feel terrible.'

Jingqiu was so furious she had to fight back her tears. So the sports school would reject me, but I could've still come first, or second, in the city, so why make me throw the contest? Isn't that worse that being rejected by the school?

Later Jingqiu's mother got to hear of it and being equally upset she went to see the coach, brandishing the logic 'you can't choose your class background, but you can choose your future' to clarify the error of his actions.

Mr Wang repeated his explanation; he had done it out of concern for Jingqiu's feelings, but despite his good intentions he did regret his decision. If he'd let Jingqiu play the school might have won the Yichang title, Shiqiao only came second. Jingqiu told her mother to forget it. It's done now, there's no point. She left the ping-pong team and joined the volleyball team instead.

But Mr Wang wanted to remedy the wrong he had done to Jingqiu, and in reality, he hadn't found anyone in the whole school better at ping-pong than Jingqiu, so he negotiated with the volleyball coach to let her continue with ping-pong so that she could compete in the next city-wide competition. The volleyball team were also in training for a competition, and along with school work, every spare moment seemed to be given over to training for the two teams.

One Thursday afternoon, when Jingqiu was practising ping-pong, Mr Wang came in and said to her, 'I just saw someone outside the canteen carrying a big bag looking for Teacher Jingqiu, maybe he's looking for your mother. I took him to your house but your mother wasn't in, no one was. Today the teachers are visiting parents so perhaps that's where your mother is. I told him to wait in the entrance to the canteen, why don't you go see what it's about?'

Jingqiu rushed over to the canteen and saw Lin crouching, as stiff and dignified as a stone lion, in the doorway. The crowds streaming in and out were giving him curious looks. Jingqiu ran over and called out. As soon as he saw her, he stood up and pointed to the bag beside him. 'Some walnuts for your mother.' Then he pointed a bit further away and said, 'Some kindling for you. I'm going.'

Jingqiu watched as Lin walked away, her heart pounding. She wanted to make him come back but she was too timid to grab him. She called out, 'Hey, hey, don't go, won't you at least help me carry it all to my house?'

As if jolted awake Lin turned back. 'Oh, they're too heavy? Let me do it.' He swung the bag on to his back, picked up the basket, and followed Jingqiu to her house.

'Have you eaten?' Jingqiu asked as she started scraping out the oven to make food.

'Yes, in a restaurant,' Lin answered proudly.

Jingqiu thought it odd that Lin would have eaten in one of Yichang's restaurants. She poured him a cup of boiled water and asked him to rest while she looked for something into which she could transfer the walnuts so that he could take his bag back with him. 'Did you go to Yumin's home town? Is her family well?' Jingqiu asked.

'Her family?' Lin looked confused. Jingqiu thought it possible that he had gone all the way there, picked the walnuts and left without saying a word to Yumin's family.

Jingqiu remembered Auntie saying Lin had been quite incapable of lying ever since he was small. His eyelids would flutter non-stop if he told a fib, making it easy for Auntie to suss him out. Jingqiu looked at his eyes and saw he was blinking a little, but the evidence was inconclusive. Inside the bag was another smaller bag with rock sugar in it. 'Did you buy the sugar?'

'My big brother bought it.'

So, even Sen had been implicated. 'You can only buy rock sugar with a doctor's prescription, where did Eldest Brother get one?' she asked, while sneaking twenty yuan of the summer's earnings into Lin's bag. She rolled the bag up and tied it with a piece of string, guessing that it would be unlikely that Lin would find the money before he got home. But if he didn't find it once he got there, Auntie or Yumin might wash the bag and the twenty yuan would be ruined. She decided to take him to the bus station, and only once the bus had started moving would she tell him about what she had put in his bag.

'Big Brother knows a doctor and he made up the prescription.'

Lin's answer sounded too prepared, nor was it like his normal way of speaking. His eyes were blinking rapidly. She decided to trick him, to find out if he'd come on his own or with someone else. 'The ticket has gone up ten per cent, it's expensive now, isn't it?'

Lin blushed, then started counting on his fingers. 'Gone up? Up to twenty yuan and eighty cents? Damn it, it's exploitation, that's what it is.'

Jingqiu now knew for certain that he hadn't come on his own. He didn't know the price of a ticket, and had calculated ten per cent to be ten yuan. Most probably he came with Old Third who must be hiding somewhere. She let Lin sit a while longer. That way Old Third would wait until, thinking Lin had lost his way, he had to come looking for him.

But Lin couldn't be forced to stay and was adamant that he should go. He had to hurry to catch the bus. Jingqiu had no option but to take him to the station. Once they reached the campus gate, however, Lin wouldn't let her go any further. He was obstinate, and looked as if he might use force to hold her back, should it be necessary.

Jingqiu had to give up. She didn't leave, however, but stood behind the window of the campus reception and watched Lin. Lin waited by the river looking around him before walking over the bank down to the river. He reappeared moments later with another person. Jingqiu could see it was Old Third. Despite his faded army uniform, he looked keen and spritely. The two of them stood by the river talking, as Lin pointed frequently in the direction of the campus gate, and the two jabbed and punched each other, laughing. Lin must have been recounting his near miss. Then Old Third turned to look in the direction of the gate. Frightened, Jingqiu ducked out of his line of sight. He must have seen me, she thought. But he hadn't. He stood looking, until eventually he followed Lin towards the river crossing.

She followed them, keeping her distance. Old Third was acting like a child, tottering along the small mud wall that had been built up along the edge of the river, rather than walking on the road. It was only just over four inches wide, and Old Third nearly lost his balance a few times, frightening her until she almost called out. He could have rolled down the bank and into the water. But he put his arms out and swayed a bit before finding his balance again, and then, picking up speed, ran as if along a balance beam.

She really wanted to call out to them, but if Old Third had been hiding from her then it would be too embarrassing to do that. He really was as Fang had described him, a soft-hearted man who couldn't bear to see people suffer. He had helped Daxiu, he had helped her, and now he was helping Lin. He must have bought the bus tickets that day, and knowing that Lin wouldn't know the way, taken him all the way to the campus gate.

Old Third must be making way for Lin, she thought, or else he never really liked me. But she couldn't believe that, hadn't his lips been up for the fight? Men always had their women before casting them aside; at least, that's what it said in the books. So did he 'have' me? She hated how ambiguous books could be, they would only hint at things, like 'he let loose his brutish behaviour, and ravished her'. What exactly did it mean, to be 'ravished'? Probably, women got pregnant after being 'ravished'. It's been six months since Old Third held me, she thought, and my 'old friend' has been making regular visits all that time, so I can't be pregnant, surely? In which case, he didn't 'have' me then, did he?

Jingqiu was also worrying about the money she had put into Lin's bag. Maybe he'd lose it, or his mother would wash it. So she followed them to the river crossing. Only once the boat had left the bank did she shout out, 'Lin, I put twenty yuan in your bag, don't let your mother wash it.'

She called out twice, then guessed Lin had heard her as he was untying the string around his bag. She saw Old Third turn to talk to the ferryman, and then suddenly he stood up, and grabbing the bag from Lin's hand he walked to the front of the boat, making it sway violently. Afraid that Old Third was going to try to give the money back, she turned and ran. After a while it occurred to her that he was on a boat, what could he possibly do? She slowed and looked back. As she turned, she saw Old Third running towards her. His army trousers were drenched all the way up to his thighs and the fabric clung to his legs. She was dumbstruck. It's October, isn't he cold?

In a few bounds he was with her, and stuffed the twenty yuan into her hands. 'Take the money, the sugar is a present, you don't need to pay. Use this money to buy your team uniforms, don't you have a competition?'

She stiffened; how did he know she needed kit for her competition? 'Lin is still on the boat,' he rushed, 'he's probably in a state of shock, he doesn't know the way. I'll be off, or we won't make the bus.' With that, he turned and ran towards the jetty.

She wanted to call after him but her throat wouldn't make a sound. It was just like in her dreams, unable to speak, unable to move, all she could do was look at him as he receded into the distance.

That day, when she got back to school, she wasn't in the mood for volleyball. Instead, she was occupied with thoughts of Old Third's wet trousers; it would be hours before he got home and could change them. Would he catch a cold? How could he be so stupid and jump into the water like that? Did he wait for the boat to come back and pick him up? Days later, she still couldn't forget the image of him running towards her in wet trousers.

What she couldn't understand, no matter how she puzzled over it, was how he had known she needed a new team uniform for her competition. Last year, the volleyball team had played in matches without proper team uniforms because of lack of money, getting them into trouble with the referee and seriously affecting their performance.

Their coach, Mr Quan, was furious. He was not the sort to let even death defeat him, and he declared that had it not been for the unhappy business of their lack of a uniform, No. 8 Middle School would have come in the top six in the city-wide championships. After the competition he forced everyone to buy one. He collected the money and their sizes and went to get them himself to ensure that they didn't all go out and buy whichever colour took their fancy, and so that the team could never again be referred to as 'a motley crew'.

This time Mr Quan was resolute. 'If you don't buy a uniform, you can't play volleyball.' The team panicked and handed over the money. But Jingqiu didn't have any to spare, and the ping-pong team also wanted her to buy one. She decided to try to convince the two coaches to buy the same colour and style, that way she could wear the same outfit for both.

But the coaches demanded that they be different. Volleyball was played outdoors and during the last competition it had been cold. Mr Quan demanded that they buy long-sleeved tops which could hold the warmth and protect their arms and shoulders from aches and pains. Ping-pong competitions, however, were held indoors, so Mr Wang wanted them to have short-sleeved tops; how can you play ping-pong with long, 'droopy' sleeves?

She didn't know how Old Third knew about all this. Did he know the volleyball coach or one of her teammates? Or did he stand somewhere watching her play? But she had never seen him at any of the matches. Perhaps he was a born reconnaissance soldier? Was he checking up on her without her knowledge? She decided to take some money from this twenty yuan to buy a new strip, but only because Old Third had risked the freezing cold to give it back to her for that purpose. She would buy it to please Old Third; if he came and saw her wearing her new strip it would be sure to make him happy.

As luck would have it, apart from the length of the sleeves, the colour and style of the strips were the same. Perhaps there weren't that many to choose from in those days. She bought a long-sleeved top and a pair of shorts so that she could wear the long sleeves when playing volleyball, and before her ping-pong competitions she could cut the sleeves short. Her needlework being what it was, she would then sew back the sleeves for volleyball and no one would be any the wiser.

Jingqiu had hoped that Old Third was going to surprise her by appearing at her competition that December, and would see her wearing her new strip. But she didn't see him on the day, and later thanked heaven that he hadn't come, as the No. 8 Middle School girls' volleyball team only came in the top six. The team put their defeat down to their poverty; they could only afford to train with a rubber ball, whereas the regulation ball used in competitions was much heavier and made from leather. Not being used to its weight, they struggled even to serve. 'Coach,' they said after the competition, 'you have to make the school get us some regulation balls to practise with.'

'I promise,' Mr Quan replied, 'but you must practise hard, otherwise it will be a waste.'

Chapter Seventeen

One chilly spring morning Jingqiu and her team were practising out in the sports field. The volleyball court was close to the back gate of the campus, and as the outer wall was only the height of the average person, the ball was often knocked over the wall. Beyond it were vegetable fields tended by the agricultural commune, so every time the ball went over the wall there would be a mad dash to get it back before their new regulation ball got drenched in water lying in the fields – water could crack and split the leather – or else was snatched by a passer-by.

To go through the campus gate, however, was quite a way and it took too long so, for fear of losing the ball, someone would have to jump over the wall to get it. Not everyone could scale the wall; only Jingqiu and two other girls could jump over and back again without requiring the help of hands pushing from below. As soon as the ball went over someone would call out one of these girls' names, urging them to hurry up and fetch it.

That morning during practice someone knocked the ball over, and as Jingqiu was closest a few voices called out, 'Jingqiu, Jingqiu, the ball's gone over!'

Jingqiu ran over and with one step and two hands she hoisted herself on to the wall. She had thrown one leg over the wall and was about to bring her other leg over and jump down when she saw a living, breathing revolutionary martyr just like Lei Feng pick up the ball and prepare to throw it back over the campus wall. He raised his head to look at her and called, 'Careful, don't jump!'

It was Old Third. He was wearing an army uniform, not of grass-green colour this time, but of that mustard-yellow kind, her favourite. She had only ever seen regional song and dance troupes wearing that colour. Old Third's ink black hair shone against the brown fur collar on his overcoat and the dazzling flash of his white shirt collar. Jingqiu felt dizzy, and spots appeared before her eyes – either from hunger and exercise or else Old Third's dashing good looks – and she nearly fell down from the wall.

He held the volley ball, already wet and covered in mud. He walked up to her and handed it to her. 'Be careful when you jump down.'

Jingqiu took the ball, lobbed it back over the wall towards the court, and remained straddling the wall. 'How did you get here?'

He raised his head to look at her, and almost as if apologising, laughed. 'The road comes here, and I walked along it.'

The girls on the other side of the wall called impatiently, 'Jingqiu, you're not taking a rest, are you? We're waiting for you to serve.'

'I've got to go and play,' she said, jumping down and running back to her position on the court. The more she played, however, the more distracted she became. Where's he going if he's come past here so early? Suddenly she realised, this day last year was the day she arrived in West Village, that is, the day she first met Old Third. Did he remember and come to see me especially? Disorientated, she had to get confirmation.

Her thoughts turned to who would next knock the ball over

the wall so she could climb over and see if he was still there. But it was as if everyone had made some prior agreement; no one hit the ball over the wall again. She waited until practice was about to finish then served the ball clear over the wall, annoying and surprising her teammates.

Without a care for what they thought she hurtled towards the wall, threw herself over it and, without wasting a moment, jumped down the other side. She picked up the ball, but couldn't see Old Third. She threw the ball back but didn't climb over the wall as she wanted to see if he was hiding somewhere. She looked all along the road right up to the gate, but there was no sign of him, so she had to accept that he had just been passing through. She was distracted for the rest of the day, and during the afternoon's sports lesson she smacked the ball over the wall a few more times, volunteering each time to go collect it. But still no Old Third.

After school she went home to eat, and then went to check on the piles of leaves she and her classmates had set fire to earlier. Each class had a small portion of the campus that was their responsibility to keep clean. Today, it had been her group's turn to sweep it, but the ground had been covered in leaves. Normally when this happened they would sweep the leaves into a pile and light them before throwing the ashes on the rubbish dump. Her group had asked Jingqiu to come back later to clean up the ashes after she'd been home to eat.

Jingqiu gathered the ashes and put them into a large woven dustpan to take to the dump. As she straightened up she noticed Old Third racing around the basketball court with some other students. He was wearing his white shirt and a woollen sleeveless top, having taken off his army uniform.

In her surprise she nearly spilled the ashes. He didn't leave! Or had he finished his business and come back? She watched him play. He's so handsome, she thought. When he jumped his black hair flew up into the air, and as the ball sailed into the net his hair fell neatly back into place.

She didn't want him to see her watching him, so she busied herself with the remnants of the leaves. She threw them on the dump, returned the dustpan to the classroom and locked the door. But she didn't go home. She sat on some parallel bars far away from the court but from which she could watch him play. There were only four players in all, playing in one half.

Old Third had already removed his tank top and was playing only in his shirt, his sleeves rolled up high, looking vigorous and handsome. She kept score for them, and counted who scored the most baskets, which turned out to be Old Third. She noticed he was wearing leather shoes. These little details made her admire him even more. Why can't he live on this court, and play for me from dawn until dusk?

The sky gradually darkened, the game finished and the team dispersed. Someone took the ball and dribbled it towards the store cupboard, obviously intending to return it. Jingqiu watched Old Third nervously, not knowing where he would go. She wanted to call out to him, just to say a few words, but she didn't have the courage. Maybe he's been sent on a work trip somewhere nearby, and having nothing to do after work, he did as the workers usually do, and came to the school to play basketball to pass the time.

Eventually she saw him start off in the direction of her house; he must be going to wash his hands, she thought. She followed behind him, at a distance. As she had guessed, he and some of his teammates stopped at the wash basins. He waited for the others to finish washing and leave, before hanging his jacket and other things on an apricot tree whose branches spread out in a Y-shape. She watched him wash his hands and face, then even pull up his shirt to wash his body. She shivered with cold.

After pulling his woollen top back on, he walked to the nearby canteen. From there, she knew, he could see the door to her house. He stood there for a while, before draping his jacket over his shoulders, picking up his bag, and walking round in the direction of the back of her house. Not far from the back of her house there was a block of toilets. She was embarrassed, and couldn't follow him. She fled, quick as a flash, back home.

Once indoors, she couldn't resist going to the window to see where Old Third would go after coming out of the toilet. Her window was about one person in height above street-level. She stood by the window and gazed out in silence but she couldn't see him. But as soon as she looked down she caught sight of him facing her house. Startled, she dropped to the ground, only to knock her head against the desk in front of the window, producing a resounding clanging sound.

'What's going on?' her mother asked.

Jingqiu waved her hands to silence her mother, and half-crouching, waddled to the other room at the front. Only when she knew there was no way he could see her through the wall did she stand up, a little puzzled as to why she was so afraid. Having waited a while, she tiptoed to the window and looked out, but he was gone. She didn't know if he had seen her. If he had, then he would know she had been watching him in secret. She stood by the window looking at the road below. She looked for a long time, but didn't see him. He must have gone. It's dark now, where did he go?

She went back to her room to knit and mull things over. After a while someone knocked on the door. It must be Old Third, she thought, flustered. She tried desperately to think of a lie to tell her mother. But when she opened the door she was greeted by the son of the school secretary, Ding Chao, who was carrying a kettle in his hand. He must have been collecting water at the taps. 'My sister wants to speak to you,' he said.

Chao's older sister was called Ling, and Jingqiu knew her a bit, but they could not be considered close friends. She had no idea why Ling would want to speak to her. 'What does she want?'

'I don't know, she just told me to fetch you. Hurry.'

Jingqiu followed Chao to the taps, and just as she was about to turn to the right in the direction of the Ding house, Chao pointed to the left. 'There, someone's looking for you.'

Jingqiu realised at once that it was Old Third. 'Thank you,' she said to Chao. 'You get your water, and don't tell anyone.'

'I know.'

She walked up to Old Third. 'You're ... looking for me?'

'I wanted to speak to you,' he whispered. 'Is it a good time? If not, then it's not important.'

She was about to respond when she saw someone emerge from the toilets, and worried that they would see her talking to a boy – and that the news would spread like wildfire – she moved in the direction of the campus back gate. After walking some way she bent over and pretended to tie her laces, turning to check that Old Third was following behind at a distance. She stood up and started to walk again, following the campus wall until she reached the place where she had collected her volleyball that morning. He caught up with her and started to speak when she interrupted him. 'Everyone here knows me, let's go a bit further,' and started walking again.

She walked and walked until she came to the ferry crossing, and only then did she realise she hadn't brought any money with her. She waited for him, and alert as always, he came up to her, bought two tickets for the boat and gave her one. They went aboard, in single file. Not until they reached the other side and walked along the river some more did Jingqiu stop and wait for him.

He bounded up towards her, and laughing, said, 'It's like in the film *In Hot Pursuit.*'

'The people on that side of the river know me, but now we're on this side no one does.'

He smiled and asked, 'Where are we going? Don't go too far, else your mother will come looking for you.'

'I know a pavilion up ahead by the river, and it has a bench. Didn't you say you wanted to talk? We can talk there.'

The pavilion was empty, probably because it was too cold for anyone to want to come down here and drink in the icy wind. It consisted of only a few posts supporting a roof and was open to the elements on all sides. Jingqiu found a place to sit beside one of the posts in the hope that it might shelter her from some of the wind.

Old Third sat down on a small stool on the other side of the post and asked, 'Are you hungry? I haven't eaten dinner yet.'

'Go and eat something at the restaurant over there. I'll wait for you here.'

But he wouldn't go. Anxious that he was hungry, she told him again to go and eat. 'Let's go together,' he suggested. 'You said no one around here knows you, so keep me company. If you don't go, neither will I.'

They found an out-of-the-way noodle stand, the type that only sells noodles and no rice dishes. Old Third asked her what she would like to eat but she insisted she wasn't hungry. 'Don't keep asking or I'll leave.' Old Third was stunned by her response and didn't ask again, telling her instead to sit and he'd go and queue.

Jingqiu couldn't remember the last time she had eaten at a restaurant. It must have been when she was a child, she reflected, with her mother and father. They used to go for breakfast; steamed buns, fried bread, hot soybean milk and savoury pancakes, that sort of thing. It must have been seven or eight years ago now. After they stopped going out for breakfast they fried up some leftovers or else bought plain steamed bread from the school canteen. Later, due to their insufficient grain ration, they had to start buying buns made from old flour, that is, the grey, rough waste left over at the mill. You didn't need a ration ticket for that type of flour, so that was what Jingqiu's family now usually ate.

Old Third bought lots of things and had to make several trips to carry it all. He passed her a pair of chopsticks. 'Don't say anything, just eat, otherwise I won't eat either.' He repeated his instructions a few times but still she didn't pick up the chopsticks. He too refused, forcing her to eat. The things Old Third had bought were the things she had loved eating most as a child. It was as if he had read her inner thoughts. He bought one large oily pancake, crispy brown on the outside and filled with sticky rice and covered with spring onions; its fragrance wafted up to her nose. He bought a couple of meat-filled steamed buns; they were milky white and let off plumes of steam, and tasted truly delicious. He also bought two bowls of soup noodles in which floated spring onions and celestial pools of sesame oil. They smelled delicious. She nibbled at the food, but was too embarrassed to tuck in.

Every time Old Third bought things it made her feel uncomfortable. She felt selfish, guzzling and slurping at restaurants behind her family's back. If I ever have lots of money I'll take my whole family out to eat at a restaurant. I won't spare any expense, and get them whatever they want. Not only was the family short of cash, they were also running out of rice. Her mother had asked someone to get them some special tickets for the leftover broken rice so that she could fill them up; each grain was as small as a granule of sand. The factory used to sell it to the farmers to feed their pigs, but now people ate anything and everything. For a half-kilo rice ticket you could buy a kilo of broken rice, so all the families that were running short bought that instead.

Broken rice was disgusting. It slid around your mouth as you chewed. Worst of all it was so dirty and mixed with little stones and husks, it took half an hour, or even an hour, to wash it properly: using a large basin and a small bowl, you had to pour in a scoop of rice and then add a bit of water. You then shook it slowly until you had skimmed off the floating husks, and then you poured the rice into another bowl, and added another bowl of water, before shaking it again.

Jingqiu always washed the rice herself; her mother was too busy and her sister too young to clean it thoroughly enough. Swallowing any of the stones or husks would give you instant tummy aches. What was more, during the middle of winter her sister's hands couldn't endure being submerged in freezing water for the hour or so necessary to get the job done. Jingqiu painfully missed her time in West Village. They didn't need tickets to collect rice, nor did they worry about the amount of vegetables they had to eat; there was always something to put on the table.

When they had finished Old Third hesitated a moment before saying carefully, 'I want to say something, but don't be angry, okay?' He waited for her to nod and then reached into his jacket pocket and took out some rice ration tickets. 'I have some of these going spare, I can't use them. Don't get upset, just take them, okay?'

'If you can't use them up, send them back to your family.'

'These are distributed here in Hubei, I'm from Anhui, there's no point in sending them. You take them. If you can't use them then pass them on to someone else.'

'How come you've got so many left over?'

'My unit buys our rice directly from West Village, we don't need ration tickets.'

Satisfied with his explanation she took them. 'Then thank you.' His face lit up, and anyone would have thought he had been the one to receive the tickets.

They walked back in single file to the pavilion. I've done it again, Jingqiu thought, taken his presents, eaten his food. How come I'm always doing this?

They sat down again, no longer feeling as cold as before their meal. 'Do you remember this day last year?' Old Third asked.

Her heart missed a beat. So this is why he came. But she didn't answer his question, instead asking coldly, 'You said you had something to say to me. What is it? The ferry will close soon.'

'It stops at ten, it's only eight now.' He looked at her, and asked quietly, 'Has anyone spoken to you about me having a girlfriend?'

'A fiancée,' she corrected him.

He smiled. 'Okay, fiancée. But it's all in the past, we haven't . . . been together for a long time.'

'Rubbish, you told Yumin that you had a fiancée, and you showed her a picture.'

'I only told her that because she wanted to set me up with Fen. That family has been so good to me, how could I just say no? But we split up two years ago, and she's married now. If you don't believe me, I can show you the letter she sent me.'

'Why would I want to read her letter? And anyway, you could easily just fake one.' Yet she reached out her hand so that he could pass it to her.

He fished out the letter and she ran to the nearest streetlamp to read. The light was dim but she could still make out the words. It accused Old Third of purposefully avoiding her and staying away from home. She had waited too long and her heart was already broken, she wouldn't wait any longer, and so it went on. It was well written, much better than the previous break-up letters Jingqiu had read. She didn't rely on Mao's poetry or maxims, you could see she was cultured, that she had been educated before the Cultural Revolution.

Jingqiu looked at the signature, Zoya. 'Isn't Zoya the name of a Soviet heroine?'

'Back then that was a popular girl's name,' Old Third explained. 'She's a bit older than me and born in the Soviet Union.'

Born in the Soviet Union! Jingqiu was speechless with admiration, and instantly imagined her to be the girl from the song, who went to ask the hawthorn tree for advice. In fact she felt rather inferior. 'Is she beautiful? Fang and Yumin both said she's beautiful.'

He smiled. 'Beauty, well, that depends on who's looking. In my opinion, she's not as beautiful as you.'

Jingqiu felt goosebumps rise on her skin. Did he just say that? He had spoiled the image she had been forming of him. I mean, would any decent person say someone was beautiful to their face? And wasn't this evidence of liberalism? Say one thing to your face, another behind your back, say one thing in a meeting and another thing outside the meeting, wasn't this what Chairman Mao had identified as liberal leanings?

Jingqiu knew she wasn't beautiful, so she knew he was lying. He must be sweet-talking me. But what are his motives? With all this to-ing and fro-ing they'd get right back to the problem of whether or not he was 'getting' his prey. She looked left and right, confirming that there was no one within a hundred metre radius. She'd led him out here for her own peace of mind, and now she realised she might have just thrown herself into his trap. She must be more vigilant. She had taken his gifts but she shouldn't be weak, and just because he had bought her food didn't mean she had to go along with whatever he said.

She gave him his letter. 'The fact that you showed me her letter means you can't keep a secret. How can I trust you with my own letters?'

He smiled bitterly. 'I didn't have a choice. Normally, I'm very good at keeping secrets, but, if I hadn't shown you, you wouldn't have believed me. Tell me, what should I have done?'

This made her feel good, he was recognising her power over him. 'As I've been saying all along, if you can toy with her, then you could do the same to someone else.'

'Why do you draw that conclusion?' he asked anxiously. 'Chairman Mao says that you can't beat someone to death with one stick. It was all our parents' idea, not mine.'

'This is the modern world, who has their parents arrange their marriage?'

'I'm not saying it was an arranged marriage, I didn't get married after all. Our parents merely encouraged it. Maybe you don't believe me, but lots of cadre families do it like that, they won't say it straight out, but they let their children know their intentions by arranging who they come into contact with, so that when it comes to it, most marriages are at least partially arranged by the parents.'

'Do you like this way of doing things?'

'Of course not.'

'So why did you agree to it?'

He was silent for a while, before answering. 'The situation at the time was rather peculiar, and it was going to have an impact on my parents' political future . . . their whole future. It's a long story, but I want you to believe me, it was over a long time ago. She and I, well, it was what you might call a political alliance. That's why I always stayed at my unit, and rarely went home.'

'How heartless,' Jingqiu said, shaking her head. 'You should have either broken it off like a decent human being, or else married her. How could you just mess her around?'

'I wanted to break it off but she wouldn't let me, and neither would our families.' He lowered his head, and stuttered, 'But it's over now, say whatever you like, but you must believe me, I'm serious about you. I will never betray you.'

That's not what the characters from the books he lent me would have said, she thought, disappointed. He sounds like Lin. Why doesn't he sound like the young men in those books? The books may well be politically poisonous, but they do describe how love ought to be, at least.

'Is that what you wanted to talk to me about?' she asked. 'Can I go back home now?'

He raised his head and looked at her, shocked by her coldness. It took him a long time to reply. 'You still don't believe me?'

'Believe what? All I know is that people who break their promises are not worth trusting.'

He sighed deeply. 'I really wish I could show you what's in my heart.'

'No one believes in all that. Chairman Mao says you can't beat someone to death with one stick, so sure, I won't. But Chairman Mao also said, "You can see someone's present from their past, and you can see someone's future from their present."'

Her words seemed to knock his voice out of him. She looked at him, feeling a little bit proud.

He looked back at her without saying anything. Finally, he replied in a whisper, 'Jingqiu, Jingqiu, maybe you've never been in love before so you don't believe that love can last forever. Wait until you fall in love, when you find that person, then you'll understand that you'd rather die than betray them.'

She trembled upon hearing him whisper her name so intensely, her whole body started to shake. The tone of his voice and his imploring facial expression made her shiver. Why do I believe him, believe that he isn't lying? Unable to reply, she took a few deep breaths to steady herself, and yet she could not stop herself from trembling more violently.

He took off his military jacket and draped it over her shoulders. 'You must be cold? Let's go back. We don't want you to catch a cold.'

She refused to leave, hiding instead under his coat until eventually she stuttered, 'You must be cold too? Why don't you wear the coat?'

'I'm not cold.' He was wearing his woollen tank top over a shirt, and watched as she shivered despite the many layers she was wearing.

'If you're cold why don't you come under the coat too,' she said softly.

He hesitated as if trying to work out if she was testing him. He looked at her with a steady gaze before shuffling closer to her and lifting one side of the coat. It covered half of his body. They shared the jacket as if it were a rain coat, but they might as well not have had anything over their shoulders, so ineffective was it at keeping out the cold.

'Are you still cold?' he asked.

'Well, not really cold. Why don't you ... wear the coat. I don't ... need it.'

He gripped her hand tentatively but she didn't react. He added more pressure and continued to hold tight, seemingly wanting to squeeze out her trembles. After holding her hand for a while he noticed that she was no longer shivering. 'Let me think of something. I'll just try it, and if you don't like it, just tell me.' He stood up and put on his coat, then facing her, pulled her towards him and wrapped her tightly inside.

She sat there, her head leaning up against his stomach, and thought it must look as if he is pregnant, his belly protruding from under his coat. She couldn't stop herself from laughing. He hung his head and looked down at her inside his jacket. 'Are you laughing because I look as if I am with child?'

He had guessed correctly, and used such an 'aerodite' expression, 'with child', making her laugh even harder. He pulled her up by the lapels of her jacket, and wrapped his arms around her firmly. 'Now I don't look like I'm with child,' but he started trembling himself. 'Did you give me your shivers?'

She leant up against his chest, and again her head felt faint from the smell of him. She desperately hoped that he would hold her harder, that he would squeeze the air out from inside her. Embarrassed, she told him, but she didn't have the courage to put her arms around his waist. She left them hanging by her side, as if standing to attention, pressing closer to his chest.

'Are you still cold?' he asked. He held her tighter still, and she felt even better, closing her eyes and hiding in the folds of his clothes. She could sleep like this, and would never want to wake up.

He shook a little longer and then said quietly, 'Jingqiu, Jingqiu, I thought ... I would never be able to do this again, I thought I frightened you too much last time. Could you pinch me, just so I can check this isn't a dream?'

She lifted her head. 'Pinch you where?'

'Wherever you want,' he laughed. 'But you don't need to do it now, I can't be dreaming because in my dreams you don't talk like this.'

'How do I talk in your dreams?'

'In my dreams you're always avoiding me and telling me not to follow you, to take my hands off you and that you don't like me touching you. Have you ever dreamt of me?'

'Yes, I have.' She told him about the dream in which he had betrayed her to the authorities.

'Why did you dream that?' he asked, hurt. 'I would never do that to you, I'm not that kind of person. I know you're worried, and frightened, but I would never get you into trouble. I only want to protect you, look after you, make you happy. But you're always confusing me. Tell me, tell me now, what do you want me to do? I'm afraid of upsetting you and not knowing why. Just tell me, I'll do anything, I can do anything for you.'

She really liked hearing him say these things, but she also warned herself, do you believe him? He's cheating you, anyone can say these things. 'I want you to promise not to come to see me until after I graduate. Can you do that?'

'Yes.'

But she couldn't help thinking of what would happen after graduation. 'After I finish senior high school I will be sent down to the countryside, and once I go I won't get called back.'

'I know you will be called back. I'm not saying that I won't love you if you don't get called back, I just believe that you will definitely be called back. And if you aren't, it doesn't matter, I can follow you to wherever you get sent.'

In fact, this wasn't really a problem for Jingqiu, because to her, as long as two people loved each other, they didn't need to be in the same place. The most important thing was their love, it made no difference if they were close together or far away, and indeed as far as she was concerned, perhaps the further apart the greater the proof of how strong their love for each other was.

'I wouldn't want you to come with me, I just want you to wait.'

'Okay, I'll wait.'

'I can't be in a relationship before I am twenty-five, can you wait that long?'

'I can wait. As long as you want me to wait, as long as it doesn't make you unhappy, I can wait a lifetime.'

'A lifetime?' She sniggered. 'Wait that long and you'll be in a coffin, what would be the point?'

'So that you'll believe me when I say I can wait a lifetime, so that you believe in an everlasting love.' He whispered, 'Jingqiu, Jingqiu, I know it's possible for you to love just one person for the rest of your life, it's just that you don't believe that someone else could love you like that. You seem to think you're insignificant, but the truth is you're so intelligent, beautiful, kind and decent, adorable. I can't be the first person to have fallen in love with you, and I won't be the last. But I do believe I will love you the most.'

Chapter Eighteen

Jingqiu was like a teetotaller who had suddenly started to drink. The first mouthful tasted hot and spicy, brought tears to her eyes and burnt her throat. How could those drunks gulp it down so enthusiastically? But after a few more tries she got used to the spicy taste, until eventually she began to appreciate its flavour. It was, perhaps, only a small step to full-blown addiction.

Old Third's whispers had brought her out in goose-pimples. They were soft and lovely to listen to. She raised her eyes and looked at him, besotted, while he told her how he felt the first time they met, of his misery when he hadn't been able to see her, how he watched her playing volleyball on top of some scaffolding near the school, how he had walked all the way to Yumin's home town to pick walnuts, and how he had 'bribed' the kid by the taps with five cents to get him to fetch her. It had happened, she was addicted to his words, the more she listened the more she wanted to listen. When he came to a pause she asked, 'And then what? Tell me more.'

He laughed, and just as he had been telling her stories on the mountain he said, 'Okay, I'll tell you more.' He carried on until suddenly he stopped and asked, 'What about you? It's your turn.'

She dodged the question. She couldn't help feeling that it would be as good as telling him she liked him outright, and that was the perfect definition of what her mother would call 'a slip'. If he liked her, it would only be because she said she liked him back, nothing unusual in that. But he could only be said to truly like her if he liked her without knowing if she liked him.

'Since when do I have so much spare time to be thinking about all that? I have to go to class, play volleyball and ping-pong.'

He hung his head, engrossed in looking at her. Her heart skipped a beat. He must be able to tell I'm lying. She turned to look the other way to avoid meeting his gaze.

'It's not immoral to miss someone, or to fall in love,' he said. 'There's no need to feel ashamed, everyone falls in love sooner or later.' He was persuasive and she was almost drawn into making her confession. But suddenly she thought of a scene from *Journey to the West*, when Sun Yukong challenges a monster to a fight. The monster has a small bottle, and if the monster calls your name and you answer you get sucked into it and turned to water. It felt like Old Third was carrying a similar such bottle, and all it would take for her to be sucked in, and never come out, would be to say that she liked him.

'I don't think it's shameful, but I'm still young, I'm still at school. I can't make these sorts of plans.'

'Sometimes it's not about planning. You just can't stop yourself from feeling it. I don't want to disrupt your studies, and neither do I want to lose sleep over this every night, but I can't seem to control it.' He looked at her, and pained, appeared to come to a decision. 'You study in peace, I'll wait until you've graduated, and then I'll come see you, how about that?'

It occurred to her suddenly that her graduation was very far away. Did he mean that they wouldn't meet for all those months? She wanted to explain that that wasn't what she had meant, that 'as long as no one found out, he could still come to see her'. But she thought his expression showed that he had already read her thoughts and he was just making her nervous on purpose so that she would reveal her true feelings.

'Graduation?' she said. 'That's ages away. Let's talk about it then, who knows how things will look then.'

'No matter how it looks, I'll come see you. But, if you need anything before then, you must tell me, okay?'

He had decided, she could see that, and she was hurt. It was as if it was of no matter whether he saw her or not, nothing like the yearning day and night he had just described. 'What would I need from you?' she asked angrily. 'What I really need from you is that you don't come to see me.'

Confused, he smiled. It took him a while before he replied. 'Jingqiu, Jingqiu, does it make you happy to torture me like this? If yes, then I have nothing to say, as long as you are happy. But if you . . . are also upset, why do you have to torture me?'

He can read exactly what's on my mind. She started shaking uncontrollably, and continued firmly, 'I don't know what you're talking about.'

He pulled her closer, and comforted her. 'Don't be angry, I didn't mean anything by it, I was just talking rubbish. If you don't like me . . . well, that's fine. But I like you.' He rubbed his face against the top of her head.

As he stroked her like that she felt the top of her head grow hotter, and the heat shot down into her face and neck until she felt feverish. She didn't know what was wrong, and taking it out on him said, 'What are you doing? Rubbing someone's head like that makes a mess of their hair. What happens when they have to go home?'

He laughed, and mimicking her strange way of putting it said, 'I'll help them neaten their hair.'

'What do you know about neatening hair? Don't make my hair look like a bird's nest.' She threw him off, undid her braids, and brushed it out roughly.

He cocked his head and watched. 'You look really good with your hair out.'

'Eugh, stop it!'

'I'm only seeking truth from facts. Hasn't anyone ever told you you're beautiful before? Lots of people must have said it.'

'Stop talking nonsense. I'm not listening. If you say any more I'll go.'

'Okay, I've stopped. But it's not a bad thing to be beautiful, and if someone says that it doesn't mean they have bad intentions. Don't be so modest, and definitely don't get angry.'

Seeing that she was about to start braiding her hair again he said, 'Don't, wear it down and let me see.'

His expression was pleading and, moved, she unconsciously hesitated to let him take a look. He looked and looked and, breathless, suddenly said, 'Can I kiss your face? I promise not to kiss you anywhere else.'

She thought his face looked pained, as if he hadn't enough air to breathe. It scared her a little, that if she didn't say yes he might die. She carefully reached her cheek across to him. 'If you promise.'

He didn't answer but held her tightly and pressed his lips against her cheek, covering it with small kisses, never straying beyond the agreed area. His beard was scratchy and his breath hot, exciting and frightening at the same time. His lips moved towards the edge of her lips a few times. Fearing a repeat of last time she became flustered, and prepared to bite her mouth shut, but he moved his lips away.

He continued to kiss her like that and she started to worry that his beard would scratch her face until it was red-raw.

How can I go home with one cheek red, and one white? She carefully pushed him away, and while brushing her hair grumbled coyly, 'Why didn't you stop?'

'I won't see you again for a long time.'

She started to laugh. 'What, so you thought you'd save them for later?'

'If only I could save them.' He seemed out of sorts, fumbling with his hands, his chest rising and falling. He stared at her.

'What's up? Are my plaits a mess?'

'No,' he said, 'they're nice. It's getting late, I'll take you back, who knows, your mother might be looking for you.'

At this she suddenly remembered that she hadn't said anything to her mother as she had left. Flustered, she asked, 'What time is it?'

'Nearly half past nine.'

'Quickly, I can't get back after the ferry stops.' They ran towards the jetty and she asked anxiously, 'Where are you going to spend the night?'

'Wherever, a hotel, at some organisation's guesthouse.'

There were no hotels or guesthouses near the jetty so she said, 'Then don't come with me across the river or else you won't be able to get back, and there are no places to stay on my side.'

'No problem.'

'Don't follow too close, I don't want anyone to see when we get to the other side of the river.'

'I know, I'll follow far behind. I just want to see you get to the campus.' He reached into his bag and brought out a book and gave it to her. 'Careful, there's a letter in it. I was afraid I wouldn't get to speak to you, so I wrote it all down.'

She took the book and pulled out the letter and stuffed it into her pocket.

*

'Where did you go?' her sister grumbled when she got home. 'Mother's been looking everywhere for you. She fell into a sewer on the way back from Wei Hong's house.'

Jingqiu saw that her mother's leg was covered in a large red gash down the shin. Stained by the antiseptic she had dabbed on it, it looked truly horrific.

'Back so late. Where have you been?' her mother asked in a loud voice.

'I went . . . to Zhong Ping's house.'

'Mother asked me to go look for you at Zhong Ping's, but he said you didn't go round,' her sister said.

Jingqiu was irritated. 'What were you doing looking for me all over? A friend from West Village came to see me so I went out. What were you doing dragging other people into this, everyone will think I've been—'

'I didn't go around dragging people into this. I heard when Zhong came round looking for you. Then when it started to get late and you hadn't come back I asked your sister to go to his place. I only told Wei Hong that I was wanting to borrow something – your mother is not that stupid. I wouldn't go telling people my daughter hadn't come back.' Her mother sighed. 'But going out and not telling me, and not a word about what time you'd be back . . . It's dangerous these days, if a girl like you should come across some . . . villain your life would be ruined.'

Jingqiu hung her head and didn't respond. She knew she was in the wrong. Luckily her mother had only hurt her leg – had she had a more serious accident then Jingqiu would have been eaten up with guilt.

'This friend from West Village, was it a he or a she?'

'A she.'

'Where did you girls go so late?'

'Hung around the riverbank.'

'Mother and I went to the river, you weren't there.'

Jingqiu didn't dare say anything more.

'I always thought you were a clever, sensible girl. How could you do something this stupid? Some men go for young girls like you, a few kind words, some nice-looking clothes, and they've got you. If someone like that fools you, that's it, it's over. You're still at school. The school will expel you if you get mixed up with any bad types. If you behave like this ...' Jingqiu's mother saw her daughter hang her head, and asked, 'Was it that Lin boy?'

'No.'

'Who was it then?'

'It was someone from the geological unit. There's nothing going on between us. He was sent here on a work trip, that's all. He had a few rice ration tickets that he didn't need so he asked me to come get them.' She pulled out the ration tickets in the hope that they would get her off the hook.

Her mother was even angrier. 'This is exactly the kind of trick I was talking about, they use little gifts to suck you in.'

'He's not like that, he just wants to help.'

'He's not like that? But he knows you're still at school, so why did he have you out until the middle of the night? If he really wants to help you why didn't he come to our house, in an upright and honest way? Would a decent person be so sneaky?' Jingqiu's mother let out a pained sigh. 'I've always worried that you'd be taken in. One slip leads down a road of hardship. I've told you so many times, and still you don't listen?' She turned to Jingqiu's little sister and said, 'Go to the other room for a bit, I want to talk to your sister.' The girl left, and her mother whispered, 'Did he ... do anything to you?'

'Do what?'

Her mother hesitated, and then said, 'Did he hug you? Kiss you? Did he ...'

Jingqiu was flustered. Her heart was thumping wildly, but she braced herself and lied, 'No.'

Her mother was relieved. 'That's good. Don't have any more contact with him. He can't be a good person, coming all this way to seduce a girl who's still at school. If he ever comes again and bothers you, tell me. I'll write a letter to his unit.'

Chapter Nineteen

It took a long time for Jingqiu to get to sleep that night. She didn't know if the ferry had still been operating when Old Third had turned back.

The school was on a little island in the middle of the river so they were surrounded by water. The river split when it came to Jiangxin Island. To the south the 'Big River' was still quite wide, but to the north is was narrower, so they called that branch the 'Little River' onto which faced the campus gate. The two rivers joined up again to the east of the island. In the summer the waters rose, often nearly to the level of the bank, but the island had never flooded; the old people said that Jiangxin Island was resting on a turtle's back, so it never would.

On the other side of the river the region known as Jiangnan, literally 'south of the Yangtze River', stretched out into the distance. Not the Jiangnan known to the Chinese from their ancient poetry, however, but rather a landscape of poor villages. A suburb of Yichang was located on the other side of the 'Little River' but it wasn't easy to get to. The island itself had only a few factories, some fields managed by one of the farming communes, a few schools, some restaurants and a vegetable market, but no hotel.

Jingqiu worried that if Old Third hadn't managed to cross, he would have had no choice but to spend the night on Jiangxin

Island. It was cold, might he have frozen to death out there? And even if he had crossed the river, would he have found a place to stay? Didn't you have to have a letter from your work unit to be able to get a room?

Her head was crammed with images of Old Third wrapped up in his coat, his neck pulled in, wandering the streets. Then she visualised him spending the night in the pavilion, his body freezing solid, and being discovered by street cleaners the next morning. If she hadn't been worried about scaring her mother sick she would have run outside to look for him, to find out if he had found somewhere to stay or whether he was spending the night by the river. If he freezes to death tonight he will have died for me, and I'll have to follow him. The thought of death didn't scare her because that would mean they would always be together, and she would never have to worry about him betraying her, or worry that he might fall in love with someone else. This way, he would always love her.

If this really happened she would ask for them to be buried together under the hawthorn tree outside West Village. But that didn't seem very possible, as they weren't anti-Japanese heroes. They didn't die for the people but only for love, one by the elements, the other by her own hand. According to Chairman Mao's words, their deaths would be lighter than a swan's feather, not as weighty as Tai Mountain.

Jingqiu was tossing to and fro in her bed, and could hear her mother doing the same in the other room. She knew her mother must be anxious about the day's events. She trusted her not to go to Old Third's unit without her permission. For her mother to do so would be cutting off her nose to spite her face, as it wouldn't just get Old Third into trouble, but would drag her into it too. She wasn't stupid, and nor was she that meddling. But Jingqiu imagined that from that day on her mother would be even more worried about her, and if she was out of her sight for only a few minutes she would instantly assume she was seeing that 'bad boy'.

She wanted to tell her mother, you don't need to worry, he won't come to see me these next six months, he told me. He's going to wait until I've graduated. And who knows, he might have forgotten me by then. Or else have found another girl. He's such a smooth talker – he managed to convince me, so wouldn't it be easy for him to convince someone else?

She thought through the evening's events over and over again, reviewing the two key scenes; when he held her, and when he kissed her. Why am I so fixated? Was it because she was so consumed with unhealthy thoughts, or because her mother had turned white at the mere mention of these things? They must be serious crimes if they could affect her mother like that, and to make matters worse, she had actually committed them; so now what? What harm will come of me by being held and kissed? She felt muddled. Last time he had embraced her and kissed her too, and nothing seemed to have happened. But if there is no harm involved, then why is Mother so scared? Mother knows a lot of the world, so surely she must know what's worth worrying about and what's not?

Old Third had been a bit excited, so was that evidence of some 'brutish nature'? But what exactly did that mean? To be 'brutish' is to be like a wild animal, to eat people, right? But he didn't eat me, he only kissed me tenderly – nothing wild about it.

It was not until the next day that she got the opportunity to read Old Third's letter. That week it was her turn to lock the classroom, so she waited until everyone had left and sat in a corner of the classroom, pulled out the letter and opened it. It was beautifully written, tender and passionate. When he wrote of how much he longed for her she was moved and felt safe. But when he came to writing about her, his style wasn't quite to her taste.

If he had only written about how much he loved her and how he missed her, and not written her into his letter as his accomplice, then she would have really liked it. But he kept referring to 'we' this and 'we' that. He had overstepped the mark. She had received a few love letters before, mostly written by boys in her class. No matter how good they were at writing the thing she hated the most was when they assumed that she must reciprocate their feelings.

She couldn't understand why such an intelligent person as Old Third couldn't see that she didn't want him to put her passionate side into writing. He should portray her as cold, should imply that he loved her bitterly, and that only at the end – and notice, not until the very end, even if she didn't know when exactly that was – had she given him the smallest sign of her affection. She believed real love was like this; that he starts to chase her in the first chapter and only in the last does she relent.

After finishing the letter she thought of tearing it up and throwing it down the toilet but then she realised it might be the last letter he ever wrote to her, and so she couldn't bear to destroy it. She waited instead until her mother had gone out to visit the parents of her pupils, and sewed it into her padded jacket.

She could tell that her mother was keeping a close eye on her, asking her repeatedly where she was going every time she left the house. She didn't even trust Jingqiu when she said she was going to visit Wei Hong, in case this was a pretext to go running off with the boy from the geological unit.

It wasn't fair; her brother Xin had had a girlfriend from a young age, and her mother had never been so overprotective of him. In fact, she had welcomed his girlfriend Wang Yamin most enthusiastically. Whenever she came to visit, their mother would do everything she could to get hold of meat to feed them. She would gather up the bed mats and sheets to wash them. In fact, she wore herself out with these preparations to the point that once or twice she made herself sick.

Her mother always said, 'People like us, with no money, no power, and with bad class status as well, what can we hope for other than a bit of affection?'

Jingqiu knew that her mother was grateful to Yamin, almost to the point of tears, because it wasn't easy for her brother to find someone so tolerant of the family's poverty and low status. Xin was three years older than Jingqiu. His girlfriend had been Jingqiu's classmate in junior high school, and the prettiest girl in the whole year. Her eyes were round, her nose was pronounced and she also had long black, slightly curly hair; in other words, she didn't look Chinese. When she was small photographs of her used to hang in the photo shop window as adverts.

Yamin's family were not badly off, her mother was a nurse and her father a manager at a tyre factory. After she graduated from middle school her father helped her get a certificate saying that she had problems with her legs, so she didn't get sent to the countryside and went instead to work in a clothing factory in Yichang. From the beginning she kept the relationship a secret from her family.

One day, Yamin came to Jingqiu's house, her eyes bright red and a quiver in her voice. 'Mrs Zhang, can I speak to Xin? I know he's here, he's hiding from me. I told him that my parents don't approve, they're afraid that once he's sent to the countryside he won't come back. He said we should break up to avoid trouble. He said my parents want the best for me, but this is only what my parents think, not what I think.'

'He also wants the best for you,' Jingqiu's mother said, her eyes reddening too.

Yamin started to sob. 'First my parents do this to me, and now so does he. What's the point of living?'

Jingqiu's mother started in surprise then told Jingqiu to fetch her brother from a friend's place where he was hiding.

'I'll go with you,' Yamin said.

When Xin opened the door and saw Yamin, his eyes filled with tears. Jingqiu turned quickly to leave, knowing that her brother would no longer hide from Yamin and that he really liked her. In the time he had been avoiding her, he had lost a lot of weight.

That evening, Yamin and Xin came over to eat. 'I don't care what my parents say,' Yamin said. 'I just want to be with Xin. If they tell me off again, I'll move in here with your family, and sleep in the same bed as Jingqiu.'

During Spring Festival she came over nearly every day, spending time with Xin in Jingqiu's room, often returning home after eleven o'clock at night. Who knows how she managed her parents' disapproval.

One evening, when it was nearing eleven, some teachers who were in charge of patrolling the school came to find Jingqiu's mother. 'Your son has had an accident.' Jingqiu and her mother went immediately with the teachers to the office only to find Xin locked in one room and Yamin in another.

The teachers wanted to speak to her mother alone so Jingqiu waited outside, her chest burning with anxiety. Finally one of the guards brought Yamin outside and told her to go. But Yamin refused to leave saying, 'We didn't do anything. If you won't release him, I'm not going either.'

'How dare you stand here shouting? Don't you know the meaning of the word shame? We could send you right now to the hospital to be checked, see if you're so cocky then.'

Yamin didn't back down. 'Sure, I'll go, only someone

immoral would refuse, but if they find I haven't done anything, you'd better watch out, you dog.'

Jingqiu had never seen Yamin so plucky; usually she was cautious and measured in her speech. 'Your brother's still inside,' she said to Jingqiu. 'I'm not leaving 'til they let him go.'

So Jingqiu waited outside with Yamin. She ventured to ask, 'What's going on?'

'Those guards are busybodies. It was cold tonight so we were sitting on the bed, using a blanket to cover our legs, and they came knocking on the door. They led me off to the office to question me, then they said they'd take us to the police.'

Jingqiu didn't know how serious that was. 'What will they do?'

'The police are completely unreasonable. Beat you first, ask questions later.'

'What did they mean about sending you to the hospital for a check-up?'

Yamin hesitated before answering. 'They mean ask a doctor to check if I'm . . . still as a young girl should be. But I'm not afraid, we didn't do anything.'

Jingqiu still didn't quite understand. Yamin said herself that she and her brother had been on the bed – so hadn't they 'shared a room'? What did she mean by saying they hadn't done anything?

Eventually the guards let Xin go, deciding that nothing could have happened if Yamin was so eager to go to the hospital for a check-up. Afterwards, Yamin continued to come round almost every evening, but the school guards didn't come knocking again. Her mother liked Yamin even more after that; she had never anticipated that such a gentle girl could turn so fierce, like a tiger, just to save her son.

Jingqiu was happy that her brother had found such a good girlfriend. But she couldn't stop herself from thinking, if it had been me and Old Third in that room, mother would probably have sent Old Third to the police herself.

As she had no way of knowing if he had found somewhere to stay or not, Jingqiu feared for Old Third's life that night. She was terrified that Fang would appear suddenly one day to tell her that Old Third had been found, frozen to death, and that she was invited to the memorial service.

Every day she found reasons to go to her mother's office so that she could flip through the newspapers in search of news of frozen bodies found around the city. But probably the newspapers would not report it anyway because Old Third had brought it on himself, he had not died trying to save someone else. Why bother reporting that?

She thought of going to West Village to see if he was still alive, but she couldn't ask her mother for the bus fare and she could think of no excuse that would let her be away for a whole day. She had no choice but to wait anxiously for news.

It occurred to her that she knew a doctor called Cheng who worked at the city's largest hospital. She went looking for him. Dr Cheng told her that he had not received any patients suffering from frostbite. 'Could someone freeze to death outside in the kind of weather we're having?' she asked.

'If they're wearing too little then, yes, perhaps.'

Old Third had been wearing a military jacket so he was probably okay, she thought.

Dr Cheng reassured her that nowadays people did not tend to freeze to death; if they were caught out in the cold they could go to the station waiting room or the one by the pier, or else the police would pick them up as a vagrant. His logic comforted her somewhat.

Dr Cheng's mother-in-law and Jingqiu's mother had been

colleagues. As both women had the same last name, many of the families on Jiangxin Island had, for several generations, been taught by a Mrs Zhang. Dr Cheng's mother-in-law had already retired, but they lived by the school. Dr Cheng's wife was also a teacher in the city as well as a proficient accordion player and passers-by often stopped to listen as husband and wife sang and played together.

Jingqiu was entirely self-taught at the accordion. She had initially started playing the organ as her mother's school had one in the music room where she could go to practise, but the students often went travelling around singing revolutionary songs, and they needed someone to accompany them. The organ was too heavy for that so she started to learn the accordion instead. She often heard Dr Cheng's wife Mrs Jiang practising as she passed by their house, and she admired her music immensely, so she asked her mother if she could study with Mrs Jiang. Before long she had got to know the family well.

Dr Cheng didn't look very Chinese: his nose protruded and his eyes were deep-set, earning him particular fame on the island, the nickname 'foreigner', and the islanders' curious looks. Some of the young children boldly called 'foreigner' after him as he walked by, but as he was a good-tempered man he would only turn around, laugh and wave. Dr Cheng explained his 'foreign' looks by claiming to have Kazakh blood in his veins, but as no one had met either of his supposedly Kazakh parents people preferred to believe that he was a special agent or the product of an illicit relationship.

For some reason Old Third had always reminded her of Dr Cheng, and although Old Third's nose was not as big nor were his eyes as deep-set, and people would never gather around him, curious, like they did with Dr Cheng, she still thought there was a resemblance. She wasn't sure if she had been so attracted to Old Third at first sight because she liked Dr Cheng's looks, or whether it was the other way round, but the two were firmly connected in her imagination.

Dr Cheng had reassured her that it was unlikely that Old Third had frozen to death, but only a letter would truly put her mind at ease. That day Jingqiu's mother brought her a letter sent by someone from West Village. She nearly fainted; Old Third must have gone crazy from the cold, otherwise why else would he send a letter directly to her mother's school? She had told him that very first day when they met in West Village that he shouldn't send letters to her there because students didn't receive letters, and if they did they could only contain wicked secrets. The receptionist would be sure to give any letter to her mother even if it was addressed to her.

Her mother had not opened it, however. This was probably the first letter that she had ever received through the post. It stated clearly that the sender was Fang and the handwriting looked right, so she opened it in front of her mother. The letter was straightforward, informing Jingqiu that her studies had been going well and her family was fine. It went on to invite Jingqiu to come back to visit them in West Village, and she hoped that Jingqiu's family was well.

Jingqiu could tell, however, that the real sender of the letter was Old Third, and she couldn't help but laugh inside: how sneaky, he's brave enough to try to fool my mother. So he was fine. She burned the last letter that she had sewn into her coat as the pocket had started to bulge with all the letters she had stuffed in there and she feared her mother would find her hiding place. She kept his first letter, however, because in that one he had not written anything using the pronoun 'we'.

Chapter Twenty

As her graduation drew closer Jingqiu felt more and more torn. She was aching for the day to arrive so that she could see Old Third again, but she was also scared because soon afterwards she would be sent down to the countryside. Once permanently registered in her new rural home she would no longer be a citizen of the city, and thus would no longer be allowed to take on odd jobs in the summer. She would have to do the same as her brother and borrow money to supplement her rations. There was no way she could let her twelve-year-old sister go out to work.

Policy had recently changed and the students from Yichang were no longer sent to random production units but instead went to special teams for sent-down youths, grouped according to their parents' work units. Children of Yichang's education and culture workers were sent to a remote mountain area where they worked in the forest. It was an extremely tough place where it was next to impossible for them to earn any money. They were there to forge 'red hearts', to be loyal to the revolution. The students relied on their parents to provide the money for their rations, and all parents asked for was that their children endure a few years of hardship before seeking to be transferred back to the city.

Every July a new batch of students was sent away. That year, however, the authorities had decided to start providing extra classes to the teenagers about to be sent down. Every day they were told that 'a loyal heart requires two types of preparation'. The bureau of education organised a few large meetings, inviting students who had already been sent down – and especially those who had settled fully in their new homes – to describe to that year's students how they had integrated with the poor and lower peasants. Some of the model youths had married, or as they called it, had 'put down roots in the name of the revolution'.

Jingqiu listened to them describe these glorious deeds, but she couldn't say whether they really loved their peasant husbands and wives. One thing she did know: as soon as you marry a local there is no way you can get back to the city. Wei Ling was a few years older than Jingqiu and had already been sent down. Whenever she came back home she would tell Jingqiu about how hard it was in the countryside. The work was exhausting and their daily life boring; all she longed for was the day when she would be called back to the city to bring an end to her suffering. She sang some of the songs popular among the students for Jingqiu:

My waistband's loose from slaving all day,
someone's cooking sweet-smelling rice
as I go back to my room, cold and grey.

Jingqiu was in the same year as Wei Ling's sister Wei Hong. Wei Hong and Jingqiu had decided to share a room once in the countryside so together they started to prepare their belongings. Wei Hong's family had a bit more money than Jingqiu's as her parents were both teachers at No. 8 Middle School. With two salaries, raising three children presented them with no great difficulties. This meant that Jingqiu couldn't afford to buy the same things as Wei Hong. The only thing that they both purchased was material to make pillowcases, on which they embroidered 'sweeping lands, vast potential'.

Animated, they busied themselves with their preparations until one day Jingqiu received an unexpected visit from Fang. The only moment they had alone together was just as Jingqiu was seeing her off home on the bus, and Fang pushed a letter into Jingqiu's hands. 'It's from Old Third.' Jingqiu waited for Fang's bus to draw out of the station before she sat down to open it. Perhaps out of consideration to his courier Old Third had not put the letter in an envelope, but in it he expressed his feelings without reservation. Jingqiu blushed, and her heart pounded. Wasn't he afraid that Fang might read it?

In the letter Old Third told her that there was a new policy which allowed children to replace their parents after retirement. The policy had not been made public yet, and final decisions were to be made by the individual work units concerned. Old Third urged her mother to make enquiries at her school or the bureau of education. Perhaps Jingqiu could replace her mother, and that way she wouldn't be sent down. You would be perfect for the job, he said, you'd make an outstanding teacher.

Jingqiu read the letter a few more times in disbelief. She hoped with all her heart that her brother Xin, rather than her, might be able to replace their mother because he was in such a wretched situation. Since their father had been persecuted just as her brother was finishing junior middle school, Xin had been sent straight to the countryside rather than being allowed to attend the last years of high school. He had been there for so many years and still he had not been called back.

Yamin often came to Jingqiu's house to collect letters from Xin as he wouldn't send them to her house. Every time she came she would sit with Jingqiu and tell her the story of how they had met: how they had been in the same class, how Xin had told someone to go to her house to ask her to come and see him, and how there had been another very pretty girl in his class who had liked Xin, but how he only had eyes for her. But the thing she talked about most was how to get Xin called back to the city, as once he was back in the city her mother would no longer oppose the match so vehemently. Jingqiu hoped desperately that her brother might be called back so that the distance would no longer threaten to extinguish the love between them.

Overjoyed about this new employment policy, Jingqiu sped off at once to tell her mother. She would not say it was Old Third who had told her, but rather that she had heard someone at school talking about it. Her mother was not instantly convinced considering that the news came from someone at school, but said it would not hurt to ask as long as no one got their hopes up. She went to ask Mr Zhong, the secretary, but he said he had not heard anything about it. His daughter had long since graduated but was still in the city, a situation about which everyone had an opinion. Mr Zhong was therefore very interested in this new policy and went directly to the bureau of education to have it confirmed or otherwise. He made straight for their house on his return. This policy had indeed been introduced, but as there was no directive on how to implement it, it was up to each work unit to take care of it.

'Mrs Zhang, thank you for telling me about this,' he said. 'I am still not of retirement age but my wife soon will be. Her health is not so good so she can get early retirement on those grounds, and that way my daughter can replace her. Why don't you do the same and let Jingqiu stay in the city? It is always a worry to let the young girls be sent down.'

Jingqiu's mother had not expected someone as important as Mr Zhong to worry himself about her daughter being sent to the countryside, to take pity on a normal parent's suffering.

But she understood from the tone of his voice that if she were to seek retirement on the grounds of ill health then the school would let Jingqiu replace her. Excited, she thanked him profusely before sending him off.

She told Jingqiu the good news, that after years of worry a huge weight could be taken off her shoulders. 'I'll apply to retire and you can replace me, that way you won't be sent down. Sorting it out will put my mind at rest.'

'We should let Xin replace you, he's been away for so many years and has suffered so much. And Yamin's family only oppose the marriage because he's in the countryside. If he can come back everything will be fine.'

Jingqiu told Yamin and she was ecstatic. 'We can finally be together and my family won't be able to stop us.' Yamin went to write a letter to tell Xin the news. But he would not agree to the arrangement. He had been away for so long that it was only a matter of time before he would be called back. He said he'd only be using up someone else's opportunity, Jingqiu should do it, that way she wouldn't be sent down at all.

Jingqiu's mother too was determined that she was not to be sent down. She frequently had nightmares in which Jingqiu had had some terrible accident and she would go to her, only to find her daughter lying on a pile of rice straw, her hair matted and dishevelled and her eyes glazed over. 'I won't let you go,' her mother said. 'You're still young and you don't know the kinds of dangers young girls face in the countryside. Since ancient times beautiful girls have suffered bad fates. Here at school you have so many boys taking a fancy to you, causing you trouble, would it be any different there?'

Despite her mother's feelings Jingqiu persuaded her to go to the school to suggest that Xin should replace her. They responded, however, that as he had only finished junior middle school he was not a suitable candidate. Jingqiu, on the other hand, was; not only was she a senior student, but she was intelligent, morally upstanding, and physically strong. She would make a good teacher, and they agreed to the arrangement.

With no other option available to her Jingqiu agreed too. They couldn't waste such an opportunity, after all. But she was upset about her poor brother, and she vowed with all her heart to find some other way for him to return.

She was extremely grateful to Old Third that he had told her about the policy, and just in time, for there was no other way that her mother would have found out about it. She wanted him to know but she didn't know how best to tell him. She had no telephone and she couldn't write a letter, much less go to West Village herself. She would just have to wait until he came to see her. He, however, was taking his promise not to come as seriously as if it had been made to the Party.

She was sick with longing, just as he had described it in his letters. All she wanted was to see him. Everything that had even the smallest connection to him made her feel close to him. Her heart would thump whenever anyone said the words 'third', 'geological unit', or 'army district', as if they were making secret references to him. She had never dared to call him by his real name, not even to herself, but now when she saw someone with the last name 'Sun' or the first name 'Jianxin', her heart melted.

Nearly every day she made her way to Dr Cheng's house to practise the accordion with his wife, Mrs Jiang, or to cuddle their little baby. When Dr Cheng was away she grew restless, and only when he came home and she heard the sound of his voice did she feel that her task for the day was complete and she could return home contented. She didn't have to speak to him, nor see his face; as long as she heard the sound of his voice she felt at ease. He spoke Mandarin just like Old Third. Most people in Yichang didn't speak Mandarin, so she rarely heard it being spoken. If Dr Cheng was speaking in the next room she would stop what she was doing and listen quietly. Often she imagined that it was Old Third next door, that she was sitting in Old Third's home, one of the family. Her exact relationship with him was left unspecified. It didn't matter. If only I could hear his voice every day, it wouldn't matter.

Mrs Jiang wanted Jingqiu to knit her son a woollen jumper. Once she had finished, Mrs Jiang gave Jingqiu money as the pattern had been complicated and it had taken a long time, but Jingqiu refused it. 'I don't take money for helping someone with their knitting.'

Mrs Jiang thought of another method to repay Jingqiu. Mrs Jiang only ever made the odd thing like a pair of shorts on her sewing machine, whereas Jingqiu had to do her sewing by hand. 'My machine sits here unused and gathering dust. I don't have time to use it, why don't you come and use it, else it'll rust.'

Mrs Jiang's offer was heaven sent. Unable to resist, Jingqiu soon got the machine's wheel spinning. Mrs Jiang bought some pieces of material so that Jingqiu could help her and Dr Cheng's mother make overalls for her two sons. Jingqiu cut the pattern and sewed them together, each fitting perfectly.

At that time Jingqiu was only comfortable making tops for women and children. Men's clothes were difficult and pockets and trouser waists seemed nigh-on impossible. Mrs Jiang bought material and told Jingqiu to treat the couple as test dummies by making tops from cotton and woollen cloth, and a Mao suit for Dr Cheng. 'You can do it. I've bought the material now so don't make me waste it. Don't be afraid, if you make a mistake in the cutting you can always use the material to make my eldest something, and if not, then his brother. It won't go to waste.' Jingqiu cut and sewed and in the end, the clothes turned out pretty well.

But making clothes for Dr Cheng made her blush and her heart pound. One day she was making him some trousers and she needed to take his leg, waist and crotch measurements. Taking the tape measure, she decided to start with his waist. Dr Cheng lifted his woollen jumper. Despite the fact that he was still wearing a shirt and there was not an inch of flesh in sight Jingqiu was so startled that she ducked away and said, 'No need to measure, just find an old pair of trousers and I'll use those.'

Once, when she was making a woollen jacket the material was so nice that she couldn't bring herself to use an old top for her measurements so she asked Dr Cheng to stand before her so that she could do it properly. She reached her arms behind his back and around his chest trying her best not to brush against him. On making the two ends of her tape measure meet she was unable to catch her breath; she had recognised Old Third's manly scent. She felt dizzy and spots clouded her eyes. 'I'll just use one of your old tops,' she said. With that she rushed away. From then on she resolutely avoided measuring Dr Cheng. Once she finished the clothes she wouldn't even have him try them on to check that they fitted properly.

Polyester trousers became very fashionable around that time. To make them, however, you had to use an overlock stitch, which was not possible on most sewing machines. On seeing Jingqiu run off to ask someone to help her every time she made trousers, Mrs Jiang decided to ask a friend to help her get hold of a second-hand machine to do the job. Not many people on Jiangxin Island had even simple sewing machines as they were one of the 'three treasures', along with bikes and watches, that brides would ask for as a wedding present from the husband's family. An overlock machine, therefore, would drive people wild with envy. With such 'modern weapons' at her disposal, Jingqiu was like a ferocious tiger given wings; not only could she make nice clothes, but she could make them quickly.

Mrs Jiang introduced Jingqiu to her colleagues and friends so that she could make clothes for them too, and they would usually come on Sundays at lunchtime to order them. Jingqiu would measure, cut and sew on the spot so that within a couple of hours they were finished and ironed, with buttons sewed on, and ready to be worn on the way home. Tailors were not common in those days as the labour was more expensive than the materials. Not only that, but you also had to wait a long time for your clothes to be ready, and even then they might not fit. More and more people, therefore, asked Jingqiu to make their clothes.

Mrs Jiang told Jingqiu to ask for a bit of money for her work but Jingqiu refused on the grounds that she was helping Mrs Jiang's friends while using Mrs Jiang's machine. 'How can I ask for money? And if I do, that would make me a "black market factory". It'd be a disaster if anyone found out.'

On reflection, Mrs Jiang agreed that it was best for her not to risk it, so instead she asked her friends to bring small gifts to express their gratitude. They brought anything and everything; notebooks, pens, a few eggs, a few kilos of rice or fruit. Whatever the gift Mrs Jiang did her best to persuade Jingqiu to take it. 'Don't bite the hand that feeds you,' she would say. 'They're only thanking you.' Jingqiu accepted some of the gifts, but gave back those that she deemed too large. 'It's like we've hit oil!' her mother joked when Jingqiu brought them home.

Chapter Twenty-One

In May Fang came to Yichang, bringing with her some bright red hawthorn flowers wrapped in plastic. Jingqiu understood at once that Old Third had asked her to bring them. Neither, however, dared say anything in front of Jingqiu's mother or sister. Only when Jingqiu took Fang to the bus station did Fang confirm it, 'Old Third asked me to bring them.'

'How is he?'

Fang scrunched up her face. 'Not well.'

'Is he sick?' asked Jingqiu anxiously.

'Yeah, he's sick all right.' Seeing just how anxious Jingqiu was on hearing this, Fang started to laugh. 'Lovesick, that is. So, you two are together. Why didn't you tell me?'

'Don't talk rubbish,' Jingqiu said quickly. 'What do you mean, together? I'm still at school, how could we possibly be together?'

'What are you so scared of? I don't go to your school, what's the point of lying to me about it? Old Third has told me everything. He really likes you. He dumped his fiancée just for you.'

Jingqiu was stern in her reply. 'He didn't do it for me, they had already split up.'

'Wouldn't it be a good thing if he dumped her for you? It shows how much he likes you.'

'What's good about it? If he can dump his fiancée for me that means he could do the same to me for someone else.'

'He would never break up with you.' Fang reached into her bag and brought out a letter. 'I'll give it to you if you let me read it,' she said, laughing. 'Otherwise I'll take it home and give it back to him. I'll say you don't want him or his letters. He'd be so upset he'd chuck himself in the river.'

'He hasn't sealed it so are you telling me you don't know how to open it yourself?' Jingqiu said, pretending not to care.

Fang looked injured. 'What do you take me for? The fact that he didn't seal it means he trusts me, how could I open it?' She threw the letter at Jingqiu. 'If you don't want me to read it, forget it. But there's no need to say such nasty things.'

'Wait 'til I've had a look, so I know whether you can read it.'

Fang smiled. 'Forget it, I'm only joking. What's it got to do with me? It's probably all "my dear Jingqiu, I miss you day and night ... blah, blah."'

Jingqiu tore open the letter and read it quickly before folding it. She smiled. 'You're wrong. He didn't say anything like that.'

Jingqiu returned home still beaming about Old Third's letter and flowers but her mother was waiting with some bad news from Mr Zhong: the bureau of education had made some changes to the new policy. Over twenty people had already retired to be replaced by their children, but these youngsters were of uneven capability, not all teachers' children make good teachers after all. So this time it had been decided that all the sons and daughters should work as kitchen staff instead.

With the red tape for her retirement almost completed, the news that Jingqiu would not replace her as a teacher but rather as one of the kitchen staff made Jingqiu's mother so angry she nearly had a relapse. But Jingqiu took it calmly, perhaps because she always prepared for the worst. This sort of thing did not fill her with panic, and she comforted her mother. 'If I'm to work in the kitchen then that's what I'll do. There's no such thing as high- or low-status work in the revolution, and it's certainly better than being sent to the countryside, isn't it?'

'I suppose that's the only way to deal with things these days,' her mother sighed. 'But when I think that my daughter, who is so intelligent and capable, is going to spend her whole life slaving over a stove, it is hard to stay calm.'

Jingqiu repeated what Old Third had said to her as further comfort: 'Don't think so far into the future, the world is constantly changing. Who knows, after a few years of working in the kitchen I might be transferred to another job.'

'My daughter takes things more philosophically than I.'

It's fate, Jingqiu thought. How else should I take it, if not philosophically?

But by the time the holidays had started, Jingqiu's mother's retirement had been organised but Jingqiu's new job had not. What was taking the school so long? Was she to be working in the kitchen or as a teacher? All the others who had applied had had everything taken care of, and yet they had all heard of the policy from Jingqiu's mother. She had been first to apply and was the last to have everything confirmed. Her mother was afraid that they would wait, and wait, and it would all come to nothing, so she ran back and forth to Mr Zhong's house to ask him to hurry the school with the paperwork.

Jingqiu's family were now in a dire financial situation. The pension that her mother received was only twenty-eight yuan a month. Her previous income had been nearly forty-five yuan a month and that had been insufficient to support the family so, yet again, Jingqiu went to find temporary work. Even though her exact job was uncertain, people believed she was already a teacher earning big bucks, and many good friends started to distance themselves from her. Maybe people find it easy to sympathise with those who are less fortunate, but nothing makes them more unhappy than when the previously down and out stumble on a bit of luck.

'How she behaves right now is crucial,' Mr Zhong repeatedly told Jingqiu's mother. 'Tell Jingqiu she mustn't under any circumstances make a mistake. If we let her replace you lots of people will be jealous and will have something to say about it. You must be especially careful, don't make our job more difficult.'

Even the head of the neighbourhood committee, Director Li, knew about Jingqiu's application to replace her mother. The day that Jingqiu's mother took her to see the director to get temporary work, Director Li said, 'Mrs Zhang, the fact is, life is not about earning endless pots of money, a bit is enough, we shouldn't be so greedy.'

Her mother laughed awkwardly, not understanding what exactly it was Director Li was getting at.

'Isn't Jingqiu replacing you as a teacher?' Director Li said. 'How can you still be coming here for more work? We have more people looking than we have jobs, so I have to give priority to people who are struggling to make ends meet.'

'My mother has retired, but my job is yet to be finalised,' Jingqiu explained. 'We are in real difficulty, much worse than before because mother's pension is a fraction of her previous income.'

'Ah – then shouldn't you go to the countryside and wait there for your job to be organised? If I give you a job, won't I be helping you hang around in the city?'

'Jingqiu, let's go. We don't want to trouble Director Li.'

But Jingqiu wouldn't leave. 'Mother, you go back first, I'll wait a little longer.' Turning to Director Li she said, 'I'm not trying to escape being sent down, but my family is in a desperate situation. If I don't work they won't survive.'

Director Li let out a sigh. 'If you want to wait that's fine. But I'm not guaranteeing there will be a job for you.'

Jingqiu waited for two days and still Director Li did not arrange any work for her. Twice employers settled on Jingqiu before Director Li forced someone else on to their hands. 'Your difficulties are temporary, you could borrow some money to tide you over. Once you become a teacher you won't have anything to worry about.'

Jingqiu explained that it was likely she would not become a teacher, but was to work in the kitchens, to which Director Li shook her head disapprovingly. 'Why is that necessary? You'd rather work in the kitchens than go down to the countryside? Go for a couple of years and then come back as a worker, that'd be much better.'

On the third morning Jingqiu got to Director Li's house early and sat herself in the main room to wait for work. Just as she was contemplating what she would do if she didn't get any work that day she heard a voice call out, 'Jingqiu, are you waiting for a job?'

Jingqiu looked up and to her surprise she saw her former classmate, Director Li's son, Kunming, wearing a grass-green army uniform and matching jacket.

'I've joined the army,' he said exuberantly. At school his classmates barely registered his existence and no one could have imagined that he would join the army. He must be trying to avoid being sent down. 'Waiting for a job?' he repeated. Jingqiu nodded and with that he went through to the inner room to ask his mother, 'Mother why haven't you given Jingqiu any work?'

Jingqiu could hear her respond, 'What do you mean, not given her work? There have been more people looking than jobs available.'

'Hurry up and sort something out, she's waiting in there.'

'It doesn't matter where she waits, I have to have a job to give first.'

Jingqiu heard him say something quietly to his mother but what that was exactly she couldn't make out. She was very grateful to Kunming, but she also felt uncomfortable, as if she were asking him a favour.

After a while Director Li emerged. 'Wan Changsheng from the paper factory came yesterday looking for workers. It's hard work so I didn't suggest you, but if you think you're up to it, go now and see him.'

Jingqiu thanked Director Li and left. Out on the road she heard the sound of a bike approaching before the bell rang out. She twisted her head around to see Kunming, glowing like a flower, riding towards her. 'Jump on, I'll take you to the paper factory. It'll take you ages to walk.'

Jingqiu's face turned bright red. 'There's no need, I'll be there in no time.'

He rode his bike closer and repeated, 'Get on. We've graduated now, what are you afraid of?' Jingqiu still refused so he jumped down from his bike and walked with her. Jingqiu noticed that everyone they met on the road looked at them curiously. She felt uncomfortable all over.

At the factory Kunming helped her find Mr Wan Changsheng. This Mr Wan turned out to be a weedy and slightly hunchbacked middle-aged man of not more than five-foot five with a look of death about him, reminiscent of an opium addict. It looked as if he had yet to wipe away the morning's gunk from his eyes. The fact that his first name, Changsheng, meant 'prosperous' added a dint of irony to the situation.

'Mr Wan, this is my classmate Jingqiu. My mother has sent her to you for work, can you take care of it?' Kunming's professional tone surprised Jingqiu. He turned to her. 'I'm off, but be careful. If the job's too heavy just ask my mother to get you a different one.'

Jingqiu answered with a 'thank you', but didn't know what else to say.

'Is he your other half?' Wan Changsheng asked once Kunming was some distance away.

'No.'

'I thought not. If he was, his mother would never let you do this kind of work.' He sized her up before saying, 'Don't you worry, today you can follow me to buy some things, I need to go to the docks.'

That day Jingqiu pushed a flat cart behind Wan Changsheng to the river to buy goods. On the way he boasted of his love of books and asked Jingqiu to lend him some to read in return for easier work at the factory. Jingqiu agreed reluctantly, thinking to herself, I wonder what kind of medicine he's got in his gourd?

At four in the afternoon they finished and Wan Changsheng praised Jingqiu, saying that next time he would call on her specially to help him. 'We don't work on Sundays because I like to rest then, and most of the temporary workers slack off if I'm not here. But I don't think you would. If I find you some work to do, are you game?'

Jingqiu had never had Sundays off before when working, so she replied without hesitation, 'Of course.'

'OK, tomorrow you push this cart to the city distillery, wharf number eight, and collect the bags of grain I ordered. We use it to feed the factory's pigs. This job is especially for you, so don't go telling the other temporary workers otherwise they'll accuse me of favouritism.'

Jingqiu thanked him as tears collected in her eyes. This puffed up Mr Wan's sense of self-worth and he continued his praise. 'You only have to look at you to know you're capable and level-headed.' He took two pieces of paper out of his pocket. 'This one is for collecting the goods tomorrow, and this one is a meal ticket, you can exchange it for two steamed buns at the canteen. That'll be your lunch. Just deliver the grain to the canteen before five.'

Chapter Twenty-Two

Early the next morning Jingqiu got up and went straight to the paper factory to collect the cart and the steamed buns before setting off for wharf number eight. The wharf was right on the river some ten or so li away. There was a freight ferry further up the river where she could pull the cart across. As it was summer the water was high, nearly reaching the bank, so there was no need to climb up and then down again, you just had to be careful not to fall in the water.

As she did every time she went out to work, as soon as she walked out of the door she took off her shoes – she only put them on for her mother to see – so as not to wear them out too quickly. Today she was dressed from head to toe in her brother's old clothes, with a sailor's striped shirt on top and a pair of patched trousers that Jingqiu had cut off just below the knee. The sun was high so she wore an old straw hat pulled low over her face so that no one would recognise her.

By the time she got to the other side of the river she needed the toilet, but she couldn't go to the public toilet in case someone made off with her cart. There was no way she would be able to replace it.

She stood pondering the problem when a voice from behind her said, 'Go on, I'll watch your cart.'

Jingqiu didn't need to turn around, she already knew who

it was. Her faced boiled with embarrassment. Why couldn't he have come sooner, or later? Why just now when it was most awkward?

Old Third walked round to face her and, taking hold of the cart's handle, repeated, 'Go, I'll look after the cart.'

'Go where?' she asked, her face burning red.

'Don't you need the toilet? Go, I can watch the cart.'

She felt extremely uncomfortable to hear him speak so frankly. Even if you can tell someone needs it you don't just say it straight out. 'Who says I need the toilet?' she said.

His short-sleeved white shirt was unbuttoned revealing a white vest trimmed with blue tucked into his army trousers. This was the first time she had seen him wearing short sleeves and it was strange. His skin was unexpectedly white and his forearms bulged; they were even more muscled and defined than his biceps. Boys' arms were really strange.

'I've been following you since yesterday.' He smiled. 'But you were being escorted by a fellow army man so I didn't come to say hello. Breaking up an army marriage is, without exception, dealt with very harshly and if you're not careful can result in a death sentence.'

'What army man? Oh, that was an old classmate.'

'He looked very brave and imposing in his army uniform. So are you going to the toilet? If not, then we should head off.'

'Where? I don't have time, I'm working.'

'I'm off to work with you.'

She started laughing. 'You want to go to work with me? Aren't you scared people will laugh at you dressed up all posh and yet walking with me and this cart?'

'Who's going to laugh? Laugh at what?' He removed his white shirt and rolled up his trouser legs and asked, 'How about like this?' Seeing her shake her head he pleaded, 'You've already graduated and no one around here knows you, let me go with you.'

It didn't take any more to convince her. She had been longing to see him for so long that she couldn't bear to let him go. Today they would take the risk. Blushing she replied, 'Wait a second,' and ran to the toilet. On her return she said, 'Let's go. Just you wait, you'll soon be crying tears of exhaustion.'

'What a joke,' he boasted. 'Pushing a cart will make me cry? I haven't cried in years.'

Seeing that she was walking barefoot he removed his shoes and placed them on the cart. 'Sit on top.'

She resisted but he insisted so she climbed up. He took her old straw hat and draped his white shirt over her head. 'This will cover your shoulders and arms as well as your head.' Then they set off.

She sat on top, giving him directions. After a while he said, 'It's a shame my shirt's not red, otherwise it would look like I was pushing my new bride in her red bridal veil.'

'Oh, so you're trying to take advantage of me!' Then, as if driving an ox, she called, 'C'mon! Go!'

'Ah yes, you're just like a real wife, already bossing me around,' and with that he started gathering speed.

Only once they got to the distillery did Jingqiu realise how lucky it was that Old Third was there to help, otherwise she would never have been able to deliver the grain back to Mr Wan. The grain was still being stored in a deep pool of hot water. They had to scoop it out themselves and put it into sacks, each one weighing more than fifty kilos. Furthermore, the distillery was located on a small but steep hill. Just pushing the empty cart up had been tough enough, never mind taking it down again when loaded with grain. If they weren't careful it would tip over and cause them a serious injury. Old Third lifted the shaft up high but still the cart raced down the hill and the two of them struggled until they were drenched in sweat. So much for Mr Wan's promise of an easy job!

Once down the hill, however, the road followed the river and was much easier to manage. Old Third took hold of the handle and Jingqiu pulled a rope attached to the side. They walked and talked until without thinking they arrived at the small pavilion that had been the site of their last meeting. 'Let's rest here a while,' Old Third suggested. 'Didn't you say it had to be delivered before five? It's only three now. Let's take a seat.'

They stopped the cart by the pavilion and went to rest inside. It was a hot day, so Jingqiu used her straw hat to fan herself and Old Third went to buy ice lollies. 'Who was the other man you were taking a walk with yesterday?' he asked as they ate.

'Taking a walk? Didn't you see me pushing the cart? That was my boss, Wan Changsheng.'

'He doesn't look like a nice guy, I don't think you should work for him.'

'Where else will I work? It took a lot of pain and effort to get this job. What makes you dislike him? You don't know him.'

Old Third smiled, 'There's something about him. Watch out, don't be alone with him.'

'What could he possibly do?'

'You're too naive. Just find a way to tell him that your boyfriend is in the army, it doesn't take much for us army men to draw our swords. If he does anything untoward, tell me.'

'And what would you do?'

'I'd sort him out.' He reached into his bag and took out a Swiss army knife, and started fiddling with it.

'I didn't know you were so tough,' she joked.

'Don't be afraid, I would never do anything to you. I just

don't like your boss, there's something not right about him, you can see it in his eyes. I followed you two the whole day and I had to force myself not to go up to him and give him a warning. I thought you wouldn't want me to.'

'It's best that people don't see us together. Even though I've left school my new job still isn't sorted and lots of people at school are already jealous.'

'I know, so I'll only approach you when you're on your own.' They sat in silence for a while before Old Third spoke again. 'Let's find somewhere to eat lunch.'

'I brought a steamed bun. You go and find a restaurant, I'll wait here with the cart. That grain is so smelly it's attracting the mosquitoes. I don't want to park the cart in front of someone's restaurant.'

Old Third thought a while. 'Okay, I'll buy some things and bring them back here to eat. You wait, don't run away. It's too dangerous for you to push the cart over the river on your own.'

After a while he came back with a pile of food in his arms, along with a red swimsuit. 'Let's eat, rest then take a swim in the river. It's so hot today we're covered in sweat. The water looks really inviting.'

'How do you know I can swim?'

'Jiangxin is surrounded by water, how could you not have learned? Everyone on the island must be able to, surely?'

'Well, yes.' Jingqiu opened the packet containing the swimsuit. It was a figure-hugging model, the top part shaped like a vest and the bottom part like a pair of briefs. It was the most old-fashioned and conservative type, but Jingqiu had never worn one like it before, and neither had anyone else she knew. Everyone wore a short-sleeved T-shirt and shorts when swimming. 'How do you wear it?' she asked, her face turning crimson.

Usually she wore boxer-style pants and sports bras, she had

never worn briefs nor bras with thin straps. The thought of wearing such a revealing costume horrified her. She was always desperate to cover up what she considered to be her large thighs and breasts. 'You bought it without asking me. Can it be returned?'

'Why return it?' Old Third said.

After their lunch and a rest Old Third continued to urge Jingqiu to go to a nearby public toilet to change into her new swimsuit. She was too shy but she did want to swim, so after a lengthy period of persuasion she decided to try it on. I'll put my shirt and trousers over the top and when I get to the water I'll ask Old Third to turn away so I can quickly remove them and slip in, she decided. Okay, she thought, and ran to the public toilets to get changed, emerging again with her shirt and trousers over the top of the swimsuit.

They parked the cart close to the bank so that they could watch out for potential thieves as they swam. Jingqiu ordered Old Third to go in first and, laughing, he obeyed, stripped off his vest and trousers until he was standing in only a pair of boxer shorts, and in he went. After a couple of steps he turned and shouted, 'Hurry up, the water's lovely and cool.'

'Turn around.'

Again, he obeyed. Jingqiu removed her clothes quickly and started pulling at her swimsuit around her chest and bottom, painfully aware that it didn't cover her up sufficiently. After tugging at the cloth for a while she could see no improvement and so gave up. Just as she was about to step into the water she noticed that he had already turned around and was watching her. 'How can you be so sneaky?' she finally managed to stutter.

He turned around again quickly and sank into the water. She dived in and swam towards the middle of the river before turning back to look behind her. He hadn't followed and was, instead, still crouching in the shallows. What's he up to? She swam back towards him until she was close, and standing in the water up to her chest she asked, 'Why aren't you swimming?'

'You go first, I'll chase you,' he said.

She turned and swam out again to the middle of the river, but after turning she realised that he still hadn't started swimming. Maybe he doesn't know how to swim? He's so funny, he can't swim but is so insistent that I should jump in. She swam back again and called out, 'Are you a duck raised on dry land?'

He sat in the water, laughing, but didn't reply. She too stopped swimming and stood in the deeper water, talking to him. After a while he said, 'Let's have a race.' With that he took off towards the middle of the river. So he can swim! He had a beautiful front crawl, making not even the slightest splash of water as he swam into the distance. She wanted to catch up but she couldn't swim that fast, so followed behind.

Tired, she called to him, 'Come back, I'm exhausted.'

Quickly he returned, and as he drew near asked, 'So, do you think I'm a duck raised on dry land now?'

'No, but why were you sitting so long in the shallows then?'

'I wanted to see how good you were at swimming.' He laughed.

What a bad boy, waiting to see I wasn't better than him, so I'd make a fool of myself! She followed him again before making a surprise attack. She grabbed him by the shoulders so that he could pull her back to land. She floated on the surface and gently hung herself around his shoulders kicking her legs. I can't be giving him too much extra weight. But he suddenly stopped, straightened his body, and started treading water. Her body seemed to glue itself to his, so she let go as quickly as she could.

Together they swam back to the shore and he sat in the water, shaking slightly.

'Are you tired?' she asked.

'No ... You go first and get changed, I'll come in a second.'

He had a strange look on his face. 'Have you got cramp in your legs?'

He nodded. 'You go and get changed. Unless you want to go for another swim?'

'No more.' She shook her head. 'We need some energy left in order to deliver the grain. If you've got cramp don't swim any more either. Where does it hurt? Do you want me to give it a rub?'

'Never mind me.'

He was behaving very strangely, so she stood firm and asked, 'What's wrong? Is the cramp in your stomach?'

He looked back at her intently until she realised that she was still wearing the swimsuit. She ducked down into the water; he must have seen my thighs, he thinks they're huge. 'It's my legs, they're horrible, aren't they?'

'They're really nice, don't say that. You go on.'

She refused to leave because she didn't want him to see her bottom hanging out of the swimsuit. 'You go first.'

'Okay, turn around.'

She couldn't help laughing. 'You're not a girl, why should I turn around? Are you afraid I'll think your legs are ugly?'

He shook his head. 'You're impossible.'

They remained in a stalemate until Old Third eventually conceded and got out first while Jingqiu faced the other way, waiting for him to shout 'okay' before turning back. He had already pulled his army uniform over his wet shorts. 'It's hot today, they'll dry in a second.' Jingqiu had got him out first, and yet he had to walk even further away until she could no longer see him before she would come out of the water. She too pulled her clothes over her costume, drenching them so that they clung to her body, and dashed to the public toilets to get changed properly.

She asked him to take the swimsuit back with him because she was too afraid to take it home with her; he could bring it next time.

Old Third helped her push the cart across the river but after that Jingqiu wouldn't let him come any further. She went on her own and he followed at a distance all the way to the paper factory where they parted as previously agreed, she to deliver the goods and return the cart, and he to the ferry crossing to catch the last bus back to West Village.

Only afterwards did it occur to Jingqiu that someone might have seen them together and reported it to the school. After a few days of worrying, however, no one had said anything about it and so it seemed that perhaps they could continue meeting in secret after all. She knew he had to swap shifts with someone else to be able to have two days to come to Yichang, so at most he would be able to come only once every two weeks. If she was not alone when he came, however, she wouldn't let him come up to her to say hello, so it was entirely up to the gods how often they would come face to face.

Chapter Twenty-Three

Perhaps it was because Old Third had suggested Wan Changsheng seemed dishonest, but Jingqiu began to think so too. He stood too close to her when speaking, brushed dirt from her clothes and squeezed her hand when passing her things, making her feel incredibly uncomfortable. She wanted to give him a piece of her mind but she was also worried that were she to offend him she would lose her job. Yet it was also true that Mr Wan took good care of her, giving her lighter work to do and making clear that he was doing so as a favour. 'I'm doing this to help you. If it was anyone else I wouldn't give them such easy work.'

'Thank you,' she would always reply, 'but I would be happy to do the same as the other temporary workers. I'd have people to talk to, my day would be more lively.' But in the end it was up to Mr Wan to assign the work, and she would do whatever he told her to.

One day he told her to sweep the dormitory blocks assigned to unmarried workers as within a few days the factory was expecting a delegation of important people for an inspection. 'It's your responsibility to make sure these buildings are clean. You don't need to do inside the rooms, just the corridors and the outer walls. In the corridors the most important thing is to clean away the rubbish and take it to the dump.'

Jingqiu set to work on the dormitories. The female block

did not pose too many difficulties and she swept the corridors quickly. The male dormitory block, however, made her very uncomfortable. It was the height of summer and the men were very casually dressed. The more considerate among them had hung pieces of cloth over the middle of the doorway, leaving a gap at the top and bottom to let some air into the rooms. The others had merely flung open their doors and walked around topless, wearing only a pair of shorts.

Jingqiu bent over her broom and got on with cleaning the space before each door without looking up for fear of seeing their bare torsos. Some swooshed the door shut on seeing her, but others not only kept the door open but came out in their shorts to speak to her, asking her questions like what school she went to and how old she was. Blushing, she spluttered a few words in response and declined to say any more.

A couple of the young men asked her to clean inside their rooms but she refused to enter, telling them her boss had specifically told her to clean only the corridors. Laughing, they brushed their rubbish out into the corridor. After she had swept it into her bamboo scoop they brushed another pile into the corridor in order to detain her longer. Frustrated, she left to clean elsewhere so that they would give up on this stupidity. She would return to finish the patch around their door.

At one door a hand appeared underneath the cloth that had been hung across it just as she was clearing away their rubbish and emptied a cup of tea dregs and stewed leaves on to Jingqiu's foot; the water was still very hot, scalding it. He probably didn't see me, she thought, so she left to pour some cold water on it without saying anything. A young worker was walking by when this happened and he shouted into the room, 'Hey! Watch where you're pouring that water.' As he turned to Jingqiu, a flicker of recognition came across his face. 'Oh, it's you? How come you're doing this?'

Jingqiu looked up to see an old classmate, Zhang Yi, the naughtiest boy in her class, if not her whole school. All through primary school their teacher sat them at the same table, entrusting Zhang Yi to Jingqiu's care. Her job was to restrain and discipline him during class. This continued into junior middle school, where Zhang Yi was still considered Jingqiu's patch of field, her own 'household responsibility'. But he had just got naughtier and naughtier, and Jingqiu was forced to run around after him. She had both hated and feared him and had spent her school days wishing every day that he might call in sick. When Zhang Yi left school after junior middle school Jingqiu had felt a burden lift from her shoulders, so she had never imagined that they would have to endure such an awkward reunion.

'What are you doing here?'

'I work here,' he said, while eyeing her up and down. 'Why are you here? You working here too now?'

'No, I'm just doing temporary work.'

'I'll help you,' he said boldly, trying to grab the brush out of her hand. 'Are your feet all right?'

Jingqiu looked down at them, and could find no blisters. 'They're fine. You get on with your work, I'll do mine.'

Seeing that she was unwilling to give him the brush he started calling from door to door, 'Hey! Sweep your floors and bring all your rubbish out at once, don't go doing it bit by bit. No tipping out tea water, my friend is cleaning out here and you'll burn her feet.'

His broadcast had the effect of bringing all the men to their doors so they could take a look at 'Zhang Yi's friend'. 'Zhang Yi, is this your bird?' 'I've seen her, wasn't she the girl playing accordion when No. 8 Middle School's propaganda team came to perform?' 'This is Mrs Zhang's daughter, I recognise her. Why is she working here?'

Jingqiu wished she could shoo them back into their rooms and lock the doors so that they wouldn't stand staring at her as she worked, looking her up and down and making comments. What was Zhang Yi thinking? She put her head down and continued sweeping the floor while the men called to her to come back and sweep a bit more, to take away the rubbish over there, or to 'come in for a chat and drink' or 'come in and teach us to play the accordion'. She gave no reply, working hastily to finish the cleaning so that she could escape.

The next day Wan Changsheng sent her back to the dorm blocks; she was to work there until the leaders came for the inspection. She asked him to give her some other work to do, a thousand times more strenuous if necessary. She'd rather do work like that than go back to the dormitories. 'Okay,' he replied, after thinking it over, 'you can work with Master Qu today.'

Mr Wan took her to the south end of the factory to a small river on the other side of the boundary wall, where, on the river's edge, sat a solitary, forlorn little building which belonged to the factory. She was to repair a hole in one of its walls. Mr Wan instructed Jingqiu to fetch some bricks from the factory complex and then mix up the mortar in a barrel from cement, lime, sand and water. Master Qu, the bricklayer, was over fifty years of age and walked with a limp.

As Mr Wan was about to leave Master Qu said, 'Send along another worker, how can she transport all those bricks over the factory wall? We're not talking about one or two bricks here. Send along someone else. One can stand on the wall, and they can help throw the bricks down to me.'

'Where exactly do you want me to find someone else? And once this person's finished chucking the bricks what'll he do then? Just stand watching you two work? I'll help you,' Mr Wan replied.

Jingqiu fetched a cartload of bricks and then climbed on to the wall as Mr Wan and Master Qu positioned themselves on either side. Once they finished throwing the bricks over Mr Wan dusted his hands and said, 'What did I say? Didn't we just save ourselves another worker?' Then, turning to Jingqiu he said, 'The rest is easy, just take your time,' and left.

The work was not, in fact, that tiring. Jingqiu fetched water, mixed the mortar in the barrel and generally worked as Master Qu's assistant. When the mortar was running low she would climb over the wall and bring back another barrel. Master Qu didn't talk much, preferring to keep his head down and work as Jingqiu stood to the side, letting her mind drift to thoughts of Old Third.

They had already finished by lunchtime, but as Master Qu left for lunch Jingqiu had to stay behind to tidy up the tools and clean up. Master Qu had instructed Jingqiu to leave the remaining bricks where they were, but she was afraid that stingy Mr Wan would get angry so she decided to transport them back over the wall into the factory complex. With no one to help her she had to use a bamboo basket to lift them over, one basket at a time.

As she was lifting the bricks over Wan Changsheng arrived. 'You climb back on the wall. I'll throw them to you and you can drop them down on the other side.'

Jingqiu thought this a good method, certainly much quicker than her lifting them over on her own and it didn't take them very long. As she was looking for an empty patch of ground for the last bricks, she sensed someone else on the wall. She looked up to see Mr Wan standing less than a metre away. Surprised, she stepped back. 'Have you thrown me all the bricks?'

'Yes.'

'Then what are we doing standing up here? Let's go and eat lunch. I'm starving.'

Mr Wan stood on the wall and lifted the ladder from the outside of the wall to the inside. He dusted his hands but didn't climb down, and instead stood looking at Jingqiu.

'Why aren't you going down? Aren't you hungry?' Jingqiu said.

'If you want to climb down, on you go. I want to stand here and chat.'

Jingqiu was becoming irritated. He must have had a big breakfast, she thought. 'You're standing in the way of the ladder.'

'You come over here and I'll hold you while you pass. Then you can climb down. C'mon, what's to be embarrassed about?'

Jingqiu looked around her but there was no other way down. This wall was much taller than the one at school. Not that she hadn't jumped from a wall this high, but the problem was that the ground was covered with bricks, rubble, bits of broken glass, and thorny shrubs. She might injure herself. She turned and started walking along the wall in search of another place to jump.

Mr Wan followed her. 'Where are you going? You can't jump down, you'll hurt yourself.'

Jingqiu stopped, turned and replied angrily, 'You know I can't jump so what are you doing stopping me? Let me use the ladder, I want to get down.'

'If I let you use the ladder, will you let me hold you? Or, just let me touch you. Your big breasts have been bobbing in front of me all day, every day now, it's unbearable. If you don't let me touch you I'll do it anyway.'

'What a pervert!' Jingqiu replied, wild with anger. 'I'm going to report you to your superiors!'

'Report what?' he said, coming closer. 'What have I done to you? What has anyone seen me do to you?'

Terrified, Jingqiu turned and fled along the wall. After

teetering and wobbling some way she looked back to see that Wan Changsheng was hot on her heels. Without checking what was beneath her she threw herself off the wall and into the courtyard. Quickly picking herself up she ran towards the factory in search of other people. Mr Wan was no longer chasing after her, so she slowed to check whether she had hurt herself and found that, apart from some scratches on her left palm from broken glass, she was fine.

She ran to a tap outside the men's dormitory to wash her hands. Only once she had removed the dirt did she see that there was a bit of glass wedged in her palm. She pulled it out, causing more bleeding. Using her right thumb she pressed on the cut to try and stop the flow of blood and a surge of pain shot through her hand. Maybe there's still more glass in there, she thought. I'll have to go home and use a needle to get it out.

Just then Zhang Yi came running towards her. 'Someone said your hand's bleeding. What happened?'

'I fell over.'

Zhang Yi clasped her hand to look at the cut. 'It's still bleeding! Let's go to the factory medical room.'

Jingqiu tried to make excuses but Zhang Yi paid no attention, and grabbing her by the right arm he started walking towards the medical room.

'Okay, okay, I'm coming. Don't pull me.'

Zhang Yi didn't let go. 'What are you afraid of? How many times did you pull me around when we were kids?'

At the medical room the nurse removed the last of the glass and stopped the bleeding, dressed the wound, and because Jingqiu had fallen from the wall on the south side of the factory complex, she also gave her a tetanus jab. 'It's dirty over there, what were you doing?'

'You're not going back to work today, are you?' Zhang Yi

asked after they left. 'Go home and rest, and I'll speak to the hunchback. Wait a minute and I'll take you on my bike.'

Jingqiu didn't know what to do. She didn't want to see Wan Changsheng again, but she couldn't work with her hand bandaged. 'I'll go now, you don't need to take me. You go off to work.'

'My shift doesn't start till later. Wait for me here and I'll get my bike.'

Jingqiu waited for him to leave and then sneaked off back home.

Her sister was the only person at home; her mother was out, having got a job pasting envelopes at the neighbourhood committee. She was paid according to the quantity she completed. Jingqiu didn't want her mother to work too much and get sick but she insisted. 'If I do a bit more you can work a bit less. I'm only sitting there gluing envelopes. As long as I don't get greedy and work too much there shouldn't be a problem.'

Jingqiu ate and then lay down on her bed. She worried that Wan Changsheng might tell Director Li that she was a lazy worker who didn't follow instructions, and ran away. If so, she thought, Director Li won't give me any more jobs and I won't get any money from the work I've already done as the boss has to pay it through the neighbourhood committee at the end of the month. If Wan Changsheng is dishonest and doesn't report my hours I'll get no money at all. The more she thought about it, the angrier she got. What possessed him? Was it because he's my boss? He comes from a family of wage labourers, and yet the factory knows that he'll ingratiate himself to them by exploiting the temps, that's the only reason they put him in charge. I've been taken advantage of by such a wretched-looking man, he's a complete scoundrel. If I'd fallen down and killed myself I bet they wouldn't have even provided compensation for my family. She was desperate to report him but she had no witnesses. Who would they believe, him or her?

Maybe she would tell Old Third and let him sort that Mr Wan out. But then if he beat him, or worse killed him, Old Third would be locked up forever. It wouldn't be worth it just to get back at such a horrible man. She wasn't fooled by Old Third's gentle appearance. That day when he had been playing with the knife a look came across his face that showed he was capable of violence, if necessary. It was probably best not to tell him after all.

The thought of going back to Director Li the next day put her into a terrible mood. She was not afraid of hard work and exhaustion, but she did not like to look like she was asking favours of people. If Kunming had been at home then that would have been fine, he would definitely have helped, but Jingqui knew he had already left for the army. She told her sister not to tell their mother that she had come home early that afternoon. The last thing she needed was her mother worrying.

At around six o'clock Granny Copper came to call on Jingqiu. 'The boss told me to tell you that he was joking today, he didn't realise you would take it so seriously. He heard you hurt your hand and told me to say there's no need to rush back to work. He'll count today and tomorrow as full days. You can rest for two more days without pay and he'll keep your place.'

Jingqiu couldn't help herself. 'Joking? There's no way he was joking! He was dead serious.' She explained what had happened to Granny Copper, although she couldn't bring herself to repeat his exact, dirty, words.

Granny was dismissive. 'Oh, what's the big deal? What could he have possibly done up on that wall? Why get so worked up? You can't be so precious when you're trying to scrape a living through temp work.'

Surprised and angry, Jingqiu replied, 'How can you say that? If he had done it to you would you have thought it was nothing?'

'I'm an old woman, he wouldn't waste his energy trying to touch me. I'm afraid you're going to be the one to suffer most out of this. If you had broken your leg jumping off that wall what insurance would you have to fall back on? My advice is that you rest tomorrow and go back to work the day after. If you don't go back to work he'll retaliate. He'll make sure you can't get work anywhere.'

'I don't ever want to see that man again.'

'Put your head down, and ignore him. He took advantage of you, but if it means you lose your job as well, isn't that double the misery? It's not his job to give you anyway.'

Jingqiu rested at home the next day and went back to work at the paper factory the day after that. Granny Copper had made a lot of sense. The job wasn't his so why give it up? Next time he behaves like that, she consoled herself, I'll smash him with a brick.

Wan Changsheng obviously felt guilty because he couldn't bring himself to look Jingqiu in the eye. 'Your hand still looks sore, so today you can help the propaganda team organise the noticeboard.' Then he warned her, 'I was joking with you, don't take it so seriously. If I hear you've been talking about it to anyone ...'

Jingqiu ignored him and said, 'I'm off to the propaganda department.'

Over the next few days Jingqiu helped organise the factory noticeboard, as well as distribute their magazine. The head of the department, Mr Liu, greatly appreciated Jingqiu's talents. Her writing on the noticeboard was beautiful, as were the characters she etched on to the steel plate for printing. She was excellent at drawing. When he gave her some manuscripts to look over she had so many constructive comments that he asked her to write a few pieces herself.

'Oh, what a shame the factory isn't recruiting, otherwise I would definitely have you come and work for us here.'

'I'm soon taking over my mother's job, but my brother is still in the countryside and his writing is better than mine. He also plays the violin. If the factory starts looking for workers could you call him back to the city? He can do anything, you wouldn't regret it.'

Mr Liu took out a small notebook and wrote down Jingqiu's brother's name and address saying that if they started looking for workers he would definitely recommend him.

When they finished work Mr Liu was still discussing the possibility of jobs at the factory with Jingqiu and as they both lived in the same direction they left together. Just as they were leaving through the factory gate Wan Changsheng rushed up from behind. 'Oh, you two are getting on famously, aren't you? Where are you off to?'

'We're going home,' Mr Liu replied, 'we're going the same way.'

Wan Changsheng didn't say anything else and left them. Feeling uncomfortable Jingqiu rushed to say goodbye to Mr Liu. 'I've just remembered I have to meet a friend, I have to go.'

Chapter Twenty-Four

Jingqiu was entering the school campus by the back gate when she heard someone calling from behind. It was Old Third! She spun round, first checking to make sure they were alone.

'No need to look.' Old Third appeared, laughing. 'There's no one else here otherwise I wouldn't have called out.'

'When did you get here?' she replied, blushing.

'In the morning. I thought it best not to look for you at the factory.'

'It's a weekday, how come you're here?'

'What's up, not welcome, am I?' he teased. 'If not, then I'll go home. You've no shortage of people to walk you home, after all.'

He must have seen her with Mr Liu. 'That's the head of the propaganda team, Mr Liu. I was asking him to help my brother get a job, we were just walking for a few minutes together.' She looked around again in case someone was watching. 'Wait in the pavilion. I'll come as soon as I've eaten.'

'Aren't you afraid your mother will come looking?'

'My mother won't be back until around nine o'clock.'

'Then let's walk a bit now, we can eat together.'

'My sister's at home, I have to go speak to her quickly.'

'Okay, off you go. I'll wait in the pavilion.'

Jingqiu floated home in a state of euphoria. Once through the door she no longer had any appetite for dinner but went straight to wash. That day she'd got her period and was afraid that she might be giving off a bad smell. She changed into a dark-coloured skirt that she had made. It had originally been white but she had dyed it red at one point. Then, after it had faded in the wash, she re-dyed it a dark blue and re-sewed it in a different style. She matched it with a short-sleeved nearly new blouse that Yamin had given her. She grabbed her bag and filled it with toilet paper.

She ate distractedly and as she left she said to her sister, 'I'm going to my friend's to ask about my teaching job. Will you be all right on your own?'

'Yes, Zhong Qin is coming soon to play. Which friend?'

Perhaps I'm looking a bit dressed up, she thought, even my sister has noticed. 'You don't know them. I'm off. I'll be back soon.' She felt guilty leaving her sister all alone, but she comforted herself that Zhong Qin would soon be there.

She walked to the ferry crossing, excited, thinking, this is our first date. Every other time they had met by chance and she had had no time to get changed. Would he like what she was wearing? He knows a thing or two about life, he must have seen lots of pretty, well-dressed people, how can someone like me, not particularly good-looking and not especially well dressed, hope to catch his heart?

It felt like everyone she met on the way was looking at her as if they knew she was going to meet a boy. She was extremely nervous, and couldn't wait to get across the river where no one knew who she was. As she stepped on to the bank on the other side of the river she caught sight of Old Third standing near the pavilion. As she had done last time, Jingqiu walked on ahead before eventually stopping to wait for him.

Old Third rushed up and said, 'You look amazing today, I hardly recognised you. Pinch me, I want to know if I'm dreaming. Is such a beautiful girl really waiting for me?'

'I've got used to your sweet-talking, it doesn't give me goose pimples any more,' she teased. 'Live with a fishmonger and you no longer smell the stench of fish. Let's walk by the river. That way if my mother gets home from work early she won't see us, she walks home this way.'

'Have you eaten?' she asked. He hadn't, he was waiting for them to eat together. She had learned her lesson from last time, there was no point in refusing politely, he always found a way.

They returned to the pavilion after they had eaten, but as it was summer, and still early, some people were milling around, so they escaped to an empty part of the river, and sat on the bank.

'It's not Sunday today, how come you're free to visit?' she asked.

'I'm here trying to get work. I want to move to Yichang.'

She was surprised and delighted, but asked pointedly, 'You're doing so well at the geological unit, why would you move to Yichang?'

'You have no idea why I want to move to Yichang?' He laughed. 'Then I'm just wasting my time going to all this trouble, aren't I?'

'Which work unit do you want to move to?' Jingqiu asked.

'I'm still contacting people. Maybe the performance troupe, or another would be fine, wherever they need me as long as it's in Yichang. I could be a street cleaner, or better yet a street cleaner on Jiangxin Island, as long as I got to clean outside your house.'

'What do you mean, outside my house? It's a passage about a metre wide, there'd be no room for you to dance your broom through there. Try for the performance troupe, you could play the accordion for them. But as soon as you're one of them you'll forget all about your old friends.'

'Why would I do that?'

'Because the girls in the performance troupe are beautiful.'

'I used to be in the army's one, but I didn't think the girls were that beautiful.'

'You used to be in the army performance troupe?' she asked in amazement. 'How come you don't walk like the performers do, with their toes pointing outwards?'

He chuckled. 'Does everyone in the performance troupe walk with their feet pointing outwards? Anyway, I wasn't a dancer, I played the accordion. I think you're the one that walks with their toes pointing out, you danced in the model opera *The White-haired Girl*, didn't you?'

She nodded. 'When I was at primary school. At first I was one of the leading dancers in the paper-cut dance, and then I got to play the lead, Xi'er. Then after that I didn't like dancing so I played the accordion while the others danced. Will you teach me to play when you get into the Yichang performance troupe?'

'Once I move to Yichang, are we going to be spending our time together with me teaching you the accordion?'

Jingqiu didn't understand what he meant. 'What else would we be doing?'

He didn't reply to her question, but said instead, 'If I move to Yichang we can see each other all the time. Once your job is sorted out we can meet every day, in the open. We can take walks in the street. How does that sound?'

The scene he was describing sounded as alluring, and far-fetched, as Communism. She saw things more realistically. 'Once my job is organised I'll be working in the kitchens, or I may even be a teacher, and you'll be in the performance troupe. Will you still want to meet me every day?'

'Even if you were the canteen's pig I'd still want to meet you every day.'

'You dog, are you calling me a pig?' She laughed, and gave

his forearm a pinch. How could I do that? I'm just like one of those bad girls in books, showing off and flirting, she thought. Worried that he might think her loose she explained, 'I didn't do that on purpose, I—'

'What are you apologising for?' he laughed. 'I like you pinching me, here, do it again.' He took her hand, put it on his arm and told her to pinch.

'Pinch yourself.'

Seeing that she was embarrassed, he decided not to tease her any more, and instead asked about her brother. 'Where was your brother sent?'

She told him the story of her brother and Yamin, although she left out the part about the bed. Somehow she couldn't bring herself to talk about that.

'Your brother is very lucky,' he said, 'to have found such a good girl. But I'm even luckier, because I found you.'

Although she said she was used to his flirting talk, she was still embarrassed. 'Me? What's so good about me? I haven't protected you the way Yamin has my brother.'

'You would, if it was necessary, it's just that up until now it hasn't been, that's all. I would do the same for you. I would do anything for you, I would agree to anything. Do you believe me?' Then, changing the topic suddenly, he asked, 'How's your hand?'

Unconsciously she put her right hand behind her back. 'What do you mean?'

'I've already seen it. Tell me, what happened? Was it that Wan guy? Did he take advantage of you?'

'No, how could he? Cut my hand with a knife? I was using a small knife to scrape the old notices off the board when I hurt myself.'

'It has nothing to do with him?'

'Really.'

'But if you were holding the knife with your right hand, how could you cut your right hand?'

She looked back at him, unable to come up with a reply.

He didn't ask her again. 'I've always thought you shouldn't do that temporary work,' he sighed. 'You should let me look after you, but I'm too scared to say it to you in case you get angry.' He looked at her. 'I worry about making you angry. Do you worry about making me angry?'

'Yes, I worry about making you angry and that you will then stop liking me.'

'Silly! How could I? Whatever you say, if you snub me or treat me coldly I could never be angry with you, never stop liking you, because I believe that whatever you do you must have your reasons. I'll do whatever you want me to, even the things I can't explain. So you absolutely mustn't tease, because I take everything you say as the truth.'

He took her injured hand and rubbed it lightly. 'Does it still hurt?'

She nodded.

'If I hurt my hand, if I wore myself out, would it upset you?' She couldn't say the words, but nodded. 'Then why do you always do this work, injure and exhaust yourself?' he asked. 'Don't you know how much it upsets me? It hurts, as if someone has stabbed my heart with a knife. Have you ever experienced that kind of pain before?' His expression was solemn and she didn't know how to respond. 'You can't have, you don't know what it is like. Forget it, I don't want you to know how it feels.'

Why hasn't he held me in his arms today? she thought, slightly petulantly. He just talks and talks and talks. That day she was especially hoping that he would hold her close, although she didn't know why. Not far away she could see people, some swimming while others were strolling around.

Perhaps it's not quiet enough here, that's why he's not holding me. 'There are lots of people around here, let's go somewhere else.'

They stood up and walked along the river to find a new spot. As they walked Jingqiu kept casting glances at him to see if he could read her feelings, or if secretly he was laughing at her. But he looked serious, as if he was still thinking of what they had been talking about. They had walked a long way before they found a place empty of people and sat down shoulder to shoulder on a rock.

'What time is it?' she asked.

'Past seven,' he said, looking at his watch.

We'll be heading back soon, and still he hasn't tried to hold me. Is it because it's too hot? The last times he had embraced her, the weather had been cold. 'You don't like the heat, do you?'

He looked at her without replying, as if trying to work out what she really meant by this question. Her face was burning. He sees right through me, she thought. The more she wanted to hide it the hotter her face felt.

He pulled her to her feet and took her in his arms, whispering, 'I don't mind the heat, I'm just too scared . . . '

'Why? I didn't mind last time.'

'I know, I'm just afraid—' but he didn't finish his sentence and instead leaned close to her ear and whispered, 'Do you . . . like me doing this?'

Her blood felt as if it was circulating quicker than usual and then indeed something gushed. Damn! she thought. I need to go to the toilet to change the paper.

He continued to pull her in tight. 'Do you like this? Tell me, don't be afraid, do you like me holding you like this?'

His breath felt scalding hot in her ear. She couldn't wait any longer and whispered, 'I need to go to the toilet.'

He took her by the hand and they went together but all they could find was a very old, filthy toilet. She had no choice, however, and bracing herself, went in. Quickly, she replaced the thick pile of toilet paper and ran outside.

This time he took her in his arms without any need for hinting from her, and he didn't let go again.

It was strange, usually when she got her period for the first few days it was very light, but uncomfortable. Her back would ache and it would feel like she had a horrible weight in her belly and the pain would only ease once her period was coming to an end. Today, however, it was different. As he held her close the pain seemed to disappear.

Were boys like medicine that could cure period pains? However, it was now obvious to her that she hadn't taken enough toilet paper. 'I . . . need to buy something,' she faltered.

She found a grocery shop which sold toilet paper, but a young man there made her too embarrassed to buy what she needed. She hesitated at the door worrying that it would stain her clothes but felt unable to move.

'You wait here, I'll buy it.'

She didn't even have time to ask Old Third 'Buy what?' before he entered the shop. When he came out swinging two bundles of toilet paper she rushed up to him, and tried to stuff them in her bag. She managed to fit in one bundle and she pushed the other underneath his shirt. Once they were some distance from the shop she said, 'Why aren't you hiding it under your clothes? How can you be so brazen?'

'What do you mean, brazen? It's natural, it's nothing people don't know about.'

Chapter Twenty-Five

The next day Jingqiu went back to work at the paper factory, and although she knew that Mr Liu's propaganda department still had work she went straight to see Wan Changsheng to await instruction, as the rules determined. She went to Mr Wan's office-cum-tool cupboard but he pretended not to see her and busied himself assigning tasks to the other temporary workers. Only once he had finished with all the others did he turn to Jingqiu and say, 'There's no work for you today, why don't you go home. And there's no need to come back.'

'What do you mean? Are you sacking me? Mr Liu says he wants me to carry on with the magazine today.'

'If Mr Liu wants you why didn't you go straight to him? What are you doing here?'

Jingqiu thought he was being difficult and this made her angry. 'You're the boss, you're the one responsible for my work, that's why I came to you. Aren't you supposed to be the one who sends me to Mr Liu?'

'I told you to go help with the noticeboard, did I tell you to go for walks with him?'

'When did I go for walks with him?'

'I thought you were a decent girl,' Mr Wan spluttered. 'Spending all that time pretending to be a decent girl, more like. You work for whoever you want to work for, but I don't want you here working for me.'

Jingqiu was fuming.

'Aren't you going? I'm going to get breakfast.' With that, he walked off in the direction of the canteen.

Jingqiu was left behind, cursing herself that she had come back to work for him. How totally spineless, she thought. If only she had not been persuaded to come back by Granny Copper she wouldn't have had to face the humiliation of being fired. She was certain that Wan Changsheng was going to talk to Director Li, and spread nasty rumours about her and Mr Liu. He'll drag my name through the dirt.

Shaking with anger, she thought of finding someone to report Mr Wan to but Mr Wan would be able to clear himself with just the one question: 'If I did something to her that day, why did she come back to work?'

Feeling wronged, she headed for the factory exit. As she passed the factory noticeboard she saw Mr Liu working frantically, but rather than say hello she slid past. As she left the factory compound she caught sight of Zhang Yi coming towards her eating a fried dough stick.

'Jingqiu? Aren't you working today?'

'The boss fired me,' she said, betraying her plan to keep silent about the injustice.

Zhang Yi stopped. 'Why did he fire you?'

'Never mind, it's got nothing to do with you. You get on.'

'I'm not busy, I've just come off my night shift. I didn't want the canteen food so I popped out for breakfast before heading back to sleep. Tell me, what happened? Why did he fire you?'

Feeling that it was more than she could bear, Jingqiu told Zhang Yi all about Mr Wan's behaviour, although she glossed over the parts she thought particularly embarrassing.

Zhang Yi flew into a rage, flung the remainder of his dough stick to the ground, then grabbed Jingqiu's hand and pulled her back towards the factory. 'C'mon, I'll settle things with that hunchback. He must have been aching these last few days, I'll give him a run around, no problem.'

Seeing him raging, looking for a fight, frightened Jingqiu, and just like she used to do when they were young, she pulled at his hand to hold him back. Zhang Yi struggled free from her grip and said, 'Are you scared of him? I'm not scared of him, a man like that only responds to force, the more you're scared of him the fiercer he becomes.' Fuming, he stomped off towards the factory.

Jingqiu had no option but to follow him to the factory. If something happens, she thought, I'll have put Zhang Yi in danger. He was speaking to someone ahead, probably asking them if they had seen Wan Changsheng, and then he made straight for the canteen. Alarmed, Jingqiu ran after him. By the time she got to the door she could hear them arguing inside.

She saw Zhang Yi shoving Wan Changsheng, shouting, 'Hey, hunchback, what are you doing firing my friend? Looking for a fight?'

Wan Changsheng looked pitiful, and repeated one sentence over and over, 'Say what you have to say. Say what you have to say . . .'

Zhang Yi grabbed him by the front of his shirt and pulled him outside. 'Let's go, we can talk at the scene of the crime.' He dragged Mr Wan to the southern wall of the compound, and though they attracted plenty of looks on the way, no one seemed bothered about getting involved. Even though a couple of people called out, 'Fight! Fight! Someone call security,' nobody actually responded, and nor did anyone come forward to mediate. Only Jingqiu followed, startled, calling to Zhang Yi to stop.

Once at the wall Zhang Yi released Mr Wan, and pointing at him shouted, 'You son-of-a-bitch scoundrel, you took advantage of my friend, do you still want to live?'

Mr Wan continued to deny it. 'How could I possibly take advantage of your friend. Don't listen to her rubbish, she's the one that's loose.'

Zhang Yi walked up and kicked Mr Wan in the shin. Mr Wan let out an 'ai-ya!' and slumped on to the ground, picked up a brick and then surged forward.

Jingqiu called out, 'Watch out, he's got a brick in his hand!'

Zhang Yi seized Mr Wan's hands and started shouting and kicking him. 'Stop it or you'll kill him!' Jingqiu called out, frightened.

Zhang Yi stopped. 'I'm going to report you, you scumbag, taking advantage of my friend like that, do you know who I am?'

'I didn't take advantage of her, honest. If you don't believe me go ask her, I didn't lay a finger on her.'

'Do I need to ask? I saw with my own eyes, you fucking pig's head.' Zhang Yi's fist flailed in the air.

Mr Wan protected his head with his hands and shouted, 'What do you want? You want me not to fire her, is that it? If you hit me, will you get away with it?'

'I only hit people for pleasure, I never worry about whether or not I can get away with it.' Zhang Yi let go of Mr Wan. 'It must be your lucky day. Hurry up, what job are you assigning her, so I can go sleep?'

'You can help Mr Liu with the factory notices,' Mr Wan said quietly to Jingqiu.

'Thank you,' Jingqiu said after Mr Wan left, 'I was really worried that you were going to do something stupid.'

'Don't worry, he won't dare touch you again. Worthless guys like that, if you don't hit them they don't know how tough you are. You go and help Mr Liu, and if that hunchback gives you any more trouble come tell me and I'll sort it out.'

Now she owed Zhang Yi, and she wasn't sure how to repay

him. She hoped he didn't want to go out with her, but Zhang Yi didn't appear to be acting any differently. Yes, he always said hello when they met, and sometimes carried his lunch over to say a few words, or else watched as she worked at the noticeboard, but he hadn't asked her to be his girlfriend, so she relaxed.

Mr Wan behaved much better than before. When handing out work he wouldn't speak to her and while the work he gave her was a bit on the heavy side, she preferred it that way.

She arranged to meet Old Third by the river. It was the first time he had seen her with her top tucked into her skirt. He leant in close to her ear and whispered, 'Your outfit looks really good.'

She had always been embarrassed by her large breasts. All the young girls she knew were the same, they all wore bras that made them look flat. If when they ran their breasts bobbed, they would be laughed at. She was unhappy that Old Third had noticed. 'You're just like that hunchback Wan, he said the same thing—'

'What did he say?' Old Third interrupted.

She had no choice but to tell him, as well as the part where Zhang Yi had hit Wan. His face went ghastly pale and he bit his lips together tightly. The same look that Zhang Yi had had appeared in his eyes. 'You don't understand how it makes a man feel when he hears that the girl he loves has been taken advantage of by another man.'

'But he didn't take advantage of me.'

'He made you jump down from a wall. What if you'd hurt yourself? What then?'

She tried to soothe him. 'Don't worry, next time I won't jump, I'll push him off. It's already in the past,' she urged him repeatedly, scared that he would do something to Mr Wan. 'Don't get involved, he's not worth it.'

'Don't worry,' he said, his voice cracking, 'I won't do anything stupid. I just want to move to Yichang as soon as possible, so I can take care of you. Being so far away, every day I worry about someone taking advantage of you, or that you'll exhaust yourself with work, or injure yourself. I don't ever get a good night's sleep. When I'm at work all I want to do is sleep, but when it's time for bed I'm thinking of you.'

His words touched her, so for the first time she took the initiative and embraced him. He was sitting and she stood before him. He rested his head on her chest and said, 'I really could sleep like this.'

He really mustn't be sleeping well, she thought, and then he rushes over here during the day to see me. It's tiring him out. She sat down beside him and he lay down, made her lap his pillow, and fell asleep at once. Her heart ached to see him so tired, and she feared that even the smallest movement might startle him awake.

At nearly eight-thirty she woke him. 'I have to go back otherwise if Mother gets back before me she'll worry.'

He looked at his watch and asked, 'Did I just fall asleep? Why didn't you wake me? You go back at once . . . Sorry.'

'Why are you apologising?' she smiled. 'As long as we're together that's all that matters. Or is there something else?'

He laughed, embarrassed. 'No, not exactly, it's just that we so rarely get to see each other and you let me fall asleep.' He sneezed a few times, his nose seemed blocked and his voice raspy.

'I should have used something to cover you just now.' She was shocked. 'You must have caught a chill while sleeping. We're right by the river here, and this stone bench is cold.'

Holding her he said, 'I'm the one who slept and you're apologising? You should be hitting me instead.' He sneezed again, turned his head to one side. 'I haven't been exercising so I'm in such bad shape, I'm like those glass whistles, blow and I break in an instant.'

'You've probably caught a cold. Remember to take some medicine when you get back.'

'It's nothing, I hardly ever get sick. I don't need to take medicine.'

He took her back home and she told him not to cross over with her as it was possible her mother was also on her way back. 'But it's already dark, how can I relax knowing you're crossing on your own?'

'If you're worried you could walk with me but on the other side of the river.'

So they walked on either side of the river, she taking special care to walk right along the edge so that he could see her. He was wearing a white vest and he carried a white short-sleeved shirt in his hands. A little way along she stopped and looked across to the other side where she saw him stop level with her. He raised his white shirt and flapped it in a circle.

Laughing to herself she wanted to say, Have you surrendered? Why are you flying the white flag? But he was too far away and wouldn't be able to hear her. She continued before stopping again to look over in his direction. He stopped and flapped his white shirt again. They walked and stopped like this until she got to the gate of the campus. The last time she stopped to look over at him she waited for him to leave but he didn't move. She waved her hand at him, shooing him away to find a place for the night. But he too started waving, perhaps to tell her to go first.

Then she saw him stretch out his arms, this time he was not waving, but rather it looked as if he was holding her. She checked that there was no one around and then reached out to him. The two of them stood, on either side of the river, their arms wide, holding each other. Tears welled in her eyes so she turned and ran into the campus where she hid behind the gate.

He was still standing there, with his arms reached out. Behind him stretched the long riverbank and the street lights shone above him. He was wearing white and looked so small, so lonely, so bleak.

Chapter Twenty-six

That night Jingqiu slept badly and had several dreams about Old Third. One minute she was dreaming that he was coughing until he started bringing up blood, the next that he was fighting hunchback Wan. She kept thinking in her dream, as long as this is only a dream, as long as this is only a dream.

Later, when she woke and discovered it really had been a dream she let out a sigh of relief. The sun still hadn't risen but she couldn't get back to sleep. She didn't know if Old Third had found a place to stay the previous night. He said that sometimes he couldn't find a place because he didn't have the papers that said he was on a work trip required by all hotels, so he would stay in the pavilion overnight. Before midnight there would be people in the pavilion playing chess and cooling off after the day's heat, and then after midnight he would be left on his own, he said, thinking about her.

She didn't know when she would next see him – they hadn't been able to fix a time – though she knew that as soon as he had the opportunity he would come see her. Before, she had been afraid that he would tease her and not come, but it wasn't like that any more.

The next morning she went to the paper factory and as before went first to Wan Changsheng's office to be assigned her job for the day. As his door was still closed she sat on the ground outside and waited. Soon other workers came and sat down to wait too.

'The boss must've tired himself out burning the midnight oil and now he can't get up,' someone said. 'As long it all gets counted I don't care when he comes, the later the better.'

They waited until half past eight but Mr Wan still hadn't arrived and everyone was concerned because if they delayed much longer they wouldn't get any work that day. Some of them discussed going to find someone else at the factory to see if anyone knew what had happened to him.

After some time the factory sent a section manager who told them, 'Last night Mr Wan was beaten up so he can't come today. I don't know what work he had planned to give you so I can't organise any. Why don't you all go home and come back tomorrow.'

The temporary workers made their way out of the factory, swearing and muttering, if we aren't going to work today they should've told us earlier. Half the day's already gone before they say anything, they've wasted our time.

Jingqiu started to fret, it must have been Old Third. But, she reasoned, after he took me back to the campus he stood there for ages, surely the crossing must have closed? He can't have swum across to beat Mr Wan up, surely? If he had wanted to swim across, though, it was perfectly possible. Was he saying goodbye to me yesterday when he reached out his arms and stood there for such a long time? Maybe he knew he would go to jail for what he was about to do?

She simply had to find out what exactly had happened, how badly Wan had been hurt and whether they had caught the person who had done it. Did the police even know who it was? She didn't know who to ask, and in desperation she tried everyone. She even ran to Mr Liu's office to ask him if he knew what was going on.

'I've only just found out myself that he was beaten up,' Mr Liu replied. Seeing Jingqiu so worked up he became curious and asked, 'Mr Wan usually stirs up negative feelings in people. I never thought you would be so worried about him.'

Jingqiu had no intention of explaining, and instead stuttered a few words in reply before running off to find Zhang Yi. Zhang Yi was still asleep and was woken by his roommates. He emerged in the hall, rubbing his eyes. 'Have you heard? Someone beat up Mr Wan last night, he couldn't come to work.'

'Really?' Zhang Yi replied excitedly. 'Serves him right. Who did it? Whoever it was is more ruthless than me.'

'I thought it was you,' Jingqiu replied.

'Why did you think it would be me? I was working the night shift.'

'I thought you might have been teaching him a lesson for last time,' Jingqiu replied, now thoroughly disappointed. 'I thought you might be in trouble over it.'

'Don't worry about me,' Zhang Yi replied, visibly touched. 'It wasn't me, honest. Since coming to work here I've not been in a fight once. I only did that last time because he took advantage of you. You've always been good to me, helped me, ever since primary school.'

Jingqiu recalled all the times she had wished he would call in sick and felt ashamed. 'What do you mean helped you, didn't the teacher tell me to do it?'

'Did you notice I only ever listened to you? That's why the teacher asked you to look after me.'

Jingqiu didn't know whether to laugh or cry, and thought to herself, no matter how I tried to hold you back I couldn't, and you say you only listened to me.

'If you're not working today,' Zhang Yi said, 'let's go and watch a film.'

'You've just got off your night shift,' Jingqiu said quickly. 'You go to sleep, otherwise you won't have energy for work tonight.'

'I'll go back to bed now then. See, I still listen to whatever you say.' He went back to his dorm to sleep and Jingqiu went back home.

At home Jingqiu was as fidgety as before, and the image of Old Third having his hands tied and being led away by the police kept floating before her eyes. How could you be so hot-headed? Is it worth giving up your life for this hunchback? But then she blamed herself. Why did she go blabbing about it in the first place? If she hadn't said anything, how would Old Third have known about it? If he got caught it'd all be her fault.

She thought about running to the police station to confess that it was all her doing, that she had hit him because he had taken advantage of her, that she'd had no alternative. But they would never believe her, and anyway, Mr Wan would definitely know if he'd been beaten up by a boy or a girl.

There was no way she could stay at home, so she ran back to the factory to see if there was any news. More and more people had heard about the incident. It really did seem that Mr Wan roused feelings of hatred in people. Not one person who had heard that he had been beaten up expressed any sympathy, and although they did not express pleasure at his misfortune, they did discuss it with gusto.

'It must have been someone who really hates him,' someone offered. 'I heard that they chose a strategic spot, and kicked him several times in the stomach and between his legs. It sounded terrible, his balls must have been totally smashed. He won't be having any sons.'

On hearing this Jingqiu knew that at least Mr Wan wasn't dead. The situation could still be resolved, Old Third wouldn't get the death sentence. But she also thought that if Mr Wan wasn't dead, that meant he could describe the person who had beaten him, which was in some ways worse. But Old Third was so intelligent, surely he wouldn't have let Mr Wan see his face?

The next day she went early to the factory and sat outside Mr Wan's office without knowing exactly what it was she was waiting for. It was immaterial now whether or not she had a job, the important thing was to find out about the latest developments. Had Old Third been captured? After a while the other temporary workers came one by one. The favourite topic of conversation, naturally, was the incident with Mr Wan.

One of the workers, known as Beady Eyes, had, up to now, always appeared a well-informed individual, and today was no exception. 'It all happened in front of Mr Wan's door.' She spoke with authority. 'He had just returned from taking a walk to cool off in the evening air when the person came out of the dark with a bag or something covering his head, and then he punched and kicked him. Apparently the attacker didn't say anything, so it must have been someone he knows well otherwise why would he cover his head and not want Mr Wan to hear his voice?'

Another middle-aged woman known as Crazy Lady Qin spoke up. 'He must be an army guy who doesn't know his own strength.' Crazy Lady Qin had a particular affection for army guys because she had once dragged the head of an army propaganda department 'into trouble', bringing with her an illegitimate child.

'It was your propaganda guy, wasn't it?' someone teased. 'The boss must have had a thing for you for your army man to come back and retaliate.'

Crazy Lady Qin didn't try to defend herself but stifled a grin. 'Men are always beating each other up over some woman.

The boss must have been beaten over one of ours,' she said, looking sideways at the women present. She had a squint, so even if the person she wanted to look at was right in front of her she had to turn her whole body to one side.

This talk made Jingqiu even more scared that Granny Copper might tell everyone about what had happened between her and the hunchback. If other people found out that Mr Wan had taken advantage of her they might suspect her boyfriend or older brother. She had always believed that people who broke the law could never escape the police.

That day they waited until nearly nine o'clock before the factory sent someone to tell them that for the next few days Master Qu would assign them work until Mr Wan was better. Master Qu handed out the tasks, asking Jingqiu to help him tidy a long disused and dilapidated workshop. While working, Jingqiu asked Master Qu when the boss would come back to work.

'Your guess is as good as mine,' he replied, 'but the factory has asked me to fill in for a week at first.'

'You went to Mr Wan's house today. How bad were his injuries? Serious?'

'He won't be back at work for at least ten days, if not a couple of weeks.'

'Do you know who did it? Why did they hit Mr Wan?'

'It's all rumours at the moment. Some people say he took part of someone's wages, and others say he picked on someone's relative. Who knows? Maybe they got the wrong person.'

'Have they caught the person yet?'

'Doesn't look like it, but you've got nothing to worry about, they definitely will. It's just a matter of time.'

Jingqiu was dumbstruck. The fact that Master Qu was so certain that the police would catch the person meant that they had leads and Old Third would struggle to escape. She was heartbroken. She didn't dare cry, nor continue her questioning. If Old Third gets caught and sentenced I'll wait forever for him, I'll visit him every day, all I ask is that he isn't sentenced to death. As long as he's going to be released one day I'll wait a lifetime until he is set free.

Jingqiu plucked up the courage to ask Master Qu, 'Do the police have a lead? Or else how do you know that he will be caught sooner or later?'

'I'm not a policeman, how do I know if they'll catch him or not? I only said it to reassure you, you seemed so worried about the boss. It happens all the time that people don't get caught. My foot got badly hurt by someone, I even know who did it and I told the police, but did they catch him? No. If you're just an average man, who is going to waste their energy catching your wrongdoer?'

This was brilliant news. But over those next few days she was constantly worrying. Later she heard that the hunchback hadn't reported the incident, maybe because he had committed some reprehensible act and was afraid that if he reported it to the police they would weasel it out of him during questioning. It would be better just to keep it to himself. Jingqiu relaxed when she heard this, although she still worried that Mr Wan was creating a smokescreen, so she continued to be on her guard. Old Third would only be safe once the hunchback was dead.

Under Master Qu's tutelage, things were easier because he didn't assign work as Mr Wan had done, using it to extract praise and suggestions. Master Qu didn't let things get personal, and distributed the heavier and lighter work fairly. It didn't matter to Jingqiu if she was physically exhausted.

But this beautiful communist ideal didn't last long, as Mr Wan was soon back at work. There were no scars on his face, but if you looked closely you could detect that the beating had been serious. His back seemed to hunch over even more than before and he looked even closer to death. Someone who didn't know him would have guessed that he was at least fifty years old.

But his former acid tongue seemed to have been neutralised, he no longer lectured people harshly for the smallest thing, and instead simply said, 'Today everyone will transport the materials for fixing the basketball court, and then start resurfacing it.'

All the temporary workers began to complain, this was the hardest work. 'What do you take us for – coolies?'

'What are you moaning about?' the hunchback shouted back impatiently. 'Those who aren't willing can leave now.'

This shut them up. Everyone went to the basketball courts in silence to start work. As Jingqiu was going to the storeroom to collect the tools, Granny Copper said, 'Girl, hasn't anyone told you that you should be wearing rubber boots?'

Jingqiu looked and saw that most of them were indeed wearing rubber boots, and the few who appeared not to own any had instead tied rags around their feet. Jingqiu had never resurfaced a court before so she didn't know to wear rubber boots – she didn't own any anyway – and couldn't find any rags either, so she had to wade in barefoot.

Everyone measured out the correct proportions of cement, lime and a type of coal cinder. Once these were thoroughly mixed with water they were to spread the mixture on to the court, and after that layer had dried they were to spread a layer of concrete. And there you had it, a simple basketball court. As this was apparently a money-saving technique, the factory was using its temporary workers.

Everyone refused to work with Granny Copper because she didn't pull her weight, so Granny Copper stuck to Jingqiu. Jingqiu worried that Mr Wan might ask them to redo the work, but then, Granny Copper really didn't have any choice. How could she work as hard as the rest of them? And yet circumstances forced her to go out and slave away, to grind the last of her life down in this wretched labour. It was better that Jingqiu do a bit more.

The hunchback split them into two groups that took turns to work, swapping only when Mr Wan shouted 'change', leaving one group to rest for a bit while the other took over. Jingqiu sensed that the hunchback might be punishing her by purposefully making her group work longer than the other. Crazy Lady Qin, however, thought otherwise. 'Boss, you can't go treating that group differently just 'cos they've got a youngster with a tender pussy, it's favouritism. You're hiring her for her muscle, not her pussy, and if not, then it'd be better to take her straight home with you.'

Jingqiu was fuming. Crazy Lady Qin said whatever she pleased and you were left cowering in a corner. You'd say one thing and she'd reply with a hundred. It was not clear why, but from the start Crazy Lady Qin took a deep dislike to Jingqiu. She was always hurling obscenities to get at her. A day at work with Crazy Lady Qin felt like a year to Jingqiu. The only thing to do was ignore her.

The way Jingqiu's fellow workers didn't work together, and instead fought and tormented each other, made her spirits sink and time seemed to pass at a painfully slow pace. With great effort, she dragged herself though to the break, when she finally got to wash her feet under the hose, and discovered a layer of skin on the soles of her feet had been burned off by the lime. She hadn't noticed while engrossed in work, but now she felt a stabbing pain when she walked. After work, she went home and washed her feet again in clean water and then rubbed some cream into them, which seemed to relieve the pain a bit. That night, she didn't dare sleep too deeply in case she groaned too much and her mother heard her.

After a few days of resurfacing, she found she had adapted to the intensity of the work, but two things still troubled her. One was that Crazy Lady Qin was always picking on her, and the other that the soles of her feet were covered in blisters and sores. These weren't big but they were deep. Every day when she got home she had to spend ages picking out the bits of coal cinder with a needle, and soon her feet had swollen so much that she couldn't squeeze them into any of her shoes. Luckily her mother left early and didn't get home until late, and once home she was so exhausted by her day's work that she slept deeply, so she never discovered Jingqiu's injuries.

One morning, as Jingqiu was preparing to leave for work, she heard a strange kind of knocking at her door. It was Old Third with his hands full of paper bags. He must have used his foot to knock lightly at the door.

He didn't wait for her to invite him in, but stepped in and put the bags down. 'Don't be afraid, no one saw me.'

She looked at him, amazed. 'They haven't taken you away?' she asked quietly.

'Taken me where?' He didn't understand.

'To the police station,' she replied. She told him all about how the hunchback had been beaten up. 'So you didn't hit him?'

'No,' he replied. 'Didn't you tell me not to cause trouble?'

He's right, I did, she reflected. 'Then who else could it have been? Zhang Yi denied it too.'

'Maybe Wan's offended a lot of people. There must be more than a couple who would want to beat him up. Who cares about him anyway?' He opened one of the bags and asked, 'Have you eaten breakfast yet? I bought some food.'

'I've already eaten.'

'Have some more, I bought enough for you and your sister.'

Jingqiu took a fried dough stick to her sister in the other room and told her, 'Don't tell Mother he came over.'

'I see.'

Jingqiu went back to the front room and ate a dough stick herself. Old Third took out a cardboard box and gave it to her. 'Don't get angry,' he said quietly, 'I'm begging you.'

Jingqiu opened the box and saw inside a pair of gum boots in her favourite colour, a rice-yellow.

'They're for when you're working,' Old Third said. 'I saw you yesterday on the basketball court. How can you possibly work there and not wear gum boots?' He looked down at her feet, swollen like steamed buns, her toes red and inflamed.

'You came to the factory yesterday?'

'Relax, no one saw me,' he said hoarsely. 'Why don't you try them on?'

Jingqiu gently stroked her new rubber boots. They were so shiny you could almost see your reflection in them. She was eager to try them on but asked apprehensively, 'Wear a new pair of boots to work? Won't . . . people think I'm spoiled?'

She looked up to see him staring at her feet, his cheeks covered in tears. Flustered, she said, 'You . . . what are you doing? Since when do men cry?'

He brushed away the tears. 'Just because men don't cry over their own troubles, doesn't mean they can't cry over someone else's. I know I've told you not to do this kind of work but you won't listen. I've given you money and you don't want that either. But if you have even an ounce of compassion, if you even care about me even . . . a little bit, you'll wear these boots.'

'If you want me to wear them I will, but why get like this?' She removed her flip-flops quickly and shoved her feet into the boots, fearing that he might see the sores. If he cried at the sight of the tops of her feet, how would he react to the sight of the soles?

She just managed to get her swollen feet into the boots and paraded them for him to see. 'Look, perfect.'

But he was still crying and she didn't know how to comfort him. She wanted to take him in her arms but she was afraid her sister might appear and see them. She pointed to the other room and said under her breath, 'Don't be like that. If my sister sees she'll tell my mother.'

He wiped the tears. 'You must remember to wear them, I'll be hiding nearby to check up on you. If you take them off . . . '

'Then what?'

'I'll come, barefoot, and stomp in that lime until it burns my feet.'

Afraid that she too might start crying she broke in, 'I've got to go to work, wait for me this evening at the pavilion.'

'Don't, stay at home and rest instead. You shouldn't walk so far with those feet.'

But she didn't listen and left, saying, 'Don't forget to wait for me.'

That day the other workers called her a show-off for wearing a new pair of rubber boots to work. Her feet were already burned to a crisp so what did she need shoes for? The skin on her feet would mend, but if she ruined a pair of new boots they'd be useless.

Crazy Lady Qin started on her insinuations. 'She's young, she can sell herself to get whatever she wants.'

Jingqiu didn't care what they said and carried on wearing the boots in case Old Third came to check up on her. One pair of burnt feet was enough.

Chapter Twenty-seven

When she got back from work that afternoon, she found her younger sister putting the finishing touches to their dinner. Jingqiu ate, washed and then changed into her skirt and short-sleeved blouse and said to her sister, 'I'm going to a friend's house.'

'Going to ask about your job again?' her sister asked, seeing Jingqiu had put special effort into her appearance.

She gave an 'uh-huh' and thought, she mustn't tell Mother. 'I've got something on, something very important. Don't say anything to Mother.'

'I know. Is it the same person as this morning? He really likes you.'

Jingqiu's face turned crimson. 'What do you know about that sort of thing? You're too young.'

'How could I not know?' Using her forefingers she acted out Old Third crying, and like a traditional story-teller clapped as she recited, 'Old Man Sob, sold his cob, to a certain Mr Bob. Then Bob sold it on, to Mr Long. Long's dog came up, to make a ruck, scaring Old Man Sob away.'

'Did you see him crying? Don't tell Mother.'

'I know. Sister, if a boy cries over you that means he really likes you.'

Jingqiu was startled. Not only had her little sister seen everything but she understood as well. She forced her to promise not to tell their mother before eventually setting off to meet Old Third.

She couldn't wear shoes so she slipped on a pair of her brother's old flip-flops, the type she normally most detested wearing as it was so uncomfortable having them wedged between your toes. Today she had no option, however. Surely she couldn't go see Old Third barefoot? And it didn't look right to wear the rubber boots.

Her feet were so swollen she looked flat-footed, and although each step was excruciating, she walked as fast as she could, desperate to see Old Third. She had only just boarded the boat to cross the river when she saw him waiting for her, pushing a bike. He told her to jump on the rack at the back and no sooner had he started pedalling, they were riding up on the road by the river. 'Didn't you say your mother works near here? Now we've got a bike, we can go a bit further.'

'How did you get hold of it?'

'I hired it. There's a bike repair place by the pier, and they hire bikes too.'

It had been a long time since she heard of anyone renting bikes; it must have been when she was small, when her father had hired a bike from the very same bike business by the pier. He had put her on the crossbar, and they had ridden the streets, wind in their hair, her father riding and she ringing the small bell. Then somehow the bell had fallen to the ground and by the time her father had discovered it they had already gone some way. Father stopped by the side of the road, pulled out the bike stand and placed her on top while he went to look for the bell. Terrified that the bike would topple over, she had started bawling. She cried with such force that it shook the skies above and ground below, drawing in a crowd of onlookers.

Remembering this she started to chuckle. 'What are you laughing about?' Old Third asked. 'Aren't you going to share the joke with me?'

She told him the story and he asked, 'Do you miss your father?'

She didn't reply to his question, but instead told more stories about her father, although most of them were from when she was small and were actually stories her mother had told her. Old Third listened to each one. 'Your father loves you all so much,' he sighed. 'Let's go and visit him some time. He must be really lonely on his own in the countryside, missing all of you.'

He was too bold, Jingqiu thought. 'My father is a landlord, he's being re-educated. If we go and the school finds out they'll say we haven't drawn a line between him and ourselves.'

'If we carry on like this people will never again dare talk about morality, or love,' Old Third said. 'Give me his address and I'll visit him. There won't be any problems.'

Jingqiu hesitated. 'If you really do visit my father, tell him he mustn't mention it in any letter he sends my mother, otherwise she'll know about us. Tell me when you go and I'll buy some sugared peanuts for him. He used to love eating sweet things, especially those peanuts.'

They cycled nearly all the way to quay number thirteen, which was about as far as the city buses went. They found a place by the river empty of people and sat down. Her feet were especially swollen by the evening, and it was getting difficult to wear her flip-flops. As soon as she sat down they fell from her feet and tumbled down the bank towards the river. He chased after them and caught them before returning to her side so that he could slip them on her feet. 'No, don't, I don't need my flip-flops while I'm sitting.' She drew her feet under her skirt as she spoke.

'Why won't you let me touch your feet?' He crouched before her and lifted her skirt, grabbing one of her ankles. She tried to fight him off but didn't succeed. When he discovered that her feet were covered in sores, he cried out softly, 'Jingqiu, Jingqiu, don't work like this. Let me help you, if you keep going I'm afraid I'll go mad ...'

'Don't worry, I've got boots now, there'll be no more trouble.'

He slipped the flip-flops on to her feet and pulled her up. 'Come on, we're going to the hospital.'

'What would we do at the hospital now? Won't they have finished for the day?'

'The emergency room is always open. With sores like this you could have got poisoned, your feet could become infected.'

'No they won't, anyway, it's not just me. Lots of people have feet like this.'

He was stubborn, and he continued to pull at her. 'I don't care about anyone else, I only care about you. You're coming with me to the hospital.'

'The doctors will ask my name and work unit, and I didn't bring my medical papers. I'm not going.'

He suddenly let go of her and pulled out his knife, and slashed the back of his left hand. Blood started to pour from the wound.

Frightened, Jingqiu scrabbled around for a handkerchief to wrap up his hand. 'Are you crazy?'

She wrapped the handkerchief tight but the blood continued to seep out. Her legs began to give way with fright. 'Let's go to the hospital, now! You're still bleeding.'

'So you'll go? Okay, come on.'

'I'll take you on the bike.'

'You can't ride, your feet are too sore. You sit on the front and I'll ride.' He sat her on the crossbar and told her to hold on to the handlebars, and with his good hand on hers, he rushed them to the hospital.

He spoke to a doctor who then looked at Jingqiu's feet, while another in a white coat took Old Third to a separate room. When Jingqiu spotted a flash of red peeping out from under his white coat she thought he might be an army doctor; she had never been here before.

The doctor kept calling her Little Liu. Old Third must have given a fake name. The doctor looked over her feet and wrote out a prescription for some cream along with some disinfectant and sterilised cotton. 'Once you get home wash your feet, pick out the bits of coal from the sores and then rub on this ointment. Don't put them in unsterilised water, boil it first, and certainly don't let any more bits of coal get into them.' He filled out another form and told her to go to the room opposite where a nurse would clean her feet and bandage them so that she could get home. The nurse helped Jingqiu to tie her flip-flops to her bandaged feet. She told Jingqiu to wait for Sun on the bench in the corridor outside.

After a while Old Third appeared, his left arm in a sling. 'Is it serious?' Jingqiu asked nervously.

'No. How about you?'

'I'm okay, the doctor wrote me a prescription.'

He took her prescription and told her to wait there. Presently he returned, patting his shoulder bag. 'Got the medicine, everything's sorted. Let's hurry home so you can put on some of this cream.'

As soon as they were outside Old Third removed his sling and stuffed it into his bag. 'If I have my arm in a sling people will think I'm starring in that model opera, what it's called? *Shajia River*.'

'What about your cut? What did the doctor say?'

'He said my blood wasn't clotting properly so he gave me two stitches. But how could I have problems with blood clotting? I'm as healthy as they come. I even got into the air force and only didn't join because my dad was scared I would be killed if there was a war.'

'Aren't you just dying with regret?' Jingqiu asked, overcome with envy.

'Regret what?' He glanced at her. 'Would I have met you if I had gone into the air force?'

Jingqiu let him take her back on his bike. Once they got to the ferry crossing he refused to leave her. 'It's only just past eight, your mother won't be back yet. Let me take you to the campus gate on my bike. Your feet are so swollen, you can't walk.' He took off his short-sleeved shirt so that Jingqiu could drape it over her head. 'No one will recognise you.' When they drew up to the campus gate he said, 'Let me take you in, that way you won't get your feet dirty.'

Jingqiu lifted the shirt from her head and looked in the direction of the gate. There was no one around, but then she turned to discover her mother making her way towards them from the ferry crossing. They might even have passed her on the way without realising it.

'Damn,' she whispered. 'My mother is coming, you'd better go quickly.'

'It's too late to escape,' he said under his breath.

Jingqiu's mother came up to them and stopped. 'Where are you going?'

'I ... I went to the hospital to get my feet checked. This is ... this is the person I was telling you about ... my friend Sun Jianxin from the geological unit.'

'Jingqiu, go home,' her mother said. 'I want to say a few words to Sun here.'

'Then please let me take her home first,' Old Third

interjected. 'Her feet are terribly swollen and infected, she can't walk.'

Her mother saw the bandages on Jingqiu's feet and said, 'All right, but I want to speak to him. I'll go first, but don't hang around outside and let people see you, it'll create a bad impression.' She walked through the campus gate.

'Let me get down,' Jingqiu said to Old Third. 'I'll go by myself. You should leave now, my mother will only send you to the police.'

'Don't be afraid, I'll take you. Your mother only wants to speak to me.'

'How can you be so stupid?' Jingqiu responded, fidgeting anxiously. 'She told me ages ago not to have any contact with you. Now she's caught us, do you really think she wouldn't take you to the police? Let me get down and then go, quickly.'

He pushed her towards the school. 'Won't your mother be furious with you if you let me run away? It's just like Yamin said, we haven't done anything. What can anyone do?'

Jingqiu allowed him to take her home. Once they got to the house Old Third pulled down the bike stand and supported her as she dismounted. He locked up his bike, then followed her inside.

Mother told Jingqiu to close the door and invited Old Third into the inner room, asking him to sit down. It was hot and stuffy, and Old Third was now soaked in sweat. Jingqiu's younger sister was perceptive; she scuttled out and returned with a bowl of cold water so that Old Third could wash his face, and seeing the bandage on his hand even wrung out the towel for him. Old Third was too scared to take it, and looked over to Jingqiu's mother as if awaiting instruction.

'It's too hot, maybe it will make you feel better,' Mrs Zhang said.

He was extremely grateful and washed his face. He used one hand to splash the water on his face, and then took the towel Jingqiu's sister was holding for him and wiped it. He sat obediently, waiting for Jingqiu's mother to start the trial.

Jingqiu was so nervous she stood to one side looking at the other three act out the scene. She had only one thought: I haven't gone to bed with Old Third, I haven't shared a room with him, I would definitely pass any physical examination. She didn't know if her mother had already called the police from the campus reception – probably not, because they had been so close behind her and they hadn't seen her stop there to make a call. But still, she listened carefully for any noise outside. Were she to hear anything she would tell Old Third to get on his bike at once and escape.

Old Third got up and offered his chair to Jingqiu. 'Sit, your feet must hurt, you shouldn't stand. I can stand.'

'Jingqiu, go to your room and let me talk to Sun,' her mother said.

Jingqiu went back to her room. In fact, the two rooms were really only one room with a wall just taller than head-height down the middle. You could hear everything, so if she really wanted her not to hear her mother should have sent her outside. She sat on her bed near the door so she could see Old Third but not her mother who was sitting opposite him.

Her sister was also sent out, making a face at Jingqiu as she went. She stood nearby and she too watched the play unfold in the other room.

'Sun boy,' Jingqiu heard her mother say, 'I can tell that you are a cautious person, that you are patient with our Jingqiu. I am very grateful that you took her to the hospital today, and I've heard that you've done a lot to help her. I'm grateful for all that you've done. You could say,' her mother continued, 'that you and I have the same aims when it comes to Jingqiu.

Our feelings are the same. I can tell that you are very sincere about her.'

Her mother's opening remarks didn't seem to be pointing in the direction of the police so Jingqiu started to worry that she might be diverting their attention before making her attack and that a 'but' was on its way.

Jingqiu listened to Old Third add unnecessarily, 'I am indeed sincere about Jingqiu, I do hope Mother will believe that.'

'People call me Teacher Zhang, why don't you call me that.'

'I do hope Teacher Zhang will believe that,' Old Third corrected himself hastily.

Jingqiu didn't dare laugh at his terror-stricken, fawning manner, but listened anxiously for her mother to continue. 'I believe that,' her mother said, 'and that is why I feel the need to talk to you. If not, I wouldn't have anything to say to you. We care about Jingqiu, we cherish her, so we need to take the long-view, not just live for the present. No plans for the future makes for trouble tomorrow. Jingqiu is taking over my job and lots of people are jealous. They're making all sorts of comments behind our backs. Her job is still not finalised, so if these people see you two together it will be terrible for Jingqiu . . . '

'Yes, indeed.' Old Third nodded again.

They were silent for a while until he cleared his throat and said, 'Teacher Zhang, please don't worry, I will go home and I won't come back until her job is sorted out.'

Jingqiu saw Old Third look at her mother smugly, as if waiting for her praise. But instead she said, 'The situation is not improved even when she has her job. Until it has been made permanent, the school can get rid of her whenever they please.'

Old Third sat, silenced for a while, and then replied, 'Then I'll wait until her job has been made permanent. Her probationary period is what, a year? Then I'll come back in a year . . .' He stopped to calculate. 'In thirteen months, taking into consideration that she hasn't started yet.'

Whether it was his willingness to cooperate or the precision of his calculations that moved her, Jingqiu's mother was warm in her reply. 'Do you know this couplet? "When love is long-lasting, why must we meet day and night?" If you and Jingqiu are meant to be then you won't mind waiting a year or more, isn't that right?'

Old Third's face was veiled in sadness. 'Yes, of course, you're right.' He then elaborated, although it was not obvious who it was he was trying to persuade. 'It's only a year, we're still young, we've still got many years left.'

'I can tell that you are a reasonable person,' Jingqiu's mother said approvingly, 'there's nothing left for me to say. I'm not one of those feudal mothers, I understand how you young people feel, but this is the reality. Gossip is a powerful thing, we need to be careful.'

'I understand, you're doing this for us.'

Her mother must have stood up and signalled for her guest to leave as Jingqiu saw Old Third stand and implore, 'Just let me get some water to wash Jingqiu's feet. Her soles are infected and covered in sores, and she has bits of dirt inside them. She can't see them herself, so I can help her pick them out, and put the cream on. Then I'll leave at once. I'm begging you, please.'

'You shouldn't go walking around out here, I'll get the water.'

When Jingqiu's sister heard this she jumped up and said, 'I'll go, I'll go,' returning promptly and placing the bowl by her sister's bed. Jingqiu felt like those mothers who are not allowed to go out for a month after giving birth, but who lie in bed all day being served. She wanted to get up, but the three of them wouldn't let her.

Old Third removed the bandages from her feet and her mother examined them carefully. With tears in her eyes, she said to him, 'Please do help her, Si and I will go outside to get some fresh air.'

Jingqiu wouldn't let him wash her feet in case he got his bandage wet. She washed them herself and he helped her dry them. He then switched on a nearby lamp and pulled the bulb closer. He asked Jingqiu for a needle and started picking out the bits of coal dust from her sores. 'Does it hurt? If I go too deep just tell me.'

Jingqiu shook her head. She thought of the scene that had just passed earlier with her mother and began to laugh at him. 'You were just like Fu Zhigao, the traitor from Red Crag. Grovelling and fawning.'

He laughed too. 'I was scared to death.'

'Were you worried my mother would send you to the police?'

'I wasn't worried about that, I was worried that she wouldn't let me wait for you, that she would shout at you. Thank god we weren't born in Fu Zhigao's day, else I'd definitely have been a traitor,' he joked. 'If the Nationalists took you hostage to threaten me then I would tell them everything, no doubt about it.'

'Do you hate my mother?'

'Why would I hate your mother?' he asked, surprised. 'We have the same interests at heart, she said so herself. Don't you think she likes me? She agreed that I could come back in thirteen months, she even said our love was "long-lasting".'

'You're certainly full of revolutionary optimism.'

'It's like Chairman Mao said, "When our comrades are in trouble we must look to success, to the light, we must be even braver." 'Deep in concentration, he picked out the bits of soot while she gazed at him.

Her heart sank; another thirteen months before I get to see him again, how will I get through it? 'Will you really wait thirteen months before you come see me again?'

He nodded. 'I've promised your mother, and if I don't keep my word she will never believe me again.' He looked at her staring at him, utterly miserable. 'You want me to come and see you? You don't want to wait that long?' She nodded. 'Then I won't wait, I'll come in secret, is that okay? So, I'm a traitor after all, I made a promise to your mother and all it took was one word from you.'

'Traitor or not, as long as you don't get caught,' she smiled.

Once he had cleaned out all her sores he rubbed the cream into her feet, emptied the basin of water outside and returned to sit beside her on the bed. 'Give me a picture, so when I'm missing you I can look at it.'

She thought she looked ugly in all the photos she had of herself, and she rarely had her picture taken anyway, so it took her some time to find one, and even then it was one of her at six years of age. The girl in the picture had bobbed hair and a straight fringe across her forehead, and was wearing a light green dress. The photo was in black and white but her father had coloured it himself, not very neatly in some places, especially in the green of her dress. She gave him the photo, promising to send him a new one.

He had previously sent her two passport-sized photos in between the pages of books and letters. He took another from his bag, taken outside. He was wearing a white shirt and a pale pair of trousers, in his hand he was carrying what looked like a roll of paper, and he was standing beneath a tree. She recognised it to be the hawthorn tree. He looked very young in the photo, distinguished even, with a slight smile spreading across his face. She really liked the photo, and now that her mother knew about their relationship she wasn't scared about having it in the house.

'Do you like it? I went especially to the tree to take it. Once you've got your job, and it's permanent, I'll take you to that tree and we can have our photo taken there. I've got a camera and I can develop my own pictures. I'll take lots of pictures of you in all sorts of poses, from all angles, I'll develop lots, big ones even, and put them all over my walls.'

He took out some money from his pocket and put it on the table by her bed. 'I'm leaving this money for you. If you don't want me to cut my hand again you'll take it. You mustn't work for that hunchback Wan again. If the cardboard factory has work then that's fine, but if you don't listen to me and go back to work for that man, or do any kind of dangerous work, I'll be angry. I won't leave you, but I will cut myself again. Do you believe me?'

She nodded. 'I won't ever go back to work for that man.'

'Good. The problem is only temporary. That is why I'm leaving this money here, there is no way your mother will be angry with you.'

He knelt by the side of the bed and took her in his arms. They remained wrapped in each other's arms until he stood up decisively and said, 'I'm going. You stay there, don't get up, you've only just put the cream on your feet and you don't want them to get dirty.'

She sat on the bed, listening to him leave, unlock his bike, and ride it away, until everything was once again plunged into silence.

CHAPTER TWENTY-EIGHT

A short while after Old Third left her mother and sister returned. Jingqiu looked at the clock; it was nearly eleven.

'Did Sun say where he was staying tonight?' her mother asked, a hint of worry in her voice.

'Whenever he doesn't have somewhere to stay he spends the night in a pavilion by the river, but by now the crossing will have closed. Maybe he'll sit on the bank . . . ' The words caught in her throat, and she faltered.

Her mother sat on the bed. 'I know you don't want to let go of him, and he doesn't look like a bad boy, but what are the options? You're still so young, and even the girls and boys over twenty in relationships invite criticism. You've started so early – your job isn't yet sorted out – and I'm telling you you can't see him, for now. It will be a test of his intentions. If he's sincere he won't run away just because he can't see you for a year, but if he can't pass the test . . . '

'Mother, you don't need to explain, I know you only want the best for me. You go to bed, we've got work tomorrow.'

'Are you working tomorrow? Your feet are so badly injured and you didn't say a word to me about it.'

'It would only have made you worry, what would have been the point? It's fine, he told me not to go tomorrow and I agreed.'

'If you're not working tomorrow then you won't need your rubber boots,' her sister said.

'What rubber boots?' her mother asked.

'That Sun boy bought them for her,' Jingqiu's sister piped up. 'He came one morning with them and he cried when he saw how bad her feet were.'

'He's just like your father,' Jingqiu's mother sighed. 'He also cried easily. When men cry it's either because they are especially empathetic or because they are weak. Sun seems like an empathetic boy. What about his family?'

'I'm not quite sure,' Jingqiu replied. 'I know he's got a younger brother and a father. His mother killed herself . . .'

'I've heard that that sort of thing runs in families. The children of depressed people are easily depressed themselves. What is Sun like? He seemed a bit particular when he was calculating how long it'd be before he got to see you.'

Jingqiu thought back to when he was making those calculations; it was cute. Her mother asked her some more questions about Old Third, how old he was, whether he smoked or drank, fought and swore, where he went to school, what his hobbies were, where he was from, that sort of thing. 'Why didn't you ask him yourself when he was here?' Jingqiu asked in turn.

'He would have thought I was checking him out as a prospective son-in-law, I couldn't give him that impression lightly. My goal in speaking with him was to tell him not to come to visit you.' Jingqiu recalled the proud way Old Third had said that her mother had already agreed to their relationship, and she felt touched with sadness on his behalf. 'What does his father do?'

'He's a district level commanding officer.'

Her mother fell silent before saying, 'I thought he seemed different from most boys. Someone from that kind of background can't easily understand people like us. Who did the People's Liberation Army liberate? Workers and farmers oppressed by landlords and capitalists. His father and your father belong to two irreconcilable classes. His family obviously doesn't know about you ...'

Jingqiu hadn't thought about that before, but now that her mother mentioned it, it was a serious question. She hoped with all her heart that it wasn't true. 'But his mother was the daughter of a capitalist, and his father didn't abandon her.'

'You're right, the Communist Party takes a very different attitude to capitalists than it does to landlords. In those days capitalists represented the rising, progressive, productive forces, whereas landlords represented a declining force. The first thing the Communist revolution wanted to do was get rid of the landlord class. Don't get your hopes up. His family is a barrier you can't easily overcome and he might lose interest sooner rather than later.'

Jingqiu said, 'He said he would wait a lifetime ...'

'Who can't say that? Who hasn't said it? To open your mouth and say "a lifetime" is naive. Who can predict the way things will go at such a young age?' Her mother saw a look of rebellion in Jingqiu's eyes. 'You're still young, you haven't got much experience of people so you believe him as soon as he says it. Wait until you've grown up, then you'll discover every man will say that when he is chasing you, they all say they can wait a lifetime. But if you ignore him for a year, you see if he'll wait. He'll have gone already.'

If mother knows men won't wait a year, thought Jingqiu, why did she tell Old Third to wait? She's using it as an excuse to test him. She was desperate to tell Old Third what her mother had said, but she also thought that if she told him he wouldn't really be tested at all.

Do all men exaggerate and not keep their word? I probably should test Old Third to see how long he will wait for me. The problem is, say he waits for a year, that doesn't prove he could wait two. If he waits two years that doesn't prove he could wait a whole lifetime.

She didn't even really know what 'making him wait' meant. If she made him 'wait' for her did that mean he had to 'love' her? By asking 'could you wait a lifetime for me?' wasn't she really asking 'could you love me for a lifetime?' She wasn't used to using that word, 'love'. But these two words, 'wait' and 'love' still seemed to mean slightly different things.

Lost in her own thoughts, she had no idea if her mother had spoken or not, she only heard her sister say, 'I'm asking you, what happened to his hand? When he came this morning it was fine.'

'He told me to go to the hospital but I wouldn't, so he cut himself. He bled lots.'

'He seemed so sensible,' her mother said, her brow furrowed. 'How could he do such a crazy thing? That shows he's immature. Erratic people are dangerous and easily take to extremes. If they like you, they can like you too much, if they hate you, they hate you too much, it's like that whatever they do. It's better to keep a distance from people like that.'

Jingqiu had thought that her mother would be moved by this, but she called it dangerous. Her mother had once told her that when her father was young he had a tendency towards extreme behaviour, and that when her mother either paid him too little attention or didn't believe him he would start tugging furiously at his hair, pulling it out in large clumps. She knew that their courtship had been complicated. Her father's parents had originally arranged a marriage for him back in his village, and in fact not just one; as he had been set to inherit from two branches of the family, from his grandfather's real son (his father), and also from his grandfather's younger brother, who had no son, each branch of the family had arranged a wife for him. In order to escape these marriages he ran away to study, but as his grandfather was dying he was forced to marry both of the women chosen for him.

Later, Father had met Mother, and he went through all kinds of hardships in order to leave his two wives and remarry. Mother waited a long time to marry, until she was almost thirty. Father and Mother worked in different cities after they were married, so father only came to visit once every couple of weeks, but they wrote to each other frequently. During the Cultural Revolution, when Mother was being criticised at No. 8 Middle School, these letters were used as evidence that Jingqiu's parents were living a capitalist lifestyle.

It was her granny who had talked to outsiders about the letters. She lived with Jingqiu's mother, Jingqiu and her brother and sister, while her father lived on his own. Granny was old-fashioned and thought her mother had bewitched her father in order to make him leave his first two wives. According to Granny, only the first wife was truly legal, and it simply wasn't proper to divorce and remarry. She couldn't stand seeing them being affectionate towards each other, so she used to say that they were extravagant, wasting their money on trains and stamps.

After her father was sent home to be re-educated through labour they discussed divorce, mainly because they were worried about what effect his denunciation would have on the children. But Mother thought that Father was already so desperately poor and lonely that were they to divorce, he might not survive. She had sought the children's opinions, saying that they were only really considering a divorce for their sake, and that they would only go through with it if the children were worried about how their father's class status would impact on them.

They replied that she shouldn't do it. This was just how it was, even if she divorced him they would still be his children and people wouldn't necessarily regard them as innocent anyway. So her mother didn't divorce her father, but neither did they have much contact in person in case people criticised them for it.

Through all this, though, her parents continued to write to each other frequently. Her father sent his letters to a sister of his who had married a man with a good class status, and who in this way had avoided attack during the Cultural Revolution. Her mother would go regularly to their house to collect the letters, but she never let the children go in case people made the connection between them and their father.

Jingqiu was lost in her thoughts until she heard her mother ask, 'Has Sun ever had a girlfriend?'

Jingqiu knew if she said that Old Third had previously had a fiancée it would give a bad impression, so she stuttered, 'Not that I know of.'

'Men always hide that kind of thing if they can. If you don't ask he definitely won't bring it up himself. But at his age, and as the son of a cadre, if he says you're the first I wouldn't quite believe it.' Her mother hesitated before asking, 'Has he ever asked you back to his room on his own?'

'No, he has lots of roommates.'

'Is he normally ... disciplined when he's with you? He hasn't ... stroked or touched you, has he?'

The words 'stroked' and 'touched' nearly made Jingqiu vomit. How can Mother use such horrible words about Old Third? But she thought carefully. Had he been disciplined? Apart from the time when he had been too forward on the mountain, he had been very disciplined, and he had never 'stroked' or 'touched' her. He had held her, and had rested his head on her chest, but he had never stroked her chest, or anywhere else for that matter.

'No,' she said firmly.

Her mother let out a long breath and explained, 'A young girl should have backbone, there are some things that you should only do after you're married, and before that you should say no, firmly. It doesn't matter how nice he is to you, nor what promises he makes, you must say no. He can promise you the world, but as soon as you do it he won't respect you, he'll think you're nothing. When that happens the power is all his, if he wants you he can have you, but if he wants to dump you it'll be nearly impossible to find another boyfriend.'

Jingqiu really wanted her mother to explain more clearly what those things were that you couldn't do until you were married, but she couldn't find the words to ask, so instead she pretended not to be interested.

'Ah,' her mother sighed. 'I always thought you understood how things are, I never imagined you'd get involved in all this so soon. These days they are promoting a policy of later marriages and you're only eighteen, so even if you marry at twenty-three you've still got four or five years to wait. If he clings on so tightly then . . . things can easily happen between you two, and your reputation will be ruined.'

Her mother followed this with numerous examples of 'ruined' girls: Little Wang who worked at No. 8 Middle School's factory had originally been part of the city song and dance ensemble, as had been his girlfriend of the time. They were not yet married but she got pregnant, and when their work unit found out Little Wang was demoted to factory work and the girl was sent to work in No. 3 Middle School's factory. Everyone knew about their bad behaviour, so now they scarcely dared show their faces around town.

Then there was Mrs Zhao, a teacher at the same school as Jingqiu's mother. She gave birth only seven months after she got married, and although she had not been punished, people had looked down on her since. Then there was . . . .

Jingqiu knew every one of these 'ruined' girls, and they had all received various punishments for getting pregnant out of wedlock, or some other misdemeanour. Whenever anyone spoke of them they would curl their lips and speak in disparaging tones.

'Lucky I found out before it was too late, otherwise who knows what might have happened. Don't have any more contact with him. Spoiled sons of officials like him are experts at playing with girls' feelings. He hasn't got his prize yet so he's chasing you with all he's got, but once he's got you he'll tire of you in a heartbeat. And even if he doesn't tire of you his family will never agree to it … And even if they agree, you're so young, and he's already … so mature. I think he'll struggle to get through the next four or five years. Something will happen sooner or later.'

Chapter Twenty-nine

The next day Jingqiu went to the paper factory to give in her notice. Hunchback Wan was, surprisingly, very polite. 'I'll calculate your hours at once and you can take the note yourself to Director Li, that way you won't have to worry about it.' This was exactly what had been troubling Jingqiu. If it hadn't been for her concerns that hunchback Wan might not give her her hours, she wouldn't have come all the way to give in her notice. She took the form Mr Wan had written for her, said thank you, and left his office.

Jingqiu had also wanted to say thank you to Zhang Yi but he was working the day shift, as one of his roommates had informed her on the bus. As she was leaving she bumped into Mr Liu so she thanked him, and reminded him about her brother. Mr Liu promised he wouldn't forget.

Once back at home she took over preparations for the evening meal, letting her sister go out to play with Zhong Qin. She boiled the mung bean congee and then lay down on her bed to think. She was very worried about Old Third's cut. It must have been very deep, otherwise why would he need two stitches? She wasn't too worried about the fact that his blood wasn't clotting properly as the doctor was always saying the same about her mother, that she had 'a reduced platelet count'. As soon as she bumped herself she would bruise, so she was often green and purple all over. Jingqiu hadn't inherited the problem, but neither did it seem very serious.

Yet, some fears lingered as she recalled the scene of Old Third slicing his hand; how could he have been so quick? She had seen him take out his knife, but before she could ask what he was doing he had cut himself. He was crazy, but she was willing to excuse it as a moment of desperation.

She had not dared tell her mother about the money Old Third left the previous evening because she already sensed that the more her mother knew about Old Third, the more things she found to criticise. If her mother knew that Old Third had given her money she would definitely say he was using it as bait.

Jingqiu stayed at home the whole day, and the next she accompanied her mother to the other side of the river to glue envelopes. Her mother had not agreed at first, saying that she needed to rest her feet a little longer, but for some reason suddenly changed her mind and took Jingqiu with her, showing her how to glue the envelopes. Jingqiu was a fast learner, working at great speed. The neighbourhood committee had rules about how much work they would assign, and as her mother had a pension they would only let her earn a small supplement based on the proportion of her earnings that she had lost. This meant that her mother could only take home around seventeen yuan a month.

Now that Jingqiu knew how to paste envelopes, and where to collect and return the goods, she told her mother to rest at home, and not go all the way to the neighbourhood committee to do the work. Secretly, she was hatching a plan: if her mother didn't come, when Old Third visited she could go swimming with him and tell her mother she had been at the neighbourhood committee, gluing envelopes. But her mother seemed to be able to read her mind and insisted upon coming, even bringing Jingqiu's little sister. Every day mother and her two daughters got up early and crossed the river while the sun was not yet too high. Then, once they had finished gluing the day's envelopes, the three of them would walk back home together.

Her mother didn't offer any more stern words of wisdom, but walked around with a serious expression on her face, as if about to oversee a defensive campaign. Even when Jingqiu and her sister went to the river to swim, her mother came along and sat on the bank, watching them. She was one step behind when they went to cool down in the evening breeze; the three of them would sit together by the river, their mother in the middle, a fan in her hand, swatting away the mosquitoes for her daughters. Sometimes Jingqiu would get a strange feeling, as if Old Third were like the naughty monkey Sun Wukong from *Journey to the West*, using his magical powers to change into a mosquito so that he could whisper in her ear. But her mother swatted and swatted him, until he flew off.

Twice Jingqiu thought she saw him; he seemed to be following them. But when she got the chance to turn around and look properly he was nowhere in sight. She had no idea if she had been seeing things, or if he had hidden, afraid that her mother might spot him.

One day the headmaster Mr Wang asked Jingqiu to go work at the cardboard factory; he had recommended her as soon as his son had mentioned that they were hiring workers. Jingqiu was immensely grateful, thinking that she could finally slip her mother's tight surveillance. But despite the fact that her mother would no longer be following her like a shadow, Jingqiu would still not be able to move freely as one of the teachers at No. 8 Middle School, Mrs Li, was sending her daugher Li Hong to work there too. She was a year younger than Jingqiu, and this was her first job, so Mrs Li had asked

Jingqiu to take her to and from the factory every day. It was as if her mother had hit upon treasure, and she replied at once on Jingqiu's behalf that she would.

The two of them talked and chatted merrily all the way to the factory. But deep down, Jingqiu's mind kept drifting to thoughts of whether or not Old Third would come to Yichang, and if he saw her with Li Hong, would he dare come up to her? A few times she thought of shaking off Li Hong, but she couldn't think of an excuse. And now her mother was getting better at gluing envelopes, she managed to finish and get home before Jingqiu; by the time she got back her mother would often be standing by the ferry or at the school gate, waiting for her.

Gradually Jingqiu gave up hope, and instead she focused on the beginning of term again in September. The education bureau took another two weeks before they finalised arrangements for Jingqiu's new job in the school's kitchens. Her place of work was now only one step away from her front door, in the canteen opposite.

Apart from the fact that she couldn't see Old Third, life for Jingqiu was getting better, reaching higher, like sunflowers nourished by the sun. The first happy event was when she started to draw a salary. That day, the director of the general affairs department, Mr Zhao, came personally to tell Jingqiu her first paypacket was ready.

'Jingqiu, you started after the fifteenth, so you'll only get half a month's wages for September,' he said with a smile. To Jingqiu he sounded almost apologetic, but this was already more than she had expected; it had nearly been the end of the month when she started and yet the school was giving her half a month's wages!

Mr Zhao gave her an envelope which contained nearly fifteen yuan as well as a small piece of paper half an inch wide by eight inches long: her wage slip. She took it out and read it over several times to check. It really did have her name on it. The thought that from now on she would collect a slip of paper like this every month made her so excited she knew she wouldn't be able to sleep that night.

She gave all her wages to her mother for the family to use, as well as to save for her brother Xin's wedding, or at the very least so that he would have money to buy Yamin's family a present at New Year. Until now, Yamin had always bought the present and given it to Xin to take to her family, but each year Yamin's father threw it out of the front door. Yamin reassured Xin that lots of girls' parents didn't agree to a match at first, but time usually wore them down.

Yamin's prediction soon came true, because at last Xin was called back to Yichang to work in a state-owned factory. Yamin was thrilled, and went out to buy a New Year present for him to take to her parents, despite the fact that it was a long time before New Year and Xin had yet to start his new job.

All Yamin's parents' objections melted away when they realised that he had been called back to the city, and to such a large factory at that. Not only did the present not get hurtled out the door, but Xin was even invited in to eat with them. Her brother had finally passed the first test for sons-in-law, and he was honoured with the new job of being Yamin's coolie. All the heavy work in the house, such as buying coal, rice and firewood, was left to him from then on. It had been a struggle for him to be entrusted with this heavy work, so he was happy to do it.

Sometimes, just as he had sat down to eat, Yamin would call, 'Xin, Mum wants you to go and buy coal.' Without a word in protest he would put down his chopsticks and head out. Jingqiu's mother teased her son: 'If I were to ask you to do anything you'd drag your feet all right, but as soon as Yamin's parents say anything, you jump up at once.'

'What can I do?' he laughed in response. 'That's the fashion these days. Jingqiu, why don't you hurry up and get someone to carry the family's coal.'

'Don't make stupid jokes!' her mother snapped. 'Jingqiu's job isn't yet permanent, don't go ruining her chances just so we can have someone carry the coal.'

Her brother's unexpected success made Jingqiu twitch with excitement, and she started to draw up in her mind a blueprint for Old Third to achieve the same. Most probably they'd have to wait until she had been made permanent, then her mother wouldn't have so much to worry about, and she and Old Third would be able to spend time together in public just like Yamin and her brother. Old Third would then collect the family's coal. The thought of it was funny; her brother collected the coal for Yamin's family and Old Third for hers. But who would get the coal for Old Third's family?

Suddenly it seemed as if they couldn't keep good fortune from knocking on their door. The headmaster, Mr Wang, revealed some important inside information to Jingqiu's mother. He had suggested to the school that when the time was right they might let Jingqiu teach instead of work in the kitchens. Because the area around No. 8 Primary and Middle Schools was cut off by the river, very few people agreed to be transferred there from the city. It was the kind of place that the Bureau of Culture and Education sent either teachers who had committed some misdemeanour, or else naive young teachers from the teacher training college, who as soon as they figured out the situation, got themselves transferred elsewhere. The schools were always short of teachers. They could use this excuse to petition the Bureau of Culture and Education to let Jingqiu become a teacher.

'Tell your Jingqiu to behave herself, and you go and try to influence some of the other senior staff at the school.'

Even though Jingqiu had officially replaced her mother the school still treated her as a child, and everything went through her mother. Her mother went to see the school's leaders and begged them to let Jingqiu teach when the situation allowed. A few of them made promises. They knew Jingqiu had had good marks and was good teacher-material, it was just a matter of time before they would let her teach, she needn't worry. 'But just now, she's only just started work and she's not the only one who's replaced their parent. If we let her start teaching now other people might have something to say about it. We have to wait until it won't cause trouble.'

Jingqiu was ecstatic to hear this latest piece of news, and was desperate to tell Old Third at once. But she had heard nothing from him since the day he left. She grew more nervous by the day; she couldn't work out why he wasn't coming to see her. There were three possible reasons, she thought. The first was that he had contracted tetanus but she reassured herself that should Old Third have died of tetanus Fang would have told her. The second was that Old Third was keeping the promise he had made her mother, and that he was waiting for her position to be made permanent before visiting. But he had also acknowledged his planned deceit. 'So, it turns out I'm a traitor,' he had said. Had he subsequently decided not to be a traitor after all?

There was one more possibility, that her mother's interrogation had angered him so much that he wasn't going to come back. She knew of many such stories, where the girls' parents were so harsh towards their future son-in-laws that the young men stormed off in anger. When she thought of this third possibility she started to get angry herself. If he ran away because of that discussion he'd definitely failed the test.

But then she thought that perhaps he was waiting for her, suffering even. Perhaps he often came to Yichang to see her but just didn't have the chance to speak to her. This thought made her angry with her mother. My brother was my age when he had a girlfriend, why are you singling me out to be watched so closely?

After working a while in the canteen, Jingqiu was informed that she was being sent to the school's farm for six months. If she didn't go people would object to her becoming a teacher. If she did go, however, there would be nothing they could say.

The school had just set up a farm in a small village called Fujia Plateau, just beyond Yanjia River, in order for students to take turns working on it. The reason for choosing Fujia Plateau was because one of the heads of the school, Mr Zheng, was from the village, and it was only due to this connection that the village had agreed to give the school some land, and had even helped them construct some buildings.

The school sent a few teachers to the farm, along with Jingqiu. The women were to take charge of the meals and the men were to lead the students in their physical labour. This first group was the vanguard, preparing the farm for the other students' arrival. Jingqiu was overjoyed to be sent as it meant that she could escape her mother's close surveillance and, furthermore, West Village was only a few kilometres away from Fujia Plateau, so she would be very close to Old Third.

Her mother was a bit nervous but she wasn't nearly as worried as she would have been if Jingqiu had been properly sent down. Jingqiu had a job, and after six months she would be back and teaching. Moreover, she was going with other teachers, so her mother was relatively confident about the arrangement. Most importantly, though, her mother didn't know how close Fujia Plateau was to West Village.

Mr Zheng took this first group to the farm. They were accompanied by a young female teacher in her twenties, Miss Zhao, and another male teacher in his forties, Mr Jian, who had previously taught Jingqiu physics and had often played volleyball with her team. Mr Jian was not tall, but he had previously been a gymnast so his arms were strong, and he often did forward rolls when catching the ball, gaining cheers of admiration from the girls.

Not far from the farm, on the other side of the mountain, a road big enough to drive the smallest tractor along wound its way down to a small town called Chrysanthemum Field, from which buses left for Yanjia River. The school had one of these small tractors, the type known as 'Little Hauler', which they used to transport goods to market. The young man in his twenties who drove the tractor was called Zhou Jianxin or 'Little Zhou'. His father was headmaster of Yichang's No. 12 Middle School. Little Zhou wasn't sent down after graduation due to a heart condition, and instead learnt to operate these tractors. Jingqiu had seen Little Zhou transporting goods before, usually when she was working in a factory as part of her school work. Later, once she started working in the school's kitchens, she used to see him regularly, his face covered in engine oil, tinkering with a 'Little Hauler', encircled by a group of small children watching him while he desperately tried to jig it back to life using a crank.

Little Zhou was not only called Jianxin – just like Old Third – but he also looked a bit like him. They were of similar height, although Little Zhou was a bit skinnier, his skin a little darker, and his back wasn't as straight. They shared one special characteristic, however: when they laughed their whole faces would crinkle up.

The four teachers, including Jingqiu, took the bus from Yichang to Yanjia River and from there they walked to Fujia

Plateau and then to Chrysanthemum Field. On the walk up the mountain, the teachers sang a series of songs known as the Songs of the Long March, and as there were no other people on the mountain even the more shy among them gathered their courage and really let go, singing at the tops of their voices. Little Zhou drove the tractor the thirty or so kilometres from the school although he had to stop just short of the farm as the road ahead had yet to be repaired.

The buildings on the farm were basic. The sleeping quarters had earth floors that had not even been flattened, but were just made from clods of earth. There was no glass in the windows, nor was anything put to cover them, so they used bamboo hats. The beds were made from heaped-up earth with a couple of wooden boards laid on top. Jingqiu and Miss Zhao shared a room, and as there were no bolts across the door, they propped a large wooden stick against it in lieu of a lock.

The first thing they did was build a toilet by digging a hole and resting two planks across it. Then they stuck a few poles made from a nearby sorghum tree in rows into the ground, creating walls on all sides. According to legend, a dangerous animal that the local people called a *balangzi* stalked this part of the mountain, and it especially liked to attack people who were doing their business at night. It would come up to you and lick your bottom with its tongue, which was covered in long quills, before it gouged out your intestines and gorged on them. Everyone carried an axe with them whenever they went to the toilet for fear of such an encounter. People did their utmost to avoid going after dark, and if they really couldn't avoid it, the men would run round the back of the house and relieve themselves there. Jingqiu always needed to go once or twice in the evenings, so she had no choice but to brave the couple of hundred metres to the toilet, axe in hand.

Little Zhou also lived at the front of the building and if he didn't close his door he could see when Jingqiu went out. She soon discovered that every time she came back from the toilet Little Zhou would be standing by the path, smoking, perfectly positioned so that she wouldn't feel awkward and yet were anything to happen he could run up to save her. When she walked past they would greet each other and walk back to the building, one behind and one in front.

The first days after they arrived there were no vegetables on the mountain for them to eat, so everyone brought out their own private supplies. When the weather was clear they would all go to collect wild onions and wild garlic, and when it was raining they went picking *dijianpi*, a sort of black fungus they cleaned and fried. Miss Zhao and Mr Jian would always go off together leaving Jingqiu on her own, but before long Little Zhou would appear and they would work together.

Life was hard on the farm, but the teachers were lively and witty, so for Jingqiu the days passed quickly. During the day they worked and in the evening, before going to sleep, they would gather and tell stories. Jingqiu discovered that Mr Jian was particularly good at telling historical stories, Mr Zheng and Mrs Zhao were better at folk tales, and Little Zhou's speciality was stories involving Sherlock Holmes.

Once they were more or less finished with their preparations the farm welcomed its first group of students. Their first task was to repair the road up on the mountain so that the tractor could drive all the way up to the L-shaped building on the farm. Once they finished Little Zhou and his tractor became regular features of the landscape. He loved wearing an old army uniform with a pattern of wrinkles that seemed to suggest he might be stuffing it in the pickling barrel every evening before bed. The army hat he wore was a sort of floppy cap, and looked like the ones the soldiers of the routed Nationalist army used to wear. He was very focused when driving, riding at lightning speed, leaping up and down in his seat like an unstoppable force, before screeching to a halt at the kitchen door. As soon as the students heard the 'du-du-du' sound of his tractor they poured out of their rooms. The tractor was their only connection to the outside world.

As usual, Little Zhou's face was smeared with engine oil, a look that had almost become a badge of his professionalism and skill. Sometimes Jingqiu would point to the oil on his face, and he would wipe it with his sleeve, more often than not spreading it still more widely across his cheeks. Jingqiu would double over in laughter and he would lean towards her so that she could wipe it for him, startling her into running away.

The five adults worked well together. At regular intervals either Jingqiu or Miss Zhao would ride with Little Zhou on his tractor to buy vegetables and rice. After a couple of times Miss Zhao said she didn't want to go any more, she couldn't stand the smell of diesel oil, and after a few kilometres of du-du-du her bottom came out in blisters. Jingqiu was not bothered by the smell so she went instead. They would leave after breakfast and try their best to be back in the afternoon in time to make the students' dinner so that Miss Zhao wouldn't have to do it on her own.

Since she and Little Zhou got to know each other quite well, she decided to ask him to drive her to West Village. She wanted to know what Old Third was doing. So the next time they went to buy vegetables she asked him if they could make a detour so that she could give a book back to a friend.

'Is your friend a girl or a boy?' he asked.

'What does it matter?' Jingqiu asked in return.

'I'll take you if it's a girl, if it's a boy I won't,' he shot back, grinning from ear to ear.

'Forget it, if you think it's inconvenient.'

Little Zhou had made no mention of it being inconvenient. After they had bought the rice they started out on their return journey but he kept stopping to speak to people on the road. Jingqiu had no idea what he was up to so when he said, 'We've arrived at West Village, where do you want to go?' her mind was all of a muddle. She had never approached West Village by this road before. She stood for a long time trying to get her bearings before eventually pointing in the direction of the geological unit: 'It should be that way.'

Little Zhou drove the tractor right up to the unit's sheds, stopped and said, 'I'll wait for you here, but if you take too long I'll come running in to save you.'

Jingqiu told him, 'No need, I'll be out at once,' and walked over to the sheds, her heart thumping so fast she thought it would jump out of her mouth. She took a deep breath and knocked on Old Third's door, holding the book she had taken as cover. She stood for some time, waiting, but no one answered. She realised that Old Third was probably working. She was disappointed, but she was not going to give up, so she went from room to room to see if someone could tell her where he was. She couldn't find a single soul.

She went back to Old Third's room, and with almost all hope of finding him gone she knocked one last time. To her surprise, the door opened. A man came to the door, whom she recognised as the middle-aged man she had met the last time she came. She glanced into the room and saw a woman combing her hair; she looked as if she had just got out of bed.

The man recognised Jingqiu. 'Hi, "mung bean soup", isn't it?'

'Is she your "mung bean soup"?' the woman asked, as she came to the door.

The man laughed. 'No, she's Sun's. I said that eating venison stoked the old fires, and she said a bit of mung bean soup would sort it out.' He laughed again.

Jingqiu didn't care what they were talking about. 'Do you know when he gets off work?'

'He? Who d'you mean?' the man joked.

'Do you know Old Cai here?' the woman asked, pointing at the man. 'He's my husband. I've come for a visit, and I've only just arrived today. You must have been here a while, do you know if my Cai has any mung bean soup of his own in the village? They're all having things on the side, not one of them's decent or honest, got one in each village, they have.'

'Sun's been transferred,' he said, ignoring his wife. 'Didn't you know?'

'Where did he get transferred?'

'To the second unit.'

Jingqiu was struck dumb, how could he be transferred and not tell her? She stood rooted to the spot, before eventually plucking up the courage to ask, 'Do you know ... where the second unit is based?'

Cai's wife tugged at his sleeve. 'Don't go causing trouble. This Sun belongs to someone else, if he'd wanted her to know, wouldn't he have told her? Be careful not to stir up trouble.'

'You've got it all wrong,' Jingqiu stuttered awkwardly. 'I just wanted to give him back this book. I've disturbed you ...' With that she ran away.

Little Zhou saw her return, out of sorts, and asked her a few times if she was okay, but she didn't reply. They had already started cooking when they got back to the farm, so Jingqiu ran straight to the kitchen to lend a hand. After they had finished serving the students and the teachers were sitting down to eat, however, her head started hurting and she completely lost her appetite, so she made her excuses and went to her room to sleep.

Chapter Thirty

The next day, Little Zhou wanted to go with her to fetch the water, but Jingqiu refused. 'Don't, you've got heart problems, you shouldn't be collecting the water.'

'My heart problems came about because I was scared to be sent down, that's all, let me help you. You're always the one who collects the water, why doesn't Miss Zhao ever do it?'

This had never occurred to Jingqiu; when the water ran out she just went to get more. But she was worried that people might not approve if Little Zhou helped her, so she insisted, 'Look, I'll do it, okay?'

'Do you think people will gossip?' he laughed. 'In that case you shouldn't have gone to lie down instead of eating your dinner. Any gossip now isn't going to match yesterday's.'

'What were they saying yesterday?'

'That we got up to things on our drive yesterday . . . '

'What exactly were they saying?'

'That I did you, of course,' he grinned cheekily.

Jingqiu felt faint; she thought she knew what 'doing someone' meant. 'Who . . . who said that?' she said, shaking. 'I want to speak to them.'

'No, don't,' Little Zhou said. 'If you go asking them I won't tell you anything ever again.'

'Why would they say such things?'

'We were back late yesterday, and you were in a strange

mood. Then you didn't eat but went straight to bed. Not to mention the fact that I have a reputation for being a bit of a rascal, so it's no wonder they jumped to that conclusion. But I already explained, so you don't need to say anything more. The bigger deal you make of it, the more people will talk.'

'Then, did you say where we went yesterday?' Jingqiu was extremely nervous.

'Of course not, relax. I may be a rascal, but I have my own sense of honour.' Then a grin spread again across his face, and he continued, 'Anyway, with you being so pretty it'd be worth me getting a bad reputation . . . '

Jingqiu was starting to suspect that it might all just be Little Zhou talking it up. He had always loved to suggest something was going on, saying that other people were gossiping about them. She didn't say any more. She started out to collect the water, but he pulled at her shoulder pole and wouldn't let her leave. 'What exactly was going on yesterday? Were you visiting your boyfriend? He wasn't there, or was he hiding from you?'

'Don't go making wild guesses, there's no boyfriend . . . ' She thought for a moment and then asked, 'Do you know what "mung bean soup" means?' She explained the circumstances behind the first time she heard the phrase, and added some selected passages from her conversation with Old Cai and his wife.

'Don't you understand anything?' Little Zhou looked at her. 'They're talking about when a man feels hot, when he wants to . . . do it to a woman. But you didn't get it, and told them to eat some mung bean soup to cool off. Do you think mung bean soup helps for that kind of fire? They were laughing at you for being so stupid.'

'Forget it,' she muttered. 'I can't be sure with you, I don't get what you're talking about, and you don't understand what it is I'm asking.'

Jingqiu had not yet recovered from her sulk since returning from West Village and after hearing Little Zhou's explanation of the meaning of mung bean soup she descended even deeper into it. So, Old Third was two-faced, and had been all along; to her face he acted like their relationship was sacred, yet behind her back he was talking about her in this way with his friends. It was disgusting. He went without saying anything, and he didn't even try to tell me, she thought, making me go all the way there for nothing, to be humiliated and set everyone talking.

The problem was she couldn't be sure that Old Third really was like that, it could all be a misunderstanding. The thing she was most afraid of was that she might never find out, that she would be kept guessing and in a state of fear and anxiety. No matter how bad the situation was, as long as everything was brought out into the open, there would be nothing to be scared. She decided that the next time she went to Yanjia River with Little Zhou to do the shopping she would visit Fang at the middle school and ask for Old Third's address, then she would ask Little Zhou to take her there so that Old Third could explain what was going on, to her face.

But Mr Zheng never sent her to do the shopping with Little Zhou again. When they needed anything he called on Miss Zhao to go or else went himself. Not only that, but when he went back to the school to report on their work he told Jingqiu's mother about what had happened with Little Zhou. Her mother immediately wrote a letter for Mr Zheng to take back to the farm.

When Jingqiu saw her mother's letter she felt dizzy. How come everyone loves to make something out of nothing? Can't it just be that two people went out to buy rice and were just a bit late coming back? Do they really need to see hidden meaning in it? But it was not easy for her to get angry as these people were all her former teachers, and she still greatly respected them.

She pondered the problem from all angles but she couldn't accept what was being implied, so she ran to find Mr Zheng. 'Mr Zheng, if you think I have done anything wrong you can tell me to my face, don't tell my mother. She is a nervous person, these rumours will only make her sick.'

'I only did it for your own good. Little Zhou has a violent temper and is an ignorant boy. What are his good points exactly?'

Jingqiu said, wounded by the injustice of it all, 'But we are not ... boyfriend and girlfriend. We've only had contact because of our work, why did you have to go suggesting all of that?'

Mr Zheng did not answer her question and instead said, 'The thing is, our school has lots of good comrades, such as Mr Quan from your volleyball team. He's a good man, he's made a lot of progress over the last few years, he's joined the Party, been promoted to cadre, he's honest and dependable ...'

Jingqiu couldn't believe her ears, everyone was always telling her she was too young and that she shouldn't be thinking about this sort of thing and now Mr Zheng was suggesting that she should find herself a nice young comrade then she could start thinking about this sort of thing. He seemed to be saying, I told your mother not because you shouldn't have a boyfriend, but because you shouldn't have *that* boyfriend. She was too scared to say anything more apart from repeat her innocence, before heading back to her room.

Part of her also found it quite amusing; before, when she was in junior middle school, she had had some feelings for Mr Quan, especially when he had first come to No. 8 Middle School. He was young and inexperienced, and as none of the students were scared of him they would often tease. But after that he started to get friends in high places. She didn't know why, but from the moment Mr Quan started to climb his way upwards in status she rather stopped liked him, maybe because she liked underdogs the best. Now, hearing Mr Zheng speak like that about him, she was starting to detest her former teacher. It was almost as if he was using his connections in order to push Little Zhou aside and get ahead.

She had planned to remain friendly towards Little Zhou, while distancing herself from him in order to avoid more gossip, but after seeing Mr Zheng put him down just to promote another teacher, she began to sympathise with Little Zhou. He was only a temporary worker, and she was reminded of her own time as a temp. Furthermore, he preferred to have a bad reputation rather than reveal what exactly had happened that day they came back late. She respected his 'honourable rascal' code of ethics.

A few days later it rained heavily, damaging the huts on the farm and the mountain road. Mr Zheng used this as an excuse to ask Mr Quan to come from Yichang to help for a week on the farm. Jingqiu didn't have an ounce of feeling for Mr Quan, she couldn't even be bothered speaking to him, so when they bumped into each other she only greeted him quickly and went on.

It was not until the last week of November that Jingqiu had another opportunity to leave the farm with Little Zhou, this time because the students had not brought enough money for their mess fee and they were fast running out of rice. They couldn't let the students run back home to collect more money so Mr Zheng had no option but to send a teacher to go from door to door collecting ration tickets. Miss Zhao knew that this was a terrible job that would result in aggravation from the parents, it would be hard work with no reward in other words, so she made excuses and it was left to Jingqiu to do it.

Mr Zheng called Jingqiu to one side and spent ages warning her of the dangers, before eventually allowing her to return with Little Zhou to Yichang to 'collect their debts'. Once they had finished collecting the money, they were to buy rice in the city, and Little Zhou would take it back to the farm. She, in the meanwhile, could take two days' holiday.

Little Zhou was also aware that Mr Zheng was purposefully keeping them apart, and he complained a great deal about it on the way. As she listened to him she started to form a plan. Once they got to Yanjia River she asked Little Zhou to stop, saying that she wanted to see a friend and it would only take a couple of minutes.

'Boy or girl?'

'Girl,' she replied firmly.

'If it's a boy again, I'm coming in for a fight,' he joked. 'Last time it got me a bad reputation, I'm not going along with it this time.'

Once they arrived at Yanjia River she asked where the middle school was. Luckily it was not a big town so the school was located close to the main road. Little Zhou drove the tractor to the school and switched off the engine. 'This time I don't have anything in the tractor, so I don't need to watch over it. I'll come with you.'

Jingqiu wouldn't let him come, which only caused him to be more curious. 'Didn't you say it was a female friend? Why won't you let me come? Are you afraid that your friend will take a liking to me?'

There was no way to win against him. The more she tried, the more he talked, and anyway, she was about to ask him to drive to the second unit so she wouldn't be able to hide anything from him. She gave up, and let him come with her into the school. They stood under one of the school's trees, waiting for the school bell. Jingqiu asked a pupil where Fang's classroom was, and then she asked someone else to ask her to come out.

Fang looked at Jingqiu, then at Little Zhou, and said sadly, 'Brother is in the county hospital, can't you go and visit him? You may not want him any more, but . . . you could at least be a friend to him. Go and see him, it's . . . terminal.'

Jingqiu was extremely upset Lin had contracted a terminal illness. She wanted to explain that it wasn't that she didn't want him, it was just that she didn't love him, but the word 'terminal' scared her stiff, she couldn't get the words out. 'Do you know which ward he's in?' she asked quietly.

Fang wrote the address of the hospital and the number of his ward on a piece of paper and gave it to her, then stood, silent, her eyes filled with tears. Jingqiu also stood in silence, then asked carefully, 'Do you know what it is he's got?'

'Leukaemia.'

Jingqiu felt that it would be an inappropriate moment to ask for Old Third's new address, and even if she asked she wouldn't have time to go. It would be better to sort it out after she had been to visit Lin.

The school bell rang again and Fang whispered, 'I'm going back to my classroom. You go by yourself . . . don't take your friend.' Jingqiu was frozen to the spot.

'Who's sick?' Little Zhou asked. 'Your face has turned as white as a ghost . . . '

'It's her older brother. I used to live with them, I want to go and see him, he helped me a lot. Do you know how you get leukaemia?'

'I heard someone say that it only appeared after the atomic bomb, but someone at my school had it and died from it. Apparently it's . . . incurable.'

'Then let's go quickly.'

They rushed to the local county town and bought some

fruit, before they found the county hospital as Fang's note had described. Jingqiu recalled that Fang had instructed her to go alone so she negotiated with Little Zhou. 'Could you wait for me outside?'

'You won't let me come in? He's got a terminal illness, what are you afraid of?'

Jingqiu had also not quite understood why Fang had said that. 'I don't know what they're worried about either, but my friend said that we shouldn't, so perhaps you should wait outside anyway.'

Little Zhou had no choice but to wait outside, but he warned her, 'Don't be too long, we still have to get back. You've got to collect money today, and if we're late and you don't get the money we won't be able to buy the rice . . .'

'I know,' Jingqiu said, and then ran into the hospital.

Chapter Thirty-One

The county hospital was quite small and it was made up of only a few buildings, so Jingqiu quickly found the ward. It had four beds. She was surprised to see Old Third sitting on one, writing in a notebook. What's he doing here? Is he looking after Lin? Why isn't he at work? Perhaps the second unit is nearby, and he got transferred so that he could look after Lin?

Old Third looked up, and a startled expression came across his face. He put down his notebook and pen and walked over to her. He didn't invite her in, but stood in the corridor. 'Is it . . . really you?'

'What about Lin?'

'Lin?' he asked, surprised. 'Isn't he in West Village?'

'Fang said her brother was in the hospital . . . '

'Oh,' he smiled, 'I'm her brother too . . . '

Jingqiu's heart missed a beat. 'How are you her brother? She said her brother was ill, she didn't say you were ill. You must be here looking after Lin? Aren't you? Don't joke around. Where's Lin?'

'You're . . . here to see Lin? You wouldn't come if it wasn't Lin . . . ?'

'You know I don't mean it like that. Why did Fang say I didn't want you? That's why I thought she meant Lin, because she knows I didn't want him.'

'Oh. I wrote a few letters to you at the farm, but they were all sent back. I used Fang's address, and they all went back to her, so she said you don't want me any more.'

'You wrote to me at the farm? Why didn't I get a single letter? What address did you use?'

'I wrote, Yichang No. 8 Middle School Farm, Fujia Plateau Production Team, Yanjia River Commune, Yiling. I also put your name on the envelope. All the letters came back with "Person unknown, return to sender" written on them.'

Jingqiu thought that it must have been Mr Zheng's doing, because he was trying to set her up with Mr Quan. What despicable methods! But he wrote Fang's name on the letters, so why would Mr Zheng have suspected they were from a boy? Could he tell that it was a boy's writing? Or did he open the letters and read them?

'What did you write in the letters? You didn't write anything I should be worried about, did you? It must have been our Mr Zheng that did it, I'm worried he might have ... opened them and read them.'

'He can't have. If he'd opened them I would have been able to tell.'

She was starting to be very angry with Mr Zheng. 'Isn't it against the law to go around secretly reading other people's letters? I'm going to have a word with him when I get back, see if he really has the guts.'

'Why would your teacher be interested in your letters? Does he ... have those sorts of feelings for you?'

'No way,' she reassured him. 'He's old, and married. He's acting on someone else's behalf.'

'The guy who drives the tractor?'

'How do you know about the guy who drives the tractor?' she asked, looking at him in surprise.

'I saw you two together,' he smiled, 'in Yanjia River. It was raining and he lent you his raincoat.'

'It's not him, Mr Zheng hates him. It's another teacher, the one who taught us volleyball. But don't worry, I don't like him. What were you doing in Yanjia River?'

'The second unit is nearby, I often go there during our lunch break to wander around in the hope that I might bump into you.'

'Have you been to our farm?'

He nodded. 'I saw you once cooking, barefoot.'

'The roof leaks in there. As soon as it rains the ground is mud soup for a week. Barefoot is the only way.' Thinking this might worry him she added, 'But it's colder now, so I wear my rubber boots. Haven't you seen me in them?'

He looked sad. 'I haven't been for a while.'

She was too scared to look at him. 'What's . . . wrong with you?' She was extremely anxious, afraid that he would say the terrible word.

'Nothing, just a cold.'

She exhaled slowly, but she didn't quite believe him. 'You're in hospital for a cold?'

'People do if it's bad.' He laughed quietly. 'I'm a glass whistle, remember? I'm always getting colds. Are you going home or back to the farm? How long can you stay?'

'I'm heading home, and I have to go now. A colleague is waiting for me, I need to collect money so we can buy rice.' She saw the disappointed look on his face and promised to come back. 'I'll be back the day after tomorrow. I've got two days of holiday, so I can leave home a day early.'

His eyes filled with happiness. Then he began to worry. 'Aren't you worried your mother will find out? '

'She won't find out.' She wasn't actually that sure, but she couldn't worry about that too. 'You won't leave over the next few days, will you?'

'I'll wait for you here.' He rushed back into the ward,

grabbed a paper bag and stuffed it into her hands. 'Such good timing, I bought it yesterday. See if you like it.'

She opened the bag and took a peek. Inside was a length of hawthorn-red corduroy with small black flowers embroidered on it. 'This is my favourite colour and type of material, it's like you read my mind.'

'I knew you would like it,' he said proudly. 'When I saw it yesterday I had to buy it, but I never guessed that you would come the next day. You make something from it and let me see it when you next come.'

He walked her to the main entrance and saw Little Zhou and his tractor in the distance. 'Your colleague is waiting, I'll stay here so he doesn't see me. What's his name?'

'He's got the same name as you, but his last name is Zhou.'

'As long as he doesn't have the same fate too.'

'What ... do you mean by that?' she stuttered.

'Nothing. I'm just ... jealous. I hope he's not chasing you too.'

As they drove to Yichang, Old Third's words echoed in her head, 'As long as he doesn't have the same fate too.' He may have explained, but she still felt that it wasn't jealousy he was talking about, but something else entirely.

Fang said that her brother had contracted a terminal illness, and it was true Old Third did not look too good. He was pale, but perhaps that was because he was wearing black. Yet he said that it was only a cold. Was it possible that, were he really terminally ill, he could be so calm and collected, as if nothing was wrong? And, if he was that ill, would the doctors tell him?

Fang must have been mistaken, or else she did it on purpose so that she would go visit Old Third. Fang thought that she didn't want him any more, so maybe she came up with this story to trick her into visiting him at the hospital. But what had he meant?

Once they arrived in Yichang, Little Zhou stopped the tractor before a restaurant. 'Let's eat first, it's better to wait until everyone's home from work before going to collect money.' She nodded, and gazed absent-mindedly as Little Zhou bought some food.

After they had finished eating, Little Zhou drove them to Jiangxin Island where he took them to each student's home, one by one, to collect the money. He asked her to give him the piece of paper with their addresses, and he took charge of navigation. For her, it was as if she was floating in a dream; she followed Little Zhou in a daze, first here then there. When he told her to keep the accounts she did so, when he asked her to find change she did so. He spoke to the parents while she stood dumbly by his side. Eventually, Little Zhou took the paper and money bag from her and organised the whole thing by himself.

They worked until past nine o'clock, when they had more or less collected all the money. Little Zhou took her home. 'I'll come tomorrow morning and we can go and buy the rice. Don't think about it too much, a county hospital can deal with leukaemia, pneumonia, whatever, right?' This startled her. Can Little Zhou tell I'm worried about Old Third? She told herself she mustn't look sad, in case her mother could tell.

Her mother was surprised but happy at her return, and hurried to make some food for her. But Jingqiu said she was not hungry, that she had already eaten. She took out the material Old Third had given her and started washing it first in cold water and then in hot in order to shrink it. Then she wrung it out and hung it up where the breeze could dry it quickly, so that she could make something from it as soon as possible.

Early the next morning Little Zhou came round early to collect her. Her mother was uneasy as she watched Jingqiu climb up on the tractor. Perhaps she was tempted to jump on too so that she could keep an eye on them. Jingqiu made a special effort to speak animatedly with Little Zhou because she was not afraid of her mother thinking there was something between them. In fact, the more she suspected the better. If her mother was taken up with worrying about Little Zhou she wouldn't be suspicious when Jingqiu went to visit Old Third the next day.

Once they had bought the rice Little Zhou drove her back home and gave her the receipt to keep safe. Then he left to deliver the rice back to the farm. With the danger gone, Jingqiu's mother relaxed and began to warn her daughter that she mustn't, under any circumstances, have anything to do with this Little Zhou.

In the afternoon Jingqiu went to the school to report on their progress at the farm. She also went to the homes of Mr Jian and Miss Zhao in order to collect their private supplies of pickles. Once everything was taken care of, she went to Mrs Jiang's house to borrow her sewing machine. She popped home in the evening for dinner before returning to Mrs Jiang's house to carry on sewing.

Once she had finished she still couldn't bring herself to leave, as if she still had some unfinished business, something she wanted to do but didn't dare. After a great deal of thought it occurred to her that she wanted to ask Dr Cheng about this leukaemia business. She crept up to his bedroom, the door was open, and she could see Mrs Jiang sitting reading, and Dr Cheng playing with their son on the bed.

'Jingqiu, have you finished sewing?' Mrs Jiang asked on seeing her.

Jingqiu nodded blankly, and then plucked up the courage to ask, 'Dr Cheng, have you ever heard of leukaemia?'

Dr Cheng gave their son to Mrs Jiang and moved to the side of the bed to talk to her. 'Who's got leukaemia?'

'A close friend.'

'Where were they diagnosed?'

'At Yiling hospital.'

'That hospital is very small, they might not have made the correct diagnosis.' Dr Cheng asked her to sit down, and reassured her, 'Don't worry, wait and see what it really is.'

Jingqiu couldn't explain, all she knew was what Fang had said. 'I don't know for sure what it is either, I just want to know if a young person can get ... that kind of disease?'

'Most people who get it are young, usually teenagers or those in their twenties, and perhaps young men more than women.'

'If ... you get it ... does that mean you'll definitely ... die?'

'Fatalities are ... rather high,' Dr Cheng said, choosing his words with care. 'But didn't you say they were examined at the county hospital? The county hospital is badly equipped, they are very constrained. Your friend should get themselves to the city or provincial hospital as soon as possible. You shouldn't worry yourself sick over an inconclusive diagnosis.'

'Didn't that happen at our school?' Mrs Jiang joined in. 'The hospital said this boy had cancer and scared him half to death, and in the end it wasn't. When it comes to these sorts of situations you won't find three hospitals that give the same diagnosis, you just can't trust them.'

Jingqiu sat in silence while Mrs Jiang and Dr Cheng continued to give examples of misdiagnoses, but she couldn't see that they had any relevance to her situation. 'If he really does have it, how long has he got?'

Dr Cheng bit his lips together nervously, as if afraid that the answer would fly out of the side of his mouth. She asked again and he replied, 'Didn't you say that he's only been to the county hospital?'

Jingqiu was so anxious she had to fight back the tears. 'I'm asking "if". If ... if ...'

'That depends . . . I . . . can't say how long exactly, it might be six months, it could be longer.'

Jingqiu got back home and started packing her things until she realised that it was already evening and there would be no buses to Yichang County until tomorrow. She lay on her bed and did what she did best: she prepared for the worst. As she didn't know whether it was the county hospital that had diagnosed him, her thoughts alternated between peaks of optimism and the deepest depths of despair. Such wild ups and downs were the most painful of all.

Now, if he had not been diagnosed by the county hospital, what would that mean? That he really did have leukaemia. If that was the case, then he would not have long to live. But how long was not long? When she was fourteen or so her mother had had an operation to remove a tumour from her uterus, and Jingqiu had looked after her. There had been a woman with late-stage ovarian cancer in the same ward who everybody called Granny Cao. She was as thin as a ghost, and spent most nights groaning in pain, so that no one else on the ward was able to sleep.

Then one day, Granny Cao's family came to take her home, and beaming with joy, she left. Jingqiu had envied her on her mother's behalf, thinking that Granny Cao was the first on the ward to be cured and allowed to leave. Only later did she hear from another patient that Granny Cao had been 'sent home to die'.

Old Third was still in hospital, so you could say he was being 'kept to live'. If he was discharged then she would ask her mother if he could come and stay with them. Her mother did like Old Third after all, she was only afraid of what others might say, or that his family would not approve the match. But if people knew that Old Third only had three months to live then surely there'd be nothing for them to say, it wouldn't matter if his family didn't approve, and nothing could possibly happen between them, so her mother could not be worried.

She wanted to be with him, feed him whatever he wanted, let him wear whatever he wanted, take him wherever he wanted to go. The money that he had left for her last time amounted to nearly four hundred yuan, which was the equivalent of one year's wages. She had yet to use a cent, so it should be enough to satisfy his every desire.

She would wait until he had died, and then she would follow him. She knew that her death would devastate her mother, but if she carried on living she would only suffer, and that would be even worse for her mother. She would wait three months in this world with Old Third, and then accompany him to the next, where they could be together forever. It didn't matter where they were, as long as they were together.

This had to be the worst case, that Old Third only had three months to live. If he had six months left, then they would gain three months in this world. Or if the hospital had made a mistake, a whole lifetime. Thinking it through like this made Jingqiu feel calmer, like a general before a battle planning every attack and retreat. There was nothing to worry about.

The next day she got up even earlier than usual and told her mother that she had to return to the farm. Her mother was surprised, but Jingqiu stood her ground and said that that was how things were organised, she had only been sent to collect the money and then return the following day. 'If you don't believe me, ask Mr Zheng.'

'How could I not believe you?' her mother said. 'I just thought ... you'd stay another day.'

Jingqiu went to the bus station and bought a ticket. Then she went to the toilets and changed into her new outfit. She guessed that Old Third would be waiting for her at the bus station because she had told him when she was returning, so it would be better to change now. That way, when he caught his first glimpse of her, she would be wearing the clothes she had made from the material he had given her. She wanted to do everything in her power to please him, whether that meant letting him see her in her clothes or out of them.

Chapter Thirty-Two

Old Third was waiting at the station, just as she had expected, wearing his black woollen clothes, with an army jacket draped over his shoulders. If she hadn't known that he was sick she would never have guessed that he was dying. She was definitely not going to bring it up, to say that word. She would pretend she didn't know, so as not to break his heart.

He ran up to her, took her bag and said, 'You're wearing it! How beautiful, you work so fast.'

She hadn't meant to let him take her bag in case it tired him out, but she realised that if she refused she would be treating him differently, like an invalid. They walked close, side by side. As they were passing a shop he pointed to her reflection in the window. 'Beautiful, isn't it?' he said.

What she saw was the two of them. He was leaning in towards her, looking young and healthy, smiling broadly. People said that if you saw a skull floating above someone's reflection in a window that meant they were about to die. She looked carefully, but there was no skull above Old Third's head. She turned to look at him: he really did look young and full of life. Maybe the doctors at the county hospital were wrong. It's only a tiny hospital, did they know leukaemia from pneumonia?

'Are you going back to the farm tomorrow?' She nodded. 'Then you can stay tonight?'

She nodded again. 'I had a feeling that you might, so I asked Nurse Gao if I could borrow her bedroom. You can sleep there.' He took her to the town's largest department store and bought a towel, toothbrush and plastic wash bowl, as if she was moving in permanently. They then went to buy some fruit and snacks. She didn't try to restrain him, but let him shop to his heart's content.

'Let's take these things back to the hospital first,' he said, after they had finished their shopping spree, 'and then I'll take you wherever you want. Do you want to see a film?'

She shook her head, she didn't want to go anywhere, she just wanted to be with him. She noticed that he was heavily wrapped up. He really must be sick. 'Didn't you say you borrowed someone's room? Why don't we go there, it's cold outside.'

'Do you ... want to go and see the hawthorn tree?'

Again, she shook her head. 'No, it's not flowering now, and it's such a long walk. Let's go another time.' He didn't say anything in response and it struck her: perhaps he knows he hasn't got long in this world, maybe he wants to keep his promise. She started to feel shaky, and looked at him intently. He was looking back at her.

'You're right,' he said, tilting his head to one side, 'let's go another time, we'll go when it's in bloom.'

They returned to the hospital and he took her to Nurse Gao's room. It was a very small room on the second floor, with a single bed made up with the hospital's white sheets and blankets. 'Nurse Gao lives in town, so she only uses this room when she's on night shift. She hardly ever sleeps in here, and she changed the bedding yesterday, so it's clean.'

There was only one chair in the room, so she sat on the bed. He went to clean the fruit and collect some boiled water before sitting down on the chair to peel the fruit for her. She noticed the scar over an inch long on the back of his left hand. 'Is that from when you cut yourself?'

He followed her gaze. 'Mmm. Do you think it's ugly?'

'No.'

'It's only because I cut myself that the hospital told me to get checked for . . .' He stopped, realising that he'd said too much. 'To change my medicine. This scar marks me out, so you will always be able to find me. Do you have some kind of mark too? Tell me, that way I will always be able to find you.'

Find me where, she wanted to ask. But she was too scared, and instead she remembered a scene that she had often dreamt of in which the two of them were searching for each other through a dense veil of mist. She wanted to call out his name, but for some reason she couldn't. He was hidden from view, but she could hear him shouting 'Jingqiu, Jingqiu'. She followed the sound of his voice until she caught sight of him from behind, enveloped in the fog. It occurred to her that this was the other world.

She sucked air deep into her lungs. 'I've got a red birthmark on the back of my head, it's covered by my hair.'

'Can I see it?'

She undid her plaits and pointed to the place on her scalp. He parted her hair and gazed at it for some time. She turned around, and saw that his eyes were bloodshot. 'What's happened?' she asked, flustered.

'Nothing. I've had so many dreams in which it's all hazy, and I can't see clearly. Then, I see someone that looks like you from behind, and I shout "Jingqiu, Jingqiu", but someone else turns around and it's not you after all.' He smiled. 'Now I know how to find you, I just need to look for this birthmark. I like the sound of your name. I may have one foot in the grave, but when I hear it I feel that I can take it out . . .' He was silent for a while, then contined, 'Tell me about when you were little, or what you've been doing on the farm. Anything, everything, I want to hear it all.'

So, she started to tell him stories from when she was little, and from her life on the farm. She also wanted him to tell her his stories, stories from his home town. They gave the day over to talking, eating lunch at the hospital canteen and dinner in a local restaurant. It was already dusk by the time they finished eating, and everyone had gone home, so they took a walk around the town, holding hands. It was completely dark by the time they got back to Nurse Gao's room. He fetched a few bottles of hot water so that she could wash her face and feet.

He left the room and went to fetch a bed pan as there were no toilets on that floor. She blushed a deep shade of red.

A few minutes later he was back and closed the door behind him. 'Why don't you get under the covers. If you stand here in your bare feet you'll freeze solid.' He unfolded the blanket, spread it across the bed, peeled back one corner and urged her to get in. I'll keep my clothes on and just sit on the end of the bed with the blanket over my legs and feet, she thought to herself.

He pulled the chair over to the bed and sat down. 'Where are you going to sleep tonight?' she asked.

'I'll go back to the ward.'

She hesitated before asking, 'And what if you don't go back tonight?'

'If you want me to stay, I will.'

She stripped down to her woollen jumper and long johns and dived under the blanket.

He tucked her in, and began stroking her through the blanket. 'Sleep, I'll look after you.' He sat back on the chair and covered himself with his army jacket.

This was the first time she had spent the night alone with a boy, but she wasn't scared. Chairman Mao was right when he said, 'The Chinese are not afraid of death itself, how can they be afraid of a bit of hardship?' She was prepared for anything, even death, so what could possibly scare her now? Whatever people wanted to say, that was their business. They could sprain their tongues talking, she wouldn't care.

There was one question, however, that she was afraid to ask, did he really have leukaemia? She had spent the whole day afraid of asking this one question. She kept her eyes closed but didn't sleep, her head spinning. When would she muster the courage to ask Old Third this question?

Furtively, she opened her eyes to check if he had fallen asleep. As soon as she opened them she saw him looking back at her, his eyes filled with tears. He quickly turned his head, and wiped his eyes with a towel. 'I was just ... remembering that scene from *The White-haired Girl*, where Yang Bailao watches Xi'er fall asleep and sings, "Xi'er, Xi'er, you're asleep, but you don't know that I'm in debt to your father ... "'

He stopped. She scrambled out from under the blanket and took him in her arms. 'Tell me ... Do you have ... . leukaemia?' she whispered.

'Leukaemia? Who told you that?'

'Fang.'

'She ... said that?'

'I want you to tell me if it's true. If you lie to me then I'll feel even worse. Tell me the truth, I have to know ... '

He said nothing before eventually nodding slowly, and tears streamed down his face. She wiped them for him. 'I'm no real man, am I? You said men don't cry.'

'I said ... men don't like to cry in front of strangers. I'm not a stranger.'

'I'm not afraid to die, I just ... don't want to. I want to be with you, always.'

'We will be together, I won't let you go on your own. I'll

come with you. It doesn't matter which world we're in, we'll always be together. There's no need to be scared.'

'What are you saying? Don't talk nonsense. I was too scared to tell you the truth because I was worried you'd talk rubbish like this. I don't want you to come with me. As long as you're alive, I'm not dead. Do you understand? Do you hear me? I want you to live, live for both of us. You've got to help me live. I'll use your eyes to see the world, use your heart to feel it. I want you to . . . marry, have children. We will live in your children, and they will have children, and that way we will live forever.'

'Will we have children?'

'You will, and if you do then so will I. You will live for a long, long time, you will marry, be a mother, be a grandmother, you will have children and grandchildren. Then, in many years' time, you will tell them about me. You don't need to tell them my name, just that I am someone you once loved, that's enough. Thinking of that day is what gives me the strength to face the present. I'm only going somewhere else, where I'll be watching you, living happily—'

He talked and talked, until he realised that she wasn't wearing much. 'Quick, get back under the blankets, else you'll catch cold.'

She said, 'Why don't you come under the blankets too.'

He thought for a moment before he stripped down to his underwear, and crept under the blankets. He stretched out his arm and let her lie on it. They were both shaking. 'I never imagined I would ever get to sleep in a bed with you. I never thought I'd get the chance.' He turned on to his side and held her tightly. 'I wish we could do this every day.'

'Me too.'

'Could you sleep if I held you like this?' She nodded. 'Then you sleep, sleep sweetly.'

She tried to sleep but couldn't. She buried her head in his armpit and, using her hand, 'read' his face.

'Would you like to see what a man is like?' he asked suddenly. 'I mean, would you like to see what I look like?'

'Have you ever shown anyone else?' He shook his head. 'Have you ever seen a woman?'

He shook his head again. 'I might die without experiencing that pleasure,' he said. He started to wriggle out of his clothes under the blankets. 'Don't be scared, I won't do anything. I just want to fulfil a . . . desire.'

He threw each item of clothing one by one on top of the blankets, and then grabbed hold of her hand and laid it on his chest. 'Use your hand to look.' He held on to her hand and moved it across his chest. 'I'm not too thin yet, am I?' Then he placed her hand on his stomach and let go. 'Take a look for yourself.'

She was too afraid to move her hand because she knew what she would find further down. She had seen those of very little boys; they weren't embarrassed about peeing in public. She had also once seen a man's thing on an acupuncture chart, but she hardly dared look at it more carefully.

He took hold of her hand and started edging it lower down until she touched his hair. 'Men also have hair down there?' she asked, shocked. The acupuncture chart didn't have any hair on it, it was perfectly smooth.

'Did you think only girls have hair there?' He laughed.

'How do you know girls have hair there?' she asked, even more shocked.

'That's common knowledge, it says so in books.' He led her hand to his hot, hard place.

'Do you have a fever? Why is it swollen?'

He groaned. 'Don't . . . be scared, I'm fine. Take hold of it, it likes that, hold it tight . . . '

She held it tightly, but her hands were only small, so she couldn't hold all of it. She squeezed it lightly. It moved and Old Third shook. 'It doesn't seem to like me holding it, it keeps trying to get away . . .'

'It likes it, it's not running away, it's . . . jumping. Do you remember the time by the river, when we were swimming? I saw you in your swimsuit, and it . . . was doing this then. I was scared you would see, so I hid in the water.'

It all started to fall into place. 'And what about the time when you carried me across the river, was it doing this then?' He closed his eyes and nodded. 'But I wasn't wearing a swimsuit that day, why would it . . . ?'

He laughed, and suddenly took her in his arms, kissing her all over her face in a frenzy of passion. 'I only have to brush against you, see you, think of you, and it gets like this. Grab it, grab it tight, don't be scared.'

She still didn't understand what it was she was supposed to do. She felt it turn hot inside her hand, it seemed to be twitching. I must be squeezing too tight. She was about to loosen her grip when he grabbed her hand, he wouldn't let her. She wrapped her other arm around him and felt his back drenched in sweat. 'Are you all right? Shall I get the doctor?'

He shook his head. Then after some time replied quietly, 'I'm fine, I'm great. When we're together, I feel as if I'm flying. I want to take you with me. But I can't be with you for much longer.' He took the towel and wiped her hand. 'Do you think it's disgusting? Don't be scared, it's not dirty. It's . . . what babies are made of.'

She used a pillowslip to wipe his back and body. His sweat had even soaked the sheets. Then, as he had done earlier, she stretched out her arm and let him rest his head on her chest. He curled up and lay like that, exhausted. Even his hair was soaking wet. The flying must have tired him out. Her heart ached as he drifted off to sleep in her arms. She listened to his steady, light breathing, as she slipped into a dream.

She woke some time later with Old Third burning hot like an oven on her chest. It was so nice to sleep together but now she felt red-hot. Her woollen underwear was jabbing into her all over, and her sports bra was pressing into her uncomfortably. Her mother had always taught her to undo her bra before bed because, she said, you could get cancer if you were bound in too tight. She wanted to take off her top and long johns and undo her bra, but she was afraid to wake him up.

As she was hestitating, he opened his eyes. 'Aren't you sleeping?'

'I was, I'm just too hot. I want to take my clothes off.' She wriggled out of them. 'Do you want to look at me? Didn't you say you'd never seen a woman before? I'll show you . . .'

'There's no need, I was just rambling.'

'Don't you want to look at me?'

'How could I not? I want to so very much, every day, every moment. But I . . .'

Just as he had done, she placed each item of clothing, one by one, on top of the covers, then she took his hand and laid it on her chest. 'Use your hand . . .'

He pulled his hand away as if he had just been scalded. 'No, don't, I'm scared I . . . won't be able to stop myself . . .'

'From doing what?'

'From doing the thing husbands and wives do.'

'Then do it.'

He shook his head. 'You're going to get married one day, save yourself for your . . . husband.'

'I won't get married, I want to marry you. If you go, I'm coming with you. Do whatever you want. Otherwise, you'll die without having that pleasure, and so will I.'

He used his hand to explore her. To her, his touch felt like an electric shock, wherever his hand roamed her skin tingled, even on her scalp. He used his hands to squeeze her breasts. She melted, and it felt as if something was gushing out down below.

'Wait, wait,' she said, flustered, 'I think … my old friend is back. Don't let the sheets get dirty.' They both sprang out of bed. But when she looked at the sheets there was no sign of blood. It was something clear that looked like water. 'I was wrong, I had it only last week anyway,' she apologised.

She saw him standing there, naked, his eyes fixed on her naked body. She could see everything and, she thought, he must be able to see all of me too. She leapt under the covers, her whole body shivering.

He followed her, took her in his arms and, trying to catch his breath, he said, 'You're so beautiful, so perfect, just like a Greek goddess. Why don't you like your … that they're so big, they're so beautiful.' He held her tightly. 'I want to take you flying …'

'Then take me flying.'

He sighed quietly, and then carefully climbed on top of her.

CHAPTER THIRTY-THREE

It was evening the following day by the time Jingqiu arrived back on the farm. Old Third insisted on accompanying her up the mountain to the point where they could see the farm's L-shaped building, before, reluctantly, they separated.

Old Third said he was still waiting for the last, conclusive test results, and he'd lose his temper if she didn't go back to work on the farm. They arranged to meet again at Nurse Gao's room in two weeks' time when she would next have some time off, and were he to have been discharged already, he would come back. He agreed to write to her at once if the tests confirmed that he had leukaemia, but if there was no news it was good news.

That evening, Jingqiu went to speak to Mr Zheng to ask him not to send back any more letters. 'I have a friend who teaches at Yanjia River Middle School, and she said that she sent me some letters here to the farm, using the address you gave me, but they were all returned to sender. Do you know what might have happened?'

'The address is right.' Mr Zheng was perplexed. 'Who would have sent them back?'

He's a good actor, she thought. 'Who delivers the letters up here?'

'The letters only get as far as the production brigade. Usually my father brings them back when he goes down there, and I bring them here when I come back from visiting. My father knows everyone's names here, so he wouldn't have sent them back. Do you think I sent them back? I swear on my Party membership, it wasn't me who returned your letters.'

Jingqiu couldn't very well say anything more after this declaration but she was sure that he wouldn't dare send back any more letters.

She spent the days making food for the students and, when she had time, working in the fields. In the evenings, when she went to bed, she closed her eyes and thought of the day and night she had spent with Old Third, especially the night. It sent waves of emotion through her. On occasion she would touch herself, but she didn't feel anything. How strange, how come when Old Third did it, it felt electric? She longed to fly away with him, they should soar away together, while they still could.

She had heard someone say that the thing boys and girls do together transformed your body shape, the way you walk, even the way you urinate. 'Young girls pee like fountains, women pee like waterfalls.' But they had never explained exactly how it transformed your body, nor how it would make you walk differently. She didn't think she walked any differently, although she did feel somewhat on edge, constantly afraid that people would detect a change in her gait.

The week passed slowly, and that Sunday evening Miss Zhao, who the day before had gone home for a holiday, had still not returned to the farm. After another two days a letter arrived saying that she had had an abortion and would need to rest at home for a month. Jingqiu was stunned by this news. If Miss Zhao wasn't coming back for a month that would mean Jingqiu couldn't go back to Yichang the following week. There were only the two of them in charge of the food, so someone had to stay.

She was burning with anxiety, and she rushed to find Mr Zheng. 'I promised Mother I would go home next weekend, and if I don't, she'll be worried sick.'

'Miss Zhao is staying in the city, your mother will know that, and that you have to stay on the farm. She won't be worried. The school will send someone to replace Miss Zhao. If you wait just a week or two I'll give you a couple more days' holiday. You're the only one preparing all our meals now, so work will be a bit tough, but you'll be helping all of us at the farm.'

Jingqiu was so miserable she could barely speak. She had no idea how she was going to let Old Third know that she couldn't make it. Thankfully there had been no letter from him, so that meant that there was no definite diagnosis yet. She would just have to be patient for a few more days, and trust that Old Third would understand.

After a few days, the school sent Miss Li to the farm and Jingqiu begged Mr Zheng to let her take time off to go back home. Mr Zheng had planned that Jingqiu stay another week so that she could teach Miss Li how they did things, but Jingqiu flatly refused. Mr Zheng had never known her to refuse an instruction like this and he was not happy about it, but ultimately felt he had no choice and let her go.

It was already a week later than their prearranged date, but Jingqiu believed that Old Third would wait for her. She set off very early on Saturday morning and made her way from Fujia Plateau to Yanjia River, where she caught the first bus to the county hospital. She went straight to Old Third's ward but he wasn't there and the other people in the ward were all new so they had never heard of Sun Jianxin.

Jingqiu went to Nurse Gao's room but Old Third wasn't there either. She ran to find Nurse Gao but was told it was her day off. She begged and pleaded to be told where Nurse Gao lived and she rushed to her house, but Nurse Gao was not home. She waited there until well into the afternoon when Nurse Gao finally returned from her mother-in-law's house. Jingqiu introduced herself as Sun Jianxin's friend, and said that she was trying to find out where he had gone.

'Oh, you're Jingqiu? You're the one Sun borrowed my room for that day?' Jingqiu nodded. 'Sun left the hospital a while ago,' Nurse Gao continued. 'He wrote you a note, but I left it in my room at the hospital. Come, we can go and get it.'

Jingqiu was overcome with emotion, the events of that night crowding her thoughts.

Old Third's note. It wasn't in an envelope, but folded into the shape of a dove. A bad feeling came over her.

> I am so sorry that I lied to you, this is the first time, and will be the last time that I ever do so. I don't have leukaemia, I made it up so that I could see you one last time before I left.
>
> My dad hasn't been well recently, and he wants me to go back home to look after him, so he secretly arranged for me to be transferred. I should have gone back ages ago, but I wanted to see you, so I waited for an opportunity. It was heaven's will that I got to see you one last time, that I spent such a wonderful day and night with you. Now I can leave with no regrets.
>
> I once promised your mother that I would wait for you for thirteen months, and I also promised you that I would wait until you turned twenty-five. It seems like I can't keep these promises. The love between a man and woman cannot do anything to resist an order from one's superiors. Blame me if you want, it is all my fault.
>
> The man with the same name as me can protect you

from future tempests, he will do everything for you, I
trust that he is a good person. If you let him grow old
with you then I will be happy for you both.

The letter was like a blow to the head with a cudgel. Jingqiu felt dull, she couldn't understand what it was Old Third was saying. He must have leukaemia. He's lying so that I will forget him, so that I will move on and live a happy life.

'Do you know what was wrong with Sun?'

'Didn't you know? He had a very bad cold.'

'Why did I hear that he has ... leukaemia then?' Jingqiu asked carefully.

'Leukaemia?' Nurse Gao's surprise confirmed that she wasn't pretending. 'I didn't hear that. If he did have it, he wouldn't be in this small hospital, surely? We don't have much here and anyone with anything the least bit serious gets transferred elsewhere.'

'When did he leave?'

Nurse Gao thought for a second. 'It must have been two weeks ago. I was on the day shift, and I change every week, so yes, it must have been two weeks ago.'

'Did he come back last weekend?'

'I don't know, but he had given back the keys to my room.'

Did he write the letter because I didn't come? Did he overreact? But Old Third wasn't the type to read so much into her missing their appointment.

She didn't know why she was still sitting there, it wasn't going to bring Old Third back. She thought of going to find him at the second unit, but when she asked Nurse Gao the time, she discovered it was too late, there were no more buses to Yanjia River. All she could do was thank Nurse Gao and on the bus to Yichang.

Once at home, it was impossible for her to be calm. The worst of it was that she didn't know what was really going on. She had never been so depressed and she found it difficult to talk to family and friends.

Officially, she had three days off, but first thing on Monday morning she left for the farm. The excuse she gave her mother was that the newly arrived Miss Li didn't know how to prepare the food, and it would be better for her to go back early. But she got off the bus in Yiling and went back to the hospital. She headed straight for Old Third's old ward. He wasn't there, of course, but she just wanted to make doubly sure.

Then she went to the in-patient department to see if they could tell her why Old Third had been in hospital, but they told her to speak to Dr Xie. She found Dr Xie's office, and discovered two middle-aged female doctors talking about knitting. When Jingqiu said that she wanted to speak to Dr Xie, she was asked to wait for a moment outside.

Jingqiu could hear them arguing over a rather simple knitting pattern, so she walked in and told them roughly how it should be done. The two women closed the door, took out their needles and wool, and asked Jingqiu to show them, then to write it down on a piece of paper. The doctors discusssed it a bit longer, making sure they had understood, until one of them, who turned out to be Dr Xie, eventually asked what she could do for Jingqiu.

'I just wanted to ask why Sun Jianxin was admitted to hospital.' She explained her concerns, that he had a terminal illness but was afraid of hurting her and so had run away. If that was the case she would go to him, and look after him for the next few months.

The two doctors sighed and gasped. She was so brave, they said. 'I don't remember, but I'll check for you,' Dr Xie said and rifled through some papers in a large cabinet. She pulled out a notebook and flicked through it. 'He had a bad cold. The injection, medicine, and drip we gave him are all used to cure colds.'

Jingqiu left the hospital with her stomach in knots. She was happy for him that it was only a cold, but the fact that he had disappeared leaving only that note puzzled her deeply.

As soon as she got off the bus at Yanjia River, without thinking she found herself running towards the middle school in search of Fang. She didn't care that she would be in the middle of a class, she stood outside one of the classroom windows and waved until the teacher came out to see what was the matter. She told her that she was looking for Miss Zhang Fang and the teacher left, fuming, to find Fang.

'What brings you here now?' Fang said, rather surprised.

'Why did you say it was your brother in the hospital that day when it was clearly ... him?'

'We all call him brother ...'

'The illness you said he had that day, how come the hospital says he doesn't have it? Who told you he had it?'

Fang hesitated before replying. 'He said so himself, I wasn't lying.'

'He's been transferred back to Anhui, did you know that?'

'I'd heard. Do you want to go to Anhui to look for him?'

'I don't have an address for him there. Do you have it?'

'Why would I have it?' Fang grumbled. 'If he didn't give it to you, why would he give it to me? I don't know what dirty secret's going on between you two.'

'There's no dirty secret, I'm just worried that he's got leukaemia, and that he doesn't want me to know, to worry about him. And now he's run off to Anhui. Jingqiu pleaded with Fang. 'Do you know where the second unit is stationed? Could you go with me? I want to go but I'm scared that he's avoiding me.'

'I've still got classes. I'll tell you where it is, but you have to go on your own. It's close, I'll point you in the right direction.'

Jingqiu walked in the direction Fang had pointed and found it without any difficulty. It was only half a kilometre from Yanjia River, so no wonder Old Third spent his lunch hours wandering around the town. She asked the men who were working there where Sun Jianxin was and they replied that he had already left for Anhui. 'His father's a high-ranking official. He organised a new work unit for him ages ago. He's not like us other guys, we don't have anyone behind the scenes pulling strings for us, we'll have to spend the rest of our lives working out here.'

Jingqiu didn't know what to think. Maybe Old Third is scared I'll be worried about his health and so he lied to me, and has now run off to die on his own. But all the evidence seemed to refute this conclusion; the hospital's records suggested that he was being treated for a cold, and his friends in the second unit confirmed that he'd had all the paperwork in order to transfer to Anhui a long time ago. It didn't seem possible that Old Third had bribed all these people to trick her. In the end it was only Fang and Old Third who had said that he had leukaemia; she had never seen any concrete evidence. But Jingqiu couldn't understand why Old Third would want to lie to her about this. He said it was so that he could see her one last time, but he only told her it was leukaemia after they had met, not before.

But there was another problem, one she hadn't allowed herself to think about before, one that shook her to her core: her old friend was late. It was normally very regular, and it was only ever early, never late. This could mean only one thing, that she was pregnant. This much at least she knew from the many stories she'd heard.

Those stories had all, without exception, ended tragically,

and because they were all girls who Jingqiu knew personally, that made them even more terrible. One girl from No. 8 Middle School, who everyone called Orchid, started going out with a rascal who got her pregnant. Apparently Orchid tried every possible way of getting rid of the child, including carrying an incredibly heavy shoulder pole while jumping from a height. The baby was born in due course, but perhaps as a result of the jump or the fact that she had used a long strip of material to tie up her bump in the last months, the baby was born with two sunken ribs. Her boyfriend was sentenced to twenty years in prison because of this pregnancy, and for getting into numerous fights. The baby was given to her boyfriend's mother to bring up, and the two families were left to suffer in unspeakable misery.

Orchid's story wasn't even the most tragic, all the harm it really did her was to her reputation, lessening her chances of making it back to the city; at least her boyfriend acknowledged the child as his own, which saved Orchid her life. There was another girl, called Gong, who got pregnant. Her boyfriend came home with some herbs which he claimed could get rid of the child. She secretly boiled them with water and drank the bitter mixture, and it ended up killing her. Her story was much discussed at No. 8 Middle School; the girl's family wanted the boyfriend to pay with his life, and the two sides slogged it out in public until the boy's family had to move away.

Jingqiu had heard that you needed a certificate from your work unit in order to have an abortion at the hospital, and maybe even a certificate from his work unit too. This has to be why he's run away. So he's taken off, leaving me to deal with it on my own. Yet, it didn't matter how she twisted and turned it, she couldn't see that Old Third was that kind of person, he had always been so good to her, always so considerate in every respect. How could he put her in such an awkward position and not care? Even if he really did have leukaemia, that was surely no excuse for letting her deal with this all on her own? He could always have waited until this was sorted before disappearing on her.

There was only one explanation for his behaviour: he had only wanted to get his way with her. All of it, he had done it just to 'succeed' with her. The more she thought about it, the more this seemed to explain Old Third's behaviour. He had worked so hard for so long, all for that night at the hospital. If he really didn't want her to worry about his illness he would never have said he had leukaemia, he would have taken the secret with him to the grave. Why, exactly, did he reveal that he was terminally ill? It could only be so that he could get what he wanted. He knew how much she loved him, and he also knew that she would do anything for him if she thought he was about to die, including letting him do that.

Her chest felt like it was burning, she didn't know what to do. If she was pregnant there were only two options; one was to end her troubles by ending her life, but her death would only be a relief to herself and not to her family, they would forever be the subject of gossip. The second option would be to have an abortion at the hospital, but that would be a great cost to both her pocket and her reputation, and she would have to live with the shame of it for the rest of her life. She couldn't even begin to imagine giving birth to it, that would be too unfair to the poor child. It would be one thing for her to have to live with the shame, but to implicate an innocent baby!

The next few days after she got back to the farm were a living hell for Jingqiu. She was in a constant state of anxiety. Thankfully, however, her old friend arrived, and she was so relieved that she sobbed. It really was like setting eyes on a long-lost friend, and the discomfort became something worthy of celebration. As long as she wasn't pregnant, everything else was manageable.

There were two reasons why people said that it was awful for a young girl to be cheated into losing her virginity: because it would ruin her reputation, and because she couldn't be married off afterwards. Jingqiu no longer needed to worry about being pregnant, so the only thing left to be concerned about was whether or not she could be married. But if Old Third was only ingratiating himself with her to get what he wanted, she couldn't imagine there was anyone in this world who could really love her.

She didn't even blame Old Third. If I was worth his love, he would have loved me; if he didn't, that's because I'm not worth it. But if he didn't love her, why did he spend so much time and effort trying to get her? Maybe all men were like that: the harder it was to get you, the harder they tried. He pretended to be interested for so long, but it was all because he was yet to get what he wanted.

And then there was all that stuff about 'mung bean soup'. He must have been bragging with his roommates, saying that she was the 'mung bean soup' he used to cool off. To her, he called it 'flying', to them it was all about 'putting out his fire'. Just the thought of it was disgusting.

Then there were the letters. He said he wrote to her at the farm, but Mr Zheng promised on his Party membership that he hadn't sent them back. At first she had suspected Mr Zheng of lying, but now she realised it must have been Old Third, and that he hadn't written to her at all.

And ...

She didn't want to think about it any more, it seemed like everything could be explained, it had all been a game from beginning to end, sitting by the river in the evenings, crying, cutting himself, each scene more desperate than the last, until, when he thought there was no hope of prevailing, he thought up the idea of telling her he had leukaemia.

The strange thing was that as soon as she had seen through him, seen him for what he was, her heart no longer ached and she was no longer consumed by regret over her actions. Wisdom comes from mistakes. Knowledge doesn't just come from nothing. People may draw on their own experiences to tell you what to do, but you can't learn everything that way. True wisdom can only really come from your own experience. And so every generation must make its own mistakes.

CHAPTER THIRTY-FOUR

Jingqiu had not yet finished her six months at the farm when she was sent back to Yichang to teach. It was a sort of good fortune wrought from disaster, only it was someone else's disaster, not her own. She took over class 4A at No. 8 Middle School's adjoining primary school from a Mrs Wang. She was the kind of teacher who was of even temper, honest in her work, and yet was simply not that suited to teaching, especially when it came to discipline. Every day was a struggle and she couldn't keep control of her class.

Recently it had fallen to Mrs Wang's class to begin their labouring duties. Every school was given the task of collecting scrap iron. The school had a deal with a factory over the other side of the river whereby the students could rummage for scrap screws and nails in their rubbish bins and give them to the national iron-smelting commission. One day when Mrs Wang was bringing her troops back from the factory her students began to fall out of line. She rushed to and fro trying to maintain discipline and didn't notice a few of the naughtiest kids disappear.

The river in front of the school had nearly completely dried up, leaving only a narrow stream of water. People had made a walkway across the mud to enable them to get to a small boat that could take them over what was left of the river. On either side of the walkway the mud had dried in patches, the large cracks revealing only a glimpse of the thick sludge beneath the surface. One of the naughtiest boys from Mrs Wang's class, a boy called Ceng, escaped the class and went to play in the mud. All on his own, he ventured out too far, and started to sink into the silt, but the more he flailed the deeper he sank.

It was only two days later that the boy's body was found near the makeshift walkway. When Ceng's father saw his boy's face and mouth slathered in stinking mud he was overcome with anger and bitterness. He placed all the blame on Mrs Wang's shoulders. Had she been a more competent teacher his son would never have run away, would never have met with this awful fate. Ceng's father rallied his friends and relatives to harass Mrs Wang every day, demanding that she should pay with her life. The school had no choice but to send Mrs Wang to the countryside to hide for a while. No one dared take over her class, so the school assigned it to Jingqiu.

Jingqiu knew that if she refused to take this class the school would not let her teach another. So, returning to Yichang, she took over Mrs Wang's class 4A. Ceng's father had no complaints about Jingqiu, so he caused her no trouble. As far as the other parents were concerned, they were merely grateful that the class would finally get a new teacher.

Jingqiu threw herself body and soul into her work, preparing classes, teaching, visiting the parents, talking with her students; she was busy until late every day. She also began to practise volleyball again, and set up a girls' team at the primary school. Sometimes she would even take the class on outings, much to the students' delight, and they quickly became the best-behaved class in their year.

Jingqiu had very little time during the day to think about Old Third. But at night, when it was quiet and there was no one else around, she would lie in bed thinking of the past, and doubt would enter her mind. Is Old Third really such a scoundrel? Could he be lying in a hospital somewhere, dying?

It suddenly struck her that she hadn't tried the army hospital in Yichang where Old Third had taken her when he cut himself with the knife. Maybe this was where he had been diagnosed with leukaemia. The more she thought about it the more uneasy she felt. She would ask Dr Cheng to ask for her.

Dr Cheng told her that that hospital wasn't part of Yichang's medical system and was under the direct jurisdiction of the central government. It had been set up as part of Chairman Mao's call to educate the people to 'prepare for war, fight against natural disasters', and was built for senior-ranking cadres only. It was still difficult for ordinary folks to be treated there.

Dr Cheng spent a lot of energy trying to find out about Sun's condition, and discovered from his medical records that it did appear that Sun Jianxin showed signs of a slight decrease in his blood platelets, but that was not a conclusive sign of leukaemia.

Jingqiu gave up all hope. She had repeated the same story that had been playing out for thousands of years. She wasn't the first girl to be tricked, and she wouldn't be the last. In fact, she was starting to believe that it wasn't Old Third who she had always been in love with, but Dr Cheng. She had only fallen for Old Third because he resembled Dr Cheng in so many ways. But when it came to fundamentals they were completely different.

The production team on Jiangxin Island specialised in growing bean sprouts, so the local families based their diet around them. Jingqiu thought that Old Third and Dr Cheng were like two beans growing from the same crisp, white stem; one was blackened and rotten, while the other was still a healthy shade of yellow. The thing that made them different was their attitude to 'success'. Dr Cheng had been married for so many years, but he was as loyal and devoted to Mrs Jiang as ever. By contrast, as soon as he had 'succeeded' with her, Old Third had run away from her.

She started going to Mrs Jiang's house more and more often just to hear the sound of Dr Cheng's voice, to see his honest devotion to his wife. Dr Cheng was, quite possibly, the only man on Jiangxin Island who carried away the dirty water after his wife and mother-in-law had washed their feet. In the summer, everyone used large wooden tubs to collect water and wash in. Not one woman on the island was able to lift the tubs, and instead they would have to empty them out one ladle at a time. But Dr Cheng would always carry out the tub himself.

Jingqiu never once thought that this compromised Dr Cheng; on the contrary, she thought him a magnificent man. It was his love for his two children that particularly moved her. On summer evenings you could often see Dr Cheng taking his eldest son to the river to swim while Mrs Jiang sat with their youngest on the bank, watching. When not out swimming, Dr Cheng would play with his sons on the bed, letting them ride him like a horse.

Dr Cheng and his wife were everyone's idea of a loving couple, two zithers in perfect harmony. One played the accordion while the other sang along; watching them together was one of the most heart-warming sights on the island. In Jingqiu's eyes, only a man whose thoughts and actions were one, who was constant, just like Dr Cheng, was worthy of her love.

His tender love for his wife and sons inspired her to compose fragments of poetry in her head; each scene, each feeling had to be captured. They wouldn't leave her, as if calling out to her to be written down. When back in her room she would do so, never mentioning his name, but using only the pronoun 'he'.

Jingqiu had moved now into a small room of about ten square metres belonging to the school which she shared with another teacher, Miss Liu. Their room contained a desk with two drawers, one each. This was her small corner of the world where she could lock away her secrets.

Miss Liu's family lived by the river and every weekend she went back to visit, so at the weekends the room was Jingqiu's sole domain. She would lock the door, take out Old Third's letters and photographs and imagine that they had all been given to her by Dr Cheng. She was happy when engaged in these thoughts, intoxicated almost, because these words could only have meaning coming from someone like Dr Cheng. Otherwise, they were worthless. She copied out some of her poems so that she could show them to Dr Cheng. She didn't know exactly why, she just wanted to.

One day, she slipped these small poems into Dr Cheng's jacket pocket as he was taking his son back from her arms. For the next few days she was too scared to go back to Dr Cheng's house. She didn't feel that she had done anything wrong because she had made no effort to take Dr Cheng away from his wife. She worshipped him, that was all, loved him. She had written those poems for him, so she wanted him to read them. The real reason she avoided their house was that she feared Dr Cheng would laugh at her writing, laugh at her feelings.

One evening that weekend, Dr Cheng came looking for her. He gave back the poems and said, with a smile, 'Little girl, your writing is beautiful, you will become a great poet, and you will meet the "him" in your poems. Keep them, keep them to give to him.'

Jingqiu was flustered and confused, and kept trying to explain. 'Sorry, I don't know what I was writing, nor why I put them in your pocket. I must have gone crazy.'

'If you've got anything on your mind, talk to Mrs Jiang. She's got experience, she'll understand you. And she can keep a secret.'

'Please don't tell Mrs Jiang about these,' Jingqiu begged. 'She would be so angry with me. Please don't tell anyone.'

'I won't. Don't worry, you haven't done anything wrong, you've only written a few poems, and asked someone with no clue about poetry to comment on them. I'm afraid I don't have much to say when it comes to poetry, but when it comes to real life problems, I can help.'

His voice was soft, sincere. Jingqiu didn't know if it was because she trusted him, or because she wanted to show that she felt nothing but admiration for him, but she began to tell Dr Cheng more about her relationship with Old Third, leaving out only the night at the hospital.

'Maybe he really has got leukaemia, in spite of what I found in the records,' Dr Cheng said after she had finished, 'otherwise there's no good reason for him to avoid you. He may well have been at the county hospital to be treated for a cold. Leukaemia weakens the immune system, so it makes all these illnesses easy to catch. There is no cure for leukaemia at the moment. They can only treat the symptoms, and try to keep sufferers alive as long as possible. The county hospital might not be aware that he has it, maybe it was the army hospital that diagnosed him.'

'But didn't you say that the army hospital diagnosed him with a reduced platelet count?'

'It's possible he might have asked the hospital to keep it a secret. I'm only guessing, I might not be right. But if it were me, I'm afraid that I might do the same, because you said you wanted to die with him. What choice did he have? He couldn't really let you go with him, could he? And how could he stand letting you see him getting thinner, more gaunt by the day? If it were you, you wouldn't let him see you fading away like that, would you?'

'So, you're saying that he's all alone in Anhui, waiting to die?'

'I can't say,' Dr Cheng said, after giving it some thought. 'He might even be in the city. If it were me, I would come back to Yichang, so that I could be . . . a bit closer.'

'Could you possibly help me by asking around all the local hospitals then?'

'I can ask for you, as long as you promise not to do anything stupid.'

'I won't, I . . . I . . . won't say that ever again.'

'Not that you won't say it, that you won't do it either. He's worried about you, and this is adding to his worries. Maybe he's . . . already prepared himself for his fate, maybe he's come to peace with his death, but if he thinks you will go with him, he will be angry with himself. At the hospital I regularly see the inconsolable grief of families when they lose loved ones. The thing that strikes me most is that our lives don't just belong to us, we can't do whatever we please with them. If you followed him, how would that affect your mother? How awful would it be for your brother and sister? We would all be upset, and this would be of no benefit to him. While he is still alive it will only add to his worries, and after he's gone . . . you must know there is no afterlife, there is no other world, that if two people die together they will not be reunited. He was right, as long as you're alive he won't die.'

'I'm scared . . . that's he's already . . . Can you ask around, as soon as possible?'

Dr Cheng asked everywhere, but not one of the hospitals in the city had Sun Jianxin as a patient, and that included the army hospital. 'I've exhausted all avenues, I must have been wrong, maybe he's not in Yichang.'

Jingqiu had also exhausted all avenues; the only thing that comforted her was the thought that Dr Cheng had been wrong. 'If it were me . . .' he had said, but Old Third wasn't him, in the most important respects they were like chalk and cheese. She hadn't made this clear to Dr Cheng, so maybe his predictions were inaccurate.

One day, in April 1976, Jingqiu's friend Wei Ling, who was studying at the district teacher training college, came to visit Jingqiu. She had visited her parents every weekend and she and Jingqiu often spent time together.

This time, as soon as Wei Ling saw Jingqiu she blurted out, 'I'm in deep trouble, you're the only person who can save me.'

Startled, Jingqiu asked what had happened.

Wei Ling faltered, and managed to stutter, 'I . . . might be . . . carrying a baby. But my boyfriend never put that stuff in there, so how can I be pregnant?'

'Put what stuff there?'

'The stuff that makes babies, of course, boy's sperm.'

Jingqiu didn't really want to know the details. She wanted to help, but she didn't want to go into the nitty gritty. But the details were important, so she had to ask. 'Put the stuff for making babies where?'

'Eugh, you've never had a boyfriend, you've never done it, you wouldn't understand. Put the stuff for making babies where your old friend comes out.' Wei Ling was angry. 'He didn't actually put it in there, but it went all over my front, so some of it must have got in there, otherwise how could I now be pregnant? Did it fall from the sky? I'm certain, I haven't done it with any other man.'

Jingqiu was shocked. Put that sticky stuff in 'there'? Disgusting!

She suddenly realised that Old Third really was everything he had seemed. He hadn't 'done' anything to her, he hadn't spread his stuff down there inside her. And if he hadn't 'succeeded' with her, then all her explanations of his behaviour were wrong. He really must be sick. He must have lied to her out of fear that she would kill herself and felt compelled to run away to Anhui. In doing so, he might have made her hate him, but he was also saving her life.

She was heartbroken. She had no idea how to find him, or whether he was even still alive.

Chapter Thirty-five

Jingqiu had never imagined that she was this ignorant, that she didn't even know what sharing a bed really involved. If Wei Ling hadn't come to her, she would have continued to blame Old Third unfairly. She had thought that 'sleeping together' simply involved sharing a room with a man.

He had said that he daren't touch her, scared that he wouldn't be able to stop himself from doing what husbands did to their wives. She had told him not to worry, that he should do it, that if he didn't they would both die without having experienced it. Then, Old Third had climbed on top of her, and she believed what had followed was exactly that, what husbands did to their wives.

That evening she had been ignorant but curious, and as a result had said some inappropriate things, which must have upset Old Third. If only I could cut my tongue out! That night, after they had been 'flying', she wiped the creamy stuff from her stomach with a towel. 'How do you know it's not urine?' she had asked.

'It's not,' he said awkwardly.

'But doesn't pee usually come out of there too?' He nodded, and she continued, 'Then how do you know that it wasn't pee this time? When isn't it? Could you make a mistake?'

He was hesitant, and could only reply in a muddle. 'You can feel it. Don't worry, it definitely isn't . . . pee.' He got out of the bed and poured some water into a wash basin, wrung out the towel and wiped her hands and stomach carefully. 'Feeling less worried?'

'I'm not calling you dirty,' she explained. 'I'm just scared of this creamy stuff.'

He took her in his arms and laughed silently. 'I didn't ask to be made this way, maybe you should ask God.'

Then he told her about his first time. He was only in primary six at the time, and was sitting an exam. The question was very difficult, and he wasn't sure he could do it, and as he grew nervous it felt like he was peeing, but it was also strangely pleasurable. Only later did he discover that this was what people called 'ejaculating'.

'You were such a ... bad boy when you were in primary six?'

'It's not naughty, it's a normal, physical process. When boys hit puberty they start to develop, and then this sort of thing happens. Sometimes it happens while you're dreaming. Just like you girls, once you get to a certain age you get your ... "old friend".'

It was all becoming clear, boys had their own 'old friends'. But why did girls feel ill when their old friends came to visit, while for boys the experience was 'strangely pleasurable'? It didn't seem fair.

She then told him about her first time. It happened when her mother was in hospital, about five or so kilometres from their home. Her sister was still small, and couldn't walk great distances, so she spent the night with their mother in the hospital, sleeping in the same bed. Jingqiu, on the other hand, would spend the day looking after her mother, and then went back in the evenings, to stay with her friend Zuo Hong.

One day, in the middle of the night, they both got up to use the toilet and Zuo Hong said, 'You must have got your period, the bed's all red. I haven't got mine yet.'

Zuo Hong helped her find some toilet paper, and used a length of bandage to hold it in place. Jingqiu was scared and ashamed, and didn't know what to do. 'Every girl gets her period at some point,' Zuo Hong told her. 'Some of your classmates might have got it already. Just tell your mum when you go to the hospital and she'll teach you all about it.'

The next day Jingqiu went to the hospital, but couldn't seem to get the words out; she um-ed and ah-ed until she eventually told her mother.

'What timing!' her mother said. 'And so life carries on in its mysterious way.'

When Old Third heard this he said, 'I hope you will get married, have children, have a daughter, and then another and another, and they will all grow up just like you. That way there will be a Jingqiu in every generation.'

She didn't want to hear it, so she covered his mouth with her hand. 'I won't get married to anyone else, I'll only marry you, have your children.'

He pulled her in closer. 'Why are you so good to me?' he mumbled. 'I want to marry you too, but . . . '

He looked so upset that she had changed the subject: 'The right side of my body is bigger than the left.' She put her thumbs together to show him, then her arms, and sure enough, the right was a fraction larger than the left.

He looked at her for a while and then took hold of her breasts and asked, 'Do you have a big and a small one of these then?'

She nodded. 'The right one is a little bit bigger, so when I make my bras I have to make the right cup a bit bigger too.'

He wriggled under the covers and stayed under there for a long time, looking, until he eventually stuck his head out and said, 'You can't tell when you're lying down. Sit up and show me.' She sat up and he confirmed that one was just a little bit bigger. 'Can I draw you?' he then asked. 'I've studied drawing a bit. When it gets light I'll go back to the ward and get paper and a pen.'

'What would you draw me for?'

'So I can look at you every day . . . If you don't want me to we don't have to.'

'It's not that, it's just that you don't need to. I can show you myself every day.'

'I still want to draw you.'

In the morning he went to fetch pen and paper, and positioned her on the bed, draping the blanket over her shoulders. He looked at her and then let her lie under the covers. He drew her for a while, looking up and then drawing some more. It didn't take him long to finish his picture. He showed her, and even though it was just a rough sketch it still looked a lot like her.

'Don't let anyone else see it or they'll lock you up for being a pervert.'

'How could I bring myself to let anyone else see it?' he laughed.

That day she lay naked under the covers while he ran out to empty the bedpan, collected water for her to wash with, and food from the canteen for them to eat. With a top draped over her shoulders, she sat up in bed, eating. Once she was finished she dived back under the covers, and he too removed his clothes and got in with her. They snuggled together until there was only half an hour before the last bus left for Yanjia River. Then they jumped out of bed, flung on their clothes, and ran to the bus station.

Now, looking back on that day, she realised that he had planned it so that she could go on living, and she had falsely accused him of being selfish and immoral. He really hadn't done anything wrong. She was overcome with regret. It had already been nearly six months since they last saw each other, and if he had been diagnosed on the day when he had cut himself, that was eight or nine months ago. He might have died at the end of last year.

Did that mean he was still relatively strong and would live for a long time? She was suddenly optimistic. Maybe his health was better than that of most people, maybe he was still alive? She had to find him, and if he had gone, she wanted to know where he was buried. She needed everything to be out in the open.

Jingqiu realised that her first lead was Fang, because she had known about his condition, and it was possible that she might know his address in Anhui. Fang had said that she didn't, but Old Third might have told her to say that. If she promised Fang that she wouldn't commit suicide, surely she would tell her Old Third's address.

That Sunday Jingqiu made a trip to West Village, and went straight to Fang's house. Auntie Zhang and the rest of them were surprised to see her, but very welcoming. Lin had already married; his wife was from a small mountainous area very far away. She was really quite beautiful, and the two of them lived with Auntie Zhang while preparing to build a new house.

Jingqiu greeted everyone and then went with Fang to her room to talk.

'I really don't know his address in Anhui,' Fang replied to Jingqiu's questions, injured. 'If I knew, would I not have told you before? I would have gone with you to help look after him.'

Jingqiu didn't believe her. 'He didn't tell anyone that he was sick, only you. He must have told you his address.'

'He didn't tell me he had leukaemia, it was my brother who

overheard that when Old Third was making a telephone call at Yanjia River. He's the second guy in the second unit who's had it, so he was asking the unit to send someone to investigate, to see if it had anything to do with their working environment.'

'Then why didn't you tell me when I came to the school after he left?'

'You told him that you had heard it from me, and he came over to ask how I knew. I told him, and he told me not to tell you, to say instead that he had told me himself. He said it was lucky that you hadn't got those letters because in them he told you that he was afraid it had something to do with the environment around here and he wanted to warn you.'

Jingqiu said meekly, 'So is it an environmental problem?'

'Probably not. The other person who got it was in the geological unit. He left after a while, and no one knows what the cause was . . .'

'Did Old Third leave with the unit?'

'He left at the end of the year, said he was going to Anhui. We haven't had any more news.'

Jingqiu decided to use the Labour Day holidays to go to Anhui to look for Old Third in the hope that she could see him again. If she didn't get to meet him she hoped that she could visit his grave. She knew that Old Third came from Hefei, the provincial capital, but she didn't know exactly where. If his father is a district level military commander then all I have to do is find Anhui's district headquarters, and from there it must be possible to find a commander. Once I've found his father, I'll obviously find his son.

She would have to ask Mrs Jiang to help her buy a ticket to Hefei for the Labour Day holidays. The father of one of Mrs Jiang's pupils worked at the station so he could buy a ticket for her. The trains were always jam-packed during the holidays. She didn't have time to go and queue herself and, anyway, she might not be able to get hold of a ticket even if she did.

Mrs Jiang agreed, but she was very worried. 'Are you going to go on your own? It's not safe. Your mother won't let you.'

Jingqiu told her that she was going to look for Old Third, and she asked Mrs Jiang to help her no matter what. If she didn't go during the Labour Day holidays she would have to wait until the summer holidays, and by then there would be even less hope of finding him alive.

Mrs Jiang had bought the ticket within a few days, but she bought two, saying that she would go with her, so that Jingqiu wouldn't have to go on her own. Mrs Jiang went to talk to Jingqiu's mother, saying that she wanted to take her youngest son, Little Brother, to visit friends in Hefei, but it would be difficult to look after him on her own, and she wanted Jingqiu to accompany them to help look after the little one. Jingqiu's mother had no objections, and agreed readily.

Jingqiu and Mrs Jiang took Little Brother on the train, and once they arrived in Hefei, stayed with Mrs Jiang's friend, Mrs Hu. The next day Jingqiu and Mrs Jiang took Little Brother on several different buses until they finally found the district army headquarters. It was located in a place called Peach Blossom Ridge, and surrounded by a high wall. From outside you could see the trees on the hills behind. They were all in bloom and it looked like paradise on earth. What a good thing that Old Third came back home, Jingqiu thought on seeing the beauty of the place. It's much nicer here than staying in my small room. I only hope he's still here.

The gates were guarded by an armed soldier. They said they

were looking for District Commander Sun, but the guard wouldn't let them in, saying that the District Commander here was not called Sun. Perhaps they were mistaken. 'Then is there a deputy commander by the name of Sun, or some other leading cadre?'

The guard checked but said no, there wasn't. 'What is the District Commander called?' Jingqiu asked.

The soldier refused to answer. 'It doesn't matter what he's called,' Mrs Jiang said. 'We're here to see the District Commander.'

The soldier had to make a call to ask for permission. They waited a while until he came out, upon which he said that the District Commander was not at home.

'Is there anyone else at home?' Jingqiu asked. She only wanted to ask after his son.

The soldier went to make another call. Each call took ages. 'Why does it take so long?' Mrs Jiang asked him when he came back.

'You can't get through on a direct line to the District Commander,' he explained. 'You have to phone an office first and they put you through. It wastes quite a lot of time.'

After all that to-ing and fro-ing they hadn't discovered anything, only that the District Commander's family were all out, on holiday perhaps. When they asked where the leading cadres went on their holidays the soldier refused to reply, as if afraid that they might ambush them on the road.

Jingqiu was downhearted. She should never, ever, have told him that she wanted to go with him. If she had wanted to go with him she should just have done it, why did she go announcing it to him? Wasn't she worried about scaring him?

Chapter Thirty-six

Crestfallen, Jingqiu caught the train back to Yichang. On the way to Anhui, she had been filled with hope that even if she didn't get to see Old Third, she would at least get to see his family, and if he had already died, they would tell her where his grave was. How was she to know that they wouldn't even be allowed through the main gate?

'Maybe they didn't let us in because we didn't have a letter from our work unit,' Mrs Jiang said. 'Next time we'll remember to get our work unit to write one for us, then we'll definitely get in.'

'But the soldier said that the District Commander isn't even called Sun . . .'

'Maybe he took his mother's name. Didn't he say that when his father was being struggled against the whole family was chased out of the army compound? They must have moved back only after he was pardoned.'

Jingqiu thought that Mrs Jiang's analysis might have some truth to it, but it would be the summer holidays before she could return, and who knew if he would still be there then.

'The whole family was away,' Mrs Jiang continued, 'which is both good and bad news. The bad news is obviously that we didn't see them, but the good news is that if they are all away on holiday, there can't have been a family tragedy recently.'

Mrs Jiang might be right. If Old Third was in hospital, or had died, how could his family go off travelling? He must have recovered, or the army hospital in Yichang must have misdiagnosed him. Old Third had returned to Anhui and had himself checked out by different hospitals, which confirmed that he didn't have leukaemia after all, much to everyone's delight. Or perhaps the geological unit had been disbanded, and so Old Third had decided to stay in Anhui.

She imagined that Old Third was with his father and younger brother, visiting some beautiful place, taking photographs of each other, even asking passers-by to take photos of the three of them. She could see it so clearly, so vividly, she even thought she could hear the sound of his laughter.

Jingqiu immediately began to doubt her own fantasy. 'If he's better, then why hasn't he come to see me?' she asked Mrs Jiang.

'How do you know that he hasn't gone to look for you? He might be in Yichang right now, and we went to Hefei. We might have passed each other. That is a strong possibility. Maybe you'll get home and he'll be sitting in your house, waiting for you, while your mother gives him a grilling.'

Jingqiu recalled the look on Old Third's face the last time her mother had interrogated him and she couldn't help smiling. Now she was anxious to get home, she longed for the train to go faster. It was already late into the night by the time they arrived. Old Third wasn't there but her mother told her that Zhou Jianxin came, but he wouldn't say what he wanted. He sat waiting for a while, and then left.

Jingqiu was bitterly disappointed. Why was it Little Zhou, and not Sun Jianxin?

That evening she couldn't sleep, so she wrote a letter to the Anhui District Commander. She wrote about Old Third's illness, and reluctantly included one of her few photos of Old

Third, begging the District Commander to help her find this Sun Jianxin. She had started to believe that Old Third's father was not in fact the District Commander, but rather some lower-level cadre in the army. But she was sure that the District Commander would be able to find him for her.

The next day she sent the letter by registered mail, knowing that, even though it was a bit slower, it was guaranteed to arrive. She had already given up on miracles and had no option but to prepare for the worst, the possibility that not even the District Commander would be able to find Old Third. If that was the case, she would return to Anhui every summer until she did.

On the morning of Youth Day, 4 May, No. 8 Middle School put on a celebration. As usual, Jingqiu played the accordion for each class's performance. Just as she finished playing for one class, a teacher came up to say there was a comrade from the People's Liberation Army waiting for her outside, and it was urgent. He was in the reception by the main gate. She had only just sent the letter so it seemed impossible that Old Third's father could have received it already. It could only be that he had come back from holiday, and on hearing that she had been looking for him, had sent someone to see her.

But this didn't seem possible either, she hadn't told the soldiers her address, so how would he know where to find her?

Filled with confusion, she ran to the reception, and at once caught sight of a young soldier who looked incredibly like Old Third. On seeing her he walked towards her and asked, 'Comrade Jingqiu? I'm Sun Jianmin, Sun Jianxin's younger brother. My brother is in a very bad way at the moment, will you come with me to the hospital?'

Jingqiu's legs felt as if they were giving way beneath her. 'What's wrong?'

'Let's get in the car and I'll tell you on the way. I've already been waiting a while. I had thought of going straight in to find you, but you're having your celebrations today so they locked the campus gate.'

Jingqiu was too preoccupied to ask permission to leave, and instead said to the person in reception, 'Will you ask Mrs Jiang to come play the accordion for the rest of the show, and ask my mother to take my class in the afternoon. I have to go to the hospital, my friend is in a bad way.'

The guard agreed, and Jingqiu rushed after Sun Jianmin to the jeep that was standing outside the gate. While they were driving Sun Jianmin told her the long sad story. After Old Third was discharged from the county hospital he didn't go back to Anhui, but stayed with the third unit in Chrysanthemum Field, for two reasons: so that he could assist in the geological unit's investigations into the two recent occurrences of leukaemia; and because it was only a few kilometres from No. 8 Middle's School's farm, and he could drive or cycle to see Jingqiu easily.

Jingqiu sat in silence while Sun Jianmin told her that after she was transferred back to the primary school in Yichang, Old Third had followed her, being transferred to the city's military hospital. He had only returned to Anhui for a brief visit during the Spring Festival. Their father wanted him to stay in Anhui, but he wouldn't, so the District Commander had had no choice but to let him return with a nurse from home who would stay with him, and look after him. Their father couldn't stay in Yichang, but made regular visits, because the distance could be covered in ten or so hours by car.

Sun Jianmin looked Jingqiu in the eye and told her sadly and slowly that right now Old Third's father, sister-in-law, uncle, aunt, cousins and even a few friends were all staying at the hospital. He smiled a little. 'When he was well enough, we took him to your school to see you, and together we watched you taking the volleyball class. We could also see you teaching your regular class from the road outside. Later, when he was confined to his bed, he would ask me to go instead, and I would tell him what I had seen. He wouldn't let us tell you he was here in the city, nor that he had leukaemia. He said, 'Don't let her know, let her live like this, so carefree.'

Jingqiu could see that he was struggling to say more. 'According to his instructions, we weren't going to disturb you, but he's been in pain for too long. He's been on his death bed for several days now. The doctors have stopped giving him his medicine or trying to save him, but he won't take his last breath, close his eyes.' He took her hand. 'We thought he must want to see you again, so we've gone against his instructions and have come to find you without his permission. We believed that you would understand, that you would come and see him one last time.' He held her hand and shook it slightly. 'But you mustn't do anything extreme, otherwise his soul will blame us from heaven.'

Jingqiu couldn't speak. She hoped this was a dream, a nightmare. She hoped that she would wake to see Old Third bending over her, telling her that it was all fine now.

She heard Sun Jianmin speak. 'Comrade Jingqiu, are you a member of the Party?'

Jingqiu shook her head.

'Part of the Communist Youth League?'

Jingqiu nodded.

'Then in the name of the Youth League, promise me you won't do anything to hurt yourself.'

Jingqiu nodded again, unable to speak. She was numb.

The jeep drove up outside Old Third's ward. Sun Jianmin helped her down, and led her to the first floor. There were lots of people in the room, each of them with red, swollen eyes. A man who looked like a leading cadre, it must have been

Old Third's father, came forward and said, 'Are you Comrade Jingqiu?'

She nodded, and he took her hand, tears streaming from his eyes. 'He must be waiting for you,' he said, looking over to the bed. 'Go ... say goodbye.' He went out into the corridor.

Jingqiu looked at the person lying in the bed. She couldn't believe that it was really Old Third. He was so thin, and his eyebrows looked particularly long and bushy. His deeply sunken eyes were half open, and she could see that they were bloodshot. He had lost a lot of hair, and what remained was spread thinly over his scalp. His cheekbones were protruding, and his cheeks were like two pits. His face was as white as the hospital sheets.

Jingqiu was too scared to go any closer. This couldn't possibly be Old Third. She had seen him only a few months ago, and he was still a handsome, lithe young man. The figure before her was almost too ghastly to look at.

Hands pushed her gently towards Old Third, and she gathered all her courage to walk up to the edge of the bed. She found his left hand under the covers, and saw the scar where he had cut himself. His hand was now so thin and bony that the scar looked even longer than before. Her legs gave way beneath her and she fell to the floor.

People were trying to pull her to her feet but she couldn't move.

She heard people call out, 'Say it! Say it!'

'Say what?' she asked in confusion.

'His name, call his name! If you don't say it, he won't go!'

Jingqiu couldn't make a sound. She hadn't often said his name out loud, and now it seemed impossible. She only knew how to hold his hand, and look at him. His hand was not yet completely cold, it still had a bit of warmth to it, so he was still alive, but his chest was neither rising nor falling.

People continued to urge her to 'say it, say it', so she held his hand tightly and said, 'It's me, Jingqiu, it's me, Jingqiu.'

She held his hand tightly, hoping with all her heart that he could hear and called louder this time, 'It's me, Jingqiu, it's me, Jingqiu.'

She didn't know how many times she had said it, her legs were going numb, her throat was dry. Someone beside her couldn't stand it any longer, and said, 'Stop, stop shouting, he can't hear you.'

But she didn't believe them, his eyes were half open, she knew he could hear her, it was just that he couldn't speak, he couldn't reply, but he could definitely hear her.

'It's me! Jingqiu!'

She moved closer to his face, to his ear, pleading, 'It's me, it's me, Jingqiu!' He could hear her, it was just that he was being covered by a layer of white mist, he needed some time, he just needed to see her birthmark to be sure that it was her.

She heard the sound of a muffled cry, but it wasn't hers. 'It's me, Jingqiu! It's me, Jingqiu!'

His eyes closed and two tears rolled down his cheeks. Two red, crystal tears . . .

Epilogue

Old Third had gone, and as he had wanted, he was cremated and buried under the hawthorn tree. He wasn't a war hero but they let him be buried there. At the beginning of the Cultural Revolution, the gravestones of fallen soldiers were considered one of the 'four olds' to be smashed, and were therefore removed. So Old Third didn't get a gravestone.

'He insisted upon being buried there,' Old Third's father said to Jingqiu. 'But we're so far away, so we entrust his ashes to you . . .'

Old Third had put his diary, the letters he had written to Jingqiu that the postman had returned, and some photos in an army shoulder bag, and he had given this to his brother to look after. 'If Jingqiu is happy,' he had said, 'don't give it to her. But if she is unlucky in love, or is having problems with her marriage, then give it to her, let her know that there was once someone who loved her with his entire mind and body, let her know that there is such a thing as eternal love.'

On the first page of one of his notebooks he had written, 'I may not be able to wait thirteen months for you, nor until you are twenty-five, but I can wait for you a lifetime.'

The only things he had with him when he died were a photo of Jingqiu when she was six years old and that short note from his notebook. He had kept it with him always. They too were put in the army bag, and Sun Jianmin gave it to Jingqiu.

Every year, in May, Jingqiu went to the hawthorn tree to see the flowers. Perhaps it was just her imagination, but she thought they were even redder than the ones Old Third had sent her.

Ten years later Jingqiu passed the university entrance examinations and started a Master's degree at the English deparment of Hubei University.

Twenty years later Jingqiu made the long journey across the Pacific to America to start her PhD.

Thirty years later Jingqiu had a job teaching at an American university.

This year, she will take her daughter back to the hawthorn tree to visit Old Third.

She will say to her daughter, 'Here sleeps the man I love.'

To find out more about Ai Mi
and other Virago authors,
visit our websites

www.virago.co.uk
www.viragobooks.net

for news of forthcoming titles and events,
exclusive interviews and features, competitions
and our online book-group forum.

And follow us on Twitter @ViragoBooks